As a child **Sarah Morgan** dreamed of being a writer and, although she took a few interesting detours on the way, she is now living that dream. With her writing career she has successfully combined business with ple_____ ___ _irmly believes that reading romance is _____ ___ ___ _atisfying and fat-free escapist plea____ ___ ___ stories are unashamedly optimistic, ___ ___ _s pleased when she receives letters from reade__ _____ _hat her books have helped them through hard times.

Sarah lives near London with her husband and two children, who innocently provide an endless supply of authentic dialogue. When she isn't writing or reading Sarah enjoys music, movies and any activity that takes her outdoors.

Readers can find out more about Sarah and her books from her website: www.sarahmorgan.com. She can also be found on Facebook and Twitter.

Praise for

Sarah Morgan

'Sarah Morgan puts the magic in Christmas'
—*Now* magazine

'Full of romance and sparkle'
—*Lovereading*

'I've found an author I adore—must hunt down everything
she's published.'
—*Smart Bitches, Trashy Books*

'Morgan is a magician with words.'
—*RT Book Reviews*

'Dear Ms Morgan, I'm always on the lookout for
a new book by you...'
—*Dear Author blog*

Once Upon a Christmas

Sarah Morgan

MILLS & BOON

All the characters in this book have no existence outside the imagination of the author, and have no relation whatsoever to anyone bearing the same name or names. They are not even distantly inspired by any individual known or unknown to the author, and all the incidents are pure invention.

All Rights Reserved including the right of reproduction in whole or in part in any form. This edition is published by arrangement with Harlequin Enterprises II B.V./S.à.r.l. The text of this publication or any part thereof may not be reproduced or transmitted in any form or by any means, electronic or mechanical, including photocopying, recording, storage in an information retrieval system, or otherwise, without the written permission of the publisher.

This book is sold subject to the condition that it shall not, by way of trade or otherwise, be lent, resold, hired out or otherwise circulated without the prior consent of the publisher in any form of binding or cover other than that in which it is published and without a similar condition including this condition being imposed on the subsequent purchaser.

® and ™ are trademarks owned and used by the trademark owner and/ or its licensee. Trademarks marked with ® are registered with the United Kingdom Patent Office and/or the Office for Harmonisation in the Internal Market and in other countries.

Mills & Boon, an imprint of Harlequin (UK) Limited,
Eton House, 18-24 Paradise Road, Richmond, Surrey TW9 1SR

ONCE UPON A CHRISTMAS
© Harlequin Enterprises II B.V./S.à.r.l. 2012

Originally published as *The Doctor's Christmas Bride* © Sarah Morgan 2004 and *The Nurse's Wedding Rescue* © Sarah Morgan 2004

ISBN: 978 0 263 90232 7

024-1012

Printed and bound by
CPI Group (UK) Ltd, Croydon, CR0 4YY

Part One

PROLOGUE

'Mummy, I've written my letter to Santa.'

Bryony tucked the duvet round her daughter and clicked on the pink bedside light. A warm glow spread across the room, illuminating a small mountain of soft toys and dressing-up clothes. 'Sweetheart, it's only just November. Don't you think it's a little early to be writing to Santa?'

'All the decorations are in the shops. I saw them with Grandma.'

Bryony picked up a fairy outfit that had been abandoned in a heap on the floor. 'Shops are different, Lizzie.' She slipped the dress onto a hanger and put it safely in the wardrobe. 'They always start selling things early. It's still ages until Christmas.'

'But I know what I want, so I thought I might as well write to him now.' Lizzie reached for the stuffed mermaid that she always slept with. 'And anyway, this present is special so he might need some time to find exactly the right one.'

'Special?' Bryony gave a groan and picked up the book

they'd been reading all week. 'Go on.' Her tone was indulgent. 'Hit me with it, Lizzie. What is it this time—a horse?' She toed off her shoes and curled up on the end of her daughter's bed with a smile. This was the best time of the day. Just the two of them, and Lizzie all warm and cuddly in her pink pyjamas. She smelt of shampoo and innocence, and when she was tucked up in bed she seemed younger somehow, less like a seven-year-old who was growing up too fast.

'Not a horse.' Lizzie snuggled down, her blonde curls framing her pretty face. 'Bigger.'

'Bigger than a *horse*?' Bryony's eyes twinkled. 'You're scaring me, Lizzie. What if Santa can't find this special present?'

'He will.' Lizzie spoke with the conviction of youth. 'You said that Santa always gives you what you ask for if you're good.'

'Ah—did I say that?' Bryony took a deep breath and made a mental note to concentrate more when she answered her daughter's questions in future. 'Well, it does depend on what you ask for,' she hedged, and Lizzie's face fell.

'You said he *always* gives you what you ask for if you're good.'

'Well, he certainly does his best,' Bryony said finally, compromising slightly and hoping that the request wasn't going to be too outlandish. Her doctor's salary was generous, but she was a single mother and she had to watch her expenditures. 'Do you want to show me this letter?'

'I've sent it already.'

'You've sent it?' Bryony looked at her daughter in surprise. 'Where did you post it?'

'I went into the post office with Grandma and they said that if I posted it there it would go all the way to Santa in Lapland.'

'Oh.' Bryony smiled weakly, her heart sinking. 'So it's gone, then.'

Which meant that there would be no chance to talk Lizzie out of whatever it was that she'd chosen that was obviously going to cost a fortune and be impossible to find in the wilds of the Lake District.

Bryony sensed a trip to London coming on. Unless the internet could oblige.

'Uh-huh.' Lizzie nodded. 'And he's got until Christmas to sort it out.'

'Right. Are you going to give me a clue?'

'You'll like it, I know you will.'

'Is it something messy?'

'Nope.'

'Something pink?' Everything in her daughter's life was pink so it was a fairly safe bet that whatever was top of her Christmas list would be pink.

Lizzie shook her head and her eyes shone. 'Not pink.'

Not pink?

Feeling distinctly uneasy, Bryony hoped that her mother had managed to sneak a look at the letter before it was 'posted' otherwise none of them were going to have the first clue what Lizzie wanted for Christmas.

'I'd really like to know, sweetheart,' she said casually, flipping through the pages of the book until she found where they'd left off the night before. She wondered whether the post office had binned the letter. At this rate she was going to have to go and ask for it back.

'OK. I'll tell you, because it's sort of for you, too.'

Bryony held her breath, hoping desperately that it wasn't a pet. Her life was so frantic she absolutely didn't have time to care for an animal on top of everything else. A full-time job and single parenthood was the most she could manage and sometimes she struggled with that.

A pet would be the final straw.

But then she looked at Lizzie's sweet face and felt totally overwhelmed by love. More than anything she wanted her daughter to be happy and if that meant cleaning out a rabbit…

'Whatever it is you want,' Bryony said softly, reaching out and stroking her daughter's silken curls with a gentle hand, 'I'm sure Santa will get it for you. You're such a good girl and I love you.'

'I love you, too, Mummy.' Lizzie reached up and hugged her and Bryony felt a lump building in her throat.

'OK.' She extracted herself and gave her daughter a bright smile. 'So, what is it you want for Christmas?'

Lizzie lay back on the pillow, a contented smile spreading across her face. 'A daddy,' she breathed happily. 'For Christmas this year, I really, *really* want a daddy. And I *know* that Santa is going to bring me one.'

CHAPTER ONE

'SIX-MONTH-OLD baby coming in with breathing difficulties.' Bryony replaced the phone that connected the accident and emergency department direct to Ambulance Control and turned to the A and E sister. 'That's the third one today, Nicky.'

'Welcome to A and E in November.' The other woman pulled a face and slipped her pen back in her pocket. 'One respiratory virus after another. Wait until the weather gets really cold. Then everyone falls over on the ice. Last year we had forty-two wrist fractures in one day.'

Bryony laughed. 'Truly?'

'Truly. And you wouldn't laugh if you'd been working here then,' Nicky said dryly as they walked towards the ambulance bay together. 'It was unbelievable. I wanted to go out with a loudhailer and tell everyone to stay at home.'

As she finished speaking they heard the shriek of an ambulance siren, and seconds later the doors to the department crashed open and the paramedics hurried in with the baby.

'Take her straight into Resus,' Bryony ordered, taking one look at the baby and deciding that she was going to need help on this one. 'What's the story?'

'She's had a cold and a runny nose for a couple of days,' the paramedic told her. 'Temperature going up and down, and then all of a sudden she stopped taking any fluids and tonight the mother said she stopped breathing. Mother came with us in the ambulance—she's giving the baby's details to Reception.'

'Did she call the GP?'

'Yes, but he advised her to call 999.'

'Right.' Bryony glanced at Nicky. 'Let's get her undressed so that I can examine her properly. I want her on a cardiac monitor and a pulse oximeter—I need to check her oxygen saturation.'

'She's breathing very fast,' Nicky murmured as she undid the poppers on the baby's sleepsuit. 'Poor little mite, she's really struggling. I suppose we ought to call Jack—even though calling him will massage his ego.'

Bryony looked at the baby, saw the bluish tinge around her lips and heard the faint grunting sound as she breathed.

'Call him,' she said firmly. 'This baby is sick.'

Very sick.

She didn't care if they massaged Jack's ego. She trusted his opinion more than anyone else's and not just because he was the consultant and she was a casualty officer with only four months' A and E experience behind her. Jack Rothwell was an incredibly talented doctor.

Nicky finished undressing the baby and then picked up the phone on the wall and dialled, leaving Bryony to carry out her examination. She watched the baby breathing for a moment and then placed her stethoscope in her ears, strands of blonde hair falling forward as she bent and listened to the child's chest.

When she finally unhooked the stethoscope from her ears, Jack was standing opposite, looking at her with that lazy, half-bored expression in his blue eyes that always drove women crazy.

And she was no exception.

She'd known him for twenty-two years and still her knees went weak when he walked into a room. She'd often tried to work out why. Was it the sexy smile? The wicked blue eyes that crinkled at the corners when he smiled? The glossy dark hair? The broad shoulders? Or was it his sense of humour, which had her smiling almost all the time? Eventually she'd come to the conclusion that it was everything. The whole drop-dead-gorgeous, confident masculine package that was Jack Rothwell.

When she'd started working in A and E in the summer, she'd been worried about how it would feel to work with a man she'd known all her life. She was worried that finally working together would feel odd. But it didn't.

She'd fast discovered that Jack at work was the same as Jack not at work. Clever, confident and wickedly sexy.

'So, Blondie,' his deep masculine tones were loaded with humour. 'You need some help?'

Blondie...

Bryony grinned. He'd called her 'Blondie' when she'd been five years old, and now she was twenty-seven he was still calling her 'Blondie'. She'd even had a brush with being brunette at one point in her teens but it had made no difference. He'd still called her 'Blondie'. It was one of the things she loved about their friendship. The way he teased her. It made her feel special. And, anyway, it meant that she could tease him back.

'This baby's sick.'

'Which is presumably why she's in hospital,' Jack drawled, leaning across and reaching for her stethoscope, the fabric of his shirt moulding lovingly to the hard muscle of his shoulders. Despite his teasing words his eyes were on the baby, looking, assessing, mentally cataloguing his findings.

Bryony watched him with admiration and more than a touch of envy. His instincts were so good. If anyone she loved ever ended up in A and E, the doctor she'd want them to see would be Jack. He had a brilliant brain and an amazing ability to identify medical problems based on seemingly scanty information. And she'd learned more from him in her four months in A and E than she had from any other doctor in her career so far.

'So what did you notice, Blondie? Apart from the fact that there's a little patient on the trolley?'

He stood back while Nicky attached leads to the baby's chest and connected them to the monitor.

'She's cyanosed, has intercostal recession and she's grunting,' Bryony said immediately, her eyes on the baby. 'Her resps are 60 per minute and she's becoming exhausted.'

Jack nodded, his eyes flickering to the monitor, which was now operational and giving them further clues to the baby's condition.

'She has acute bronchiolitis. We need to get a line in this baby fast,' he ordered softly, holding out a hand to Nicky who immediately proffered the necessary equipment. He handed it to Bryony. 'Go on. Impress me.'

'You want me to do it?' Bryony looked at those tiny arms and legs and shook her head. 'I'd rather you did it.'

She could see how ill the baby was and she didn't have the confidence that she'd get the line in first time. She knew Jack could. And with the baby that sick, his skill was more important than her need to practise.

His eyes narrowed and his gaze was suddenly serious. 'Don't doubt yourself,' he said softly, his blue eyes searching as he read her mind. 'Do it.'

He was still holding out the equipment and Bryony sucked in a breath. 'Jack, I—'

'Can do it,' he said calmly, those wicked blue eyes locking on hers. 'In three months' time you're going to be working on the paediatric ward and you're going to be taking blood all the time. You need the practise. Go for it.'

Bryony hesitated and Jack lifted an eyebrow, his blue eyes mocking.

'You want me to hold your hand?' His voice was a lazy drawl and Bryony blushed. How could he be so relaxed? But she knew the answer to that, of course. During her time in the A and E department she'd learned that panic did nothing to improve a tense situation and she'd also learned that Jack's totally laid-back attitude to everything rubbed off on the rest of the staff. As a result, they operated as a smooth, efficient team.

Looking at the baby, Bryony bit her lip and lifted the child's tiny wrist.

'Relax. Take your time.' Jack closed long, strong fingers around the baby's wrist and squeezed. 'OK. Here's one for you. What do you call a blonde with half a brain?'

Bryony was concentrating on the baby's wrist. She found a tiny, thready vein and wondered how she was ever going to hit such a tiny target. It seemed almost impossible.

'Gifted,' Jack said cheerfully, squinting down at the baby's hand. 'You'll be fine. She's got good veins. Stop dithering and just do it.'

So she did and the needle slid smoothly into the tiny vein on her first attempt.

Relief and delight flooded through her.

'I did it.' She looked up, unable to hide her pride, and Jack smiled, his eyes creasing at the corners.

'As I said. Gifted. Now you just need the confidence to go with it. You're a good doctor. Believe in yourself.' His eyes held hers for a moment and then he looked at Nicky. 'OK, we need a full blood count, U and Es, BMG, blood culture and viral titres. And Nicky, let's give the child some humidified oxygen.'

Believe in yourself.

Well, she did believe in herself. Sort of. It was just that she was afraid of making a mistake and Jack Rothwell never seemed to be afraid of anything. He just did it. And it turned out right every time.

Bryony busied herself taking the necessary samples. 'Should I do arterial blood gases?'

'They can do them on the ward,' Jack said immediately. 'Nicky, can you call Paeds and get them up here? This little one is going to need admitting. She's a poorly baby.'

Bryony looked at him. 'You think it's bronchiolitis?'

'Without a doubt.' He smothered a yawn and looked at her apologetically. 'Sorry. I was up half the night.'

It was Bryony's turn to look mocking. 'Was she nice?'

'She was gorgeous.' He grinned, that wonderful slightly lopsided grin that affected her knees so acutely. 'She was also eighty-four and had a fractured hip.'

'You love older women.'

'True.' He checked the monitor again. 'But generally I like them mobile. OK, Blondie. What's the likely causative organism here? Exercise your brain cell and impress me twice in one evening.'

'RSV,' Bryony said immediately. 'Respiratory syncytial virus causes 75 per cent of cases of bronchiolitis.'

He inclined his head, his expression mocking. 'All right, you've impressed me. And you've obviously been studying your textbook again. Now we'll do some maths. What's two plus two?' His eyes were dancing. 'No need to answer immediately and you can use your fingers if you need to. Take your time—I know it's tricky.'

'No idea,' Bryony returned blithely, batting her eye-lashes in a parody of a dumb blonde and handing the bottles to Nicky for labelling. 'Jack, should we pass a nasogastric tube?'

'No. Not yet.' He shook his head, his gaze flickering over the baby. 'When you've finished taking the samples we'll set up an IV and get her to the ward. I've got a bad feeling about this little one. She's going to end up being ventilated.'

'I hope not,' Bryony murmured, but she knew that Jack was always right in his predictions. If he thought the baby was going to need ventilating, then it was almost certain that she would.

He looked at her quizzically. 'Is the mother around?'

As he asked the question the doors to Resus opened and the paramedics came back in, escorting a tall woman wrapped in a wool coat. Her face was pale and her hair was uncombed.

'Ella?' She hurried over to the trolley, her face lined with anxiety, and then she looked at Jack.

Bryony didn't mind that. She was used to it. Women always looked at Jack.

Even before they knew he was the consultant, they looked at him.

And it wasn't just because he was staggeringly, movie-star handsome. It was because he was charming and had an air of casual self-assurance that attracted women like magnets. You just knew that Jack would know what to do in any situation.

'I'm Dr Rothwell.' He extended a hand and gave her that reassuring smile that always seemed to calm the most frantic relative. 'I've been caring for Ella, along with Dr Hunter here.'

The woman didn't even glance at Bryony. Her gaze stayed firmly fixed on Jack. 'She's been ill for days but I thought it was just a cold and then suddenly today she seemed to go downhill.' She lifted a shaking hand to her throat. 'She wouldn't take her bottle and she was *so* hot and then tonight she stopped breathing properly and I was *terrified*.'

Jack nodded, his blue eyes warm and understanding. 'It's always frightening when a baby of this size is ill because their airways are so small,' he explained calmly. 'Ella has picked up a nasty virus and it is affecting her breathing.'

The woman blanched and stared at the tiny figure on the trolley. 'But she's going to be OK?'

'We need to admit her to hospital,' Jack said, glancing up as the paediatrician walked into the room. 'This is Dr Armstrong, the paediatric registrar. He's going to take a look at her now and then we'll take her along to the ward.'

'Will I be able to stay with her?'

'Absolutely.' Jack nodded, his gaze reassuring. 'You can have a bed next to her cot.'

Deciding that Jack was never going to be able to extricate himself from the mother, Bryony briefed Dr Armstrong on the baby's condition.

She liked David Armstrong. He was warm and kind and he'd asked her out on several occasions.

And she'd refused of course. Because she always refused.

She *never* went on dates.

Bryony bit her lip, remembering Lizzie's letter to Santa. She wanted a daddy for Christmas. A pretty tall order for a woman who didn't date men, she thought dryly, picking up the baby's charts and handing them to David.

Dragging her mind back, she finished handing over and watched while David examined the baby himself.

A thoroughly nice man, she decided wistfully. So why couldn't she just accept his invitation to take their friendship a step further?

And then Jack strolled back to the trolley, tall, broad-shouldered, confident and so shockingly handsome that it made her gasp, and she remembered the reason why she didn't date men.

She didn't date men because she'd been in love with Jack since she'd been five years old. And apart from her one disastrous attempt to forget about him, which had resulted in Lizzie, she hadn't even *noticed* another man for her entire adult life.

Which just went to show how stupid she was, she reflected crossly, infuriated by her own stupidity.

Jack might be a brilliant doctor but he was also the most totally unsuitable man any woman could fall for. Women had affairs with Jack. They didn't fall in love with him. Not if they had any sense, because Jack had no intention of ever falling in love or settling down.

But, of course, she didn't have any sense.

It was fortunate that she'd got used to hiding the way she felt about him. He didn't have a clue that he'd featured in every daydream she'd had since she'd been a child. When other little girls had dreamed about faceless princes in fairy-tales, she'd dreamed about Jack. When her teenage friends had developed crushes on the boys at school, she'd still dreamed about Jack. And when she'd finally matured into a woman, she'd carried on dreaming about Jack.

Finally the baby was stable enough to be transferred to the ward and Nicky pushed the trolley, accompanied by the paediatric SHO, who had arrived to help, and the baby's mother.

Bryony started to tidy up Resus, ready for the next arrival, her mind elsewhere.

'Are you all right?' David Armstrong gave her a curious look. 'You're miles away.'

'Sorry.' She smiled. 'Just thinking.'

'Hard work, that, for a blonde,' Jack said mildly, and Bryony gave him a sunny smile, relaxed now that the baby was no longer her responsibility.

'Why are men like bank accounts?' she asked sweetly, ditching some papers in the bin. 'Because without a lot of money they don't generate much interest.'

David looked startled but Jack threw back his head and laughed.

'Then it's fortunate for me that I have a lot of money,' he said strolling across the room to her and looping her stethoscope back round her neck.

For a moment he stood there, looking down at her, his eyes laughing into hers as he kept hold of the ends of the stethoscope. Bryony looked back at him, hypnotised by the dark shadow visible on his hard jaw and the tiny muscle that worked in his cheek. He was so close she could almost touch him, but she'd never been allowed to do that.

Not properly.

He was her best friend.

They talked, they laughed and they spent huge amounts of time together. But they never crossed that line of friendship.

Jack's pager sounded and he let go of the stethoscope and reached into his pocket. 'Duty calls. If you're sure you can cope without me, I'll be off.'

'I'll struggle on,' Bryony said sarcastically, and he gave her that lazy wink that always reduced her legs to jelly.

'You do that. I'll see you later, then. Are you joining the team at the Drunken Fox tonight?'

'Yes. Mum's babysitting.'

The whole of the local mountain rescue team were meeting for a drink to celebrate her brother's birthday.

'Good.' He gave a nod. 'See you there, then.'

And with that he strolled out of the room with his usual easy confidence, letting the door swing closed behind him.

David stared after him. 'Don't you mind the blonde jokes and the fact that he calls you Blondie?'

Bryony shot him an amused look. 'He's called me that for twenty-two years.' She fiddled with the stethoscope that Jack had looped round her neck. 'He's just teasing.'

'You've known him for *twenty-two years*?'

'Amazing that I'm still sane, isn't it?' Bryony said lightly. 'Jack was at school with my two brothers but he spent more time in our house than his own.' *Mainly because his parents had been going through a particularly acrimonious divorce.*

'He's practically family. He and my brothers were at medical school together.'

Nicky entered the room in time to hear that last remark. 'I bet the three of them were lethal.'

'They certainly were.'

David looked at her in surprise. 'Of course—why didn't I realise before? Tom Hunter, the consultant obstetrician—he's your brother?'

Bryony smiled. 'That's right. And my other brother, Oliver, is a GP. When I've finished my rotation I'm going to join him in his practice. He's the reason for the trip to the pub—it's his birthday today.'

Not that they needed an excuse for a trip to the pub. Most of the mountain rescue team members lived in the pub when they weren't working, training or on a callout.

David looked at her. 'I can't believe that I didn't click sooner that Tom Hunter is your brother.'

Bryony shrugged. 'Well, we don't know each other that well.'

'And whose fault is that?' David said in an undertone. 'I keep asking you out.'

And she kept refusing.

Conscious that Nicky was within earshot, Bryony handed David the last of the charts. 'Here you go. Everything you need on baby Ella. I hope she does OK.'

'Thanks.' He hesitated and then gave her a smile as he walked out of Resus.

'That man fancies you,' Nicky said dryly, and Bryony sighed.

'Yes, I know.'

'Don't tell me, you're in love with Jack, the same as every other woman on the planet.'

Bryony looked at her, carefully keeping her expression casual. She'd never admitted to *anyone* how she felt about Jack, and she wasn't going to start now. 'Jack's my best friend. I know him far too well to ever fall in love with him.'

'Then you're more sensible than the rest of the female population,' Nicky said happily. 'Every woman I know is in love with Jack Rothwell. He's rich, single and sexy as sin. And most of us could scratch your eyes out for being so close to him. According to rumour, he spends half his life hanging around your kitchen.'

Bryony smiled. When she'd lived at home Jack had always been there, and when she'd moved into her own cottage he'd taken to dropping round so often that he was almost part of the furniture. 'Don't get the wrong idea. Usually he's telling me about his latest girlfriend. He's my brothers' closest friend, he's my daughter's godfather and we've been in the mountain rescue team together for years. I can assure you there's nothing romantic about our relationship.'

Unfortunately.

Nicky sighed. 'Well, it sounds pretty good to me. I'd love to have him in my kitchen, if only for his decorative qualities. The guy is sublime.'

'Nicky, you're married.'

Nicky grinned. 'I know. But my hormones are still alive and kicking.'

Bryony busied herself restocking one of the equipment trays. Strictly speaking it wasn't her job but she didn't want to look at Nicky in case she gave herself away.

Her relationship with Jack was good.

They had a fantastic friendship.

But even the most fantastic friendship didn't soothe the ache in her heart.

She was about to say something else to Nicky when the doors to Resus opened again and one of the paramedics stuck his head round.

'Has the baby been transferred to the ward? Only I've got her father here.'

'I'll speak to him,' Bryony said immediately, glad to be given an excuse to get away from the subject of Jack. She followed the paramedic out of the room.

A tall man in a suit was hovering anxiously in the corridor, his face white with strain.

'I'm Dr Hunter,' Bryony said, holding out her hand. 'I've been looking after Ella.'

'Oh, God…' he breathed out slowly, obviously trying to calm himself down. 'I came as soon as Pam called me but I was at a meeting in Penrith and the traffic was awful.'

Bryony gave an understanding smile and slowly outlined Ella's condition, careful to be realistic without painting too grim a picture.

'So she's on the ward?' He ran a hand over the back of his neck and gave a shuddering sigh. 'Sorry. I know I'm panicking like mad but she's my baby and—'

'It's OK,' Bryony said gently, putting a hand on his arm. 'You're her father and you're entitled to be worried.'

His shoulders sagged and he looked exhausted. 'You don't know what worry is until you have kids, do you?'

Bryony thought of Lizzie and shook her head. 'No,' she agreed softly, 'you certainly don't.'

'Do you have children yourself, Doctor?'

'I have a little girl.'

They shared a smile of mutual understanding. 'And the bond between a little girl and her daddy is so special, isn't it?'

Bryony tensed and then she smiled. 'It certainly is,' she croaked, feeling as though she'd been showered with cold water. 'Very special.'

She directed the man to the children's ward and stared after him, feeling sick inside.

She loved Lizzie so fiercely that she rarely thought about the fact that her little girl didn't have a father. She had plenty of father figures—her two brothers and Jack, and she'd always consoled herself that they were enough. But

Lizzie obviously didn't think so or why would she have asked for a father for Christmas?

Lizzie wanted the real thing. She wanted a father to tuck her up at night. A father who would read to her and play with her. *A father who would panic and leave a meeting because she was sick.*

Bryony gave a groan and covered her face with her hands. How was she ever going to satisfy Lizzie's Christmas wish this year?

How was she going to produce a father when she didn't even date men and hadn't since Lizzie had been conceived? And not even then, really.

Bryony let her hands drop to her sides, torn with guilt at how selfish she'd been. Because of the way she felt about Jack, she'd shut men out of her life, never thinking about the long-term effect that would have on Lizzie.

It was true that she didn't want a man in her life, but it was also true that Lizzie needed and wanted a father.

And suddenly Bryony made a decision.

She was going to stop dreaming about Jack Rothwell. She was going to stop noticing his broad shoulders. She was going to stop noticing the way his cheeks creased when he smiled. She was going to stop thinking about what he looked like with his shirt off. In fact, she was going to stop thinking about him altogether and start dating other men.

Finally she was going to get a life.

And Lizzie was going to get a daddy.

CHAPTER TWO

BRYONY paused outside the entrance to the pub, her breath clouding the freezing air. She could hear the muffled sounds of laughter and music coming from inside, and she lifted her chin and pushed open the door.

They were all there. The whole of the mountain rescue team, most of whom she'd known for years, crowding the bar and laughing together. In one corner of the bar a log fire crackled and the room was warm and welcoming.

'It's Blondie!'

There were good-natured catcalls from the moment they spotted her and Toby, the equipment officer, slipped off his stool and offered it to her with a flourish.

'Hi, guys.' She settled herself on the stool and smiled at the barman. 'Hi, Geoff. The usual, please.'

He reached for a bottle of grapefruit juice. 'On the hard stuff, Bryony?'

'That's me.' Bryony nodded her thanks and lifted the glass in a salute. 'Cheers, everyone. And happy birthday, Oliver.'

Her brother grinned. 'Thanks, babe. You OK?'

'I'm fine.' In fact, she was better than fine. She was brilliant. And she was finally going to restart her life.

As if to test that resolve, Jack strolled over to her and dropped a kiss on her cheek.

'What did the blonde say when she walked into the bar?'

'Ouch,' Bryony answered wearily, rolling her eyes in exasperation. 'And, Jack, you really need some new jokes. You're recycling them.'

He yawned. 'Well, I've been telling them for twenty-two years—what do you expect?'

'A bit of originality would be nice,' she said mildly, taking another sip of her drink and making a point of not looking at him. She wasn't going to notice Jack any more. There were plenty of men out there with good bodies. He wasn't the only one. 'Maybe I should dye my hair brown to help you out.'

'Brown? Don't you dare.' Jack's voice was husky and enticingly male. 'If you dyed your hair brown, you'd ruin all my jokes. We love you the way you are.'

Bryony took a gulp of her drink. He didn't love her. And he never would love her. Or, at least, not in the way she wanted him to love her.

'Bry, are you free on Thursday or Friday?' Oliver leaned across the bar and grabbed a handful of nuts. 'Mum wants to cook me a birthday dinner, whole family and Jack in attendance.'

Bryony put her glass down on the bar. 'Can't do Thursday.'

Jack frowned. 'You're on an early shift. Why can't you do it?'

Bryony hesitated. 'Because I have a date,' she said finally, and Oliver lifted his eyebrows.

'A date? You have *a date*?'

Jack's smile vanished like the sun behind a cloud. 'What do you mean, you have a date?' His voice was surprisingly frosty. 'Since when did you go on dates?'

Bryony took a deep breath and decided she may as well tell all. 'Since I saw Lizzie's Christmas list.'

At the mention of Lizzie, Jack's expression regained some of its warmth. 'She's made her list already?'

'She has indeed.'

'Don't tell me.' His voice was indulgent. 'She wants something pink. A new pair of pink wings for her fairy costume?'

'Nope.'

Oliver looked at her searchingly. 'Well? We're all dying to hear what she asked for. And what's it got to do with you going on a date?'

Bryony sat still for a moment, studying her empty glass. 'I'm going on a date,' she said slowly, 'because Lizzie wants a daddy.' She looked up and gave them a bland smile. 'Lizzie has asked for a daddy for Christmas.'

There was a long silence around the bar and the men exchanged looks.

It was Jack who eventually spoke first. 'Does she realise that they're not all they're cracked up to be?'

There was bitterness in his tone and Bryony frowned slightly. She knew that his parents had divorced when he'd been eight and she also knew that it had been a hideously painful experience for Jack.

But it was unlike him to ever mention it.

Like most men, Jack Rothwell didn't talk about his feelings.

'A *daddy*?' Oliver cleared his throat and exchanged looks with Tom. 'Does she have anyone in particular in mind?'

Bryony shook her head. 'No. She's leaving the choice up to Santa, but Mum gave me the letter and she's listed the qualities she's looking for.'

'She has?' Oliver gave an amazed laugh and glanced round at the others. 'And what are they?'

Bryony delved into her pocket and pulled out a rumpled piece of paper. She cleared her throat and started to read. 'I want a daddy who is strong so that he can swing me in the garden. I want a daddy who is funny and makes jokes. I want a daddy who lets me watch television before school and who won't make me eat sprouts because I hate them and I want a daddy who will meet me at the school gate and give me a hug like the other daddies sometimes do.' Bryony broke off at that point and swallowed hard, aware of the stunned silence around her. 'But most of all I want a daddy who will hug my mummy and stay with us for ever.'

No one spoke and Bryony gave a small shrug. 'That's it.'

She folded the paper carefully and put it back in her pocket, and Jack frowned.

'I never knew she wanted someone to pick her up from school,' he said gruffly, glancing between Oliver and Tom. 'We could do something about that, guys.'

'Sure.' Tom nodded agreement immediately and Bryony lifted a hand.

'Thank you, but no. That isn't what she wants. In fact,

that would probably make it worse because the person who is picking her up isn't her daddy.'

Oliver frowned and rubbed a hand over the back of his neck. 'So where did it come from, this daddy business?'

'I don't know.' Bryony shrugged. 'I suppose she's just getting to that age where children notice differences between themselves and others. Most of the kids in her class are in traditional families.'

'You've been reading her too many fairy stories,' Jack said darkly, and she shrugged.

'She's a little girl, Jack. Little girls dream of weddings.'

Oliver grinned at Tom. 'Some big girls dream of weddings, too. I find it terrifying.'

'Stop it.' Bryony frowned in mock disapproval. 'How my daughter has ever grown up to be remotely normal with you three around her is a mystery to me. She's always asking me why none of you are married.'

'Did you tell her that we're too busy having fun?' Tom drawled, and Bryony rolled her eyes.

'Actually, I tell her that none of you have met the right woman yet, but that it's bound to happen soon.'

'Is it?' Oliver gave a shudder, his expression comical. 'I hope not.'

'You're awful. All three of you.'

Tom lifted an eyebrow in her direction. 'Well, you're not exactly an advert for relationships yourself, little sister. You haven't been on a date since Lizzie was born.'

'I know that. But that's all going to change.' Bryony lifted her chin. 'I've decided that Lizzie needs a daddy.'

'So what are you saying?' Jack was staring at her, all traces of humour gone from his handsome face. 'You're going to go out there and marry the first guy you meet just so that she can have a daddy?'

'Don't be ridiculous. Of course not.' Bryony lifted her chin and looked around her, her voice quiet but firm. 'I'm just saying that I'm going to start dating again.'

Oliver glanced at Tom and shrugged. 'Well, good for you.'

'Yeah.' Tom nodded and smiled at his sister. 'I think it's great. You've locked yourself up in a cupboard long enough. Get yourself out there, I say. Paint the town red. Or pink, if you're using Lizzie's colour scheme.'

Some of the other men in the team clapped her on the back and one or two made jokes about joining the queue to take her out.

Only Jack was silent, studying her with a brooding expression on his handsome face, his usual teasing smile notably absent. 'You really think you can find her a *daddy*?'

'I don't know.' Bryony gave a little shrug. 'Maybe not. But if I don't at least go on dates, it definitely won't happen.'

When he finally spoke his tone was chilly. 'So who's your date with on Thursday?'

Bryony looked at him in confusion, thinking that she'd never heard Jack use that tone before. He sounded…*angry*. But why would he be angry? The others actually seemed pleased for her. But not Jack.

'I'm not sure it's any of your business,' she teased him gently, trying to nudge their relationship back onto its usual platform, but on this occasion there was no answering smile.

'I'm Lizzie's godfather,' he reminded her, his blue eyes

glittering in the firelight and a muscle working in his jaw. 'Who you choose as a *daddy* is very much my business.'

'You want to interview the guys I date, Jack?' She was still smiling, trying to keep it light, but he was glaring at her.

'Maybe.'

Bryony gave a disbelieving laugh, her own smile fading rapidly. 'You can't be serious.'

'You know absolutely nothing about the opposite sex, Blondie,' he said coldly. 'You've always refused to tell us who Lizzie's father was but he isn't around now which says quite a lot about your choice of men.'

Bryony gasped in shock. Lizzie's father wasn't a topic she discussed with anyone and Jack had never spoken to her like that before. He'd always been totally supportive of her status as a single mother.

'I don't know why you're looking so disapproving,' she said softly, aware that all the others had long since returned to their conversations and were no longer listening. Suddenly it was just the two of them and the tension in the atmosphere was increasing by the minute. 'You date all the time.'

His mouth tightened. 'I don't have a seven-year-old daughter.'

'But it's because of her that I'm doing this!'

Jack picked up his glass from the bar, a muscle flickering in his darkened jaw. 'That's ridiculous. You think you can just get out there and produce a happy family like magic?'

She sighed, knowing what was behind his words. 'No, I don't think that, Jack. But I think that it's time to see if I could maybe meet someone who seemed right for Lizzie and me.'

'Your life runs very smoothly,' he pointed out. 'Why complicate things?'

'Because Lizzie needs something more...' She hesitated. 'And I need something more, too, Jack. I've been on my own long enough.'

His mouth tightened. 'So basically you've suddenly decided to get out there and have fun.'

'And so what if I have?' Bryony looked at him, confused and exasperated. 'I just don't understand your attitude! You and my brothers have practically worked your way through most of the females in Cumbria.'

Streaks of colour touched his incredible cheekbones. 'That's different.'

Suddenly Bryony decided she'd had enough. 'Because you're a man and I'm a woman?'

'No.' His fingers tightened on his glass. 'Because I don't have any responsibilities.'

'No. You've made sure of that. And there's no need to remind me of my responsibilities to Lizzie. That's what started this, remember?' She glared at him, suddenly angry with him for being so judgmental. 'Lizzie wants a daddy and it's my job to find her one. And I'm more than happy to try and find someone I can live with because frankly I'm sick and tired of being on my own, too.'

How could she have been so stupid as to put herself on ice for so long? She should have realised just how deep-rooted his fear of commitment was. Should have realised that Jack Rothwell would never settle down with anyone, let alone her.

It was definitely time to move on.

'I'm going home,' she said coldly, slipping off the bar-stool and avoiding his gaze. 'I'll see you at work tomorrow.'

She heard his sharp intake of breath and knew that he was going to try and stop her, but she virtually ran to the door, giving him no opportunity to intercept her.

She didn't want to talk to him. Didn't want to hear all the reasons why she shouldn't have a boyfriend when he dated a non-stop string of beautiful women.

She'd call Oliver later and apologise for ducking out without saying goodbye, but she knew he wouldn't mind. They were a close family and she adored her brothers. At least they'd been encouraging.

Which was more than could be said for Jack.

Why had he acted like that? All right, he was absolutely against marriage, but it wasn't *his* marriage they were talking about. It was *hers*, and Jack was usually warm and supportive of everything she did. They *never* argued. They were best friends.

She unlocked her car quickly, feeling tears prick her eyes.

Well, if dating other men meant losing Jack as a friend, then so be it. She'd wasted enough time on him. He didn't even notice her, for goodness' sake!

And if she'd needed confirmation that it was time to move on, she had it now.

Jack banged his empty glass down on the bar and cursed under his breath.

'Nice one, Jack,' Oliver said mildly, clapping him on the shoulder and glancing towards the door. 'I thought the three of us agreed that we weren't going to bring up the thorny subject of Lizzie's father.'

Jack groaned and ran a hand over his face. 'I know, I know.' He let out a long breath. 'It's just that she knows *nothing* about men—'

'She's twenty-seven.'

'So?' Jack glared at Oliver. 'And we know that she hasn't been out with a man since Lizzie was conceived. That guy broke her heart! I don't want her making the same mistake again. She's obviously never got over him. What if she picks someone on the rebound?'

Tom joined them. 'I'm not sure you can rebound after seven years,' he said mildly, and Jack's mouth tightened.

'So why does Lizzie never date, then?'

Tom looked at him steadily. 'I don't know...'

'Yes you do.' Jack's eyes narrowed as he studied his friend. 'You think you know. I can tell.'

Tom shook his head and drained his glass. 'No. I don't know.' He studied his empty glass. 'But I can guess.'

Jack frowned. 'So what's your guess?'

Tom gave a funny smile and looked at Oliver. 'My guess is that she has a particular guy on her mind,' he drawled casually, 'and until she gets over him, she can't move on.'

'Precisely what I said,' Jack said smugly. 'She needs to get over Lizzie's father.'

And with that he grabbed his jacket and strode out of the pub after her.

Oliver looked at Tom. 'I always thought he was a bright guy. How did he ever come top in all those exams?'

Tom gave a faint smile. 'He'll get there in the end.'

'Unless Bry meets someone else.'

'Bryony has been in love with Jack for twenty-two years,' Tom said calmly, glancing at the barman and waggling his glass. 'She's never going to fall in love with anyone else.'

'So what happens now?'

Tom reached for his wallet. 'I think we're in for a very interesting few weeks. Happy birthday, bro. This one's on me.'

Damn.

Jack strode out to the car park, cursing himself for being so tactless. He couldn't believe he'd argued with Bryony. He *never* argued with Bryony. Or, at least, not seriously. Bryony was the nearest he had to family and their relationship was all banter and teasing and a great deal of confiding. Well, on his part at least. He told her everything about his relationships and she was always giving him little suggestions. And that was one of the things he loved about their friendship. Unlike the women he dated, Bryony never tried to change him or lecture him. She just accepted him as he was. He was more comfortable in her kitchen than any other place in the world. And now he'd upset her.

What the hell had come over him?

He looked round the car park, part of him hoping that she was still there, but of course she was long gone. He just hoped she wasn't driving too quickly. The air was freezing and the roads would be icy.

He gritted his teeth and swore under his breath. She'd been really upset by his comments and there was a very strong chance that he'd made her cry. Despite the fact that she rarely let him see it, he knew she was soft-hearted. He'd known her since she was five, for goodness' sake, and he knew her better than anyone.

Realising that he had a big apology to make, he ran a hand over his face and strolled to his car, pressing the remote control on his keyring.

He could drive over to her cottage now, of course, but she'd still be mad with him and anyway her mother would be there so they wouldn't be able to talk properly.

No. The apology was best left until they could be alone.

If he'd been dating her he would have sent her flowers, but he'd never sent Bryony flowers in his life, and if he did she'd think he'd gone mad.

He slid into his sports car and dropped his head back against the seat.

No doubt, now that word was out that she was going to start dating, flowers would be arriving for her thick and fast.

He growled low in his throat, tension rising in him as he contemplated the impact that her announcement had made.

Why had she chosen to tell the whole pub? Didn't she know that all the guys lusted after her? That with her long silken blonde hair and her fabulous curvy body, she couldn't walk across a room without stopping conversations? And he felt every bit as protective towards her as he knew her brothers did.

And now some sleazy guy would come along and take advantage of her, and she was so trusting and inexperienced with men she wouldn't even notice until it was too late.

Jack reversed the car out of its space, crunching the

gears viciously. Well, *not* while he was available to prevent it happening.

She'd become pregnant in her second year at medical school and neither he nor her brothers had been around to sort the guy out. Damn it, she hadn't even told them who he was. Just mumbled something about the whole thing being a mistake and refused to even discuss it even though Tom and Oliver had pumped her for hours.

Well, there wasn't going to be another mistake, Jack thought grimly, his strong hands tightening on the wheel. Because now there was Lizzie's happiness to think of, too. No one was going to hurt either one of his girls.

From now on, if any guy so much as *looked* at Bryony the wrong way, if there was even a *scent* of someone messing her around, he'd step in and floor them.

Satisfied that he was back in control of the situation, he stopped trying to pulverise his precious car and slowed his pace.

All he needed to do now was plan. He needed to know exactly whom she was dating so that he could issue a warning.

Bryony let herself into the house and found her mother in the kitchen. 'Is she asleep?'

'Fast asleep.' Her mother dried her hands on a towel. 'You're back early, darling. Is something wrong?'

'No.' Bryony unwrapped the scarf from around her neck and tossed it onto the chair. Her coat followed.

'Bryony, I'm your mother. I can tell when something is wrong.'

Bryony glared at her, her eyes sparkling with unshed tears. 'Jack Rothwell, that's what's wrong!'

'Ah.' Her mother gave a smile and turned to put the kettle on. 'Tea?'

'I suppose so.' Bryony slumped into the nearest chair and sighed. 'He is the most infuriating man.'

'Is he?'

'You know he is.'

Her mother reached for the tea bags. 'I know that you two have been very close for almost the whole of your lives,' she said mildly. 'I'm sure that whatever it is you've quarrelled about will go away.'

'The man dates every woman on the planet,' Bryony said, still outraged by his attitude, 'but when I announce that I'm going to start going out with men, he's suddenly disapproving. And he had the nerve to lecture me on my responsibilities to Lizzie!'

'Did he?' Her mother looked thoughtful. 'That's very interesting.'

'Interesting?' Bryony shot her mother an incredulous look. 'Irritating, you mean. And hypocritical. How many girlfriends has Jack Rothwell had since I first met him?'

Her mother poured the tea. 'Quite a few, I should think.'

'Half the planet,' Bryony said flatly. 'He certainly isn't in a position to lecture me about morals.'

'I imagine he thought he was protecting Lizzie.'

Bryony stared at her. 'From what?'

Her mother put two mugs on the table and sat down opposite her. 'Jack hasn't had a very positive experience of marriage, sweetheart.'

'You mean because of his parents?'

Her mother's mouth tightened with disapproval. 'Well, you know my opinion on that. They were grown-ups. He was a child. They should have sorted out their differences amicably. After his father walked out, Jack spent most of his childhood at our house and I don't think his mother even noticed he wasn't at home. She was too busy enjoying herself to remember that she had a child.'

Bryony bit her lip, suddenly realising why Jack might have been so sensitive about her dating. 'But I wouldn't do that. That isn't what this is about.'

'I know. But you understand Jack better than anyone,' her mother said calmly. 'He wasn't thinking about you, darling. He was thinking about his own experiences.'

Bryony bit her lip. 'Do you think I should start dating, Mum?'

'Certainly I think you should date,' her mother replied calmly. 'I've always thought you should date, but you've always been too crazy about Jack to notice anyone else.'

Bryony stared at her, opened her mouth to deny it and then caught the look in her mother's eye and closed it again. 'You know that?'

'I'm your mother. Of course I know that.'

'He doesn't notice me.'

'You're a huge part of Jack's life,' her mother said mildly. 'He virtually lives here. But that's going to have to change if you really are going to date other men.'

Bryony curled her hands round her mug. 'But I don't want it to change my friendship with Jack.'

'One day you'll get married again,' her mother said quietly, 'and I can't see any man wanting to see Jack lounging in your kitchen every time he comes home from work. Of course your friendship is going to change.'

Bryony stared into her mug, a hollow feeling inside her. She didn't want things to change. Despite their row, she couldn't imagine not having Jack in her life.

But she couldn't carry on the way she was now, for Lizzie's sake.

'Then I suppose I'll just have to get used to that,' she said, raising her mug in the air. 'Cheers. To my future.'

Her mother lifted her mug in response. 'May it turn out the way you want it to,' she said cryptically, and Bryony let out a long breath.

She wasn't really sure what *she* wanted.

But she knew Lizzie needed a daddy.

The next morning she was woken by her pager.

'Is that a callout?' Lizzie was by her bed in a flash, her eyes huge. 'Is someone in trouble on the mountain?'

Bryony picked up her pager and was reading the message when the phone rang. Lizzie grabbed it immediately.

'Hunter household, Elizabeth Hunter speaking,' she said formally, the angle of her chin suggesting that she was very proud of herself. She listened for a moment and then a smile spread across her face. 'Hello, Jack! Yes, Mummy's right here… I'll tell her. Will I see you later?'

Bryony pulled on her clothes and sprinted to the bathroom to clean her teeth. By the time she'd finished, Lizzie was off the phone.

'There's a party of Duke of Edinburgh Award boys overdue,' she said importantly. 'They're sending out the whole team but Sean wants you and Jack to be an advance party. Jack is picking you up in five minutes.'

'Five minutes.' Bryony hurried through to the kitchen, grabbed an apple from the fruit bowl and dropped some bread in the toaster. 'Get your school things, sweetheart. Jack and I will drop you at Grandma's on the way past and she can take you to school.'

Lizzie sprinted off and Bryony sent up a silent prayer of thanks that she had her mother close by. How did single parents manage without mothers?

By the time Jack hammered on the door, Lizzie was dressed and was standing by the door with her schoolbag, munching toast.

She stood on tiptoe and opened the door.

'Hi, there.' Jack stooped and swung her into his arms, squeezing her tightly. 'Are we dropping you with Grandma?'

'We certainly are.' Bryony walked into the hall and picked up her rucksack and the other bits and pieces that she'd piled by the door, avoiding Jack's gaze. She was grateful that Lizzie was there. At least it prevented her from having to continue the conversation from the night before.

She was still hurt and angry by Jack's response to her announcement that she was going to start dating.

They piled into the mountain rescue vehicle and Jack drove down the lane that led to Bryony's cottage and turned onto the main road.

'So what's the story?' Bryony twisted her blonde hair into a ponytail and pushed it under a woolly hat. Then she rummaged in her bag for her gloves.

Jack kept his eyes on the road. 'Two boys have been reported overdue. They should have been back down last night but they didn't appear.'

Bryony frowned. 'So why did no one call the team last night?'

'They were camping and didn't leave their plans with anyone so no one noticed until their friends stumbled into camp this morning and raised the alarm. The weather was foul last night, which is doubtless why Sean is worried.'

Lizzie stared at him, her eyes huge. 'Have they called the helicopter?'

'Yes, sweetheart.' Jack glanced at her with a smile. 'But the weather is pretty awful so Sean, the MRT leader, wants your mum and me to get going up that mountain in case we can help.'

'Why do you and Mummy always go together?'

Jack turned his attention back to the road and pulled the vehicle up outside Bryony's mother's house. 'Because your mum and I have always worked together in the mountain rescue team,' he said lightly. 'When your mum trained, I was her buddy. I looked after her.'

'And you still look after her,' Lizzie said happily, jumping down from the vehicle and grabbing her school-bag.

'I don't need looking after,' Bryony said crossly, glaring at Jack and calling after Lizzie, 'Sweetheart, ask Grandma to give you some more breakfast. I'll see you later.'

They waited until Bryony's mother opened the door and then Jack gave a wave and hit the accelerator.

Suddenly Bryony was very aware that it was just the two of them and she stared out of the window, for the first time in her life not knowing what to say.

'We think we know where they are,' Jack told her, flicking the indicator and turning down a narrow road. 'It's just a question of what state they'll be in when we get there.'

Which was why Sean had sent them as the advance party, Bryony thought. He wanted doctors. Which meant that he was anticipating trouble.

She picked up the map. 'What's the grid reference?'

He told her and she traced it with her finger. 'They're in the ghyll?'

'Sounds like it.'

Bryony looked at him in concern. 'But the water level is terribly high after all that rain we've had…'

'That's right.' Jack's voice was even and he brought the vehicle to a halt. 'Which is why we need to get a move on. Personally I doubt they'll be able to fly a helicopter in this. Sean has called the whole team out, but we're going on ahead.'

He sprang out of the vehicle and reached for the equipment that they'd need. They worked quickly and quietly, each knowing what the other was doing.

'You ready?' Jack lifted an eyebrow in her direction and she nodded.

'Let's go.'

Jack set off at a fast pace and Bryony followed, knowing that speed was important. After a night out in the open in the wet and temperatures below freezing, the boys would be in serious trouble.

They had to reach them fast.

The path grew steeper, the mist came down and Jack shook his head. 'It's November, it's freezing cold and the visibility is zero.' He hitched his rucksack more comfortably on his broad shoulders and squinted into the mist. 'Who the hell chooses to climb mountains at this time of year?'

'You do it all the time,' Bryony pointed out, checking her compass again. 'One of these days we're going to be out here rescuing you.'

'Never.' He winked and gave her a sexy grin. 'I am invincible.'

Bryony rolled her eyes. 'And arrogant.' She stopped dead and he looked at her questioningly.

'Why have you stopped?'

'Because your ego is blocking my path.'

Jack laughed and then the laughter faded. 'Listen, Blondie, about last night—'

'Not now,' Bryony said hastily. She really didn't want to tackle the subject again so soon, especially not halfway up a mountain.

'I just wanted to apologise,' he said softly. 'I was out of line. You're a brilliant mother and I know you'll do what's right for Lizzie.'

Stunned by his apology, Bryony lost her ability to speak. She'd never heard Jack apologise for anything before.

'Let's forget it,' she mumbled, and Jack nodded, his blue eyes studying her closely.

'All right. We'll talk about it later.' He glanced up the path and frowned. 'There is no way that helicopter is going to fly in this.'

'So we evacuate them down the mountain.'

He nodded and then turned to her, his eyes twinkling wickedly. 'Why did the blonde stare at the can of frozen orange juice?' He leaned forward and tucked a strand of hair back under her hat. 'Because it said "concentrate".'

Bryony tipped her head on one side and stared back at him. 'Why are men like government bonds?' He lifted an eyebrow, his eyes dancing, and she smiled sweetly. 'Because they take for ever to mature. Now, can we get on with this rescue?'

They stuck to the path and the mist grew thicker. Jack's radio crackled to life and he paused and had a quick conversation with Sean back at base.

'They're sending out the whole team,' he told her when he came off the radio, 'but I reckon we must be nearly at the place where they were last seen.'

Bryony stood still, listening, but all she could hear was the rush of water. The freezing air snaked through her clothing and she shivered.

'If they didn't have any protection last night, they won't have stood a chance,' she muttered, and Jack nodded, his handsome face serious.

'Better find them, fast.'

He started up the track again and then stopped, squinting down into the ghyll. 'Do you see something?'

'What?' Bryony stepped towards the edge but Jack reached out a strong arm and clamped her against him.

'If it's all the same to you, I'd rather you didn't go over the edge, too,' he said dryly, keeping his arm round her as he peered through the mist into the ghyll again.

Bryony held her breath, painfully conscious of his hard body pressed against hers.

'I don't see anything.' She wondered when he was going

to let her go and was about to ask when she spotted a flash of red below them. 'OK, I see something.'

'Me, too.' Jack released her. 'There's a path here but it's narrow and slippery. Think you can manage, Blondie? You have to put one leg in front of the other and not fall over.'

'It'll be a struggle, but I'll do my best,' Bryony assured him earnestly, relieved that their relationship seemed to have restored itself to its usual level. 'What about you? Think you can find your way without asking for directions?'

They kept up the banter as they picked their way down the path, and finally they reached the bottom and immediately saw the boys huddled together by a boulder.

Jack closed the distance in seconds and dropped to his haunches, his expression concerned. 'Hi, there—nice day for a stroll in the mountains.'

'We thought no one was ever coming,' the boy whispered, his teeth chattering as he spoke. 'Martyn keeps falling asleep and leaving me on my own.'

'Right. Put a bivouac tent over them.' Jerking his head to indicate that Bryony should deal with the conscious child, Jack shifted his position so that he could examine the other boy.

He was lying still, moaning quietly, his cheeks pale and his lips blue.

Jack spoke to him quietly and checked his pulse while Bryony checked the other boy for injuries. Once she was satisfied that he was just cold and shaken, she erected the tent and helped him to scramble inside a casualty bag.

'What's your name?'

'Sam.'

'Well, Sam, that will keep you warm until we can get you off this mountain,' she assured him, and he gave a little sob.

'Martyn fell. His leg is awful. I saw bone.'

Bryony slipped an arm round him and gave him a hug. 'Don't you worry about that now,' she said softly. 'We'll sort him out and get you both home. I'm going to pour you a hot drink and that will warm you up.'

She grabbed the flask that she'd packed and poured thick creamy chocolate into a mug.

'Here—drink this. I'll be back in a sec.' Aware that Jack was going to need her help, she slid out of the tent and moved over to him.

'Sam says that his friend fell.'

Jack nodded, still checking the child over. 'He's got a compound fracture of his tib and fib and he's bleeding a lot. We need to get a line in, Blondie, and then splint that leg.'

Bryony reached for the rucksack and found what they needed, aware that Jack was on the radio again, updating Sean on their position and the condition of the boys.

By the time he'd finished on the radio Bryony had a line in. 'Do you want to give him fluid?'

Jack nodded. 'And then we need to splint that leg. It will help the pain and reduce blood loss.' He leaned over the boy, talking quietly, explaining what they were doing, and Bryony gave a sigh. He was so good when anyone was in trouble. A rock. And he always knew what to do. Her confidence came from being with him.

She covered the wound on the leg with a sterile saline-soaked dressing while Jack carefully removed the boy's boot.

He placed his fingers on Martyn's foot, feeling for a pulse. 'That's fine—let's splint this leg. We're just going to give you something for the pain, Martyn, and then we're going to put your leg in a splint. Then we're going to warm you up and get you off this mountain.'

Bryony gave a shiver. The temperature was dropping fast and even in her top-quality gear she could feel the cold.

By the time they'd splinted the boy's leg, Sean had arrived with the rest of the mountain rescue team.

'Nice day for a walk,' he drawled, glancing around him at the thick mist. 'The views are fantastic.'

Bryony smiled. 'Absolutely fantastic,' she said sarcastically. 'Enjoy your stroll, did you?'

Sean grinned in appreciation. 'Didn't want to rush things,' he said, lifting an eyebrow in Jack's direction. 'Well?'

'We need a helicopter but I don't suppose there's any chance of that.'

'You suppose correctly.'

Jack sighed and checked the pulses on the boy's foot again. 'So we'd better carry them off, then. Good. I needed a workout.'

It seemed to take ages to organise both boys onto stretchers but eventually they managed to carry them out of the ghyll and started down the mountain.

By the time they reached the valley floor the mist had cleared and it was a sunny day.

'I don't believe this,' Bryony muttered, tugging off her hat and shaking her hair loose. 'What is it with our weather?'

Both boys were loaded into the mountain rescue team

ambulance and then transferred to hospital under Sean's supervision while Jack and Bryony followed behind.

'Are you working today?' Jack glanced across at her and she nodded.

'Yes. I'm on a late. Why?'

He returned his attention to the road. 'I thought you had a date.'

Bryony looked at him warily. 'That's tomorrow, but I don't know if I'm going because Mum has to go and visit someone in Kendal so I don't think she can babysit.'

'I'll babysit for you.'

Bryony stared at him. 'You?'

'Why not?' His eyes were fixed on the road. 'I often babysit for you. It gives me a chance to talk to my god-child. I like it.'

Bryony looked at him suspiciously. 'But last night…' She broke off and bit her lip, not really wanting to bring the subject up in case it rocked the peace that had resumed between them. 'Last night you said that you didn't think I should be dating.'

'And I've already apologised for that,' he said, flicking the indicator and turning into the road that led to the hospital. 'And to make up for it, I'll babysit for you. What time do you want me?'

Still feeling uneasy about the whole thing but not knowing why, Bryony gave a shrug. 'Seven-thirty?'

'Seven-thirty is perfect. There's just one thing…' He pulled up in the ambulance bay and yanked on the hand-brake. 'You haven't told me who you're going out with.'

There was something in his smooth tones that made her glance at him warily but his handsome face was impassive.

She paused with her hand on the door. 'David.'

'David Armstrong? The paediatrician?' Jack's expression didn't change but she sensed something that made her uneasy.

'Look, Jack—'

'I'll be there at seven-thirty. Now, let's get on. I need to get antibiotics into Martyn and call the surgeons. That wound is going to need some attention.'

And with that he sprang out of the vehicle, leaving her staring after him.

Jack was going to babysit while she went on a date?

It seemed harmless enough, generous even, so why did she have such a strong feeling that something wasn't quite right?

CHAPTER THREE

'MUMMY you look pretty.'

'Do you think so?' Bryony surveyed her reflection in the mirror, wondering whether the dress was right for the evening that David had in mind. He'd said dinner in a smart restaurant, but she never went to smart restaurants so she wasn't that sure what to wear.

In the end she'd settled for the little black dress that her mother had given her three Christmases ago and which she'd never worn.

She'd fastened her hair on top of her head, found a pair of pretty, dangly earrings and dabbed perfume over her body.

And she had to admit that she was looking forward to going out with a man.

So much so that when the doorbell rang she opened the door with a wide smile.

'Hi, Jack.' Her face glowed and she stood to one side to let him in. 'There's a casserole in the oven. I assumed you wouldn't have eaten—'

'I haven't eaten.' His eyes slid down her body and he frowned, his expression suddenly hostile.

Bryony felt the confidence ooze out of her. She'd thought that she looked good but, judging from the look on Jack's face, she obviously didn't.

'Come through to the kitchen,' she said quickly, suddenly wishing that she'd worn something different. Obviously the black dress didn't suit her. 'We've got time for a quick drink before David gets here. He was held up in clinic.'

Jack's mouth tightened with disapproval. 'So he's going to be late, then.'

'Well, only because a child with asthma was admitted at the last minute,' Bryony said mildly, tugging open the fridge and reaching for a bottle of wine. 'You know how it is.'

'Do I?'

Instead of settling himself at her kitchen table as he usually did, he prowled round the room, his eyes constantly flickering back to her dress.

Trying to ignore his intense scrutiny, Bryony poured two glasses of wine and handed him one. 'Here you are. Cheers.'

He took the wine and put it on the table, his eyes fixed on her legs.

Bryony felt her whole body warm with embarrassment. She hardly ever showed her legs. She usually wore trousers for work because they were more practical, and when she went to the pub with the rest of the mountain rescue team she wore trousers, too.

But tonight, for the first time in ages, she'd put on a

pair of sheer, black stockings and she was beginning to wish she hadn't.

'You hate it, don't you?' she croaked, and his eyes lifted and welded to hers.

'Hate what?'

She swallowed. 'The way I look. My dress. Me. You're staring and staring.'

Jack let out a breath. 'That's because I don't think you should be going out with a man dressed like that,' he said tightly. 'It sends out all the wrong messages.'

She frowned at him, totally confused. 'What messages?'

He tensed. 'Well—that you're available.'

'Jack,' she said patiently, 'I *am* available. That is the message I want to send out.'

'So you wear a skirt that's up to your bottom?' He glared at her and she stared back helplessly, totally confused by his attitude.

She'd met some of the girls that he'd dated and they were almost all blondes with skirts up round their bottoms.

'Jack, my skirt is just above the knee,' she pointed out, glancing down at herself to check that half her dress hadn't fallen off without her knowledge. 'It is nowhere near my bottom.'

'Well, it's definitely too low in the front,' he said hoarsely, reaching across the kitchen table, yanking a flower out of a vase and snapping it halfway up the stem. 'Try this.'

He walked up to her and slipped the flower down the neckline of her dress and stood back with a frown.

'That's a bit better.'

'Jack—'

Before she could say anything, Lizzie came running into the room wearing a pink gauze fairy dress and wearing wings. 'Jack, Jack!' She flung herself into his arms and he picked her up and gave her a kiss on the cheek.

'Hello, beautiful. Shouldn't you be in bed?'

'I was waiting for you.' Lizzie curled her legs round his waist and waggled her finger at him. 'Look. I'm wearing three rings. They're sweets really, but aren't they great?'

Jack dutifully studied her finger. 'Really great. And if you get hungry in the night you can eat them.'

Lizzie beamed. 'Can we play a game, Jack?'

'Sure.' Jack put her down gently and smiled indulgently. 'Any game you like. Just name it.'

'Weddings.'

Jack's smile vanished. *'Weddings?'*

Lizzie nodded happily. 'Yes, you know. You're the boy and I'm the girl and we get married.'

Jack gave a shudder. 'I don't know the rules, sweetheart.'

Bryony covered her hand with her mouth to hide her smile. Jack was brilliant at playing with her daughter but 'Weddings' was the one game guaranteed to bring him out in a rash.

'It's easy,' Lizzie assured him happily. 'We hold hands and then we get married.'

Jack ran a hand over the back of his neck and looked at Bryony for help, but she simply smiled.

'Weddings, Jack,' she said softly, her eyes dancing as she looked at him. 'That well-known game enjoyed by men and women the world over.'

His eyes shot daggers at her but he turned to Lizzie

with a resigned sigh. 'All right, peanut, tell me what I have to do.'

'Well, first I have to go and dress up.' Lizzie shot out of the room and Jack turned on Bryony.

'She's playing *weddings*?'

'She's a girl, Jack,' Bryony said mildly. 'Girls play weddings.'

'I'm breaking out in a sweat here,' he muttered dryly, and she grinned unsympathetically.

'She's seven years old. I think you can cope. Great practice for when you do the real thing.'

His gaze locked on hers, his blue eyes mocking. 'You know I'm never doing the real thing.'

'Well, don't tell my daughter that. I don't want her saddled with your prejudices about relationships.'

'I should be teaching her about reality.'

Before Bryony could answer, Lizzie danced back into the room, this time wearing a full-length sparkly dress complete with glittering tiara.

Jack blinked. 'Wow…' He cleared his throat. 'I didn't know you had a tiara.'

'I've got seven,' Lizzie said proudly, and Bryony smiled cheerfully.

'A girl can never have too many tiaras, can she, Lizzie?'

'Come on, Jack.' Lizzie grabbed his hand. 'First we have to hold hands and walk across the carpet. Mummy can video us.'

Jack glanced at Bryony who could barely stand up she was laughing so much. 'Great idea, Lizzie,' she choked. 'It would make great viewing at the MRT Christmas party. Jack finally getting married.'

Jack scowled, but his eyes were dancing. 'Revenge is going to be sweet, Blondie,' he warned softly, but he was laughing too and shaking his head as Lizzie dragged him into the sitting room and Bryony reached for the video camera.

To give him his due, Jack treated the whole occasion with the appropriate amount of solemnity, sweeping Lizzie's hand to his lips as if she were a princess.

At first Bryony was laughing so much that she could hardly keep the camera steady, but as she watched Jack playing his role to perfection and saw the delight on her little girl's face, her smile faded and she felt an ache growing inside her. Jack was so brilliant with Lizzie. And although he couldn't see it himself, he'd make a wonderful father.

She was reminding herself firmly that she wasn't going to think that way any more when the doorbell rang and she realised that her date had arrived.

She answered the door and David stood on the doorstep, flourishing a bunch of flowers.

'Are they for me? They're beautiful, thank you.' She smiled at him and was wondering whether she ought to kiss him when she heard Jack clear his throat behind her.

'You'll need a coat, Blondie,' he said coolly, the humour gone from his eyes as he held out the long woollen coat that she always wore to work and which covered her from her neck to her ankles.

'I was going to take my pashmina,' Bryony began, but Jack walked up behind her and draped the coat over her shoulders, pulling it closed at the front so that not one single inch of her was visible.

'It's too cold for a pashmina,' he grated. 'You don't want

to get hypothermia over dinner.' He stood back and gave David a nod. 'She needs to be home at eleven.'

'What?' Bryony gaped at him and then gave an embarrassed laugh. They hadn't even discussed what time he wanted her home but she'd assumed that she could be as late as she liked. She knew Jack well enough to know that he didn't go to bed early himself. And invariably he slept in her spare room. So why was he saying that she needed to be in by eleven?

David gave an awkward smile. 'Eleven is fine.'

Bryony scowled, less than impressed that he hadn't stood up to Jack. Surely he should have said that he'd bring her home when he was ready, or some such thing. She knew for sure that if someone had told Jack that he should bring a girl home by eleven he would have kept her out for the whole night just to prove a point.

But she'd promised herself that she wasn't going to think about Jack, she reminded herself hastily, taking the flowers through to the kitchen and putting them in water.

When she arrived back at the door the two men were staring at each other. David looked mildly embarrassed and Jack was standing, feet planted firmly apart, very much the dominant male and not in the slightest bit embarrassed.

Deciding that Jack had definitely gone mad, Bryony held out a hand to David and smiled. 'Shall we go?'

'Jack.' Lizzie tugged his arm and frowned at him. 'You're skipping bits.'

Jack shook himself and stared down at the book he was supposed to be reading. 'Am I?'

'Yes.' Lizzie grabbed the book from him and went back

two pages. 'You didn't read this page at all. And you've got a funny look on your face.'

'Have I?'

Jack tried to concentrate on the pink fairy flying across the page of the book but all he could see was Bryony in that dress. He hadn't seen her legs since she'd been in the netball team at school and he and her brothers had gone to matches to cheer her on, but he now realised that his best friend had sensational legs.

And if she was going to start showing them, how the hell was he going to protect her?

And it wasn't just her legs, of course…

He closed his eyes, trying to forget the shadowy dip between her full breasts revealed by the cut of her dress.

Right now they were in the restaurant and David was probably sitting opposite her, staring into paradise.

With a soft curse he stood up and the book fell to the floor.

'You said a rude word, Jack,' Lizzie said mildly, leaning over and retrieving the book.

'Sorry.' Suddenly seized by inspiration, he gave Lizzie a smile. 'How would you like to call your mother and say goodnight?'

'Now?'

'Sure, why not?' Before Dr Armstrong had time to get too hot and over-eager. Suddenly driven by an urgency that he couldn't explain, Jack grabbed Lizzie's hand and dragged her into the kitchen. 'We'll ring her mobile.'

Lizzie looked at him uncertainly. 'Grandma says we only ring if there's an emergency.'

Jack was already pressing the keys. 'Trust me, this is

an emergency,' he assured her, his mind still mentally on Bryony's creamy breasts. His mouth tightened. 'A big emergency. Her baby girl wants to say goodnight.'

Trying to ignore the fact that Lizzie was looking at him as though he was slightly mad, Jack held the receiver and waited for Bryony to answer.

As the phone rang and rang, his heart started to thud in his chest.

Why the hell wasn't she answering?

Unless she wasn't at dinner after all. What if the rat had taken one look at that dress and whisked Bryony back to his flat?

'Uncle Jack, you're breathing really fast,' Lizzie said, climbing onto a kitchen stool, her fairy wings still attached to her back. 'And you look weird.'

He felt weird.

Why wasn't she answering?

David sat back in his chair. 'Is that your phone?'

Bryony looked at him, startled, and then picked up her bag. 'Oh, my goodness, yes.' She fumbled in her handbag, her stomach turning over. 'I hope nothing is wrong with Lizzie. I don't usually get phoned...'

She delved amongst tissues, make-up, notebooks and various pink hairbands that belonged to her daughter and eventually found the phone.

Feeling distinctly nervous, she answered it. 'Jack?' She cast an apologetic look at David. 'Is something wrong?'

She listened for a moment and then frowned. 'I'm in the restaurant, Jack. Where did you think I was? Well, I couldn't find my phone.'

At that moment the waiter delivered their starter and Bryony smiled her thanks, trying to ignore his look of disapproval. She knew that mobile phones were banned from lots of restaurants but she refused to turn hers off in case Lizzie needed her.

But it seemed that all Lizzie wanted was to say goodnight. Strange, Bryony thought as she spoke to her daughter and then ended the call. Lizzie was normally fine. Especially when she was with Jack. She loved being with Jack.

'Everything OK?' David looked at her quizzically and she smiled.

'Fine. Sorry about that.'

She picked up her fork and tucked into her starter, determined to relax. Part of her mind was still dwelling on the fact that Jack had hated her dress, but she ignored it. David seemed to think she looked nice and that was all that mattered.

They chattered about work and the mountain rescue team and they were just tucking into their main course when her phone rang again.

This time Bryony heard it immediately and stopped the ringing before the waiter had time to glare at her.

It was Jack again, this time telling her that Lizzie was refusing to take her fairy wings off.

Bryony frowned. This was a guy who could save a life halfway up a mountain in a howling gale with nothing more than a penknife and a piece of string.

And he was calling her about *fairy wings*?

'Just take them off when she's asleep, Jack,' she muttered, smiling apologetically at David as she slipped the phone back into her bag.

She tried valiantly to resume the conversation but when Jack called for the third time, David raised his hand and gestured to the waiter.

'I think I'll take you home,' he said dryly. 'Then you can answer Jack's questions in person and he won't have to keep calling you.'

'Sorry.' Bryony blushed slightly. As a first date it had been less than perfect. 'I honestly don't know what's the matter with him. He and Lizzie are normally fine together.'

David drove her home and then walked her up the path to her cottage. At the front door he paused, his expression thoughtful as he looked down at her.

Bryony stared back, feeling slightly awkward. Was he going to kiss her?

Suddenly she felt a flash of panic. She wasn't actually sure that she wanted him to kiss her.

His head was bending towards hers when the front door was jerked open and Jack stood there, broad-shouldered and imposing.

'You're home. Great.'

Bryony looked at David. 'Would you like to come in for coffee?'

'He needs to get going,' Jack said coldly, his face unsmiling. 'The roads are icy tonight and they're forecasting snow.'

David was silent for a moment, his eyes on Jack. 'Right. In that case I'd better make a move.'

'OK, then.' Secretly relieved by the decision, Bryony

stood on tiptoe and kissed his cheek. 'Thanks for tonight. I enjoyed it.'

'Me, too.' David was still looking at Jack and then he gave a funny smile and turned to Bryony. 'I'll see you at work.'

With that he turned the collar of his coat up and strolled back down her path towards his car.

Bryony followed Jack into the cottage and slipped her coat off.

'I'm sorry Lizzie was such hard work tonight, Jack.' She strolled into the kitchen and flipped the kettle on. 'She never normally wants to call me. And she doesn't normally care if she's lost the book she was reading—she'll just pick another one. It doesn't sound as though you managed to relax at all.'

'I managed.' Jack sank onto one of the kitchen chairs and put his feet on the table in his usual pose. 'I expect she was just a bit unsettled by the thought of you going out with a strange man.'

Bryony frowned slightly. It was Lizzie who had suggested this whole daddy business, so why would she be unsettled? On the other hand, perhaps she hadn't really thought the whole thing through. It was certainly true that Lizzie wasn't used to seeing strange men in her life. She saw Jack and her two uncles and that was about it.

'She'll get used to it.'

'Maybe.' Jack sounded noncommittal. 'So—did you have a good evening?'

There was something in his tone that she couldn't interpret and Bryony lifted two mugs out of the cupboard, not sure how to answer. Had she had a good evening? If she was honest, she didn't really feel she'd had a chance to talk to David. Every time they'd begun a conversation the phone had rung.

Poor Lizzie.

She'd talk to her tomorrow and see how she felt about the whole thing. She certainly didn't want to go on dates if it was going to upset her daughter.

'I had a nice evening,' she said finally, not wanting to admit to Jack that it had been anything less than perfect. 'It's a shame David wouldn't come in for coffee.'

'It's not a shame. It was a lucky escape.' Jack swung his legs off the table and glared at her. '*Never* invite a man in for coffee.'

Bryony looked at him in astonishment. 'I was being polite.'

He lifted an eyebrow. 'Offering to have sex with a man is being polite?'

Bryony gaped at him, stunned. 'I did not offer to have sex with him, I offered him *coffee*.'

'It's the same thing.' A muscle flickered in his jaw, rough with stubble so late in the evening. He looked dark and dangerous and Bryony felt her stomach flip.

Why couldn't she find David even *half* as attractive? She'd been less than enthusiastic at the possibility of him kissing her, but if it had been Jack who'd been on the doorstep with her...

Reminding herself that she wasn't supposed to be noticing Jack, Bryony picked up the coffee-jar.

'Coffee is the same as sex?' She twisted the jar in her hand, looking at it with a mocking expression. 'Full of caffeine and sold in supermarkets. I don't think so.'

Jack glared at her. 'You can joke about it, but do you really think a man wants to sit around, drinking your coffee?'

'You're sitting around, drinking my coffee,' Bryony pointed out logically, and his mouth hardened.

'That's different. I'm not trying to get you into my bed.'

More's the pity, Bryony thought wistfully, putting the coffee down on the side. If Jack ever tried to get her into his bed she'd be there like a flash.

'Jack, I'm sure David didn't have anything immoral on his mind.'

'Which just shows how little you know about men,' Jack said tightly. 'Do you know the average man thinks about sex every six seconds?'

'So presumably that's why they say men are like photocopiers,' Bryony said dryly. 'Good for reproduction but not much else.'

For once Jack didn't laugh and she sighed inwardly. There was obviously something about the idea of her dating that short-circuited his sense of humour.

Suddenly she wanted the old Jack back. The Jack that called her Blondie and teased her unmercifully. The Jack with the wicked smile and the sexiest wink known to woman.

'Jack.' Her tone was patient. 'I invited David in for coffee because I was being polite. I had no intention of having sex with him.'

'And what if he'd decided to have sex with you?'

She looked at him in exasperation. 'Well, despite the colour of my hair I do have a brain and a mouth,' she said tartly. 'I can think no and say no. At the same time.

Amazing really. If I concentrate really hard I can add two and two. Jack, *what is the matter with you?*'

'I just think you're being naïve.'

'Inviting a guy in for coffee?' Bryony gritted her teeth and shook her head. 'You've gone crazy, do you know that?'

There was a long silence and streaks of colour touched his hard cheekbones. 'Maybe I have,' he said shortly, putting his half-full mug on the table and rising to his feet in a fluid movement. 'I'd better get home.'

'Fine. Thank you for babysitting.'

'You're welcome.'

As a farewell it had none of its usual warmth and Bryony turned away and poured the rest of her coffee down the sink, boiling with frustration and feeling confused and upset.

She heard Jack stride to her front door, heard him pick up his jacket and car keys and then the front door slammed behind him.

Bryony winced and let out a long breath.

Just what was going on with Jack?

Bryony was nervous about working with Jack the next day but he seemed back to his usual self, relaxed and good-humoured as they sat in the staffroom and discussed the shifts for Bonfire Night.

'It's my turn.' Sean Nicholson, one of the other consultants, looked at Jack with a resigned expression on his face. 'You deserve a year off from Bonfire Night. You've had a bad few years.'

Jack rolled his eyes. 'I won't know what to do with

myself,' he drawled, and Bryony gave him a sympathetic
smile.

'You hate this time of year, don't you?'

'I've just seen too many kids with burns after handling
fireworks,' he said grimly, scribbling something on his pad.
'OK, so Blondie and I are officially off that night, but if
you need us you can call us.' He looked at Bryony. 'Would
you be able to come in that night if we needed you?'

Bryony nodded. 'After eight. I'm taking Lizzie to her
bonfire party.'

Jack stared at her, his body suddenly unnaturally still.
'What bonfire party?'

'Her friend is having a few sparklers in the garden.
Nothing dramatic,' Bryony assured him, but he shook his
head.

'No way.' His jaw was tense. 'She shouldn't be going.'

Bryony sighed. 'She's seven, Jack. She wants to be with
her friends.'

'So? Invite them all out for a hamburger.'

'It's just a few fireworks and drinks for the parents. It
will be over by eight.'

He let out a breath. 'All right. But I'm coming with you.'

'Jack—'

'I'm off and I'm bored.' His blue eyes glittered dangerously. 'It's that or she doesn't go.'

'You're not her father, Jack!' Suddenly remembering
that Sean was still in the room, Bryony coloured with
embarrassment and shot them an apologetic look. 'Sorry,
you guys.'

'No problem,' Sean said easily, 'and I'm sure we won't
need you here so just go and have a good time.'

'Great. That's what we'll do, then.'

Jack ran through the rest of the rota and Sean left the room.

Bryony looked at him. 'So what are you planning to do? Bring the fire brigade?'

'When you've spent as long working in A and E as I have, you won't let your daughter go to domestic firework parties,' he said tightly. 'It's fine. I'll come, too. And you can tell Lizzie's friend's mother that I want a bucket of sand and another bucket of water handy.'

'Why don't we just have an ambulance on standby, just in case?' Bryony suggested tartly. 'Anne's mother will think I've gone barmy.'

'Better barmy than burned.' Jack strode to the door. 'What time does it start?'

'We're getting there at five-thirty for tea and then fireworks,' Bryony said wearily, and Jack nodded.

'Right. I'll pick you both up at five-fifteen. And I want Lizzie in gloves. She's not touching a sparkler with her bare hands.'

Bryony stood up and followed him out of the staffroom, wanting to argue but knowing that he was only being cautious.

He had dealt with a huge number of burns on Bonfire Night, all of which could have been avoided.

And he did adore Lizzie.

Deciding that she should be grateful that he was so protective of her daughter, she picked up a set of notes and called the next patient from the waiting room.

And secretly part of her was excited at spending an

evening with Jack. Even if it was in the company of half a dozen parents and their offspring.

It would be lovely to have him there, even though nothing was going to happen.

Reminding herself that Jack was not the man she was dating, she sat down in her chair and waited for the patient to arrive.

CHAPTER FOUR

THE NIGHT of the bonfire party was freezing cold and Bryony pulled on her jeans and thickest jumper and wore her long black coat.

Lizzie was wearing a bright pink hat, pink tights and a pink fleece, and Jack blinked when he arrived to pick them up.

'How are my girls?' He picked Lizzie up and planted a kiss on her cheek. 'You're looking very pink, angel.' He spoke in that lazy drawl that sent butterflies flitting through Bryony's stomach. 'Do you have any pink gloves to go with that outfit, sweetheart?'

'Somewhere.'

Jack smiled and put her back down. 'Find them for me, there's a good girl.' He looked at Bryony and she smiled, determined to have a nice evening.

'Is my dress decent enough for you, Jack?'

For a moment he didn't react and then he laughed. 'Exactly the way I like it. None of you showing.'

Bryony rolled her eyes and tried not to be offended that

he didn't actually want to see any of her body. Obviously she was lacking in something, or he would have pounced on her long ago.

Lizzie came back into the hall, holding her gloves, and Jack nodded.

'Good girl.' He opened the front door and led them towards his car. 'Now, Lizzie, tonight when the fireworks start, I want you to stay by me. The whole time. OK?'

'But what if I want to play with my friends?'

'You can play with them before and after,' he said firmly, strapping her into her seat. 'But during the fireworks, you stay with me.'

Lizzie's eyes were huge and solemn. 'Are you very afraid of them, Jack? Will I need to hold your hand?'

Bryony smothered a giggle but Jack's expression didn't flicker. 'I'm terrified of them, angel. And I'm relying on you to be beside me.'

'I'll be there the whole time,' Lizzie assured him, and Bryony rolled her eyes as she slid into the passenger seat, knowing that Jack had got his own way.

Lizzie's friend Anne lived in a house with a huge garden and they arrived to find that the trees had been decorated with fairy lights and everyone was gathered round, laughing and waiting for sausages to cook.

It felt wintry and cold, and delicious smells wafted through the freezing air.

'Hello, Lizzie.' Anne's mother greeted them warmly and drew them into the garden, introducing them to people they didn't know.

'Where have you stored the fireworks?' was Jack's first

question, and Bryony put a hand on his arm and smiled at Anne's mother.

'Jack is a consultant in A and E,' she explained hastily, 'and we doctors are always a bit nervous of fireworks. Take no notice.'

'Anne's father has it all under control,' the woman assured them, waving a hand towards the bottom of the garden. 'The children won't be allowed near them. Apart from the sparklers, of course.'

Bryony saw Jack's mouth open and quickly spoke before he did. 'That's great,' she said cheerfully, her fingers biting into his arm like a vice. 'Those sausages smell fantastic.'

'Well, we're just about ready to eat.' Anne's mother led them to a table loaded with food. 'Grab yourself a roll and some ketchup and tuck in!'

She walked away and Jack scowled at Bryony. 'You just made holes in my arm.'

'I was trying to stop you embarrassing Lizzie,' she hissed, smiling sweetly at one of the mothers who passed. 'Now, eat something and relax. Try and remember that you only see the disasters in A and E. You don't see the normal, happy bonfire parties that everyone enjoys.'

There was a long silence and then, to her surprise, Jack sucked in a breath and gave her a lopsided smile. 'You're right,' he said dryly, running a hand through his cropped dark hair. 'I'm being an idiot. It's just that I love Lizzie so much.'

Bryony's face softened. 'I know you do.' On impulse she stood on tiptoe and kissed his cheek, feeling the roughness of stubble against her lips and smelling the sexy male smell that was Jack.

He looked startled. 'What was that for?'

'For being you.' Deciding that, for a girl who was supposed to be forgetting about Jack, she wasn't actually doing that well, Bryony left him by the bread rolls and went and found Lizzie.

'You kissed Jack.' Lizzie was looking at her curiously and Bryony felt herself blush.

'Just on the cheek,' she said hastily, and Lizzie tipped her head on one side.

'Jack would make a cool dad.'

Pretending that she hadn't heard that remark, Bryony turned to chat to one of the mothers that she knew vaguely, trying not to look at Jack who was now deep in conversation with one of the prettiest mothers in the school. He looked broad-shouldered and powerful with his back to her, and her stomach twisted as she saw the woman laughing up at him flirtatiously.

Reminding herself that she was supposed to be getting a life and forgetting about Jack, Bryony joined in with the others, handing food to the children, topping up drinks and wiping ketchup from faces.

Anne's father lit the bonfire and the flames licked towards the dark sky, suddenly illuminating the massive garden.

'You kids stay here,' he ordered cheerfully. 'I'm going to start the show.'

'Mummy, can I have another drink?' Lizzie tugged at her sleeve, her cheeks pink from the cold, and Bryony took her hand and led her over to the table.

'What do you want?' She picked up some empty cartons and then found a full one. 'Apple juice OK?'

'Great.' Lizzie took the cup and looked around her happily. 'Isn't this great, Mummy? You, me and Jack together.'

Bryony swallowed. 'Well, er, we're not exactly…' Then she smiled weakly. 'Yes, sweetheart, it's great.'

There were shrieks of excitement from the other children as they played closer to the fire and Bryony felt a stab of unease.

They were too close…

Opening her mouth to caution them, she noticed the other parents laughing, totally relaxed, and closed her mouth again. She really must try and act like a normal parent and not like a doctor, seeing accidents everywhere.

'Can I go and play, Mummy?' Lizzie put her drink down and moved towards the other children, but Bryony grabbed her arm, struck by a premonition so powerful that it made her gasp. 'No, Lizzie. I think—'

Before she could even finish her sentence there was a series of horrific screams from Annie, and Bryony saw flames engulfing her little body with frightening speed.

'Oh, my God—*Jack*!' Bryony screamed his name at the top of her voice and ran forward, dragging off her coat as she ran.

Jack was there before her, knocking the girl to the ground and covering her with his jacket. 'Cold water— get me cold water *now*!' His voice was harsh and everyone ran to do as he said while Bryony stood there, so shocked she could hardly move.

All Jack's attention was on the injured girl. 'It's going to be all right, sweetheart. You're going to be fine.' Jack lifted his head and looked straight at one of the fathers.

'Call the paramedics and get me a hosepipe and cling film. Blondie, I need your help with her clothes.'

Bryony still didn't move.

'Dr Hunter.' His voice was sharp. 'I need your help here.'

His sharp reminder of her profession brought her back to reality. She nodded and breathed deeply, trying to forget that it was Annie lying on the ground.

Her daughter's friend.

Annie's mother was screaming hysterically and clinging to the other mothers while two of the fathers had fortunately listened to Jack's orders and rolled out a hosepipe.

'OK, sweetheart, you're going to be fine.' Jack carried on talking to Annie, his voice gentle and reassuring as he removed his jacket from the injured girl and took the end of the hosepipe.

Bryony dropped on her knees beside him. 'What do you want me to do?'

She felt physically sick but as usual Jack was rock-solid and totally calm.

'Her clothes are smouldering. If they're not actually stuck to her body, I want them off.'

He turned the hose onto Annie's body, the cold water taking the heat away from the burn as Bryony struggled to remove the clothing.

'Get me scissors.'

Someone quickly produced a pair and she cut the clothing away as gently as she could, careful not to disturb any that actually adhered to the burn.

'It's all below her waist,' Jack said softly, his eyes assessing the area of the burn. 'It's the skirt area. Her skirt caught fire. Has someone called the ambulance?'

'I did, Jack,' Lizzie said in a shaky voice from right beside them. 'They said they'd be here in two minutes.'

'Good girl.' Jack gave her a nod of approval. 'Sweetheart, I need some clingfilm. The stuff you wrap round food in the kitchen. The women over there are too upset to help and the men seem to have forgotten. Can you find it for me, angel?'

Lizzie nodded and shot down the garden towards the house, legs and arms pumping. She was back in less than a minute with a long, thin box.

'That's my girl. Now open it up for me,' Jack ordered, and Lizzie fished it out awkwardly and struggled to find the end.

'How much do you want?'

'I'll do it, Lizzie.' Bryony took it from her, worried about her daughter seeing her friend so badly injured. 'You can go into the house with the other children.'

'I want to help.'

They heard the sound of an ambulance approaching and Jack looked at Lizzie. 'Go and meet them. Tell them I want oxygen, two large-bore cannulae, IV fluids and morphine. Have you got that?'

Lizzie nodded and Bryony glanced at him.

'She won't remember that, Jack, she's only seven.'

'She'll remember,' Jack said firmly, his eyes fixed on Lizzie. 'Oxygen, two large-bore cannulae, IV fluids and morphine. Go, angel.'

Lizzie sped back down the garden to meet the ambulance, leaving Jack and Bryony to wrap the exposed burns.

'Can you get us clean sheets?' Bryony addressed one of the fathers who was hovering by helplessly.

'And someone put that bonfire out,' Jack added, checking Annie's pulse and breathing.

She'd stopped screaming and was lying shivering, sobbing quietly, her father by her side.

Annie's mother was still hysterical at the far side of the garden.

Seconds later the paramedics arrived with Lizzie, complete with all the equipment that Jack had asked for.

As Bryony grabbed the oxygen and fitted the mask gently to Annie's face, Jack smiled at Lizzie, his blue eyes showering her with approval and warmth.

'Good girl.'

Despite the stress of the situation Lizzie returned the smile bravely and Jack gave a nod.

'All right, I'm going to need your help here, Lizzie. Annie needs some fluid and we're going to put a line in and give her fluid through her arm. Then we're going to take her to hospital. I want you to hold this for me.'

Bryony looked at him uncertainly, still not sure that her young daughter should be exposed to the harsh realities of immediate care, but Jack seemed determined to involve her and Lizzie was frowning with concentration as she listened carefully to Jack's instructions and did as he asked.

Too worried about little Annie to argue, Bryony turned her attention back to the little girl, following Jack's instructions to the letter.

'Shall I give her morphine?'

'We're going to give it IV.' Jack murmured, picking up a cannula and searching for a vein. 'Can you squeeze for me?'

Bryony took Annie's little arm and squeezed, praying that Jack would find a vein first time.

He did, of course, and she breathed a sigh of relief.

'Give her the morphine and cyclizine in there and then we'll put a line in the other arm, too,' Jack said, holding out a hand for the syringe that the paramedic was holding ready. 'OK, sweetheart.' He looked down at Annie, his eyes gentle. 'This is going to make you feel better, I promise. And then we're going to take you to hospital. You're doing fine. You're brilliant.'

He gave the morphine and then put a cannula into the other arm and looked at Bryony. 'OK, let's get some fluid into her and get her covered or she'll get hypothermia from the cold water.'

He and Bryony worked together, each anticipating the other's needs, until finally the little girl was stabilised and in the ambulance.

'I'll go with her,' Jack said. 'Meet me at the hospital when you've dropped Lizzie at your mother's.'

'I want to come, too,' Lizzie said firmly, and Bryony shook her head.

'Sweetheart, no.'

'Bring her,' Jack said firmly. 'I'll run her home later. She can wait in the staffroom.'

He dug in his pocket and produced his car keys, a wry smile playing around his firm mouth. 'If you prang my car, Blondie, you're history.' Handing the keys to Lizzie, he jerked his head towards the front of the house. 'Go and wait for your mother by the car, sweetheart.'

Lizzie did as she was told and Jack took Bryony by the shoulders, forcing her to look at him. 'She's just seen her best friend horribly burned,' he said quietly. 'That is going to stay with her a long time and will be easier to bear if she knows she did something to help. Trust me on this one. She's tough, our Lizzie. She'll be fine. But do it my way.'

Bryony swallowed and nodded, knowing that whatever they did now the trauma had already happened for Lizzie. Maybe it was best for her to be involved.

Anne's parents came over, her mother clinging to her husband, her face streaked with tears.

'Can we go in the ambulance with her?'

Jack exchanged glances with one of the paramedics and then nodded. 'Of course. But try and be calm. I know it's a terrible shock but she needs you to be strong. If she sees you panicking, then she'll panic, and I don't want her any more scared than she is already.'

Bryony waited while they loaded Annie into the ambulance and then she joined Lizzie by Jack's car.

She pressed the remote to unlock the door and gave a short laugh. Now she knew it was an emergency. There was no other reason that Jack would have let her near his precious sports car—he never let anyone drive it.

She strapped Lizzie in the front seat and slid into the driver's seat, telling herself that it was only a car. Exactly like her car really, except that it was capable of ridiculous speed and cost about fifteen times as much.

She started the engine and flinched as the car gave a throaty growl. 'Boys with toys,' she muttered disparagingly, finding first gear and carefully pulling out of the driveway onto the road. She just hoped she didn't meet any other traffic on the way to hospital.

When she arrived she settled Lizzie in the staffroom, promising to come back and update her as soon as possible.

Jack was already in Resus, along with Sean Nicholson and a full team of staff. Jack was barking out instructions as he worked to stabilise Annie.

'Can someone check her weight with her parents?'

'I've just done it.' Bryony hurried into the room and reached in her pocket for a calculator. 'I've worked out 4 mils of fluid per kilogram multiplied by the percentage of the burn. Do you have that yet?'

'Just doing it. My estimate is twenty-two per cent,' Jack said, glancing up at her. 'Are you OK?'

Bryony nodded and studied the Lund and Browder charts that helped them to assess the area of the burn according to age. 'You're about right, Jack,' she said lightly, feeding the numbers into her calculator. 'I make it twenty-two per cent.'

She worked out the volume of fluid and showed her calculation to Jack.

'Right.' He gave a nod. 'So she needs that in twenty-four hours, but we need to give her half in the first eight hours and monitor her urine output. I want her to have a combination of crystalloid and colloid.'

'Catheter is in,' Nicky said quickly, 'and I've started a chart.'

'Great. Can you test her urine? And, Bryony, we need to take some bloods before she's transferred. Cross-matching, FBC, COHb, U and Es, glucose and coagulation.'

Bryony reached for the appropriate bottles. 'You're sending her to the burns unit?'

Jack nodded. 'The helicopter is waiting to take her as

soon as we give the word. I've spoken to the consultant, he's waiting for her.'

Bryony took the samples and then went to talk to Annie. The little girl was drifting in and out of sleep, hardly aware of what was going on around her.

'I gave her some sedation,' Jack said softly, covering the last of the burns and then giving Nicky a nod. 'OK. Let's go.'

'Are you going with her?'

He nodded. 'Take Lizzie home in my car. I'll see you later.'

'How will you get home?'

'I'll get the paramedics to drop me at your place, or I'll grab a taxi.' He shrugged, totally unconcerned, and she nodded.

'Fine. I'll see you later. Do you want me to talk to Annie's parents?'

'I'll do it,' Sean said immediately. 'That way you can get home with your little girl and Jack can get loaded into the helicopter.'

Bryony was tucking Lizzie into bed when she heard the doorbell. 'That will be Jack.'

She dropped a kiss on Lizzie's forehead and went to answer the door, praying that Annie's condition hadn't worsened during the transfer.

'How is she?'

Jack strolled into her house and gave a shiver, and it was only then that she remembered that he'd used his jacket to put out the flames and that he'd been working only in a jumper. He must be freezing.

'Come and sit by the fire,' she urged, and he did as she'd suggested, stretching out his hands towards the flames.

'It's nice and warm in here.' He looked at her. 'Is my girl asleep?'

Bryony shook her head, her expression troubled. 'No. She's very upset by it all.'

'Of course she is.' His jaw tightened. 'I'll talk to her.'

They both walked towards Lizzie's bedroom and Jack strolled in and settled himself on the edge of the bed.

'Hi, there.' His voice was soft and Lizzie stared up at him, her eyes huge in her pretty face.

'Hi, Jack.' Her smile was shaky. 'Annie is very badly hurt, isn't she?'

Jack hesitated. 'She is pretty badly hurt,' he agreed, and Bryony mentally thanked him for not lying. She knew that Annie's condition was serious and if anything happened to the little girl, she didn't want Lizzie to feel that they'd been dishonest.

'Is she going to die?' Lizzie's voice trembled and Jack shook his head.

'No, sweetheart. I'm sure she isn't going to die. I've just taken her to a special hospital where they know all about burns.'

'Can I go and see her there?'

'Sure,' Jack said immediately. 'We'll go together.'

Tears suddenly welled up in Lizzie's eyes and Jack immediately leaned forward and lifted the little girl onto his lap.

'Don't cry, baby,' he said roughly, stroking her hair with his strong hand and exchanging an agonised look with

Bryony. 'You were brilliant. My little star. All those grown-ups were panicking and you were cool as ice cream.'

Lizzie gave a sniff and pulled away from him, but her little hands still clutched at his jumper. 'I told the paramedics everything you wanted, just like you said.'

'I know you did.' Jack smiled down at her, pride in his eyes. 'You were unbelievable. And I was so proud of you. You really helped save Annie.'

'I helped?' Lizzie's face brightened slightly. 'Really?'

'Really.' Jack nodded, his handsome face serious. 'You see, you did all the right things. Everyone was scared and I bet you were, too, but you didn't let being scared stop you from doing what needed to be done. And that makes you a very special person.'

'It does?'

'Certainly. I don't know many grown-ups who would have been as calm as you and remembered all those things and done what you did.' Jack lifted a hand and stroked Lizzie's blonde curls away from her face. 'One day, if you wanted to, I think you could be a very important doctor.'

Bryony swallowed down a lump in her throat and Lizzie's eyes widened. 'Like you and Mummy?'

Jack grinned. 'Maybe not quite as important as me,' he said teasingly, winking at Bryony who smiled back weakly. 'But important, just the same.'

Lizzie gave a gurgle of laughter and punched him on the shoulder. 'That's boasting, Jack,' she said reprovingly, and wound her arms round his neck. 'I'm glad you and Mummy were there.'

For a brief moment Jack squeezed his eyes shut, his jaw tense, and Bryony knew exactly what was going through his mind. He'd been imagining a scene where he hadn't been there, a scene where there hadn't been a doctor on site to administer first aid, a scene where Lizzie might have been the one near the bonfire.

She gave a little shudder, imagining the same scene, and Jack's eyes opened and locked on hers for a meaningful second.

'Time for you to go to bed now, angel,' he said softly, lifting Lizzie off his lap and tucking her under the covers with her mermaid. He leaned across and switched her little pink lamp on. 'Your mum and I will just be eating some supper in the kitchen. Shout if you want anything.'

'I don't want you to go home tonight.'

'I'm not going,' Jack said immediately, sounding rock-solid, dependable and altogether too male for Bryony's piece of mind. 'Tonight I'm sleeping in your spare room.'

Lizzie gave a smile and they were just tiptoeing to the door when she spoke again.

'Jack?' Lizzie's voice was a little-girl whisper and Bryony saw Jack's face soften.

'Yes, angel.'

'Tomorrow when we wake up, will you play with me?'

Jack grinned. 'Absolutely.'

'Can we play Weddings?'

'My favourite game,' Jack said softly, walking back across the room and bending down to kiss her one more time. 'Now, get some sleep. I can't marry you with black rings under your eyes.'

Lizzie chuckled, sounding much happier. 'Mummy, will you leave the door open?'

'Of course, sweetheart. And I'll pop my head in later.'

Jack followed Bryony out of the room.

'Thank you for that,' she said quietly, walking through to the kitchen and opening the fridge. 'You said all the right things. In fact, you did all the right things, too. My instincts were to just get her out of there.'

'That would have been my instinct, too, if she hadn't already seen her friend engulfed by flames,' Jack said wearily, sinking down on one of her kitchen chairs with a groan. 'To be honest, I was mostly concentrating on Annie, but I did think that if Lizzie knew she'd helped, she might feel better.'

'Which she did.' Bryony removed a bottle of wine from the fridge and handed it to him along with a corkscrew. 'I just hope she doesn't have nightmares.'

'She's a tough kid,' Jack said, yanking the cork out and setting the bottle down on the table. 'She'll be fine. As soon as Annie is a bit better we can take Lizzie along to see her.'

We.

Listening to him talking as if they were a family, Bryony found it harder and harder to remember that she was supposed to not be thinking of Jack in *that* way any more.

Remembering how skilled he'd been with Annie brought a lump to her throat. 'You're amazing, do you know that?' She reached into the cupboard for two glasses, trying to keep her tone light. 'You never lose your cool, no matter what. I just saw Annie on fire and I froze.'

'Only for about three seconds,' Jack said easily, stretching out a hand for the glasses and filling them both to the top. 'And working in a well-equipped A and E department is very different from immediate care, as you know. Here. Have a drink. I think we both need it.'

'I should cook some supper first.'

'Forget cooking.' Jack took a mouthful of wine and gave a groan of pleasure. 'That's good. Let's send out for pizza or something.'

Bryony giggled. 'I can't do that. Lizzie will find the boxes in the morning and she'll kill me. Pizza is her treat.'

Jack shrugged. 'All right. Indian, then. I left a menu by your phone last time I was here.'

'It would be nice not to cook,' Bryony agreed, and Jack stood up.

'That's decided, then. Indian it is. What do you want?'

Bryony shrugged. 'You choose.'

So he did and the food arrived half an hour later and was wonderful.

They were well into the bottle of wine when they heard Lizzie's screams.

Both of them sprinted to her bedroom to find her sobbing and clutching her mermaid, her face blotched with tears.

'I keep thinking of Annie.'

Bryony cuddled her close, rocking her gently. 'Well, of course you do, darling. Annie is your friend. She's going to be fine, Lizzie.'

As she said the words she prayed that she was right. If anything happened to Annie...

Eventually Lizzie calmed down and fell asleep again and the two of them tiptoed back to the kitchen.

Bryony felt totally stressed and she was seriously worried about the effect of the accident on her daughter. As Jack had rightly said, she'd actually seen it happen. What sort of impact would that have on her in the long term?

She desperately wanted to lean on Jack but she couldn't bring herself to ask him for the hug she so badly needed.

And then he looked at her and she knew he felt the same way. 'I hate Bonfire Night.'

His voice was hoarse and for the first time Bryony caught a glimpse of the strain he must have been under.

She gave a little frown. 'We forget about you, Jack,' she said softly, stepping up to him and looking at him with concern in her eyes. 'You always seem so strong—so much the one in charge. Everyone else is panicking and flapping and you're so calm. It's easy to forget that you can be affected by things, too.'

'Hey.' He gave a sexy grin that belied the strain in his eyes. 'I'm Mr Tough.'

She smiled. 'Well, would Mr Tough like a cup of coffee?'

'As I'm not driving, I'd rather finish the wine,' he admitted ruefully, reaching for his glass. 'Do you mind me staying?'

'Of course not,' she said blithely, wondering why her heart was thumping so hard. Jack had stayed in her cottage on numerous occasions. Why did this time feel different?

'I'll get you some stuff ready,' she said formally, and he reached out and grabbed her arm.

'Don't bother. I don't wear anything in bed anyway.'

Bryony swallowed hard, trying to dispel the mental image of Jack naked in her spare room.

For a woman who was not supposed to be thinking about Jack Rothwell, she was failing dismally.

'Jack...'

'What I really need is a hug.' Without waiting for a response, he hauled her against him and she went into his arms, feeling the softness of his jumper covering the hard muscle of his chest and the strength of his arms as he held her. He gave a groan and tightened his hold, burying his face in her hair.

Bryony could hardly breathe. She felt the steady thud of his heart against her flushed cheek, felt her whole body tingle in response to the feel of his body against hers. He felt strong and safe and deliciously male.

They stood like that for a moment and she closed her eyes, wishing that it could last for ever. Wishing that it could lead to something more.

And then gradually his grip on her loosened and his hands slid slowly up her arms. His strong fingers curled into her shoulders and he looked down at her, his blue eyes suddenly intent on her face.

A warmth spread slowly through her pelvis and her whole body melted with longing.

She felt his fingers tighten, saw something flicker in his eyes and then his head lowered towards hers.

He was going to kiss her.

Finally, after so many years of dreaming about exactly that, Jack was going to kiss her.

Dizzy with excitement, Bryony stared up at him, breathless with anticipation.

And then suddenly his hands fell away from her shoulders and he stepped back, his handsome face blank of expression.

'We should probably get some sleep, Blondie.' His tone was light and he glanced at the clock on the wall. 'It's getting late.'

Bryony tried to smile but it was a poor effort. She felt swamped with a disappointment so powerful that it was almost a physical pain. *She'd been so sure that he was going to kiss her.*

But why would Jack kiss her?

She gritted her teeth, furious with herself. She was doing it again. Fantasising about Jack.

So much for her campaign to date other men. So far she'd been on one date that had been an utter disaster and she was still noticing Jack.

She had less than two months to find Lizzie a daddy, or at least someone who looked as though he had potential. It was time she made more effort.

She needed to kiss someone and see if that helped.

She needed to stop comparing everyone with Jack.

There must be another man who looked good in jeans. There must be another man who always knew exactly what to do when everyone around them was panicking. There must be another man who would make her knees wobble every time he walked into a room.

And she was going to find him.

CHAPTER FIVE

THE rest of November flew past and Annie's condition gradually improved.

'The burns are almost all round her skirt area,' Jack told Bryony one day as they snatched a quick cup of coffee during a late shift. 'I talked to the consultant last night. She's going to need extensive skin grafts.'

'Poor mite.' Bryony pulled a face at the thought of the number of hospital stays Annie was going to have to endure. 'It's going to be so hard for her.'

Jack nodded. 'But at least she's alive. And Lizzie seems to have bounced back amazingly well.'

'Yes.' Bryony smiled. 'I was worried about that but she's doing fine. We're visiting Annie a lot, which helps, and Lizzie has made it her mission to act as the link between Annie and the school. She's been taking her all sorts of books and things to do and generally keeping her in touch with the gossip.'

'She's a great girl.' Jack drained his coffee and sat back in his chair with a yawn, long legs stretched out in front of him. 'So, Blondie. December the first tomorrow.'

Bryony stared gloomily into her coffee. 'Don't remind me. I now have less than a month to sort out Lizzie's Christmas present, and I'm fast coming to the conclusion that it's an impossible task.'

Jack looked at her quizzically, a strange light in his eyes. 'So, is the romance with David Armstrong not working?'

Romance?

Bryony looked at him. 'We've been on two dates. The first one we barely had time to talk because you kept calling—not that it was your fault that Lizzie was demanding that night,' she added hastily, hoping that he didn't think that she was complaining, 'and the second date was disturbed because you called him back to the hospital to see a child. And that wasn't your fault either.'

Jack looked at her, his expression inscrutable. 'And he hasn't asked you out since?'

'Well, funnily enough, he rang me this morning,' Bryony confided, 'and he's taking me to dinner at The Peacock on Saturday. Neither of us is on call and Lizzie is sleeping at my mother's so this time there should be absolutely no interruptions.'

And this time she was going to kiss him.

She'd made up her mind that she was going to kiss him.

She was utterly convinced that kissing another man would cure her obsession with Jack.

David was a good-looking guy. She knew that lots of the nurses lusted after him secretly. He must know how to kiss.

And it was going to happen on Saturday. She was going to invite him in for coffee and she was going to kiss him.

* * *

The next day was incredibly busy.

'It's the roads,' Sean said wearily as they snatched a five-minute coffee-break in the middle of a long and intensive shift. 'They're so icy and people drive too fast. I predict a nasty pile-up before the end of the evening.'

His prediction proved correct.

At seven o'clock the ambulance hotline rang. Bryony answered it and when she finally put the phone down both Sean and Jack were watching her expectantly.

'Are you clairvoyant?' She looked at Sean who shrugged.

'Black ice. It was inevitable. What are the details?'

'Twenty-two-year-old female, conscious but shocked and complaining of chest pains.'

She'd barely finished repeating what Ambulance Control had told her when the doors slammed open and the paramedics hurried in with the trolley.

'Straight into Resus,' Jack ordered and they transferred the woman onto the trolley as smoothly as possible. While the rest of the team moved quickly into action he questioned the paramedics about the accident.

'It was a side impact,' the paramedic told him. 'She was driving and the other vehicle went straight into her side. Her passenger walked away virtually unharmed. He's giving her details to Reception now.'

Jack nodded and turned his attention back to the young woman, a frown on his face. 'She has a neck haematoma. I want a chest X-ray, fast,' he murmured, and looked at Bryony. 'Have you got a line in?'

She nodded. 'One.'

'Put in another one,' he ordered, 'but hold the fluid. And cross-match ten units of blood.'

Bryony's eyes widened. 'Why?'

'Just a feeling. Nicky, I want a BP from both arms,' he said, gesturing to the staff to stand back while the radiographer took the chest film.

'Her blood pressure is different in each arm,' Nicky said quickly, and Jack nodded.

'I thought it might be. She's only slightly hypotensive so I want minimal fluid replacement for now.'

Bryony looked at him, waiting for a blonde joke or one of his usual quips that would ease the tension, but this time his eyes were fixed on the patient.

'Fast-bleep the surgeons,' he ordered, 'and let's take a look at that chest X-ray.'

They walked across to look at the chest X-ray and Bryony looked at him, able to talk now that they were away from the patient. 'Why did you cross-match so much blood?'

'Because I think she's ruptured her aorta.'

Bryony's eyes widened. 'But a ruptured aorta has a 90 per cent mortality rate. She'd be dead.'

He squinted at the X-ray. 'Unless the bleed is contained by the aortic adventitia. Then she'd be alive. But at risk of haemorrhage.'

Bryony stared at the X-ray, too, and Jack lifted an eyebrow.

'OK, Blondie—impress me. What do you see?'

'The mediastinum is widened.'

'And is that significant?'

Bryony chewed her lip and delved into her brain. 'On its own, possibly not,' she said, remembering something she'd read, 'but taken with other factors…'

'Such as?'

Bryony looked again, determined not to miss anything. 'The trachea is deviated to the right. The aortic outline is blurred and the aortic knuckle is obliterated.'

'What else?'

'It's cloudy.' She peered closer at the X-ray. 'I haven't seen that before. Is it a haemothorax?'

'Full marks.' He gave her a lazy smile but his eyes glittered with admiration. 'She has a right-sided haemothorax caused by a traumatic rupture of the thoracic aorta, which is currently contained. In this case we can see it clearly on the X-ray, but not always.'

Bryony looked at him and felt her heart thud harder. The patient was lucky to be alive. 'So what happens now?'

'She needs urgent surgical repair. In the meantime, we need to give fluid cautiously, otherwise the adventitia could rupture and she'll have a fatal haemorrhage.'

'So presumably we also need to give her good pain relief so that her blood pressure doesn't go up?'

His eyes rested on her shiny blonde hair and he shook his head solemnly. 'Amazing.'

She poked her tongue out discreetly and he gave her a sexy smile that made her knees wobble.

Fortunately, at that moment the surgeons walked into the room and provided a distraction. They all conferred, agreeing to take the woman to Theatre right away for surgical repair.

'So what exactly do they do?' Bryony asked Jack after the woman had been safely handed over to the surgeons and they were left to deal with the debris in Resus.

'Depends.' He ripped off his gloves and dropped them into the bin. 'They'll attempt a surgical repair.'

'And if they can't repair it?'

'Then they'll do a vascular graft.'

Bryony helped Nicky to clean the trolley. 'But what made you suspect an aortic rupture? I always thought patients died at the scene of the accident.'

'Well, if they're alive it basically suggests a partial injury,' he told her. 'It's often hard to diagnose on X-ray. A widened mediastinum doesn't necessarily indicate an abnormality. But in her case there were other classic chest X-ray signs and she had clinical signs too. The neck haematoma, asymmetric BP and chest pain.'

'And if the X-ray hadn't been clear?'

'I would have talked to the consultant radiologist and we would have done a multi-slice CT scan. It's worth finding out as much as you can about the details of the accident. The paramedic told us her car had been hit on the driver's side. A significant number of blunt traumatic aortic ruptures are caused by side impact.'

Bryony stared at him in fascination. 'What's the pathology?'

'Basically a sudden deceleration such as a fall from a height or an RTA allows the mobile parts of the aorta to keep moving. It usually tears where the aorta is tethered to the pulmonary vein—'

'The ligamentum arteriosum,' Bryony intervened, and he rolled his eyes.

'If there's one thing I can't stand, it's a brainy blonde,' he drawled, and she clucked sympathetically.

'If I'm threatening your ego then just let me know.'

'My ego is shivering,' he assured her, his blue eyes twinkling as looked down at her. 'What do you get when you give a blonde a penny for her thoughts?'

'Change,' Bryony said immediately, tilting her head to one side. 'Why is a man like a vintage wine?'

Jack's eyes narrowed and his mouth twitched. 'Go on...'

'Because they all start out like grapes,' Bryony said cheerfully, 'and it's a woman's job to tread all over them and keep them in the dark until they mature into something you'd like to have dinner with.'

Nicky gave a snort of amusement from the corner of the room and Jack grinned.

'That's shockingly sexist, Blondie.'

'Just giving as good as I get.'

Jack's smile faded. 'And talking about having dinner, haven't you got a date tomorrow night?'

'Yes.' Bryony frowned as she remembered that she had all of three weeks to find a man who might make a good father for Lizzie. By anyone's standards it was a tall order.

But at least she had another date with David so he must be fairly keen.

And he was a really nice man. Her eyes slid to Jack's face and then away again. She wasn't going to compare him to Jack. All right, so Jack was staggeringly handsome and he was clever and he had a great sense of humour— She cut herself off before the list grew too long. Jack didn't do commitment. And Jack didn't notice her. Which ruled him out as a potential partner.

At least David noticed her.

And she was going to start noticing him, she told herself

firmly, leaving the room so that she wouldn't be tempted to continually look at Jack.

'I'm really looking forward to tonight.' Bryony slid into David's car and gave him a smile. 'The food is meant to be great and Lizzie is at my mother's so we are guaranteed no interruptions.'

David waited while she fastened her seat belt and then pulled out of her drive. 'Let's hope not.'

They walked into the restaurant ten minutes later and Bryony gave a gasp of delight as she saw the Christmas tree sparkling by the log fire. 'Oh—it's lovely.'

And romantic.

How could she and David fail to further their relationship in this atmosphere?

It was made for lovers.

She handed over her coat, feeling David's eyes slide over her.

'You look great,' he said quietly, and she smiled shyly, pleased that she'd bought the red dress she'd seen on a shopping expedition a week earlier.

'So do you.'

And he did. He was wearing a dark, well-cut suit and she saw several female heads turn towards him as they were shown to their table.

All right, so he didn't make her knees wobble but that was a good thing surely. With Jack she actually felt physically sick every time he walked into a room, which was utterly ridiculous. She couldn't concentrate and she couldn't breathe. All she was aware of was him. And that wasn't what she wanted in a stable, long-term relationship.

At least being with David didn't make her feel sick with excitement.

They ordered their food and then David picked up his glass and raised it. 'To an uninterrupted evening.'

She smiled and lifted her glass in response but before she could speak she gave a gasp of surprise. 'Oh—it's Jack!'

David's jaw tightened and he put his glass carefully down on the table. *'Jack?'*

'Jack Rothwell. He's just walked in with some blonde.'

Bryony felt a flash of jealousy as she studied Jack's companion. She was his usual type. Endless legs, silvery blonde hair and a skirt that barely covered her bottom. She wore a very low-cut top and Bryony glanced at Jack to see signs of disapproval, but he seemed perfectly relaxed, his eyes twinkling flirtatiously as he laughed at something the girl had said.

By contrast, David was glowering, his earlier good humour seemingly gone as he reached for his wine.

'Well…' Bryony made a determined effort not to look at Jack and not to mind that he didn't appear to have noticed her anyway. 'That's a coincidence.'

'Is it?' David's eyes glittered ominously and he sat back in his chair as the waiter poured more wine into his glass. 'Aren't you beginning to wonder why it is that Jack Rothwell would want to sabotage every date we have?'

'Sabotage?' Bryony looked at him in astonishment and gave a puzzled laugh. 'Jack has nothing to do with the fact that our last two dates haven't worked out that well.'

'No?'

'Well, he's certainly not sabotaging tonight,' Bryony

said reasonably. 'I mean, he hasn't even noticed we're here. He's with a woman himself.'

She glanced across the restaurant again and immediately wished she hadn't. Jack was leaning forward, his attention totally focused on his beautiful companion.

Bryony looked away quickly, trying not to mind. Knowing that she had no right to mind.

And, anyway, she was with David.

But he was looking at her with an odd expression on his face. 'He knows you're here,' he said quietly, 'and no man could fail to notice you, Bryony.'

She blushed at the compliment. 'Well, that's very kind of you, but I can assure you that Jack certainly doesn't notice me in the way you're suggesting.'

In fact, he didn't seem to notice her as a woman at all. Until she wore something that he disapproved of, she thought gloomily. Goodness knew how he would have reacted had she been the one dressed like his date. He probably would have had her locked up. But evidently the girl staring into his eyes at that precise moment was allowed to dress however she pleased.

Realising that she was staring again, Bryony turned her attention back to David but the atmosphere had changed. She made a valiant attempt to keep up lively conversation but it seemed like hard work.

In the end they ate their starter in virtual silence and Bryony's gaze flickered surreptitiously to Jack yet again.

Immediately their eyes locked and she swallowed hard, aware that he must have been looking at her.

His eyes held hers and everything and everyone else in the room gradually faded into the background. For Bryony there was just Jack and he seemed as reluctant to break the contact as she was.

Her heart banged against her ribs with rhythmic force and the sick feeling started in her stomach.

And still Jack's eyes held hers.

They might have stared at each other for ever if the waiter hadn't chosen that moment to deliver their next course, walking across their line of vision.

Staring down at her plate, Bryony realised that suddenly she wasn't hungry any more. Her insides felt totally jumbled up.

Why had Jack been staring at her like that?

Did he disapprove of her seeing David? Did he think that she was dating the wrong man?

She pushed her food around her plate, miserably aware that David had finished his main course and was now watching her in silence.

Finally he spoke. 'You don't seem hungry.'

'Not very.' She put her fork down and smiled at him apologetically. 'I'm so sorry.'

'It doesn't matter.'

She bit her lip, embarrassed that the evening was going so badly. 'I'm just a bit tired—it's been a pretty busy week.'

'Do you want to go home?'

She hesitated and then nodded. 'Yes. If that's all right with you.'

'Shall we have coffee first?'

She remembered her resolution to kiss him. 'No,' she croaked. 'Let's have coffee at my house.'

He looked at her thoughtfully and seemed to relax

slightly. Then he nodded and rose to his feet. 'Good idea. Come on. I'll settle the bill while they get our coats.'

'If you've finished, I'll take her home.' Jack's deep voice came from right beside her, his eyes fixed on her face. 'It's on my way.'

The two men stared at each other with ill-disguised hostility.

'She's my date,' David said tightly, and Jack smiled.

'You've had your date,' he drawled softly, 'and now I'm taking her home.'

Realising that everyone in the restaurant was staring at them, Bryony flushed scarlet and tugged Jack's arm.

'For goodness' sake, Jack! Everyone's looking at us.'

Jack gave a dismissive shrug that indicated just how little he was bothered by other people's opinions and then he smiled as his date for the evening joined them. 'Nina, this is David. He's offered to take you home.'

Nina gave Jack a longing look that left no one in any doubt as to how she felt about him. And then she sighed and shot David a dazzling smile. 'If you're sure it's no trouble…'

Wondering why Nina was giving up so easily, Bryony watched as David's eyes dropped to the neckline of Nina's dress which revealed a hypnotic amount of female flesh.

He stared in blatant fascination and then finally cleared his throat and dragged his gaze up to Nina's. 'It's no trouble at all,' he said hoarsely and Bryony resisted the temptation to scream with frustration.

Men were just so pathetic!

Boiling with anger, she said goodnight to David and Nina and followed Jack across the car park.

He unlocked the car and opened the door for her and she slid inside and yanked at the seat belt.

As Jack settled himself in the driver's seat, she let rip.

'David was my date! You had no right to interfere.'

Jack reversed out of his parking space. 'I merely offered to take you home.'

'You didn't offer, Jack,' she said caustically, 'you insisted. David was taking me home and he was ready to argue until your Nina thrust her chest in his face.'

Jack grinned, maddeningly unperturbed by her outburst. 'impressive, isn't she? I thought as I was taking you away from him, I ought to offer him something in compensation.'

'So I suppose she was the *booby* prize?' Bryony's voice dripped sarcasm and Jack's grin widened.

'Booby prize.' He repeated her words and chuckled with appreciation. 'I admit I hadn't thought of it in exactly those terms, but now you mention it…'

Bryony ground her teeth in frustration. 'You are so hypocritical, do you know that? You have the nerve to criticise my black dress and then you go out with a girl who has a cleavage the size of the Grand Canyon and shows it off to the entire population. I didn't notice you covering *her* up with a coat.'

Jack glanced across at her and in the semi-darkness she could see his eyes twinkling wickedly. 'It would have had to be a big coat and it seemed a shame to deprive everyone of the view,' he drawled, and she felt fury mix with a very different emotion.

Hurt.

When Nina wore a low-cut dress, Jack obviously thought

she looked incredibly attractive. But when *she* wore one he thought she looked awful and tried to cover her up.

David had said that she looked nice but, thanks to Jack, David was now with Nina and was doubtless enjoying the view as much as all the other men in the restaurant.

And she was with a man who didn't find her attractive and never would.

'There are times when I hate you, Jack Rothwell,' she muttered, and he gave a soft laugh.

'I don't know what you're getting so worked up about, Blondie.'

For once his use of her nickname irritated her. 'He was my date, Jack. *My date*. And you ruined it.'

To her utter humiliation she felt a lump starting in her throat. She wasn't going to cry in front of Jack.

But fortunately Jack had his eyes fixed on the road. 'How did I ruin it?'

'You really need to ask that question?' She stared at him incredulously. 'I was spending the evening with a man and you suddenly dived in and insisted on taking me home. And I really don't understand why.'

In the moonlight she saw the muscle in his jaw flicker. 'The roads are icy. I didn't want him driving you.'

Her jaw fell open. 'You think you're the only man who can drive on ice?'

'No.' His tone was calm. 'But I've never seen David Armstrong drive on ice and until I do, he's not driving you.'

'Jack, you're being ridiculous!' She looked at him in exasperation. 'And what about Nina? You were perfectly happy for him to drive Nina.'

'Nina can look after herself.'

Bryony slumped back in her seat and gritted her teeth. 'And I can't?'

'You know nothing about men.'

'I thought we were talking about ice?'

'Amongst other things.'

'Oh, right. So we're back to the fact that I haven't dated anyone for ages. It doesn't make me stupid, Jack.'

'And it doesn't make you experienced.'

'Well, it's obvious that I'm never going to get any experience while I'm living in the same town as you!' She glared at him and he gave a shrug.

'I don't know why you're making such a fuss. You had your date. You spent the evening together. Was it good, by the way?'

She opened her mouth to tell him that, no, it had not been good because she'd been staring at him all night, but she realised in time just how much that would reveal about her feelings and stopped herself.

'It was fine,' she lied, 'but it hadn't finished. I wanted *him* to take me home.' And she'd wanted him to kiss her just to see whether it was possible for another man to take her mind off Jack.

'You wanted him to take you home?' There was a tense silence and she saw Jack's fingers tighten on the wheel. 'Why?' His voice was suddenly harsh. 'Or was that where the date was supposed to begin? Keen to make up for lost time, were you?'

His tone was frosty and she gave an exclamation of disgust. 'And so what if it was? What I do with my life is none of your business. I don't need you to look out for me, Jack.'

It was only when he stopped the car and switched off the

engine that she realised that they were outside her home. The house was in darkness and suddenly she felt utterly depressed and lonely. Maybe Lizzie was right, she thought miserably. It would be great to walk into her house, knowing that someone was waiting for her. It would be great to have someone to hug her at night. She'd been without a man for almost all her life and suddenly she wanted someone special. Someone who cared whether she came home or not.

But so far her quest for a man had been a disaster.

And suddenly she just wanted to be on her own.

'Well, thanks, Jack. Thanks for ruining my evening.' She undid her seat belt and reached down to pick up her bag. 'I would invite you in for coffee but, seeing as you think that's a euphemism for sex, naturally I wouldn't dream of it. And anyway I'm sure you're dying to get back to Nina.'

'Nina is just a friend.'

'I really couldn't care less, Jack,' she lied, 'because your love life isn't any of my business, just as my love life is none of your business. A whole month has gone past since Lizzie sent her letter to Santa and so far I haven't even managed to get a man to kiss me.'

'You want a man to kiss you?' Jack's voice was a deep growl and without waiting for her answer he slid a hand round her head and brought his mouth down on hers with punishing force. His long fingers bit into her scalp and he lifted his other hand and curved it around her cheek, holding her face still for his kiss.

Utterly shocked, Bryony lifted a hand to his chest, intending to push him away, but instead her traitorous fingers curled into his shirt, then loosened a button and slid inside.

Her fingers felt the roughness of his chest hair, warm skin and solid muscle and she felt his grip on her head tighten as his kiss gentled and his tongue traced the seam of her mouth, coaxing her to open for him.

And then he was really kissing her.

Kissing her in the way that she'd always known only he could.

And it felt like magic. How could one person make another feel so different unless it was magic? She was trembling and shivering, overwhelmed by an excitement so intense that she didn't know where it was leading or how it would end. She only knew that she wanted to get closer to him, to crawl all over him but the seats in the car didn't exactly encourage that type of contact. So instead she leaned into him, sliding her hand around his body and trying to draw him closer.

His tongue teased hers gently and then dipped deeper, exploring the interior of her mouth with a lazy expertise that was so erotic it set her entire body on fire. With a maddening degree of self-control, he slid the backs of his fingers over her cheek and down to her neck, trailing his fingers tantalisingly close to her aching breasts before stopping just short of his target. Bryony whimpered with frustration. Longing for his touch, she arched against him but he didn't move his hand. Instead, he continued to kiss her with increasing intensity until none of her senses were under her control.

And then finally, just when she thought her entire body would explode with frustration, he touched her. His strong hand cupped one breast through the silken fabric of her dress and then he drew his thumb over her nipple, creating an agony of sensation so powerful that she gasped against his mouth and shifted in the seat to try and relieve the nagging throb between her thighs.

'Jack...'

The moment she sobbed his name he lifted his head, his breathing unsteady as he stared down at her. Then he released her abruptly and ran a hand over his face, obviously as shaken as she was.

Her whole body screamed in protest that he'd stopped and she looked at him in dazed confusion.

'Jack?'

She saw him tense and then he turned to face her, his handsome face totally blank of expression. 'Now do you see?'

She swallowed, finding it terribly hard to concentrate, still suffering from the aftershocks of his kiss. 'Now do I see what?'

'That kisses can get out of control.' His eyes dropped to her parted lips, still swollen and damp from the ruthless demands of his mouth and then dropped further still to the outline of her breasts which pushed boldly against her dress. He dragged his gaze away and stared into the darkness. 'That's what would have happened if you'd invited David Armstrong back for coffee.'

Bryony stared at him in silence.

She felt as though the world had changed shape. As if everything should look different. It certainly felt different.

For her, their entire relationship had changed in an instant. The moment his mouth had touched hers, everything had become different.

But evidently he didn't feel the same way.

Chewing her lip, she reminded herself that this was Jack. Jack, whose parents had divorced when he was eight and who had vowed never to get married himself when he grew up. And then he'd grown up and had shown no intention of changing his mind about that one fact. Jack didn't do relationships. Judging from the few conversations she'd overheard between her brothers, Jack did sex and not much else.

But even knowing that, her whole body flooded with disappointment as she realised that obviously the kiss hadn't meant anything at all to him. He'd actually been proving a point and in doing so he'd proved something to her, too.

That she'd been right all along about Jack.

He was an amazing kisser.

And she knew that the same thing would never have happened had she invited David Armstrong back for coffee. David might have kissed her, that was true, but she knew that there wasn't another man on the planet who would make her feel what Jack had just made her feel.

But it was totally hopeless.

And the raw, sexual attraction she felt for Jack shouldn't interfere with her determination to find a father for Lizzie, she told herself firmly.

That was just lust and lust always faded anyway. She needed a man who would be kind, good company and a caring father to Lizzie. She didn't need raw sexual attraction. In fact, raw sexual attraction was starting to turn her into a nervous wreck.

So she lifted her chin and smiled at Jack, proud of how natural it seemed. 'Well, thanks for the practice,' she said lightly, leaning forward and kissing him on the cheek, resisting the almost overwhelming temptation to trace a route to his mouth with the tip of her tongue. 'I'd forgotten how to do it, but you reminded me. Now I know I'll get it right next time I go out with David.'

And with that she opened the door, climbed out of the car and walked to her cottage without looking back.

CHAPTER SIX

DAMN. Damn. Damn.

What the hell had he done?

He'd kissed his best friend.

Jack stared after Bryony, trying to decide what shocked him most. The fact that he'd kissed her, or the fact that he hadn't wanted to stop.

He sat in the car with the engine switched off, staring into the frozen darkness feeling as though something fundamental to his existence had changed.

Where had it come from? That sudden impulse to kiss her…

Blondie was family.

As much a baby sister to him as she was to Tom and Oliver.

And until tonight he'd never thought of her in any other way.

Or had he?

Had he really never thought of her like that or was it just that he'd trained himself not to?

He sat still, watching the house, and then suddenly the lights went on. He saw her walk into her cosy sitting room and shrug off her coat, revealing that amazing red dress and an avalanche of blonde hair.

For years he hadn't seen her in a dress and suddenly she seemed to be wearing a different one every week.

He closed his eyes and breathed deeply, still able to detect the tantalising scent of her hair and skin. The instantaneous reaction of his body was so powerful that he gritted his teeth and shifted slightly in his seat, trying to find a more comfortable position.

There wasn't one.

Suddenly, somehow, she'd invaded every part of him.

He'd made an unconscious decision never to cross that boundary but now he'd crossed it there was no going back.

Whichever way he looked at her, he didn't see a surrogate sister any more. And he didn't see his best friend. He saw a woman. A living, breathing, stunningly beautiful woman.

But he couldn't do anything about it.

Lizzie was looking for a father. Someone strong who could swing her in the garden. Someone funny who'd let her watch television before school and who wouldn't make her eat sprouts.

Well, he could do that bit with no problem. He wasn't that keen on sprouts himself so he was more than happy to collude over their exclusion from their diet. And he had no trouble swinging her in the garden, hugging her and making her laugh. In fact, he was great at all those things.

The problem came with the last bit of her letter.

I want a daddy who will hug my mummy and stay with us for ever.

Jack leaned his head back against the seat and let out a long breath. He didn't do for ever. He had trouble doing next month. The whole concept of 'for ever' frightened the life out of him.

And Bryony knew that.

She knew him better than anyone.

Which was probably why she'd looked so shocked when he'd kissed her. Hell, *he'd* been shocked! And now he was confused, too, which was a totally new experience for him. He was *never* confused about women. He knew *exactly* what he wanted from them.

Everything, as long as it wasn't permanent.

Which meant that he had absolutely nothing to offer Bryony.

He started the engine and clenched his hands on the wheel. *He had to stop noticing her as a woman.* Surely it couldn't be that hard? After all, he'd only just started noticing her that way. It couldn't be that hard to go back to seeing her as his best friend.

He'd just carry on as they always had. Dropping round to see her. Chatting in her kitchen. And seeing other women.

It would be fine.

If working with Jack had been hard before the kiss, for Bryony it became even harder afterwards.

When he walked into a room she knew instantly, even when she had her back to him.

She didn't need to see him. She *felt* him. Felt his presence with every feminine bone in her body.

And she noticed everything about him. The way the solid muscle of his shoulders moved when he reached up to yank an X-ray out of the lightbox, the way his head tilted slightly when he was concentrating on something and the way everyone always asked his opinion on everything. She noticed how good he was with anxious relatives, how strong and capable he was with terrified patients and how well he dealt with inexperienced staff. He was the cleverest doctor she'd ever worked with and he had an instinctive feel for what was wrong with a patient before he'd even examined them.

If she'd had butterflies before he'd kissed her, they seemed to have multiplied since the kiss.

Which was utterly ridiculous because obviously, for him, nothing had changed.

Their relationship followed the same pattern of blonde jokes, man jokes and evenings when he sat with his feet on her table in the kitchen, watching while she cooked, a bottle of beer snuggled in his lap.

And now they were into December and there was no sign of a man who was even remotely close to fulfilling Lizzie's criteria for a daddy.

David hadn't asked her out again and she'd resigned herself to the fact that he was probably now dating Nina.

'Are you upset about that?' she asked Jack one evening, when they were curled up in front of the fire. She was writing Christmas cards and he was staring into the flames with a distant look in his eyes.

'Upset about what?'

'Nina.' She said the other woman's name as lightly

as possible. 'Someone told me that she's seeing David Armstrong.'

'Is she?' Jack suppressed a yawn and stretched long legs out in front of him. 'Well, good for him.'

'You never should have sent them home together. I'm amazed you're not upset.'

He gave her a mocking smile. 'Come on, Blondie. How long have you known me?'

She stared at him. 'You engineered it, didn't you?' Her pen fell to the floor as she suddenly realised what had happened. 'You got rid of her.'

His gaze didn't flicker. 'I encouraged her to find someone else, yes.'

'Why?' Bryony shook her head, puzzled. 'She was nice. And she seemed crazy about you.'

Jack looked at her steadily. 'She was.'

Which was why he'd ended it.

It was Jack's usual pattern.

Bryony sighed. 'Jack, you're thirty-four,' she said softly. 'You can't run for ever.'

He gave a funny lopsided grin that made her heart turn over. 'Watch me.'

'Listen…' She put her pen down and gave up on her Christmas cards. They could wait. 'I know your parents' divorce was really difficult for you, but you can't—'

'Drop it, Blondie. I don't want to talk about it.' His eyes glittered ominously and she saw the warning in the blue depths. Taboo subject.

She sighed. 'But, Jack, you can't—'

'Why did the blonde tiptoe past the medicine cabinet?'

he drawled lazily, and she rolled her eyes, exasperated by his refusal to talk about his emotions.

'I don't know.'

'Because she didn't want to wake the sleeping pills.' Jack gave a wicked smile that made her heart jump in her chest.

He was so shockingly handsome it was totally unfair, and when he smiled like that she just melted.

'How many men does it take to change a toilet roll?' She smiled sweetly. 'No one knows. It's never been done. So what did Nina do wrong?'

Jack gave a sardonic smile. 'Frankly? She said, "I love you",' he said dryly, and gave a mock shudder. 'Which is the same as "goodbye" in my language.'

Bryony rolled her eyes. 'They always say that if you want to get rid of a man, you should say "I love you, I want to marry you and most of all I want to have your children." It's guaranteed to leave skid marks.'

Jack laughed. 'That's just about the size of it. Why do you think I bought a Ferrari?'

Bryony sighed. 'Poor Nina.'

'She knew the score.'

But Bryony was willing to bet that knowing the score hadn't made it any easier. On the other hand, Nina seemed to have moved on quite happily to David so she couldn't have been that broken-hearted.

'One day you'll settle down, Jack,' Bryony predicted, licking another envelope. 'You'll be such a great father.'

'That's nonsense.'

'Look how great you are with Lizzie.'

'That's because I have all the fun and none of the responsibility,' he said shortly, frowning slightly as he looked at her.

'I don't think that's true. Lizzie expects a lot from you and you always deliver. How many netball matches have you been to this year?'

Jack grinned. 'Lots. You know me. Rugby, rock-climbing, netball—my three favourite sports.'

She laughed. 'Precisely. The sight of you standing on the side of a netball court would be funny if it wasn't so touching.' She added the envelope to the ever-growing pile. 'And it is touching, Jack. You're fantastic with Lizzie.'

A muscle worked in his jaw. 'But what she really wants is a father.'

Bryony shrugged. 'And who can blame her for that?'

'She doesn't realise that fathers aren't perfect.'

'I think she probably does, actually. But she still wants someone.'

'So how is the quest going? Any suitable candidates lined up? Obviously David is now off the scene…'

Something in his tone made her glance up at him but his expression was neutral.

'Well, it's not going that well,' Bryony muttered, licking another envelope and adding it to the pile. 'Christmas is three weeks away and I don't have another date until Saturday.'

His expression was suddenly hostile. 'You have a date on Saturday? Who with?'

Bryony blushed slightly. 'Toby.'

'Toby who?' Jack was frowning and she laughed.

'You know—our Toby. Toby from the mountain rescue team.'

'You're kidding!' He glared at her. 'Toby? He's totally unsuitable.'

'Calm down, Jack,' Bryony said mildly, gathering up all the envelopes and putting them on the table. 'Toby is nice. And he's always been kind to Lizzie.'

'Toby has a terrible reputation with women,' Jack said frostily, and she shrugged.

'So do you, Jack.'

'But I'm not dating you.'

And how she wished he was. Her gaze met his and held and then he sucked in a breath and rose to his feet, powerful and athletic.

'You can't date Toby.'

'Why not?'

There was a long silence and a muscle twitched in his jaw. 'Because he isn't right for you.'

She sighed. 'Jack, you're so jaded about relationships that you're never going to think anyone is right, but trust me when I say I'm not going to choose anyone who would hurt Lizzie.'

He took several deep breaths. 'I don't want anyone to hurt you either.'

'I know that.' She smiled at him, touched that he cared at least that much. 'You don't need to be so protective. It's nice, but I can look after myself.'

'Where are you going on Saturday?'

She wondered why he was asking and then decided that it was idle curiosity. 'Actually, I don't know. Toby is keeping it a secret.' She smiled. 'Isn't it romantic?'

'Suspicious is the word I would use,' Jack muttered,

grabbing his coat and car keys and making for the door. 'I'll talk to him.'

Bryony gave an exasperated sigh. 'Jack, you are not my minder.'

'Toby is definitely not to be trusted when it comes to women,' Jack growled. 'I want him to know that I'm looking out for you.'

'I should think he knows that, seeing as you spend half your life in my house,' Bryony pointed out mildly, and he nodded.

'Well, let's hope so. I won't have him messing either of my girls around.'

His girls.

Bryony swallowed and her eyes clashed with his. Something flickered in those blue depths and she knew that he was remembering their kiss. 'We're not "your girls", Jack.'

He hesitated and a strange expression crossed his handsome face as he stared down at her. Then he muttered something under his breath, jerked open the front door and left the house.

The next day the temperature dropped further still and it started to snow. Wrapped up in her MRT gear, Bryony was posting her Christmas cards when her pager went off.

Relieved that Lizzie was spending the day with her mother, she drove herself to the rescue base, which was less than five minutes' drive from her house.

'Two women out walking,' Jack told her, zipping up his jacket. 'One has cut herself and one has an ankle injury.'

He exchanged looks with Bryony. 'What is it with women and ankles?'

'I don't know but at least it gives you and me an excuse to climb mountains in filthy weather,' she said happily, and he smiled.

'I suppose there is that.'

The rest of the team gathered, picking up equipment and listening while they were given a brief.

'We're not sure where they are—' Sean, leader of the MRT, tapped a point on the map '—but this was where they were aiming for when it started to snow. The path is covered now and they're totally lost.'

Bryony looked at the map. 'It's really easy to lose that path in bad weather,' she said. 'I know because I've done it myself.'

Jack rolled his eyes. 'Never let a blonde loose on a mountain,' he drawled, but his eyes gleamed wickedly and she smiled back at him.

'At least a girl will ask for directions if she's lost. Men never ask for directions.'

'That's because they don't need to. Men don't get lost,' Jack returned blithely, and Sean sighed.

'Maybe you two could argue on the way,' he suggested mildly, pointing at the map. 'Ben, you go with Toby up this path and hopefully we'll come across them. Stay in touch. And watch yourselves. The weather is awful. I'll deploy the rest of the team as they arrive.'

Toby glanced at Bryony. 'I could go with Bryony…'

'No, you couldn't.' Jack's response was instantaneous, his blue gaze hard and uncompromising. 'I go with Bryony.'

Toby's eyes narrowed slightly and then he shrugged. 'Whatever.'

Bryony followed Jack out of the rescue base and they drove a short distance and parked the four-wheel-drive in a farm near the path.

Jack hoisted the rucksack onto his back and waited while she did the same thing. 'Come on. We need to get going before we freeze to death.'

They set off at a brisk pace and she glanced at the sky. 'It's going to snow again in a minute.'

'It's Christmas,' Jack pointed out. 'It's supposed to snow.'

Bryony gave a shiver and pulled her fleece up to her chin. 'Well, it looks nice on the Christmas cards but it's not so great when you're out on the mountains. Why didn't you let me go with Toby?'

'Because he'd be so busy staring at your legs he'd let you fall down a crevice.'

Bryony gaped at him. 'Jack, I'm wearing fleece trousers. They're hardly revealing!'

'Your legs would look sexy in a bin bag.'

She stopped dead. He thought her legs were sexy? He'd never said anything like that to her before. She was staring after him in confusion, wondering why he'd said that, when he glanced back at her.

'Why have you stopped? You needed to admire me from a distance?'

She grinned, suddenly feeling light-hearted. 'Why are men like placemats?' Shifting her rucksack slightly to make it more comfortable, she caught up with him. 'Because they only show up when there's food on the table.'

He smiled and as they continued up the path it started to snow again. 'I hope they've got some form of shelter,' Jack muttered, and Bryony nodded, her expression concerned.

'I hope we find them soon. It'll be dark in a couple of hours.'

They trudged on and the snow suddenly grew thicker underfoot.

'Crampons and ice axes, I think, Blondie,' Jack muttered, pausing by a snow-covered rock and swinging his rucksack off his back.

They stopped just long enough to equip themselves safely for the next part of the rescue and then they were off again.

Bryony stayed behind Jack, watching him place his feet firmly and confidently in the snow, the sharp points of his crampons biting into the snow.

They walked for what felt like ages and then suddenly heard shouts from above them.

'Sounds hopeful,' Jack said, increasing his pace and altering his direction slightly. 'We'll check it out and then I'll radio in to base.'

Bryony breathed a sigh of relief when they rounded the next corner and saw two women huddled together.

'Watch your footing here,' Jack said, frowning slightly as he glanced to his right. 'There's a slope there and a sheer drop at the end of it. I know because I climbed up that rockface last summer with your brothers. This snow doesn't feel very stable to me.'

'Shall we rope up?'

He shook his head. 'We're all right for now, but we'll rope up before we go down.'

They reached the two women and one of them immediately burst into tears.

'Oh, thank goodness…'

Bryony dropped onto her knees beside her, aware that Jack was already on the radio, giving their exact location to the rest of the team.

'You're going to be fine,' she said gently, slipping her arm around the woman's shoulders and giving her a hug. 'Where are you hurt?'

'I'm not hurt,' the woman said, but her teeth were chattering and she was obviously very cold. 'But my sister slipped on the snow and hurt her ankle and cut her wrist. I think she must have hit a rock when she landed. It was bleeding very badly so I pressed on it hard with a spare jumper that we had in our bag and it seemed to stop.'

'Good—you did just the right thing.' Bryony shrugged her rucksack off her back. 'I'm Bryony and I'm a doctor and a member of the local mountain rescue team. What's your name?'

'Alison Gayle.' The woman was shivering. 'And my sister's name is Pamela. I feel so guilty dragging you out in this weather. We've put everyone in danger.'

'Don't feel guilty,' Bryony said immediately, 'and you haven't put us in danger. It's our job and we love it. And we have all the right equipment for this weather.'

Which was just as well, she reflected ruefully, because the weather was getting worse by the second.

The snow started to fall heavily and Bryony brushed the soft flakes away from her face with a gloved hand and looked at the sky with a frown. The visibility was reducing rapidly. She moved over to check on Pamela and Jack joined her.

'All right, the rest of the team is on their way up.' He dropped down next to her and smiled at Alison. 'Lovely day for a stroll in the hills.'

Bryony moved over to Pamela and noticed that the woman looked extremely pale and shocked.

'You're going to be fine now, Pamela,' she said firmly. 'I'm just going to check your injuries and then we're going to get you off this mountain.'

She pulled off her gloves and carefully unwrapped the blood-soaked jumper so that she could examine the wrist injury more carefully. As soon as she released the pressure and exposed the wound, blood spurted into the air and Bryony quickly grabbed the jumper and pressed down again.

'It's an artery, Jack,' she muttered and he was by her side in an instant, the bulk of his shoulders providing a barrier between her and the elements.

He was strong and confident and, as usual, she found his presence hugely reassuring.

'I've put Alison into a casualty bag so she'll be fine for the time being.' He unwrapped the wrist himself, quickly assessed the extent of the injury and then pressed a sterile pad over the laceration and smiled at Pamela.

'That's going to be fine,' he said smoothly, elevating her arm and handing a bandage to Bryony with his free hand. 'We're going to bandage it tightly and keep it up just until we can get you off this mountain.'

The woman looked at him with frightened eyes. 'I can't walk down—my ankle hurts.'

'Don't you worry about that. That's why we bring my blonde friend here,' Jack said cheerfully, winking at Bryony. 'She's the muscles of the operation.'

While he chatted and teased, Bryony tightened the bandage and gave him a nod. 'All done.'

'Good. So now let's check the ankle. How painful is it, Pamela?'

The woman looked at him, her lips turning blue with the cold. 'Agony.'

'So we'll give you some gas and air to breathe while we check it out,' Jack said immediately, reaching into his rucksack. 'I want you to take some slow breaths. Great— perfect.' He looked at Bryony. 'Right, can you cut that boot off and let's see what we're dealing with here? And make it quick. She's cold and we need to get her into a casualty bag.'

Bryony sliced through the laces and gently removed the boot and then the sock. 'The ankle is very swollen,' she murmured, and Pamela gave a little groan and took several more breaths of the gas and air. 'Could you put any weight on it after you fell, Pamela?'

The woman shook her head. 'It was agony. I fell straight away, that's how I cut my wrist.'

'What do you reckon, Blondie?' Jack asked, his arm around Pamela as he supported her.

'She's tender over the distal fibula and the lateral malleolus,' Bryony said quickly. 'I think it's probably a fracture. She's going to need X-rays when we get her down.'

'So we splint it now, give her some more analgesia and then get her into a casualty bag until the rest of the team gets here with the Bell,' Jack said decisively, his arm still round Pamela. 'You're going to be fine, Pamela.'

Pamela groaned. 'Have I broken it? And why do you need a bell?'

'A Bell is a type of stretcher that we use, and it looks as though you might have broken your ankle,' Jack said, watching as Bryony pulled out the rest of the equipment. 'Don't you worry. We're going to make you comfortable. We have these amazing fleecy bags that are very snug. In a moment you're going to feel like toast. Did you hear about the blonde who ordered a take-away pizza? The waiter asked her if she wanted it cut into six slices or twelve—' swiftly he helped Bryony apply the splint '—and she said, "Six, please. I could never eat twelve."'

'Just ignore him, Pamela,' Bryony advised with a smile. 'He doesn't know the meaning of politically correct and frankly it's amazing he hasn't been arrested before now. If I didn't need him to carry you down this mountain, I'd push him off the cliff myself.'

But despite the pain she was obviously suffering, Pamela was smiling. 'He's making me laugh, actually.'

Bryony groaned. 'Don't tell him that or he'll tell you blonde jokes all the way down the mountain. Trust me, you'd rather be left on your own in the snow than have to listen to Jack in full flow.'

She and Jack kept up their banter, taking Pamela's mind off the situation she was in, working together with swift efficiency. They'd just got Pamela into a casualty bag when the rest of the team approached out of the snow. Bryony's brother was among them.

Jack rolled his eyes. 'The last thing we need up here is

an obstetrician,' he drawled. 'Who's delivering all those babies while you're wasting your time on the mountain?'

Tom adjusted the pack on his back. 'They're all queuing up, waiting for me to come back.'

'Well, you took so long you needn't have bothered coming.' Jack stood up, tall and broad-shouldered. 'You've missed all the action. Blondie and I have sorted it out as usual. Don't know why we need such a big team really.'

'If we weren't here you wouldn't have anyone to boss around,' Tom said dryly, working with the rest of the team to get a stretcher ready. 'We rang the RAF to see if there was any chance of an airlift but the weather is closing in so it looks like we're going to have to carry them down.'

Jack walked over and conferred with Sean, the other A and E consultant and the MRT leader, and discussed the best way to get the two women off the mountain while Bryony kept an eye on Pamela. Fortunately the casualty bag had zip access, which meant she was able to check on her patient without exposing her to the freezing air.

Finally Pamela was safely strapped onto a stretcher. Her sister had revived sufficiently to be able to walk down the mountain with some assistance from two bulky MRT members who roped her between them.

Bryony reattached her crampons and picked up her ice axe. The snow was thick now and she knew that one false step could have her sliding halfway down the mountain.

The snow was falling so thickly she could barely see and she scrubbed her face with her hand to clear her vision.

'Rope up, Blondie,' Jack's voice said, and as she opened her mouth to answer, the ground beneath her suddenly shifted and she was falling.

She didn't even have time to cry out, sliding fast down the slope towards the edge of the cliff that Jack had described so graphically.

Immediately she braced the axe shaft across her body, digging the pick into the snow slope and raising her feet so that they didn't catch in the snow. She jerked to a halt and hung there for a moment, suspended, her heart hammering against her chest, her hands tightly locked on her ice axe, which was the only thing holding her on the slope.

She heard Jack calling her name and heard something in his tone that she hadn't heard before. Panic.

She closed her eyes briefly and took a deep breath. She didn't want Jack to panic. Jack never panicked. Ever. Jack panicking was a bad sign. Realising just how close she was to the edge of the cliff, she kept a tight hold on her ice axe and gingerly moved her feet, trying to get some traction with her crampons.

'Hang on, Bry,' Tom called cheerfully. 'Jack's just coming to get you. You won't live this one down in a hurry.'

But despite his light-hearted tone, Bryony heard the anxiety in his voice. And it was hardly surprising, she thought ruefully, risking another glance below her. Another couple of metres and she would have vanished over the edge of a sheer cliff.

And it could still happen.

'Hang on, Blondie,' Jack called, and she glanced up to see him climbing down towards her, a rope attached to his middle.

'You think I'm going to let go?' Her voice shook slightly. 'You think I'm that stupid?'

As he drew closer she could see his grin. 'Of course

you're stupid. You fell, didn't you? And you have blonde hair. You must be stupid. It says so in all the books.'

Bryony tried to smile but then she felt the snow give under her ice axe and she gave a gasp of fright and jabbed her feet into the slope. *Jack!*

'I've got you, angel.' His voice came from right beside her and he slid an arm and leg over her, holding her against the slope while he attached a rope to her waist. 'God, you almost gave us all a heart attack.'

She turned her head to look at him and his face was so close that she could feel the warmth of his breath against her cheek and see the dark stubble shadowing his hard jaw. He looked sexy and strong and she'd never been so pleased to see anyone in her life.

Then she glanced down at the drop beneath her and thought of Lizzie. 'Oh, God, Jack,' she whispered, and she felt his grip on her tighten.

'Don't even say it,' he said harshly. 'I've got you and there's no way I'm letting you go.' He glanced up the slope and shouted something to Sean, who was holding the other end of the rope. 'They're going to take you up now, sweetheart. Try not to do anything blonde on the way up.'

She gave a weak smile and he smiled back. 'Go for it.'

And gradually, with the aid of the rope and her ice axe and crampons, she managed to climb back up the slope, aware that Jack was behind her.

Finally she reached the top and Tom rolled his eyes. 'Thanks for the adrenaline rush.'

'Any time,' Bryony said lightly, but she was shaking badly now that the danger had passed, and Jack must have known that because he pulled her into his arms and held her until his warmth and strength gradually calmed her.

He didn't speak. He just held her tightly, talking all the time to Sean and Tom as they reassessed the best way to get safely down the increasingly treacherous slope.

Bryony stood in the circle of his arms, wishing that she could stay there for ever. There was no better place in the world, she decided, closing her eyes and breathing in his tantalising male scent.

And when he finally released her she felt bereft.

She looked at him, trying to keep it light as he checked the rope at her waist. 'I didn't know you were into bondage.'

He smiled down at her as he pulled on the rope. 'There's a lot you don't know about me, Blondie,' he drawled, his blue eyes teasing her wickedly. 'There's no point in learning to do all these fancy knots if you don't put them to good use.'

She smiled and then her smile faltered. 'Thanks, Jack.' Ridiculously she felt close to tears. 'I would have done the same for you.'

He winked at her, maddeningly self-confident. 'I wouldn't have fallen, babe.'

She gasped in outrage. 'You arrogant...!' Words failed her and he smiled and flicked her cheek with a gloved finger.

'That's better. At least you've got your colour back. Let's get moving.'

He turned to Sean and she realised that his inflammatory statement had been a ploy to rouse her to anger. Which meant he must have guessed how close she'd been to tears.

She gave a reluctant laugh, acknowledging once more just how clever he was.

It was much easier to get down the mountain feeling annoyed and irritated than it was feeling scared and tearful.

In the end it took several hours to get down safely and the two women were immediately transferred to A and E in the MRT ambulance.

Jack drove Bryony home, the swirling snow falling thickly on the windscreen. 'If this carries on we're going to be busy in A and E,' he said, his eyes searching as he glanced at her.

'I'm OK.'

He nodded. 'Thanks to your ice axe technique. You did well. That's if you overlook the fact that you fell in the first place.'

She gaped at him. 'I did not fall,' she protested. 'The mountain slipped out from beneath me.'

'It wasn't my fault I crashed the car, Officer,' Jack said, mimicking her tone. 'The road suddenly moved.'

Bryony pulled a face. 'What's it like being so damn perfect, Jack?'

'I've learned to live with it,' he said solemnly, 'but I realise it's tough on those who struggle around me.'

'You can say that again,' she muttered darkly, dragging off her hat and scraping her hair back from her face. 'One of these days I'm probably going to shoot you.'

'Is that before or after I save you from falling over a cliff?'

She groaned. 'You're never going to let me forget that, are you?'

'Probably not.' He pulled up outside her house and

switched the engine off. 'So are you going to invite me to supper tomorrow night?'

There was a gleam in his eyes and she felt butterflies flicker inside her stomach. 'I have a date with Toby,' she croaked, and his eyes narrowed slightly.

'Of course you have.' He was silent for a moment and then he smiled. 'Another time, then.'

He leaned across to open the car door for her and she fought against the temptation to lean forward and hug him. He was so close—and so male...

Suddenly she wished she didn't have the date with Toby. She would rather have spent an evening with Jack.

But then she remembered Lizzie's Christmas list. She shouldn't be spending her evenings with Jack. It was a waste of time.

'Lizzie and I are going to choose our Christmas tree tomorrow,' she said, telling herself that spending time with Jack during the day didn't count. 'Do you want to come? She'd love you to join us, I know she would.'

Jack grinned. 'Will I have to play Weddings?'

'Probably, but you're getting very good at it now so I don't see the problem.'

'All right, I'd like to come.'

'Goodnight, then, Jack,' she said softly, undoing her seat belt and gathering up her stuff. 'I'll see you tomorrow.'

And she scrambled out of the car without looking back.

CHAPTER SEVEN

'I WANT the biggest tree in the forest.' Lizzie clapped her hands together and beamed at Jack, her breath clouding the freezing air. She was wearing pink fleecy trousers tucked into pink fleecy boots, a bright, stripy scarf wrapped round her neck, and she was bursting with excitement. 'The tree has to be big if Santa is going to fit my present under it.'

Bryony chewed her lip and exchanged glances with Jack. 'You know, sweetheart,' she said anxiously, 'I'm not sure we gave Santa enough notice to find a daddy. That's a pretty big present.'

'He'll manage it,' Lizzie said happily, stamping her feet to keep warm, 'because I've been extra good. Sally stole my gloves in the playground and I didn't even tell.'

Jack frowned. 'Someone stole your gloves?'

'They were new and she liked them.'

Jack looked at Bryony. 'Another child stole her gloves?'

'It's fine, Jack,' Bryony said hastily, knowing just how protective Jack could be of Lizzie. 'She'll sort it out.'

'You should speak to her teacher.'

'It's fine, Jack!' Bryony shot him a warning look. 'Now, let's go and choose this tree, shall we?'

Jack sucked in a breath and smiled. 'Good idea.' He took Lizzie's hand in his. 'We'll get you some new gloves, peanut. Any pair you want. We'll choose them together.'

They walked amongst the trees and Lizzie sprinted up to one and tilted her head back, gazing up in awe.

'I like *this* one.'

Bryony looked at it in dismay. 'Lizzie, it's the tallest tree here!'

'I know.' Lizzie stroked the branches lovingly, watching as the needles sprang back. 'I love it. It's big. Like having the whole forest in your house. And I like the way it smells.' She leaned forward and breathed in and Bryony sighed.

'It won't fit into our living room, sweetheart. How about that one over there—it's a lovely shape.'

Lizzie shook her head, her hand still locked around one branch of the tree she'd chosen as if she couldn't quite let it go. 'I love this one. I want this to be our tree.'

Bryony closed her eyes briefly. 'Lizzie—'

'It's a great tree and we can always trim the top,' Jack said firmly, and Bryony lifted an eyebrow.

'You're planning to lop six feet off the top?'

He grinned. 'If need be.' He squatted down next to Lizzie, his hair shining glossily black next to the little girl's blonde curls. 'The lady likes this one. So the lady gets this one.'

'You need to learn to say no to her, Jack.'

'Why would I want to say no?' He scooped Lizzie into his arms and grinned at her. 'So you want this tree?'

Lizzie nodded and slipped her arm round his neck. 'Can I have it?'

'Of course.' Still holding the child, Jack slipped a hand into his pocket and removed his wallet. 'Here we are, Blondie. Merry Christmas.'

Bryony shook her head. 'I'll pay, Jack.'

'My treat.' His eyes locked on hers, his expression warm. 'Please.'

She hesitated and then smiled. 'All right. Thanks.'

Lizzie tightened her arms round Jack's neck. 'Why do you call Mummy Blondie?'

'Because she has blonde hair, of course.'

'But I have blonde hair, too.'

Jack gave a start. 'So you do! Goodness—I never noticed.'

Lizzie gave a delicious chuckle. 'Yes, you did. I know you're joking.' She hugged him tight and then looked at him thoughtfully. 'Jack…'

His eyes narrowed. 'Don't tell me, you want to go home and play Weddings?'

'No.' She lifted a small hand and touched his cheek. 'I asked Santa for a daddy for Christmas.'

Jack went still. 'I know you did.'

'Well, now I wish I'd asked him to make you my daddy,' Lizzie said wistfully. 'I love you, Jack. No one plays Weddings like you do.'

Bryony swallowed hard, the lump in her throat so big it threatened to choke her.

'Lizzie…' Jack's voice sounded strangely thick and his hard jaw was tense as he struggled to find the right words.

'I can't be your daddy, sweetheart. But I'll always be here for you.'

'Why can't you be my daddy? I know Mummy loves you.'

Bryony closed her eyes, fire in her cheeks, but Jack just gave a strange-sounding laugh.

'And I love your mummy. But not in the way that mummies and daddies are supposed to love each other.'

Bryony rubbed her booted foot in the snow and wished an avalanche would consume her. But there wasn't much chance of that in the forest. So instead she looked up and gave a bright smile.

'But Santa is going to choose you a great present,' she said brightly. 'I know he is, and in the meantime we'd better buy this super-special tree before anyone else does. It's the best one in the forest and I can see other people looking at it.'

Lizzie's eyes widened in panic. 'Hurry up, then!'

Bryony took Jack's wallet and went to pay while he opened the boot of the four-wheel-drive and manoeuvred the huge tree inside, with Lizzie jumping up and down next to him.

'Most of the needles have just landed on the inside of the vehicle,' he muttered to Bryony as they climbed into the front and strapped Lizzie in. 'I think we might be decorating twigs when we get it home.'

Bryony glanced at him, wondering if he realised that he'd called her house 'home'.

'Are you getting a tree yourself, Jack?' she asked, and he shook his head, holding the wheel firmly as he negotiated the rutted track that led out of the forest onto the main road.

'What's the point? I'm going to be working for most of it.' He glanced at Lizzie who was listening to a tape through her headphones and not paying any attention. 'And, anyway, Christmas is for children.'

Bryony gave him a searching look. 'Are you coming to Mum's this year?'

Jack concentrated on the road. 'I don't know. Sean wants to be with Ally and the kids so I've said I'll work.'

'You come every year, Jack.' Bryony frowned. 'Lizzie would be so disappointed if you weren't there. All of us would. You're part of our family. At least come for part of it.'

'Maybe.' His shrug was noncommittal and she sighed. 'I know Christmas isn't your favourite time of year.'

There was a long silence and then he sucked in a breath, his eyes still on the road. 'Christmas is for families, Blondie. I don't have one.'

Bryony bit her lip. 'Have you heard from your mother lately?'

'A postcard six months ago.' He turned the wheel to avoid a hole in the road. 'She's with her latest lover in Brazil.'

Bryony was silent and he turned to look at her, a mocking look in his eyes. 'Don't feel sorry for me. I'm thirty-four. I certainly don't expect my mother to come home and play happy families after all this time. I think that's one game we never mastered in our house. When everyone else was unwrapping presents around the tree, my parents were at different ends of the house nurturing grievances.'

'Jack—'

'And that was a good thing.' He gave a grim smile. 'If

they ever met the rows were so bad I used to run and hide in the garden. Once I was out there all night and they didn't even notice. I always used to think that was why we had such a big house with so much land. Because no one wanted to live next door to anyone who argued as much as my parents.'

His experience was such a contrast to her own happy childhood that Bryony felt suddenly choked.

'You used to come to us.'

'Yeah.' He gave a funny smile. 'You were the perfect family.'

Bryony looked at him, suddenly wondering for the first time whether that had made it worse for him. 'Was it hard for you, being with us?'

He shook his head. 'It wasn't hard, Blondie. You always made me feel as though I was Santa himself from the moment I walked through the door. How could that be hard?'

Bryony smiled. She used to stand with her nose pressed against the window, waiting for Jack to arrive. Longing to show him her presents.

'You were just like Lizzie.' His voice softened at the memory. 'I remember the year you had your ballet dress from Santa. You wore it with your Wellington boots because you were dying to play outside in the snow but no one could persuade you to take it off. You were in the garden building a snowman in pink satin and tulle. Do you remember?'

'I remember tearing it climbing a tree.' Bryony laughed. 'I just wanted to keep up with my brothers.'

On impulse she reached out and touched his leg, feeling the rock-hard muscle under her fingers. 'Come for Christmas, Jack. Please?'

He gave her a funny, lopsided smile that was so sexy she suddenly found it hard to breathe. 'Better see what Santa produces for Lizzie first,' he said softly, turning into the road that led to her cottage. 'I might not be welcome.'

Bryony slumped back in her seat, the reminder that she'd so far failed to solve the problem of Lizzie's Christmas present bursting her bubble of happiness.

What was she going to do about Lizzie's present?

At some point soon she was going to have to sit her little girl down and tell her that Santa couldn't deliver a daddy. Otherwise Christmas morning was going to be a disappointment.

Trying to console herself with the thought that there must be something else that Lizzie would like for Christmas, Bryony realised that Jack had stopped the car.

'Ready to unload this tree?' He glanced behind him and winced. 'I can't believe you chose a tree that big.'

Lizzie pulled the headphones off her ears and giggled. 'It wasn't Mummy, it was you, Jack.'

'Me?' He looked horrified as he jumped out of the car with athletic grace and turned to lift the little girl out. 'I chose that?'

Lizzie was laughing. 'You know you did.'

'Well, we'd better get it in your house, then.'

Laughing and grumbling, Jack dragged the tree inside the house and proceeded to secure it in a bucket with his usual calm efficiency.

Bryony gazed upwards and shook her head in disbelief. 'It's bent at the top.'

'It's perfect,' Lizzie sighed, and Jack nodded solemnly. 'Perfect.'

Bryony rolled her eyes, forced to accept that she was outnumbered. 'OK. Well, we've got it now, so let's decorate it.'

They spent the rest of the afternoon draping the tree with lights and baubles until it sparkled festively. Lizzie produced a pink fairy to go on top of the tree and Jack lifted her so that she could position it herself.

Then Jack went into the garden and cut boughs of holly from the tree and they decorated the fireplace.

Bryony produced mince pies and they sat on the carpet, admiring their decorations and enjoying the atmosphere.

Bryony smiled as she looked around her. 'I feel Christmassy.'

'That's because of the size of the tree,' Jack told her, his handsome face serious as he bit into a mince pie. 'Any smaller and you wouldn't be feeling the way you're feeling now.'

But watching him and Lizzie fighting over the last mince pie, Bryony realised that the warm Christmassy feeling that she had in the pit of her stomach had nothing to do with the tree and everything to do with the three of them being together. They felt like a family.

But they weren't a family.

Jack didn't want to be part of a family.

Watching Lizzie climbing all over him, dropping crumbs over his trousers and the carpet, Bryony wondered if he realised that he actually *was* part of a family.

Whether he liked it or not, he was a huge part of her life. And she couldn't imagine it any other way, even if ultimately she found a daddy for Lizzie. And just thinking of how she was going to tell Lizzie that Santa hadn't managed to produce a daddy on Christmas Day filled her with overwhelming depression.

Suddenly needing to be on her own, Bryony stood up. 'I need to get ready. Toby's picking me up at seven,' she said brightly, 'and I don't want to smell like a Christmas tree.'

She half expected Jack to say something about her going out with Toby. After all, he'd been less than enthusiastic about her other attempts to date men. But he just smiled at her and carried on playing with Lizzie.

Feeling deflated and not really understanding why, Bryony ran herself a deep bath and lay in a nest of scented bubbles for half an hour, telling herself that she was going to have a really great evening with Toby.

She was going to wear the black dress again.

And it was nothing to do with Jack's comments about her having good legs, she told herself firmly as she dried herself and dressed carefully. It was just that the dress suited her and she knew that Toby was planning to take her somewhere special.

She spent time on her make-up and pinned her hair on top of her head in a style that she felt suited the dress.

Finally satisfied, she walked out of her bedroom and into the kitchen, where Jack was making Lizzie tea and playing a game of 'guess the animal'.

'You're a tiger, Jack.' Lizzie giggled, watching with delight as he prowled around the kitchen, growling. 'Do I have to eat sprouts? I hate sprouts. Can I have peas instead?'

'Never argue with a tiger,' Jack said sternly, putting

two sprouts on the side of her plate. 'Eat up. They're good for you.'

Lizzie stared at them gloomily. 'I hate things that are good for me.'

'He's only given you two,' Bryony said mildly, turning to lift two mugs out of the cupboard. When she looked back the sprouts had gone. Lizzie and Jack were both concentrating hard on the plate, neither of them looking at her.

'All right.' Bryony put her hands on her hips, her eyes twinkling. 'What happened to the sprouts?'

Lizzie covered her mouth and gave a snort of laughter and Jack tried to look innocent.

'Did you know that tigers love sprouts?'

Lizzie smiled happily. 'If Jack was my daddy I'd *never* have to eat sprouts.'

Jack shot Bryony a rueful look and ran a hand over the back of his neck. 'Lizzie, angel, we've got to talk about this.'

But before he could say any more, the phone rang. Bryony picked it up, expecting it to be her mother ringing about the babysitting arrangements for that evening.

It was Toby and when she finally replaced the receiver she was silent.

'What's the matter?' Jack was feeding Lizzie the last of her fish fingers. 'Is he going to be late?'

'He isn't coming.' Bryony looked at him, thinking that Jack didn't look that surprised. He just carried on feeding Lizzie. She frowned. 'She can feed herself, Jack.'

'I know she can, but we're playing zoos,' he said calmly, 'and at the moment I'm feeding the tigers. So why is your date off?'

'Because Sean sent him over to Penrith to pick up some equipment for the team and it's taken him ages to sort it out and he's still there.' She frowned. 'Why didn't he tell Sean that he had a date?'

Jack stabbed the last of the fish fingers, not looking at her. 'Well, I suppose it was important.'

'It sounded pretty routine to me,' Bryony muttered, facing the fact that yet another date had turned into a disaster, this time before the guy had even turned up on her doorstep. She was jinxed. Or was she?

Suddenly she looked at Jack suspiciously, remembering his attitude to Toby when they'd gone on the rescue. Had he somehow engineered this so that they couldn't go out? She knew he wasn't comfortable with the idea of her finding a daddy for Lizzie. And if she found someone, obviously that would affect his relationship because he couldn't just come and go the way he did at the moment.

Was he the reason Toby hadn't turned up?

She glanced down at herself with a sigh. 'All dressed up and nowhere to go,' she said lightly, giving a shrug. 'I suppose I may as well go and get changed.'

'Why?'

Jack stood up and suddenly all she was breathlessly aware of were those sexy blue eyes watching her.

'Well, there's no point in wearing *this*—' she gestured down to herself '—to eat baked beans.'

'Who said anything about baked beans?' he drawled softly, walking towards her with a distinct air of purpose. 'Ring your mum and cancel.'

'Cancel?'

He was so close now she could hardly breathe, and he gave her that smile that always made her insides tumble.

'Yes, cancel.' He put a hand under her chin and lifted her face to his. 'I'll cook dinner and you can wear the dress. You don't need a babysitter.'

Her heart was pumping in her chest and her whole body throbbed with a sexual awareness that was totally unfamiliar. 'You hate this dress.'

'I never said I hated the dress.'

Their eyes locked and suddenly all she could think about was that kiss. The way it had felt when his mouth had claimed hers.

She wanted him to kiss her again.

'You two are looking all funny.' Lizzie was staring at them curiously. 'Are you going to kiss?'

Bryony gasped and pulled away from Jack, her face flaming. She'd forgotten that Lizzie was still sitting at the table. *'No!'* She was suddenly flustered. 'We're not going to kiss.'

'I don't mind if you do,' Lizzie said generously, sliding off her chair and carrying her plate to the dishwasher. 'Sally says it's yucky when her parents do it, but I think it would be nice.'

'Lizzie, we're not going to kiss,' Bryony muttered, not daring to look at Jack but feeling his gaze on her. She always knew when he was looking at her and he was looking at her now.

'You blush easily, Blondie, do you know that?' His voice was a soft, teasing drawl and Lizzie clapped her hands.

'Mummy only ever goes that colour when you're here, Jack.'

Deciding that the conversation had gone far enough, Bryony glanced at her watch. 'And you should be getting ready for bed, Lizzie,' she said quickly. 'Do you want Jack to read you a story?'

'Only if he doesn't skip bits.'

Bryony risked a look at Jack. 'Is that OK with you, or do you need to get going?'

'That depends...'

'On what?'

He winked at her. 'What you're cooking me for dinner—'

She rolled her eyes. 'Don't you ever go home and cook for yourself, Jack?'

'Why would I want to when I've got you to cook for me?' He smiled and held up a hand. 'Only joking. As it happens, I'm cooking for you tonight.'

'You're cooking for *me*?'

Jack never cooked. He lounged at her table, watching while she cooked. And actually she liked it that way. She found cooking relaxing and there was nothing she enjoyed more than an evening chatting with Jack.

'I'm cooking for you. A gourmet creation right under your very nose. It's your turn to be impressed, Blondie.'

'But I was going out. How can you have the ingredients for a gourmet creation?'

He stooped to pick up Lizzie. 'I just picked up a few things on my way home, in case I was hungry later.'

'But you don't even know where the supermarket is.' Her eyes teased him. 'Or are you telling me you finally *asked for directions*?'

'No need.' He displayed his muscles, flexing his shoulders and his biceps. 'Man is a natural hunter.'

She lifted an eyebrow. 'You went to the supermarket in your *loin cloth*?'

'Of course. But I left my spear outside.' His eyes gleamed wickedly and she felt herself blush.

It was only as he walked out of the room with Lizzie that she realised that he hadn't actually answered her question about the food. How did he come to have the ingredients for a gourmet meal in his boot?

And why did he want her to keep the dress on when the last time she'd worn it he'd covered her up?

But the last time she'd worn it she'd been going out with another man.

Bryony plopped down on the nearest kitchen chair and wondered if Jack realised that he was displaying all the signs of a jealous male.

Probably not.

She hadn't realised it herself until two seconds ago.

But to be jealous you had to care, and Jack didn't care about her. Not like that.

Or did he?

She sat in silence, her mind running over everything that had happened since the night she'd walked into the pub and announced that she was going to start dating men again.

Jack had sabotaged every date.

Had he done that because of Lizzie? Because he didn't want Lizzie to have a daddy?

Or had he done it because he hadn't been able to see her with another man?

CHAPTER EIGHT

THE week before Christmas Jack, Bryony and Sean were in the staffroom discussing the mountain rescue team Christmas party, when Nicky rushed in, looking stressed.

'I just had a call from Ambulance Control,' she said breathlessly. 'Ellie has driven her car into a ditch.'

'Our Ellie?' Jack was on his feet immediately, his expression concerned. 'She's nearly eight months pregnant. Is she OK?'

Nicky shook her head. 'I haven't got many details but they had to cut her out of the car.'

Bryony was already hurrying to the door.

'She's been poorly right the way through this pregnancy,' Sean muttered, and Bryony remembered that he was very friendly with the couple outside work. 'That's why she gave up work early. Has anyone called Ben? This is his wife we're talking about.'

Ben MacAllister was another of the A and E consultants, and Ellie had worked as a nurse in A and E before she'd become pregnant.

'He's away on that immediate care course,' Jack reminded him, and Sean swore softly.

'Well, someone get on the phone.'

They heard the ambulance siren and Jack turned to Bryony. 'Call Tom,' he said urgently. 'I don't know whether there's a problem with the baby, but we're not taking any chances and I want your brother here.'

Without questioning his decision, Bryony hurried to the phone and called her brother and then hurried to Resus where the paramedics had taken Ellie.

Jack and Sean were already examining her thoroughly.

'Is Tom coming?' Jack was giving Ellie oxygen, clearly concerned about the baby.

'He's in Theatre, doing an emergency section,' Bryony told him, trying to hide her shock at seeing Ellie on the trolley. Her face was paper white and her blonde hair was matted with blood. 'He'll be down as soon as he can.'

Jack nodded and touched Ellie on the shoulder, lifting the mask away from her face for a moment. 'You're going to be fine, Ellie,' he said softly. 'The scalp wound is quite superficial. How are you feeling?'

'Worried about the baby,' Ellie said weakly, her normal exuberance extinguished by the shock of the accident and the pain she was in. 'Has someone called Ben?'

'He's on his way,' Nicky told her quickly, and Ellie gave a groan and closed her eyes.

'He'll be so worried—I wasn't sure whether we should have called him really…'

'He'd want to know,' Sean said, his face unusually white and strained as he looked at his friend lying on the trolley. 'What the hell were you doing, driving your car into a ditch anyway?'

Bryony saw Ellie smile and she lifted the oxygen mask from her face so that she could answer.

'I swerved to avoid a sheep,' she croaked, and Sean rolled his eyes.

'Well, of course you did,' he said gruffly, and looked at Jack. 'This is your show.'

Jack nodded and Bryony knew that Sean was handing over responsibility to someone who wasn't so close to Ellie. He was obviously finding it hard to be objective.

'Nicky, I need a pad for that scalp wound. We can glue it later.' Jack smiled down at Ellie. 'You're going to be fine, but I'm going to put a couple of lines in and check the baby.'

His voice was smooth and confident and he held out a hand to Nicky who'd already anticipated everything they were going to need.

Ellie shifted slightly on the trolley. 'I'm bleeding, Jack,' she murmured, her eyes drifting shut. 'I can feel it. Oh, God, I can't believe this is happening again. I'm going to lose it, I know I'm going to lose it.'

'You're not going to lose this baby,' Jack said firmly, his swift glance towards Bryony communicating clearly that she should call her brother again.

Bryony called Theatre again, and explained the situation. In the meantime Sean had put two lines in, and Ellie was connected to various monitors and had an IV running.

'Blondie, I want BMG, coagulation screen, rhesus/antibody status and a Kleihauer test. The foetal heart rate is good,' Jack said softly, his eyes on the monitor. 'Ellie,

I'm just going to feel your uterus—I want you to keep that oxygen mask on now, please. No more talking, sweetheart.'

But Ellie clutched his arm. 'If Tom can't get here, I want you to section me,' she croaked, her eyes suddenly swimming with tears. 'Don't let me lose this baby, Jack. Please, don't let me lose this baby.'

Jack's eyes locked on hers, his gaze wonderfully confident and reassuring. 'If I have to section you here, I can and I will,' he promised, 'and you are not going to lose this baby, Ellie. I swear it. Trust me, angel.' He looked at Nicky. 'Get me a pack ready just in case. And someone tell Tom Hunter that if he doesn't get himself down here in the next two minutes, he's buying the drinks for the whole of next year.'

Swallowing back a lump in her throat, Bryony took blood and arranged for it to be sent to the lab, someone delivered the portable ultrasound machine and Jack carefully scanned Ellie's abdomen, staring at the screen with total concentration as he looked for problems. He squinted closer at one area and exchanged glances with Sean who gave a discreet nod.

'The foetal heart is still 140,' Jack said, carrying on with the ultrasound until he was satisfied with what he'd seen.

Ellie tried to move the mask and Jack put a hand on hers to prevent her, anticipating her question.

'The baby is fine,' he said softly. 'I can see the heart beating and he just kicked me really hard. He's better in than out at the moment.'

Ellie gave a weak smile and closed her eyes again just as Tom strode into the room.

'Sorry, folks—tricky section upstairs. How are you doing here?'

Jack briefed him quickly and Tom listened carefully, asking the occasional question, his eyes flickering to Ellie who had her eyes closed. For once he and Jack were serious, no trace of their usual banter or humour as they conferred. Tom washed his hands and approached the trolley.

'Hi, Ellie,' he said gently, 'it's Tom. I just want to check on that baby of yours.'

Ellie's eyes opened and she looked frightened as she pulled the mask away from her face. 'I want you to deliver it, Tom,' she croaked. 'Deliver it now. Please. I've got one of my feelings. A very bad feeling…'

Tom squeezed her shoulder briefly and then slid the blanket down so that he could look at her abdomen. 'Trust me, Ellie,' he said gently. 'I'm not going to let you lose this baby.'

'I marked the top of the fundus,' Jack told him and Tom nodded as he examined Ellie thoroughly.

Five minutes later he glanced at Jack. 'She's bleeding quite a bit. I'm going to section her. Is there anything I need to know? Has she had a head injury?'

'She has a minor scalp laceration but she wasn't knocked out and her cervical spine is fine,' Jack told him. 'She's all yours.'

Tom ran a hand over the back of his neck. 'Is Ben coming?'

Ellie looked at him, her face pale. 'Just do it, Tom,' she whispered. 'Don't wait for Ben. Sean, will you stay with me?'

Sean stepped forward. 'Try getting rid of me,' he said

gruffly, taking Ellie's hand in his. 'Let's get her up to the labour ward and get this baby out.'

Everything happened swiftly after that.

Sean and Jack transferred Ellie up to the labour ward while Tom phoned around and called in the assistance of the top anaesthetist and two paediatricians, and then he sprinted up to Theatre after them.

Bryony and Nicky cleared up Resus, both of them quiet and worried about Ellie. They were still talking quietly, enjoying a brief lull in the usual run of patients, when Ben strode into Resus, his face drawn with worry.

'Where is she?'

'In Theatre on the labour ward,' Bryony said immediately. 'Tom is sectioning her.'

Ben sprinted back out of the room and Nicky sighed.

'There goes a man in love. I remember when those two met. Ellie just wouldn't let the man say no. Now he can barely let her out of his sight.'

'Ellie will be fine,' Bryony said firmly. 'Tom is a brilliant obstetrician.'

She had every faith in her brother, and every faith in Jack. Surely there was no way that anything could happen to Ellie or her baby?

'To baby MacAllister, as yet unnamed, and to Jack and Tom—' Sean raised his glass '—and a job well done.'

The whole mountain rescue team was gathered in the Drunken Fox to celebrate the safe arrival of Ben and Ellie's little boy.

Despite being just over four weeks early, he was doing well and was with Ellie on the ward.

Tom slung an arm round Jack's shoulders, his expression solemn. 'Just a question of knowing how, wouldn't you agree?'

'Absolutely.' Jack nodded sagely. 'That and natural brilliance.'

Tom reached for his beer. 'And years of training.'

'And finely honed instincts.'

Bryony rolled her eyes. 'And massive egos.' She looked at Sean. 'Better book two extra places at the Christmas party just to make room.'

There was general laughter and the conversation switched to the annual Christmas bash.

Bryony slid onto a barstool. 'So it's tomorrow night?'

'The venue has changed,' Sean told everyone, and Bryony frowned when she heard where it was.

'But that's miles away.'

'Over the other side of the valley,' Sean agreed, 'and if the weather carries on like this we'll have to all go in the four-wheel-drives or we'll be stuck in snowdrifts.'

'That would make a good newspaper headline,' Tom said mildly. 'ENTIRE MOUNTAIN RESCUE TEAM RESCUED FROM SNOWDRIFT.'

'It would be too embarrassing for words,' Jack agreed with a mock shudder, 'and it isn't going to happen.'

'Think of his ego,' Bryony said seriously, her blue eyes wide. 'It might never recover from the shock of such a public humiliation. It might shrivel to nothing.'

Sean finished his drink. 'We'll meet at the rescue centre at seven and go from there.'

'Bryony and I don't finish work until seven.' Jack reached for his jacket. 'I'll drive her there in the Ferrari.'

Sean gaped at him. 'You're taking your Ferrari out on these roads? You'll land it in a ditch.'

'I will not.' Jack looked affronted. 'I am invincible.'

'And so modest,' Bryony said mildly.

In the end they were late leaving A and E and Bryony struggled into her dress in the staff toilet, thinking longingly of scented bubble baths and hairdressers. Most people spent hours getting ready for a Christmas party. She had less than five minutes and she could already hear Jack leaning on the horn of the Ferrari.

'All right, all right, I'm here.' She fell into the seat next to him, her work clothes stuffed haphazardly into a bag, her blonde hair tumbling over her shoulders. 'I haven't even had a chance to do my hair.'

'You can do it on the way. We're already late.' Jack reversed the car out of his space and drove off in the direction of the next valley.

Bryony rummaged in her bag for her hairclips and gave a groan of frustration. 'I think I left them at work.'

'Left what at work?'

'My new hair slide.'

Jack glanced towards her and frowned. 'You look great. Leave it down.'

Bryony lifted a hand and touched her hair self-consciously. 'I look as though I've just woken up.'

'Precisely.' Jack gave her a wicked smile, his voice a lazy, masculine drawl. 'As I said—you look great.'

Was he flirting with her?

Bryony felt her stomach turn over and she looked at him, trying to read his mind, but he was concentrating on the road again. She stared at his strong profile, her gaze lingering on his mouth.

Something felt different about their relationship, but she wasn't sure what. He hadn't laid a finger on her since that one incredible kiss, but something was different. He looked at her differently.

'I can't think why Sean booked it all the way out here,' Jack grumbled as he turned the car up a narrow road and put his foot down. 'There must have been somewhere closer.'

'He wanted to just give us a grid reference and see where we all ended up,' Bryony told him, removing her gaze from his mouth with a huge effort. 'At least we managed to talk him out of that one. Do you want me to look at a map?'

'I know where I'm going.'

Bryony looked at him in surprise. 'You've been here before?'

'No.' Jack glanced across and gave her a sexy wink. 'But men have an instinctive sense of direction.'

Bryony rolled her eyes. 'Which means we're about to get lost.'

But they didn't get lost and less than twenty minutes later Jack pulled into the restaurant car park with a smug smile.

'I am invincible.'

'Unbearable, more like,' Bryony muttered, shivering as she opened the door and the cold hit her. 'It's going to snow again. It's freezing.'

'Men don't notice the cold.' Jack locked the car and held out a hand. 'Don't want you to slip, Blondie.'

'Believe it or not, I can put one foot in front of the other quite effectively,' she said tartly. 'I've been practising hard lately and I've finally got the hang of it.'

Ignoring his outstretched hand, she stalked towards the restaurant with as much dignity as she could given the amount of ice and snow on the path. She didn't dare take his hand. She was afraid she might never want to let go.

The rest of the team was already there and they had a fantastic evening, laughing and eating and drinking. Halfway through Jack looked at Bryony.

'You seem to be on water. How do you fancy driving the Ferrari home tonight?'

Her eyes gleamed. 'You trust me to drive your Ferrari on ice?'

'I'll be beside you. What can go wrong?'

But when they finally left the restaurant, several inches of snow had fallen and Bryony looked at the road doubtfully.

'I'm not sure about driving—we could cadge a lift in one of the four-wheel-drives.'

'They're full,' Jack told her, pushing her gently towards the car. 'You'll be fine.'

Bryony drove slowly but gradually she got the feel of the car and her confidence increased. Surprised by the lack of teasing from the passenger seat, she glanced sideways at Jack and realised that he'd fallen asleep.

Turning her attention back to the road, she turned right and followed the road for a while then gradually realised that it didn't look at all familiar.

She carried on for a while, hoping to see a sign of some sort, but there was nothing. The snow was falling heavily now and she could barely see the road in front of her so it was a relief when she saw the lights of a pub ahead. At least they'd be able to find out where they were.

She stopped the car and Jack gave a yawn.

'Are we home?'

Bryony slumped back in her seat and braced herself for some serious teasing. 'I haven't got a clue where we are.'

There was a moment's silence while Jack squinted at the pub. 'Well, if you had to get us lost, Blondie, at least you did it by a pub,' he said mildly, undoing his seat belt and opening the car door.

'Where are you going?' She stared at him. 'Are you asking for directions?'

He grinned. 'Of course I'm not asking for directions. I'm a man. But I'm going to check whether the road is open further on. My ego doesn't want to spend the night stuck in a snowdrift. It isn't well enough insulated.'

He vanished into the pub and reappeared moments later, his expression serious. 'As I thought, the road is blocked ahead and they won't be able to clear it until the morning. We can stay here for the night. Do you need to ring your mum?'

Bryony shook her head and unfastened her seat belt. 'She's got Lizzie until tomorrow night. They're going Christmas shopping together tomorrow.'

'Great. In which case, we'll stay here for the night and they can clear the road while someone cooks me bacon, sausages and mushrooms for breakfast,' Jack said cheerfully, holding the door open and grabbing her arm so that she didn't slip.

'I haven't got anything to sleep in,' Bryony protested,

and Jack shrugged, pushing open the door of the pub and hustling her into the warmth.

'You can sleep in your underwear,' he drawled, 'unless you'd rather sleep in mine.'

She shot him a withering look and the amusement in his blue eyes deepened.

'Just a suggestion.'

The landlady smiled at Jack and handed over a key. 'It's the last room. You're lucky. It's the honeymoon suite. We did it up specially because we have so many couples up here looking for somewhere to spend a romantic night.'

Bryony followed Jack up a flight of stairs, a frown on her face. 'The last room? There's only one room? And it's the honeymoon suite?'

'It'll be fine.' He unlocked the door. 'I'll sleep in the armchair.'

But there wasn't an armchair. Just an enormous bed draped in fur and satin, a small dressing room and a huge, marble bathroom.

They looked at each other and Bryony gave a snort of laughter as she saw Jack's face.

'It's the honeymoon suite, Jack,' she cooed, unable to resist teasing him and he shook his head, gazing round the room in disbelief.

'I knew there was a reason I never wanted to get married.' He peered at the bed in amazement. 'Hasn't Lizzie got a bed just like that for one of her dolls?'

'There's no chair,' Bryony said, glancing round for some alternative suggestion. 'You'll just have to sleep on the floor.'

'There's no way I'm sleeping on a fluffy carpet.' Jack

ripped off his jacket and dropped it over the end of the bed. 'That's an emperor-size bed at least. There's plenty of room for two of us in that. And if we shut our eyes tightly we can probably forget about the satin and fur.'

Bryony stared at him. He was suggesting that they sleep in the same bed?

Jack took one look at her face and lifted an eyebrow in question. 'We've known each other for twenty-two years, for goodness' sake. Don't you trust me, Blondie?'

Bryony looked at the bed and swallowed. She trusted him. It was herself she didn't trust. But she could hardly protest without revealing what she felt for him.

So she'd climb into the bed, turn her back on him and try and forget it was Jack lying next to her. It wasn't as if the bed was small...

Throwing a casual smile in his direction, she walked into the enormous bathroom and closed the door firmly behind her. *Oh, help!*

She stared at herself in the mirror and wondered whether she should just sleep in her dress. It was either that or take it off, and if she took it off...

She was still standing there five minutes later when Jack banged on the door. 'Have you been sucked down the plughole or something? Hurry up!'

Bryony closed her eyes briefly and then decided that she may as well get on with it. He was obviously totally indifferent to the fact that they were about to spend a night in the same bed, so perhaps she could be, too.

She used the toiletries and then opened the bathroom door and gave him a bright smile.

'All yours. You're going to *love* the mermaid taps.'

She strolled past him, waited until she heard the door close and then wriggled out of her dress and leaped into the bed, still wearing her underwear. The bed was huge and absolutely freezing and she lay there, her whole body shivering, wondering how she was ever going to sleep.

She heard sounds of the shower running and then finally the door opened and Jack appeared, a towel wrapped around his hips.

Bryony's heart started to thud rhythmically in her chest and suddenly she didn't feel cold any more.

She'd seen his body before, of course. In the summer at the beach. In the swimming pool when they'd taken Lizzie together. But she'd never seen his body when she was lying half-naked in bed. Suddenly all she could think about was the fact that he was about to slide in between the sheets next to her.

And he wasn't wearing anything.

In the dim light of the bedroom he was breathtakingly sexy. Her eyes followed the line of his body hair, tracking down over his muscular chest, down his board-flat stomach and down further still until it disappeared under the towel.

Refusing to allow herself to even think about what was underneath the towel, Bryony forced herself to breathe before she passed out. 'Are you planning to wear a towel to bed?' she croaked, trying to keep it light but feeling anything but light. In fact, her whole body felt heavy.

Jack eyed the bed with amusement. 'This bed is huge. I'm going to need a grid reference to find you.'

'You don't have to find me,' Bryony said hastily. 'It's really late. Just go to sleep.'

And with that she rolled over and closed her eyes tightly.

Not that it made any difference at all. Even with her eyes shut she could still see every inch of his incredible body. The image was embedded in her brain and when she felt the bed dip slightly and heard him switch the light off, she curled her fingers into the duvet to stop herself from reaching for him.

For a moment neither of them moved and then he cursed softly. 'I'm developing frostbite. This bed is freezing.'

'Just go to sleep, Jack.'

'I can't go to sleep, my teeth are chattering too much.'

She gave a sigh and turned towards him, telling herself that it was dark anyway so she couldn't see him and he couldn't see her.

'Well, go and put your shirt back on.'

'I'm not sleeping in my clothes.'

She chuckled. 'Put my clothes on, then.'

'Good idea. I could wear your dress as a T-shirt.' He gave a shiver. 'Alternatively, we could cuddle each other. Warm me up, woman, or I'll be found dead in the morning.'

Before she could anticipate his next move, he reached for her and pulled her firmly against him so that they were lying side by side and nose to nose.

'Jack!' She tensed and planted her hands firmly on the centre of his chest and pushed against him, but he didn't budge.

'Just relax, will you?' His voice sounded very male in the darkness. 'You know as well as I do that bodily warmth is an important source of heat.'

A source of heat?

Being this close to him, her fingers tangled with the

hairs on his chest, her palms feeling the steady thud of his heart. It wasn't heat she was producing, it was fire.

And she realised that he wasn't cold at all. His body was warm and hard and throbbing with vital masculinity and it was pressed against hers.

'Jack, I can't—'

'Shut up, Blondie.' He slid a hand round the back of her neck and found her mouth with his. His tongue traced the seam of her lips and her mouth opened under his, breathing in his groan of desire.

'Jack, this is a mistake.'

'Probably.' His mouth was warm against hers, his kiss maddeningly seductive. 'But I like making mistakes. It's the only thing that prevents me from being completely perfect.'

She chortled and thumped his shoulder. Or at least she meant to thump his shoulder, but somehow her fist uncurled itself and she slid a shaking hand over the smooth skin, feeling the powerful swell of muscle under her fingers.

'Jack...' This time her voice was a whisper and he rolled her onto her back and covered her body with his.

'Stop talking.' He brought his mouth down on hers and kissed her again and suddenly she was kissing him back. And it felt like all her dreams because darkness was where she always dreamed about Jack, and when she dreamed, this was always what he was doing.

Kissing her.

And in the darkness the rest of the world ceased to exist. There was only Jack and the seductive brush of his mouth against hers, the erotic slide of his tongue and the weight of his body holding her still.

She felt his hand slide down her body and then his fingers found her tight, aching nipple through the silky fabric of her bra. She arched into his hand and he deepened the kiss, seducing her with every stroke of his tongue and every brush of his fingers. He removed her bra with an expert flick of his fingers and then reached out and switched on the lamp by the bed.

Bryony gave a gasp and looked at him in confusion. 'What are you doing?'

'Looking at you.' The expression in his eyes was disturbingly intense. 'I'm looking at you.'

Colour seeped into her cheeks and she reached out a hand to switch off the light, but he caught her arm and pinned it above her head.

'Jack, please…'

'I want to look at you because you're beautiful, Blondie, do you know that?' His voice was hoarse and he dragged the covers back, his eyes sliding down her body with male appreciation. Then he lifted a hand and touched her hair, running his fingers through it and stroking it as if he was seeing it for the first time.

She lay beneath him, powerless to move, watching in breathless anticipation as hunger flared in his eyes. It was the look she'd always dreamed of seeing and suddenly her breathing was shallow and every nerve ending in her body tingled.

She didn't know what had finally changed for him but she wasn't going to question it.

For a suspended moment they stared at each other, and then he brought his mouth down hard on hers.

Her hunger was every bit as intense as his and she kissed him back, sliding her arms around his neck, her heart beating frantically as she arched against him. He kissed her until she was crazy for something more and then he lifted his head fractionally, his breathing unsteady as he looked down at her. His eyes glittered strangely in the dim light and for once there was no trace of humour in his expression.

'Do you want me to stop?' His voice was husky with unfulfilled desire and her own breathing jerked in response to this blatant evidence of masculine arousal.

'No.' Her hand slid down the warm, smooth skin of his back. 'Don't stop.'

Something flared in his eyes and he slid down her body, his tongue finding a path down her sensitised skin. His mouth closed over the tip of one breast and she cried out, sensation stabbing the very heart of her. He teased her skilfully with slow flicks of his clever tongue and then, when she was writhing and sobbing beneath him, he sucked her into the heat of his mouth and she gasped and sank her fingers into his dark hair, holding him against her. She shifted restlessly, trying to relieve the throbbing ache between her thighs. Immediately his hand slid downwards, ready to satisfy her unspoken request.

With a swift movement he removed her panties and then moved back up her body until he was staring down at her, his glittering blue eyes holding her captive as his hand rested on her most intimate place. He looked dark and dangerous and unbelievably sexy and she was burning with a sexual excitement so intense that she felt as though her whole body was on fire.

And then he bent his head and took her mouth in a slow, seductive kiss and she gasped as she felt his long fingers stroking her for the first time. He explored her with an expert touch, the maddening caress of his fingers driving her wild. And all the time his eyes held hers, stripping down all the barriers between them, his gaze every bit as intimate as his touch.

She lifted a hand and ran her fingers over his rough jaw, loving the male contrast to her own softness. And suddenly she wanted to touch him as he was touching her. Her hand trailed over his wide shoulders and down his powerful body until her fingers closed around the pulsing heat of his arousal. He felt hot and hard and excitingly male and she stroked him gently until he muttered something under his breath and reached down.

'Stop.' His voice was thickened as his hand closed over her wrist. 'You need to give me a minute.'

But she didn't want to give him a minute. She was *desperate*, her body driven to fever pitch by his skilled touch.

She curled her legs around him, consumed by a feminine need so powerful that she raked his back with her nails in desperation.

'Jack, *please...*'

Breathing heavily, he slid an arm beneath her and she felt the silken probe of his erection against her. She arched invitingly and he entered her with a hard, demanding thrust, filling her with a heat and passion that she'd only known in her dreams.

She cried out in ecstasy and he gave a groan and thrust

deeper still, his eyes locking with hers, fierce with passion. And she was lost in that gaze, the connection between them so powerful that she felt part of him.

'Bryony—'

It was the first time she could ever remember him calling her by her name and she stared into his eyes, overwhelmed by emotion and sensation, every part of her body feeling every part of his. And then he started to move slowly and with every measured thrust he seemed to move deeper inside her, closer to her heart. She felt his strength and his power and was consumed by a rush of pleasure so agonisingly intense that she sobbed against the sleek muscle of his shoulder. She clung to him, fevered and breathless, totally out of control and not even caring. Every time her eyes drifted shut he muttered, 'Open your eyes.' And so she did, and finally she couldn't look away as he drove her higher and higher until finally she felt the world explode and her whole body convulse in an ecstasy so powerful that it pushed him over the edge and she felt the hot, hard pulse of his own climax.

It was so powerful that for several minutes neither of them spoke. They just held each other, breathing unsteadily, their gazes still locked, sharing a depth of emotion that neither of them had felt before.

And then finally he gave a small, disbelieving shake of his head and rolled onto his back, taking her with him.

Bryony lay against him and allowed her eyes to drift shut, so utterly swamped with happiness that she started to smile.

Jack loved her.

She'd seen it in his eyes when he'd stared down at her. And she'd felt it in the way he'd made love to her.

Jack *definitely* loved her.

CHAPTER NINE

SHE awoke feeling warm and safe, wrapped tightly in his arms.

Bryony's body ached in unfamiliar places and she smiled as she remembered every tiny detail of the night before. She snuggled closer to him and kissed him gently on the mouth, watching as he woke up.

'I love you, Jack.'

Finally she could say the words she'd been longing to say for almost all her life.

And she sensed his immediate withdrawal. Physically he didn't move, but she saw something flicker in his eyes and felt his lack of response with every fibre of her being. Her insides lurched.

'Listen, Blondie.' His voice cracked slightly and he cursed under his breath and released her, rolling onto his back and staring up at the ceiling. His eyes were shut and a tiny muscle worked in his rough jaw. 'About last night…'

'*Don't* call me Blondie,' she said, her voice shaking as she lifted herself on one elbow and looked at him. *She wasn't going to let him do this.* She wasn't going to let him pretend that what they'd shared hadn't been special. 'Do you realise that last night you called me Bryony for the first time in your life? That was when you were making love to me, Jack.'

His eyes stayed closed. 'I thought we agreed that last night was a mistake.'

'It wasn't a mistake for me.' She knew she was taking a huge risk but there was no turning back now. 'I love you, Jack.'

His eyes flew open and he stared at her for a moment. Then he sucked in a breath and sprang out of bed so quickly that she blinked in amazement.

'Blond— Sorry, *Bryony*,' he corrected himself quickly as he reached for his clothes. 'You do not love me, all right? You just *think* you love me because last night we had sex and women think soppy thoughts after sex.'

She watched, thinking that she'd never seen anyone dress so quickly in her whole life. Trousers, shirt, jumper— in seconds he was fully clothed, his expression desperate as he searched for his boots.

'Why are you panicking, Jack?'

'I'm not panicking.' He found his boots and dragged them on without untying the laces. 'I just think we need to get going.'

'You are panicking. You're panicking because I told you that I love you.'

He scowled at her and ran both hands through his already tousled dark hair. 'I'm not panicking about that, because I know it isn't true.'

'It *is* true.' She took a deep breath. 'And I know you love me, too.'

He went completely still, his eyes fixed on her as if she were a dangerous animal that could attack at any moment. Then he swore under his breath and gave a sigh.

'Bryony.' He said her name firmly. 'We spent the night together, sweetheart. We had good—' He broke off with a frown '—well, *amazing*, actually…' He cleared his throat. 'We had amazing sex. It doesn't mean we're in love.'

'Of course it doesn't.' She sat up in the bed, deriving considerable satisfaction from the way that his eyes lingered hungrily on her breasts before she tucked the duvet under her arms. 'But we were in love before we had sex. The sex was amazing *because* we're in love. You felt it, too, Jack. I know you did. I saw it in your eyes. I *felt* it, Jack.'

'What do you mean—we were in love before we had sex?' He licked dry lips and his eyes flicked towards the door. 'We've been friends for twenty-two years, Blondie. We love each other, of course we do, but not *like that*.'

'I love you *like that*,' Bryony said quietly, 'and I always have.'

There was a long, tense silence and then he shook his head. 'We both know that isn't true. There's Lizzie's father for a start.'

Bryony felt her heart thump heavily in her chest. She'd never talked about Lizzie's father to anyone before. Never.

'Lizzie's father was my one attempt to get you out of my system,' she said quietly, watching as his face drained of colour. 'I've loved you all my life, Jack, but I resigned myself to the fact that you were never going to marry anyone. I decided that I needed to stop dreaming about you and get on with my life.'

He was staring at her. 'That isn't true.'

'It's true. I met Lizzie's father at a party. He was good-looking and fun to be with—'

Jack's mouth tightened. 'Spare me the details.'

'I thought you wanted the details.'

'I *don't* want to know that you found him attractive,' he grated, and Bryony stared at him in exasperation, wondering if he realised just how contradictory he was being. One minute he was saying that he didn't love her and the next he was showing all the signs of extreme jealousy.

'We spent the night together,' she said finally. 'I was determined to forget about you.'

'And it worked, yes?' His eyes glittered strangely. 'I mean, you've never given even the slightest hint that you cared about me, so it must have worked.'

She sighed. 'I didn't give the slightest hint that I cared about you because you would have done what you're doing now. Panic. And, no, it didn't work. At least, not in the sense that you mean. It taught me that I'm a one-man woman, and that man is you, Jack.'

'But you slept with him.'

She blushed and gave a wry smile. 'Just the once.'

'And then you slept with other men—yes?'

She shook her head. 'No other men. There didn't seem any point when none of them were you.'

He ran a hand over the back of his neck, visibly shaken by her admission. 'You're saying that last night was only the second time you've had sex in your life?'

She nodded. 'That's right, Jack. Why? Did I disappoint?'

There was a faint sheen of sweat on his brow. 'You know you didn't disappoint.' He let out a long breath and closed his eyes briefly. 'Blond—Bryony, I don't know what to say.'

'Say that you love me, too,' she croaked, 'because I know you do, Jack. I saw it in your eyes last night.'

He shook his head, his expression bleak as he looked at her. 'I can't say that.' His voice was hoarse. 'I wish I could, but I can't. You know I don't do commitment, Bryony.'

'Yes, you do.' She tipped her head on one side and watched him. 'You have been there for me for every second of the last twenty-two years, Jack, and since Lizzie was born you've been there for her, too. If that isn't commitment, then I don't know what is. I *know* you love me, Jack.'

She knew she was pushing him and her heart was thudding in her chest as she anticipated his reaction. Maybe it was the wrong thing to do, but what did she have to lose?

He shook his head. 'I can't be what you want me to be. I'd let you down. I'd let Lizzie down.'

'I don't believe that,' she said softly. 'I know that you had a terrible childhood. I know that your parents had a terrible marriage, but they never loved each other. That was so obvious. We do. We *really* love each other. We were always meant to be together.'

'Is that why you slept with me last night?' His eyes burned into hers. 'Because you thought I'd say—I'd say those three words?'

Which he couldn't even bring himself to say as part of a conversation, Bryony observed sadly.

'I slept with you because it felt right and because I love you,' she said quietly. 'I'm not trying to trap you,

Jack. You're my best friend. It's just that I know you love me, too.'

'That's not true.'

'Jack.' Her tone was patient. 'Since November I've been dating other men. Or, at least, I've been trying to. It hasn't been going that well and lately I've been asking myself why.'

He looked at her warily. 'And what has that got to do with me?'

'Everything.' She stared at him and sighed. 'Jack, that first night I went out with David. You hated my dress. You said it was indecent.'

'It was indecent.'

'But the other night you wanted me to wear it for you. You didn't find it indecent then.'

Hot colour touched his cheekbones and he breathed in sharply. 'That's different.'

'You wouldn't let me invite him in for coffee, you wouldn't let him drive me home…' She listed the various incidents and he grew steadily more tense.

'I never said I didn't care about you,' he said stiffly, 'but just because I don't want you to marry the wrong man doesn't mean I love you. You're reading too much into it, which is a typically female pastime.'

'Is it?' She looked at him calmly. 'Where do you spend most of your free time, Jack? Do you go home?'

'I have an active social life.'

'Which basically means that you have sex with different women,' she said gently, 'but you don't spend time with those women, do you, Jack? You have a massive house but you never go there. You spend time with me. In *my* house.

Sitting in my kitchen. Chatting about everything. Being part of my life. And Lizzie's life.'

'You're my friend.'

She nodded. 'And that's the best thing about a good marriage. I know because I saw it in my parents' marriage. In a good marriage you are friends as well as lovers.'

He backed away and stared at her incredulously. 'You're proposing to me?'

'No.' She held her breath. 'I'm waiting for you to propose to me, Jack. And then we can spend the rest of our lives having fantastic sex and enjoying the special friendship we've always had. And Lizzie gets the daddy she's always dreamed of.'

He stared at her for a suspended moment and then he grabbed his jacket. 'No.' He thrust his arms into the jacket and zipped it up firmly, his jaw set in a hard line. 'I think you've gone mad. For me it was just sex, Blondie—great sex, but just sex.'

'Jack—'

His eyes blazed into hers. 'We won't talk about it again.'

'Jack!'

'I'll go and warm the engine up.'

'Why are men like mascara?' Bryony murmured to herself, watching him go with tears in her eyes. 'Because they run at the first sign of emotion.'

'I bet Lizzie is excited about Christmas.' Nicky handed Bryony a syringe and she slowly injected the antibiotic into the patient's vein.

'Of course.' Bryony didn't look at her. 'It's Christmas Eve tomorrow.'

'What have you bought her?'

'Oh, you know, all the usual girly things. Stuff for her hair, lots of stuff for her dolls, a new doll that she likes.'

Everything under the sun except the one thing she wanted.

A daddy.

And she still hadn't confessed to Lizzie that Santa wasn't going to manage to deliver her the present she wanted this year.

'Are you all right?' As they moved away from the patient, Nicky touched her arm. 'You're so quiet and you look really pale.'

'I'm fine, really.' Bryony gave her a wan smile. 'Just tired and looking forward to the Christmas break.'

Nicky was frowning. 'Well, you've certainly been working long hours for the past few days, thanks to Jack doing a vanishing act. Do you know where he's gone?'

Bryony shook her head. After their night in the honeymoon suite, he'd driven her home in brooding silence, dropped her off without saying a word and then disappeared from her life. Even Sean didn't know where he was, although he did confess that Jack had called him and told him that he needed time off.

Bryony sighed. So not only had she frightened Jack off a relationship, she'd frightened him out of her life altogether.

She'd thrown herself into her work and had seen a steady stream of fractures and bruises as people had slipped on the ice, and she'd dealt with quite a few road accidents as people stupidly decided to drive home after Christmas parties.

And that night when she tucked Lizzie in she felt a huge lump in her throat.

'Lizzie…' She settled herself on the edge of the bed and took a deep breath. 'We need to talk, sweetheart.'

'Mmm?' Lizzie snuggled down, her beautiful round cheeks pink from excitement.

Bryony couldn't bear the thought that she was about to dim that excitement, but she knew that she had to say something. She couldn't let Lizzie carry on believing that Santa was going to deliver a daddy for Christmas.

'Sweetheart, you remember your letter to Santa?'

Lizzie nodded. 'I wrote it ages ago.'

'I know you did.' Bryony swallowed. 'But you also said you did it in November because you wanted to give Santa time, because you knew it was a pretty hard present for him to find.'

'That's right.' Lizzie smiled. 'And he's had *ages*.'

'It isn't a time thing, Lizzie,' Bryony said softly, reached out and brushing her daughter's face with her finger. 'And a daddy isn't really something that Santa can bring you.' Tears spilled down her cheeks and she scrubbed them away quickly, not wanting her daughter to see her cry. 'It's up to me to find you a daddy, and so far I haven't managed it.' She broke off, totally choked by emotion and afraid to say anything else in case she started to sob.

Lizzie sat up and curled her little arms round her neck. 'Don't be sad. You don't have to find a daddy for me. That's why I asked Santa. So that you don't have to worry about it.'

Bryony shook her head, tears clogging her lashes. 'Lizzie, no, he can't—'

'I've been good,' Lizzie said firmly, climbing onto Bryony's lap. 'I've been so good sometimes I've almost burst. And once I've got my daddy I'm never speaking to Sally again because she's just *horrid*.'

Bryony smiled through her tears and stroked her daughter's hair. 'I know you've been good, angel, but it doesn't make any difference. Santa can't get you a daddy. I should have told you that before. He can get you toys and things like that, but not a daddy.'

'Just wait and see.' Lizzie gave her a smug smile and nestled down in her bed. 'Night-night.'

Bryony closed her eyes. 'Night-night.'

What was she supposed to do? She'd just have to wait until Christmas morning and hope that all the other presents that she'd chosen would compensate in some small way for not being able to produce a daddy.

But she knew that her daughter was heading for a crushing disappointment.

Bryony worked the morning of Christmas Eve and there was still no sign of Jack.

'I think he's at home,' Sean said when she tentatively asked if he knew where Jack was.

Bryony frowned, knowing that it was very unlikely that Jack would be at home. He hardly spent any time at home, especially not at Christmas. He either stayed at her house or camped out with Tom or Oliver or stayed in his room at the hospital.

'Are you spending Christmas with your mother?' Sean pulled on his coat and reached for his mobile phone.

'Lizzie and I are staying in our house tonight,' Bryony told him, 'and then we're all going to Mum's for lunch tomorrow. Tom and Oliver will be there, too, patients permitting.'

Sean lifted an eyebrow. 'And Jack?'

She shrugged. 'I don't know. He usually comes but this year...' She broke off and flashed a smile at Sean, suddenly needing to get away. 'Are you off to see Ellie and the baby?'

Sean nodded. 'They're being discharged this afternoon, all being well.'

'Give her my love.'

They went in different directions and Bryony drove to her mother's, picked up Lizzie and headed for home.

Lizzie was so excited she was bouncing in her seat like a kangaroo and Bryony felt something tug at her heart.

'It would be great if Santa brought you that nice new doll you saw,' she said, but Lizzie shook her head.

'I don't want to be greedy. A daddy is enough.'

And after that Bryony fell silent, totally unable to find a way of persuading her daughter that her dream might not come true.

She cooked tea with a cheerful smile, hung the stocking on the end of Lizzie's bed and left a mince pie and a glass of whisky by the fire for Santa.

'Do you think he'd like more than one mince pie?' Lizzie asked, and Bryony shook her head.

'He's going to eat a mince pie in every house. That's rather a lot, don't you think?'

'Can we leave carrots for the reindeer?'

'Sure.' Bryony smiled and fished in the vegetable basket, hoping that Santa's reindeer weren't too fussy. Her carrots had definitely seen better days.

Lizzie bounced and fussed and squashed some of her other presents but finally she was bathed and in her pyjamas.

'This is going to be the best Christmas ever.' She hugged Bryony and snuggled down, her eyes squeezed tightly shut. 'Santa won't come while I'm awake so I'm going straight to sleep.'

Bryony bit her lip and then bent to kiss her daughter. 'Goodnight, sweetheart. Sleep tight.'

And with a last wistful look at the blonde curls spread over the pink pillow she switched on the tiny lamp and left the room.

CHAPTER TEN

'MUMMY, Mummy, *he's been*.'

Bryony struggled upright in bed, watching as Lizzie dragged her stocking into the bedroom.

She looked for signs of disappointment but Lizzie's eyes were shining with excitement.

'This stocking is *so* lumpy. Can I eat chocolate for breakfast?' She giggled deliciously as she poked and prodded and Bryony smiled.

'I suppose so. Come into bed and we'll open it together.'

'In a minute.' Lizzie dropped the stocking and sprinted out of the room. 'I've got to find my daddy first.'

Bryony sank back against the pillows and gave a groan. 'Lizzie, I've already tried to tell you, there won't be a daddy.'

'Well, not in my stocking,' Lizzie called back, 'because no daddy would fit in there, silly. I'm going to look under the tree.'

Bryony closed her eyes, listening to the patter of feet as her child raced downstairs, and she braced herself for

Lizzie's disappointment. It was perfectly obvious that all the dolls in the world weren't going to make up for not having a daddy on Christmas day.

She should have tried harder.

She should have used a dating agency or gone speed-dating.

She should have tried *anything*.

Deciding that she'd better go downstairs and comfort Lizzie, she swung her legs out of bed and then heard a delighted squeal from the sitting room.

Bryony froze. What could Lizzie have possibly found underneath the tree that excited her so much?

Maybe the doll was a hit after all.

And then she heard a laugh. A deep, male laugh that she would have recognised anywhere.

Jack?

Hardly able to breathe, she tiptoed to the top of the stairs and peeped down, a frown touching her brows as she saw Jack sprawled on the carpet under her Christmas tree, talking softly to Lizzie who was sitting on him, giggling with excitement.

'Jack?' Bryony walked down the stairs, holding the bannister tightly. 'What are you doing here? Why are you lying under my Christmas tree?'

He sat up, his blue gaze curiously intent as he looked at her.

'Because that's where Christmas presents are supposed to be.' His voice was husky and he gave her a lopsided smile. 'And I'm Lizzie's Christmas present.'

Bryony felt a thrill of hope deep inside her and then she buried it quickly. Lizzie's Christmas present. Of course. He was doing this because he couldn't bear to see Lizzie disappointed. But that wasn't going to work, was it? Sooner or later he'd have to confess to Lizzie that it wasn't real.

'Jack.' Her tone was urgent but he simply smiled at her and then sat up, still holding Lizzie on his lap. He reached under the tree and handed the little girl a beautifully wrapped box.

'And because I couldn't exactly wrap myself up, I wrapped this up instead.'

Lizzie fell on it with a squeal of delight. 'It's for me?'

'Certainly it's for you.' His gaze slid back to Bryony, who was standing on the bottom step, unable to move. She wanted to know what was going on.

Lizzie tore the paper off the present and then gave a gasp of delight, holding up a silk dress in a beautiful shade of pink. 'Oh, and matching shoes. And a new tiara.'

Jack's eyes were on Bryony. 'Someone once told me that a little girl could never have too many tiaras,' he said softly, a strange light in his eyes. 'And that's the sort of thing you need to know if you're going to be a decent daddy.'

Bryony gave a faltering smile and looked at the dress her daughter was holding.

It looked like…

'It's a lovely dress, Jack,' Lizzie said wistfully, stroking it with her hand. 'Can I wear it now?'

Jack shook his head. 'But you can wear it soon. Or at least I hope you can. Do you know what sort of dress this is, Lizzie?'

Lizzie shook her head but Bryony's heart was thumping like a drum and she sat down hard on the bottom stair as her knees gave way.

'It's a bridesmaid's dress,' Jack said quietly, his eyes still fixed on Bryony. 'And I want you to wear it when I marry your mummy.'

'You're going to marry Mummy?' Lizzie gave a gasp of delight. 'You're going to play Weddings?'

Jack gently tipped Lizzie onto the floor and rose to his feet. 'I'm not playing Weddings,' he said quietly, walking across the room towards Bryony, his eyes locked on hers. 'I'm doing it for real.'

He reached into his pocket and pulled out a tiny box beautifully wrapped in silver paper. It caught the light and glittered like the decorations on the tree, and Lizzie gasped.

'It's so pretty.'

Bryony was looking at Jack and he smiled.

'Are you going to stand up?'

She took his hand and allowed him to pull her to her feet. 'Jack—'

'Bryony Hunter.' His voice was sexy and seductive and a tiny smile played around his firm mouth. 'Will you marry me?'

Her stomach turned over and she stared at him, not daring to believe that this was real. Then she looked at her daughter who was leaping up and down in undisguised delight.

Bryony took a deep breath and looked at the box. 'Jack— you don't want to get married. You were never going to get married,' she began, and he pressed the box into her hand.

'Sometimes I make mistakes, remember?' He winked at her and she rolled her eyes.

'I know, I know. Mistakes stop you from being perfect.'

'Precisely.' His voice was a velvet drawl. 'Open it, Blondie.'

'Yes, open it, Mummy!' Lizzie danced next to them and Bryony pulled the paper off with shaking fingers and stared down at the blue velvet box.

'It *can't* be a tiara,' Lizzie breathed and Bryony smiled.

'You think not?' Her eyes slid to Jack's and then back to the box again and she took a deep breath and flipped it open.

'Oh, Mummy!' Lizzie gasped in awe as the enormous diamond twinkled, reflecting the lights from the Christmas tree. 'That's *beautiful.*'

'It is beautiful.' She swallowed hard and looked at Jack. 'How—? Why—?'

Jack's gaze lingered on hers for her moment and then he turned to Lizzie. 'On second thought, why don't you go up to your bedroom and try the dress on?' he suggested. 'Then we can check if it fits.'

Without questioning him, Lizzie darted up the stairs and Bryony was left alone with Jack.

Her heart was racing and she felt strange inside but she still didn't dare believe that this was real.

'You've made her Christmas, Jack.' She looked after her daughter, her heart in her mouth, not knowing what to make of the situation. 'But you can't get married just for a child.'

'I didn't do it for Lizzie, Bryony,' he said softly, taking her face in his hands and forcing her to look at him. 'I did it for me. And for you.'

She tried not to look at his incredibly sexy mouth. 'You

don't want commitment,' she croaked. 'You don't do for ever.'

'I didn't think I did, but I was wrong.'

She shook her head, forcing herself to say what needed to be said, despite the temptation just to take what she'd been given without question. 'There's only one reason to get married, Jack, and it isn't to please a child.'

'I know there's only one reason to get married,' he said hoarsely, stroking her blonde hair back from her face with a gentle hand. 'In fact, I know that better than anyone because I saw my parents together for all the wrong reasons.'

She looked at him, her mouth dry. 'So what's the reason, Jack?'

He bent his head and his mouth hovered close to hers. 'I'm marrying you because I love you,' he said softly. 'And why it's taken me so long to work that out I really don't know.'

She stood still, unable to believe that he'd actually said those words. And then a warm glow began inside her. 'You love me.'

He gave her that lopsided smile that always made her insides go funny. 'You know I love you. You were the one who told me that I love you.'

'And I seem to remember that you ran away from me so fast you left skid marks in the snow.'

He grinned. 'I know. And I'm sorry about that.'

'Where did you go?'

'I went back to my house.'

She looked at him in surprise. 'Your house? But you hardly ever go there.'

'I know that.' He pulled a face. 'Which is ridiculous really because it's a beautiful house with lots of land and a great view.'

'But it's never been a home for you, has it?' she said quietly, and he shook his head.

'No, it hasn't. And you're one of the few people that understand that.' He looked deep into her eyes. 'I went home and I sat in that house and I thought about all the years that I'd been miserable there. And I suddenly realised that home for me is nothing to do with beautiful houses and land. It's to do with people. Home for me is where you are, Bryony, and it always has been.'

She swallowed hard. 'Jack—'

'I was scared of commitment, of having a marriage that was like my parents', but we are nothing like my parents.' He pulled her into his arms. 'The other night, when you said you'd loved me for ever, was it true?'

She nodded. 'Completely true.'

He let out a breath. 'And I've loved you for ever, too. But I associated marriage with disaster so I didn't want to take that risk with our relationship.'

'There's no risk, Jack.' She smiled up at him. 'Lizzie and I will always be here for you.'

'And I for you.' He released her and took the box out of her hand. 'This says that you're mine. For ever. No more dating. No more looking for a man to take your mind off me. From now on I want your mind well and truly *on* me. All the time.'

She gave a shaky smile, watching as he slid the beautiful ring onto her finger. 'It's huge. I've just put on half a stone and I haven't eaten any turkey yet.'

His eyes dropped to her mouth. 'I love you, sweetheart.'

There was a noise from the stairs. 'This time Jack is *really* going to kiss you, Mummy, I can tell by the way he's looking at you. Sort of funny.'

Bryony rolled her eyes and pulled a face. 'Nothing is ever private,' she muttered, and Jack grinned.

'Oh, believe me, later on we're going to be very private.' He pulled her against him and kissed her gently, but it was a fairly chaste kiss, given that Lizzie was watching avidly, and Bryony was touched by that. He always did the right thing around her daughter.

She reached out a hand to Lizzie.

'So, angel, did Santa do well?'

Lizzie smiled, her whole face alight with happiness. 'I knew he'd do it if I gave him enough time. And just to make sure that I get what I want next year, I've just written my letter for next Christmas.'

Bryony looked at her in disbelief. 'Sweetheart, you haven't even eaten your turkey yet! You can't already be thinking about next Christmas.'

'I can.' Lizzie looked at them stubbornly and waved the letter under their noses. 'I know exactly what I want. And I know that if I'm *really* good Santa will give it to me. But he's going to need a lot of time to get ready for this one because it's *very* special.'

Bryony exchanged looks with Jack who swept Lizzie into his arms and gave her a hug, laughter in his eyes.

'Go on, then. What is it that you want from Santa next year?'

Lizzie smiled. 'Well…' she said, smiling into Jack's

face and wrapping her little arms round his neck. 'For Christmas next year, I really *really* want a baby sister. And I *know* that Santa is going to bring me one.'

CHAPTER ELEVEN

'WHY does Oliver get to be best man?' Tom raised his voice over the noise of the celebration going on around them. 'I'm a better man than he is.'

Jack topped up his glass with champagne. 'Someone has to give Bryony away.'

'Good point. Now you mention it, I've been trying to give my sister away since she was born and this is the perfect opportunity.' Tom winced as someone exploded a series of party poppers, sending streamers floating across the room. 'And as Oliver is the romantic in the family he can stand at the front of the church and stop you running. I'd be more likely to open the door and push you through it. I don't suppose you have a proper drink anywhere in your kitchen, do you? Champagne isn't what I need at the end of a long week.'

'There's beer in the fridge, and I won't be running anywhere. I'm ready to get married. You're looking at a family man.' Jack took a mouthful of champagne and pulled a face. 'A family man who would prefer a beer. You're right. Let's pay a visit to the fridge.'

'You are not going anywhere near the fridge. Champagne is the only proper drink for an engagement party on New Year's Eve,' Bryony said sweetly, coming up behind him and hooking her finger into the front of Jack's shirt. 'Unless you're changing your mind and you don't feel there's anything to celebrate?'

'There's everything to celebrate. I'm about to drag you off to a deserted beach for a month and have my wicked way with you.'

His mouth hovered close to hers and Bryony's heart thudded in a crazy rhythm. 'So this is all about the sex?'

'No, of course not. I want you for your fine mind and your potential future income.' But his eyes softened as he bent his head to kiss her. 'I love you. That's why I'm marrying you as fast as possible. When you've wasted as much time as I have, you don't want to waste any more. I would have married you in a muddy field without this fuss.'

Bryony wrapped her arms around his neck. 'I like the fuss. And I want to wear white and have Lizzie as a bridesmaid. Just this once we want to play weddings for real. No muddy fields in sight.'

Tom rolled his eyes. 'I, for one, am relieved you've decided to spend a month on your honeymoon. Hopefully by the time you come back you'll both be arguing like an old married couple. No more of this "I love you" every five minutes.'

Bryony was about to respond when she saw Lizzie appear in the doorway. Her daughter was wearing her favourite pink pyjamas and a tiara sparkled in her hair.

'Oops. Someone is awake.' She eased away from Jack. 'She hasn't taken that tiara off since Christmas Day. She even wears it to bed she's so excited.'

And so was she. *So excited she could hardly breathe.* And that excitement softened into something else as Jack strode across the room and scooped Lizzie into his arms, protecting her from the crush of people as he carried her back to them.

'I'll take her back up in a minute, but I don't see why she shouldn't join in the celebration for five minutes.'

'It's nine more sleeps until the wedding, Jack.' Lizzie saw Tom and held out her arms. 'I'm going to be a bridesmaid, Uncle Tom. I have a dress and a tiara.'

Tom put his drink down and took her from Jack. 'And I've just remembered that one of the best man's duties is to buy the bridesmaid a really big present, so you might want to remind Uncle Oliver of that.' He lifted her onto his shoulders. 'There. Now you're taller than anyone. Are you sure you want to live with these two? You could come and live with me instead.'

'I love Jack.'

Tom rolled his eyes and rescued his drink. 'Everyone around here seems to love Jack. The reason escapes me.'

Smiling, Bryony left Lizzie safely occupied with the two men and went in search of Oliver, who was in the middle of telling a joke to a group of besotted women. 'Sorry, folks. Urgent family business.' With an apologetic smile, she pulled him away. 'I need to ask you a favour.'

'I've already agreed to wear a suit to this wedding. That's the only favour you're getting. And you just ruined my joke.' Oliver's eyes were fixed on a girl who was wearing a tight black dress that barely skimmed her bottom. 'Do you happen to know her name?'

'No, I don't. I think she's a guest of Tom's—and talking of guests…' not wanting to be overheard, Bryony pulled him into a quieter corner of the room '…it's been crazy pulling a wedding together in such a short space of time. I'm amazed so many people can come.' She waved over his shoulder to a friend she hadn't seen for a while and then lowered her voice. 'Have you heard me talk about Helen?'

'Helen?' Oliver leaned against the wall and dug his hands in his pockets. 'Not that I remember. Is she hot?'

'No, she is not hot!' Bryony thought about her friend. 'Well, actually she is hot, but that's not— Will you please stop looking at the girl in the black dress and concentrate? This is important.' She planted herself in front of her brother to block his view. 'It doesn't matter whether you think Helen is hot or not, you're not to make a move. She's having a really bad time at the moment. I've offered her use of my cottage while we're away, so she can get her head together and have some space from everything that's happened. And that's the favour I need to ask. You're good with wounded things—I want you to keep an eye on her.'

'Wounded things?' Oliver pulled her out of the way as a group of their friends formed a line and danced around the room. 'How is she wounded?'

Bryony thought about the e-mail she'd received a few days earlier. 'It's…complicated. And I can't really talk about it because she told me in confidence.'

'Bry, if I'm expected to keep an eye on someone I should at least know why.'

'You don't need to know why.' She glanced at the clock

and saw that it was almost midnight. The start of a new year. *A new phase in her life.* 'Just be kind, that's all.'

'Kind?'

'Yes. Be a friend to her. Someone she can talk to. Women always find it easy to talk to you.' Guilt flashed through her as she realised how hard it must be for Helen to be coming to a wedding after everything that had happened. 'To be honest, I wasn't sure whether to invite her or not. Maybe I shouldn't have done, but we've been good friends for so long it just wouldn't have seemed right not to. I didn't want her to think I'd left her out. But now I'm worried she didn't want to come but didn't like to refuse in case she offended me. What do you think?'

'I think women are a species from an alien planet.'

Bryony ignored him. 'Do you think I did the wrong thing, inviting her? I feel like I'll be putting her through hell.'

'Why is your wedding going to be hell for her? Is she in love with Jack or something?'

'No, of course not! She's never even met Jack.'

Bryony turned her head to look at him and Oliver sighed.

'So I'm not allowed to look at the girl in the black dress, but you're allowed to look at Jack. That's inequality.'

'I'm *marrying* Jack. And I've wanted that for so long it all feels like a fairytale. I'm worried I'm going to wake up and find out none of this happened.' Embarrassed to have admitted that to her brother, she gave an awkward shrug. 'You probably think I'm crazy.'

He shook his head slowly. 'I think you're lucky. People search their whole lives to find what you and Jack have. It isn't easy meeting the right person in this world.'

Bryony thought about Helen. 'It seems wrong to feel so happy when she's unhappy. I feel guilty.'

'We're back to Helen again?' Oliver frowned. 'Come on, Bry, you're a doctor. You know as well as anyone how hard life can be. When happiness comes your way you have to grab it and make the most of it. And I'm sure that's what your friend wants for you.'

'Yes, of course she does. But having to come to a wedding the way she feels right now…maybe I made the wrong call.' Bryony removed a streamer from his shoulder. 'I just thought it would do her good to get away.'

'Get away from *what?*' Oliver looked at her with exasperation. 'It would be great if you could fill in the blanks here, Bry—especially if I'm supposed to be kind. If I don't know what's going on, how can you be sure I won't say the wrong thing and make it worse?'

'You never make things worse. And I can't tell you. You'll have to ask her yourself and—' Bryony broke off as people started the countdown to midnight. 'Just promise me you'll keep an eye on her. It's part of the responsibility of the best man.'

As the room erupted into cheers and howls Oliver strolled across the room to Tom.

'Next time someone invites me to be best man, remind me to refuse. Added to the discomfort of wearing a suit, and the responsibility of remembering the ring and buying a gift for the bridesmaid, apparently I now have to keep an eye on someone called Helen—nature of wound unknown.' He tapped his glass against Tom's. 'Happy New Year.'

Part Two

CHAPTER TWELVE

SHE sat on her own at the back of the tiny church, her body unnaturally still, as if the slightest movement might unleash an unstoppable tide of emotion. Her expression was haunted, her eyes fixed forward with the intense concentration of someone struggling for control.

She was beautiful, but it wasn't her beauty that caught his attention.

It was her pallor.

Her cheeks were the colour of the snow that lay thick on the ground outside and even from his prime position at the front of the church he could see the dark circles under her eyes.

She looked like a woman who hadn't slept for days, possibly weeks.

A woman who was holding it together by little more than a thread.

A woman who was about to pass out.

Oliver frowned, his instincts as a doctor battling with his responsibilities as best man. If it weren't for the fact that the bride was due in less than two minutes, he'd have positioned himself next to her because it was his professional opinion that she was about to slide off the pew and collapse onto the stone floor of the little village church.

'Stop ogling the guests.' The man standing at his side jabbed him in the ribs. 'This is my wedding. You're not supposed to be eyeing up the talent. Or, at least, not until afterwards. You're supposed to be supporting me in my hour of stress.'

Oliver dragged his eyes away from the girl and looked at his lifelong friend, a wry expression in his blue eyes. 'Stress? You're finally marrying Bryony, Jack. What's there to be stressed about?'

Jack ran a finger along the inside of his collar. 'You should know. You're still single.' He glanced nervously over his shoulder. 'Have you remembered the ring? Are you sure you've remembered the ring?'

'I've remembered the ring.'

'Show me.'

'For crying out loud…' Oliver put a hand in his pocket and then groaned dramatically, his expression horrified as he pretended to fumble for the ring. 'Oh, no! It must be in my other suit!'

'You don't own another suit and you'd better be kidding,' Jack growled, 'or you'll be sorry.'

'Trust me, I'm already sorry,' Oliver said, withdrawing his hands from his pockets and suppressing a yawn. 'This suit is *unbelievably* uncomfortable.'

Jack shot his friend a critical glance. 'That's because it doesn't fit properly.'

Oliver flexed his broad shoulders and grimaced. 'It doesn't seem to allow for muscle.'

Jack's eyes darted nervously to the door. 'Where the hell is your sister?'

'Fashionably late, and watch your language—you're in church,' Oliver muttered reprovingly. 'Stop panicking, will you? She'll be here.'

'And where's your brother? He's supposed to be in charge of getting her here.'

Oliver rolled his eyes and then glanced over his shoulder towards the girl one more time.

She still hadn't moved.

In fact, he had a feeling that if anyone touched her she might crumble. But no one else seemed to be paying her any attention. She appeared to be on her own. In every sense.

She looked so fragile and desolate that something tugged inside him. 'Jack—who is that girl?'

'Which girl?'

'As far as I'm concerned there's only one decent-looking girl in this church,' Oliver drawled, 'but obviously you've lost interest in such things since you proposed to my sister.'

Jack gave a sheepish grin. 'I admit, I'm a hopeless case. Point me to the girl.'

'The one in blue. Sitting at the back. Amazing dark hair.'

Jack looked. 'The one who is about to keel over?'

'That's her.' Oliver's mouth tightened. 'Damn, I hope she's going to be OK.'

'Now you're the one swearing in church,' Jack said mildly. 'That's Helen. One of Bryony's friends from uni-

versity. The one who's house-sitting for us. Are you sure
your sister hasn't changed her mind?'

Oliver wasn't listening. 'So she's the one Bry asked me
to keep an eye on,' he murmured softly, his eyes narrow-
ing as they swept Helen's pale face. 'I can see why she was
worried. The girl looks as though she's about to collapse.'

'She's had some sort of trauma.' Jack ran a finger around
his collar again as another stream of guests flowed into
the tiny church. 'Who are all these people?'

'Friends of my family,' Oliver said absently, his eyes still
on the girl. 'Do you know what the trauma was? Bryony
wouldn't tell me. How crazy is that? She asks me to look
after her friend for the next month but doesn't give me any
clue as to the problem.'

'That's women for you. Totally illogical.' Jack smothered a yawn. 'But I'm pretty sure it was something to do
with a man. Relationships are the pits.'

Oliver raised a dark eyebrow. 'Am I supposed to black
your eye at this point? You're standing in church waiting
to marry my sister.'

'Well, obviously I don't mean *my* relationship,' Jack
amended hastily, glancing towards the door again, 'but
think of all the women I had to date before I finally found
Bryony.'

'Bryony was under your nose for twenty-two years. It's
not her fault you're a bit on the slow side.'

Jack looked at him curiously. 'Did you know I loved
her?'

'Of course,' Oliver said wearily. 'Tom and I laid bets as
to when you'd finally click.'

'You should have told me.'

'Well, in case you've forgotten, you weren't that keen on the whole concept of commitment,' Oliver said dryly, his eyes flickering back to Helen. 'Is that what happened to her? Did some guy break her heart?'

Jack frowned. 'You're a doctor, for goodness' sake. Hearts don't break.'

'Yes, they do.' Oliver's voice was soft. 'I'm visiting an old lady at the moment who lost her husband of fifty-five years last summer. She's in a mess.'

'That's depression,' Jack said firmly. 'Trust me, her heart is still intact.'

Oliver shook his head. 'Unless I can find her another reason to live, she's going to die. I know it.' He frowned, unable to stop worrying about Hilda Graham, even though technically he wasn't working. 'She's a dear old soul but all her family have moved down south. I need to find her a surrogate family. Someone for her to worry about and care about.'

Jack sighed. 'I just don't get you, Oliver Hunter. You're Mr Rough and Tough on the outside but on the inside you're like marshmallow. I'm amazed you didn't settle down and have fifty children ten years ago.'

'My parents had the perfect marriage. I'm waiting for Miss Right. And when I spot her I'm going to be quicker off the mark than you.' He looked at the girl in the blue suit, thinking that he'd never been so drawn to a woman in his life.

'I'm waiting for Miss Right, too,' Jack muttered, his eyes still on the back of the church. 'And I wish she'd get a move on. At this rate we're going to miss our flight.'

'I still can't believe you're going on honeymoon for a

month.' Oliver looked at his friend in disbelief. 'Most people have two weeks, some have three. Four is excessive.'

'Not for what I have planned. We're sorting out Lizzie's Christmas present.' Jack gave a wicked grin. 'Your niece and my soon-to-be stepdaughter wants a baby sister for her Christmas present next year so I figure Bryony and I need to give it our best shot.'

Oliver pulled a face. 'Enough. I don't even want to *think* about you having sex with my sister. And whatever you do, don't say that to Tom. You know how protective he is of Bryony.'

'I'm marrying her, for goodness' sake!'

'I realise that. Why else would I be dressed in this ridiculous outfit?' Oliver glanced down at himself with distaste. 'I honestly can't believe I agreed to this.'

Jack grinned. 'You look beautiful, darling.'

Oliver glowered at him. 'And you're going to look beautiful with matching black eyes.'

'We're in church and your mother is watching us,' Jack reminded him cheerfully. 'You wouldn't dare.'

'Don't bet on it,' Oliver muttered darkly. 'When Ben and Ellie got married they virtually did it in climbing boots. None of this fancy stuff.'

'Your sister wanted a fairy-tale wedding,' Jack said simply, and Oliver shook his head in disbelief.

'Do you know that you've undergone a complete personality change since you put that engagement ring on her finger two weeks ago? You were the guy who was never getting married and here am I dressed like a penguin and pretty soon you're going to have 2.4 children. The world's gone mad.'

'I love your sister. Enough said.' Jack's eyes slid to the girl at the back of the church. 'Helen does look awful, doesn't she?'

'She's going to faint,' Oliver said calmly. 'The only question is, when? Is she ill? She looks ill—rack your brains and try and remember what has happened to her.'

Jack shrugged. 'I wasn't really paying attention. Something about a man and a job.'

'Well, that's helpful!' Oliver shook his head in frustration. 'You have no interest in your fellow humans.'

'Well, not like you,' Jack admitted. 'That's why you're a GP and I'm an A and E doctor. I heal them and ship them out. Frankly, I don't want to know how they got there and I'm not particularly interested in their lives. You nose around and get involved. You've always been the same— thinking that you can solve everyone's problems. Delusions of grandeur, if you ask me.'

Oliver opened his mouth to retort but at that moment there was a sudden flurry of activity at the back of the church and the organist started to play.

Oliver took a last look at the girl and finally she moved. Her body seemed to tense as the music started and her eyes lifted from the elaborate flower arrangement at the front of the church and locked on his.

Oliver felt something shift inside him.

Suddenly the music faded into the background, along with the sudden buzz of anticipation among the guests. All he was aware of was those huge blue eyes, filled with such naked desperation that he felt his heart twist in sympathy.

It was as if she was begging him to rescue her.

It amazed him that she had the courage to sit there, feeling as bad as she clearly did, and he fought the temptation to stride the wrong way down the aisle, gather her close and keep her safe from whatever it was that was threatening her.

But there was no opportunity.

His sister had already started her walk down the aisle, clutching Tom's arm.

Oliver turned back to the front, vowing to track Helen down as soon as he could. He just hoped that the girl didn't faint before the ceremony was over.

She never should have come.

Helen clutched her bag tightly, fighting the sickness and the misery, wishing that she'd made an excuse.

But how could she not have come to her best friend's wedding?

Bryony was finally marrying the man she'd been in love with for her whole life.

It would have been selfish of her not to be there for her friend's happiest moment. The fact that it coincided painfully with her most miserable moment shouldn't signify.

She sat still, reflecting that up until this moment she'd always thought of pain as being something that happened as a result of something physical. She'd nursed patients with broken limbs who'd been in pain, patients with diseases who'd been in pain.

But she was healthy. All the various bits of her body were still attached to each other and functioning perfectly well.

So why did she feel as though she'd been ripped apart?

Her emotions were so dangerously close to the surface

that she was afraid that any moment she was going to lose control and allow two weeks of shock and misery to surface in public.

No! She wasn't going to be that pathetic!

If she fell apart then David would have won, and she was not going to let a man do that to her!

Telling herself that she only had to get through the ceremony and then she could hide away, Helen swallowed hard, pressed her nails into her palms and watched as Bryony floated down the aisle, wearing a slinky cream dress trimmed in soft fur. Behind her came Lizzie, Bryony's seven-year-old daughter, dressed in pink and carrying a fluffy purple muff.

Helen's heart twisted painfully and her lips parted in a soft gasp.

It should have been her.

It should have been her walking down the aisle towards a man she loved.

She sat rigid, a lump forming in her throat as she saw Jack turn. His smile was for Bryony alone and everything he felt for her was visible in his eyes as he looked at the woman he loved.

Why did life work out for some people and not for others?

Helen watched, numb, as Jack ignored protocol and scooped an excited Lizzie into his arms, cuddling her close while he exchanged vows with the woman standing at his side.

Suddenly aware that the best man was watching her again, Helen fisted her hands in her lap and made a supreme effort to look casual. She'd never been introduced to him but she assumed that he must be one of Bryony's two brothers.

And she'd already made a total fool of herself by staring at him as though he were a port in a storm. But there was something about his searching, sympathetic gaze that had drawn her to him and she'd found it hard to look away.

She reminded herself that there had to be a reason why he was staring at her and it wasn't likely to be complimentary.

She must look like a hospital case.

Helen almost laughed but at the last moment she lifted a hand to her mouth, knowing that if she allowed the sound the freedom it craved, it would have been a sob.

Maybe she *was* a hospital case.

She felt so wounded that she couldn't see how she could possibly recover.

Next to her a woman sniffed and rummaged in her bag for a tissue and Helen felt her own tension rise another notch.

No crying.

It was supposed to be OK to cry at weddings, but she didn't dare. She just knew that if she started she would never be able to stop.

And she wished the best man would stop looking at her. Judging from the keen look in his eyes, he'd guessed that something was wrong.

Either that or Bryony had told him.

Helen gritted her teeth, wishing that the ceremony would be over quickly.

She was *not* going to cry.

She was not going to be that pathetic.

            * * *

'Great speech.' His brother Tom clapped him on the shoulder and Oliver nodded, distracted.

'Yeah—I know. I'm a one-man comedy show. Have you seen the girl in the blue suit?'

She had to be here somewhere.

Oliver peered through the crowd of laughing guests, trying to spot her.

'Why?' Tom lifted an eyebrow quizzically. 'Are you interested?'

Yes. *Very.*

But at the moment he was more worried than interested. He'd somehow missed her in the chaos of photographs at the church and her place had been empty for most of the meal. He needed to satisfy himself that she wasn't lying in a heap on the floor somewhere.

'Oliver, you were a lovely best man.' Bryony approached, her eyes shining with happiness as she stood on tiptoe to kiss him. 'Why are you looking so serious?'

His eyes slid round the room again. 'Bry, your friend, Helen…'

Bryony's smile faded. 'What about her?'

'I saw her in the church. She didn't look good. And now she's vanished.'

Bryony looked worried. 'I honestly didn't expect her to come,' she confessed, glancing around the room with an anxious expression on her face. 'I couldn't believe it when I saw her. I assumed it meant that she was holding up all right.'

'She wasn't holding up all right,' Oliver said flatly. 'She looked a mess.'

'That's why I want you to keep an eye on her for me. She

was so devastated by what happened—' Bryony broke off and shook her head. 'I just hate the thought of her being on her own in my cottage.'

'So what happened?'

Bryony bit her lip. 'I can't tell you.'

Oliver's jaw tightened. 'For crying out loud, Bry!'

Bryony sighed, obviously battling with her conscience. 'Well, I don't think she wants people to know. It was one of the reasons she came up here—to get away from the gossip and speculation. I can't tell you details but she's had a bad time. She's wounded—and you're good with everything wounded. When we were children you were always the one who dragged injured animals home. And you usually managed to heal them. You lost your two front teeth fighting with that boy who bullied me at school. Keep an eye on her, Oliver. I don't like the idea of her being on her own.'

'Neither do I.' Oliver's blue eyes glittered slightly. 'And you've let her have your damn cottage, which is in the middle of nowhere.'

'Well, what could I do?' Bryony looked at him helplessly, torn between worry and the desire to defend her decision. 'She had nowhere else to go, Olly.'

Why? Oliver wondered grimly. Why didn't she have anywhere else to go?

'I'll keep an eye on her,' he said finally, leaning forward to kiss his sister's cheek. 'You enjoy your honeymoon.'

Bryony chewed her lip. 'She's lovely, Oliver. Really gentle and kind. She didn't deserve—' She broke off and Oliver gritted his teeth.

'Didn't deserve what? Honestly, Bry, I could strangle you sometimes.'

'Keep your hands off my wife,' Jack said mildly, strolling up and sliding an arm around Bryony's shoulders. 'Is he bullying you?'

'No,' Bryony said softly, ignoring her husband, 'we're talking about Helen. Oliver's going to keep an eye on her.'

'Well, the sooner he starts, the better,' Jack said. 'I saw her vanishing to the ladies' hours ago. Just before your speech. Nearly dived for the toilet myself, in fact—didn't know what you might say.'

'The thing about living in a small community is that everyone already knows all your secrets. It ruins all the surprises.' Oliver grinned and strolled off, leaving the two of them together. There was no sign of Helen anywhere and in the end he gave a little shrug and pushed open the door of the ladies' cloakroom with his usual casual self-assurance.

Perhaps she was still in there.

Helen heard the door to the ladies' open and froze. Then she reminded herself that whoever it was just wanted to renew her make-up and return to the reception as soon as possible.

She sat silent, locked in the privacy of one of the cubicles, waiting to hear the door close again, leaving her in peace.

'Helen?'

The distinctly masculine voice startled her and she stared at the door in horror.

Oh, God, someone had come looking for her!

That was the last thing she wanted. She didn't want to have to face anyone or make small talk.

She didn't want to have to pretend that everything in her life was OK.

'Helen, I know you're in there and if you don't open this door in the next ten seconds I'm going to bust it open so you'd better stand back.'

Helen closed her eyes.

It was the best man. She recognised his voice. The one with the laughing blue eyes and the broad shoulders. The one who'd told a series of anecdotes that had had the entire room in fits of laughter.

'Helen? Please—I know you're hurting but I want you to open this door and talk to me.'

The gentleness in his voice was too much and she felt tears threaten.

No! She wasn't going to cry!

And she certainly didn't want sympathy. Sympathy would be the final straw.

'Please, go away.' Her voice sounded stiff and frozen and for a moment she thought he probably hadn't heard her, then she heard a soft masculine curse.

'Not until you come out.'

'I just want to be on my own.'

'Well, that's tough,' he muttered, rattling the door vigorously, 'because I feel like company.'

She heard a thump and another curse and then the door flew open and crashed against the cubicle wall.

Helen jumped in shock and the best man leaned broad shoulders against the door frame and gave her a smile of smug satisfaction.

'Hi, there. I'm Oliver.'

She looked at the door and back at him, a smile touching her lips despite her misery. 'Not Rambo?'

He grinned and rubbed his shoulder ruefully. 'Fortunately these doors aren't very robust otherwise you'd be giving me a lift to hospital now. It always looks so easy in the movies.'

She breathed in and out slowly, unable to believe that he was standing in the doorway of the cubicle. 'This is the ladies' toilet.'

He didn't shift. 'Then the sooner you come out of there, the less likely I am to be arrested.'

She stared at him bleakly, her face pinched and pale. 'Look, it's sweet of you to bother but I'm fine, honestly...'

'Sure you are.' He smiled a smile that undoubtedly had women falling for him in droves. 'Which is why you chose to lock yourself in the toilet for the entire reception. The food was bad, but not that bad.'

She chewed her lip. 'I can't believe anyone missed me.'

'Well, I did.' His voice was a lazy drawl. 'And I may never forgive you for missing my speech. I was funny. I would have made you laugh.'

Despite her misery, she had to smile. 'You did make me laugh. I heard you from the corridor.'

He nodded and then lifted a hand, sliding it over her cheek and tilting her face towards him. 'He isn't worth it, you know.' His tone was soft and his eyes were speculative. 'Whatever he did to you, you had a lucky escape. And now you can slap my face and tell me to mind my own business.'

His hand was warm and strong and instead of slapping him she felt a strange desire to throw herself on that broad chest and sob her heart out. But then his words registered and her features froze.

'I suppose everyone is gossiping.'

'No.' He shook his head and lifted a hand in a gesture of denial. 'In fact, Bryony refused to tell me anything. But it's pretty obvious to me that it was the wedding that was causing you major problems. My guess is you were planning one of your own.'

She stared at him in disbelief. 'Are you psychic?'

'No.' His tone was gentle. 'I'm a doctor. And I could see that the ceremony was agony for you. Am I right?'

Her eyes filled and she gritted her teeth. 'I really don't want to talk about it.' Her voice was thick with tears and she gave an impatient sigh that was almost a sob. 'I know I'm being pathetic but I can't seem to help it and I'd rather do it in private.'

'You're not being pathetic. On the contrary, I think you're being very brave.'

'Brave?'

She was falling apart in front of him and he thought she was being *brave?*

'Very.' He shrugged. 'Coming to Bryony's wedding when you didn't really want to.'

'I did want to. I love Bryony, it's just that…' Helen fumbled for a tissue and blew her nose. 'Sorry—I'm going to be OK. I just need some time on my own.'

'That's the last thing you need.' He glanced at the door and gave a rueful smile. 'We should get out of here. Sooner or later someone else is going to join us in here and then I think it could get a little bit embarrassing.'

'You go—I'll be fine.'

'I'm not going anywhere without you.'

'I don't want to go out there. I'll bump into someone I know,' she said desperately. 'I don't want anyone asking.'

'I'm a great bodyguard,' he assured her, flexing his muscles in an exaggerated pose. 'If anyone approaches you, I'll knock them down. No questions asked.'

Helen found herself laughing. 'What are you? Mr Good Guy?'

'Dr Good Guy, actually,' Oliver said smoothly, grabbing her hand and dragging her towards the door. 'Come on.'

'I can't go out looking like this.' She gestured to her face, which she knew must look pale and awful. 'I ought to put on some make-up.'

'Why?' He frowned down at her. 'You look beautiful just as you are.'

She stared at him, a lump forming in her throat.

She wasn't beautiful. If she was beautiful David wouldn't have—

'You don't think you're beautiful?' His eyes narrowed speculatively. 'The bastard really did do a good job on you, didn't he? Well, we'll deal with that later but for now we only have two choices. We can go home and I'll make you chicken soup or we can go out there and you can dance with me until your feet are sore.'

'Chicken soup?'

He gave a careless shrug. 'It's my mother's answer to life's problems. You'd be amazed how often it works.'

'Oh.' She rummaged for another tissue and blew her nose. 'You can't go home. You're the best man.'

'Which means you've decided on the dancing.' His mouth curved into a sexy smile. 'Good choice. I'm an amazing dancer. And it gives me an excuse to take this damned jacket off. It's the most uncomfortable thing I've ever worn!'

Helen looked at him helplessly, wondering why he was bothering with her.

'Look, you're being very kind but I really don't think—'

'Good idea—don't think. It's a vastly overrated pastime.' He grabbed her hand and dragged her across the carpeted floor towards the door.

'Wait.' She dug her heels in. 'Please, can you at least let me put some make-up on?'

'No point. You'll only sweat it off on the dance floor.' He pulled open the door just as a group of women approached the toilets. 'Evening, ladies.' He smiled at them warmly, as if exiting from the ladies' toilets was an everyday occurrence for him, and they simply smiled back.

'Hi, Oliver.'

He proceeded to kiss a string of women as they passed and Helen looked at him in amazement.

'Do you kiss *everyone?*'

'If I think I can get away with it.' He let the door swing behind her. 'It's my sister's wedding and this is a small town. We all pretty much know each other.'

Helen digested that. It was such a contrast from London, which always seemed to be full of people leading their own lives in parallel.

'It must be weird,' she said, 'knowing everyone's business and everyone knowing yours.'

Oliver cast her a searching look. 'Actually, it's pretty good,' he said softly. 'Only yesterday I went to see an old man who fell out of bed the night before. The reason I know he fell out of bed was because Pam, who lives next door, happened to notice that he didn't put the bin outside. For the last twenty years he's always put the bin outside on a Friday.'

'And she called you because of that?' Helen looked at him in astonishment and he nodded.

'Yes, but only after she'd let herself in and found him lying there.'

'She had a *key?*'

'Of course.' His shrug suggested that it was normal practice. 'Around here everyone keeps an eye on everyone.'

'That's a nice story,' Helen said quietly, her own problems momentarily forgotten. 'Where I live in London no one has a clue who lives next to them and certainly wouldn't be trusted with a key.'

And then suddenly she realised that she didn't live in London any more.

She didn't really live anywhere.

She didn't have a home. And she didn't have a job.

For a brief moment her heart lurched with panic and then she felt Oliver's hand close over hers, warm and strong.

'And that, my dear Helen,' he drawled cheerfully, 'is precisely why I don't live in London. Welcome to the Lake District, home of snow, rain and neighbours who know what you ate for your dinner!'

Helen laughed and the panic slowly receded. Somehow, with Oliver holding her hand firmly in his, she could pretend that everything was all right. That she'd be able to get through this and come out the other side.

He dragged her straight onto the dance floor, still holding her hand tightly in his. She glanced around her self-consciously but no one seemed to be looking at her.

Which was good, but it still didn't mean she felt like dancing.

Her whole body felt battered and limp. How could she possibly dance?

Surely dancing was an expression of happiness and there wasn't anything good inside her that she wanted to say.

The couples around them were dancing independently to the pounding music, but Oliver slid a warm hand around her back and pulled her firmly against him, forcing her to follow his lead, as if he knew that on her own she was incapable of movement.

'You move your arm, you move your leg...' He twirled her around, holding her firmly and smiled down at her. 'See? Easy.'

Actually, it felt strange. Being held by Oliver felt strange. Unfamiliar.

She felt the solid muscle of his chest, felt the strength of the arms that held her and breathed in the subtle smell of aftershave mixed with sexy man.

Sexy man?

Helen bit her lip, shocked that she was noticing how sexy Oliver was when she'd been engaged to someone else until two weeks before.

Surely she shouldn't be noticing?

But it was impossible not to notice Oliver Hunter. He was powerfully built, very good-looking and so self-confident that almost every woman in the room was casting wishful glances in his direction.

And he was so different to David. For a start David

had been the same height as her and quite slight in build. Oliver was taller and broader and more solid. She knew that Bryony and both her brothers were in the mountain rescue team and she found it easy to imagine Oliver in that role. He was the rugged outdoor type, his dark hair cropped short, his hard jaw showing the beginnings of stubble. And he looked totally out of place in formal dress. On his way to the dance floor he'd discarded his jacket and rolled his sleeves up, revealing strong forearms covered in dark hairs. She had the feeling that he'd much rather be in jeans.

He looked tough and capable and very, very male.

'What?' He gave her a lazy smile, his blue eyes trapping hers. 'You're giving me funny looks. Should I be flattered or offended?'

She blushed. 'I've just realised I'm probably hogging the only available male in the room.'

His smile faded and he pulled her closer and swung her in time to the music. 'I'm not available. I'm with you.'

His words made her heart miss a beat and her first thought was one of guilt.

She shouldn't be responding to another man.

And then she remembered that she no longer had any reason not to respond. She could flirt with anyone she liked. *Except that it had been so long since she'd flirted with a man that she'd forgotten how to do it.*

Her cheeks grew pink under his steady gaze. 'You're unbelievably kind.' Her voice sounded croaky and she wondered if he could hear her above the music. 'But I don't want you to spend the evening being kind to me and miss out on the opportunity to meet someone exciting.'

'I've met someone exciting.'

His expression was serious and she gave a little laugh. 'Then you'd better be getting back to her.'

Oliver laughed, too. 'Glad to see that your sense of humour is returning.'

'Returning?' She lifted an eyebrow. 'How do you know I have a sense of humour to return?'

His gaze slid over her face in slow motion. 'Because you have smile lines around your eyes. Dead give-away.'

Helen's smile faded and she felt her tummy tumble. Those compelling eyes locked with hers and tension hummed between them.

Sexual tension. It felt dangerous and deliciously unfamiliar.

As if aware of her thoughts, he stroked a warm hand down her back. 'Just relax and have fun, Helen. Stop thinking. It's a dangerous pastime.'

She stopped moving, trapped by the expression in his lazy blue eyes and by the feel of his strong hands on her body as he coaxed her closer still.

Close enough to feel the warmth and strength of his body against hers.

Close enough to feel the evidence of his arousal.

Desire curled low in her pelvis and she gave a little gasp and leaned her forehead against his chest, shocked by the power of her own response. *Confused.* Suddenly the dominant emotion she was feeling wasn't pain.

Her fingers tightened on his shirt and she felt the steady thud of his heart through the thin fabric, felt the strength of his body against hers as he held her.

And then she caught a glimpse of Bryony across the dance floor.

The bride.

And reality came rushing back.

She wasn't free to flirt with Oliver Hunter, however sexy he was. She was carrying too much baggage.

'I'm really sorry but I have to go.' She dragged herself out of his arms, cast a last look at Bryony and then fled across the dance floor.

CHAPTER THIRTEEN

OLIVER swore fluently and followed her, grabbing his jacket and car keys on the way out of the manor house.

Outside, snow lay thickly on the ground and it was easy enough to spot her footprints forming a pattern that led away from the house.

He gritted his teeth.

Where did she think she was going?

They were in the middle of nowhere and she was wearing ridiculous heels and a thin suit that wasn't designed for winter weather. She was going to freeze to death. And so was he, if he followed her on foot dressed in this ridiculous suit. He glanced down at himself in disbelief, watching as snowflakes settled on his arms, merging with his white shirtsleeves.

Without bothering to put on the jacket, he sprinted to the car park and slid into his car. Switching on the headlights, he drove slowly, squinting into the darkness, until he spotted her halfway down the long drive.

He pulled up next to her and sprang out of the car. 'Are

you mad?' He paced in front of her, blocking her path, forcing her to stop. He was still in his shirtsleeves, his bow-tie hanging around his neck. 'It's below freezing out here and you're not even wearing a coat!'

She looked at him blankly, her cheeks pale in the glow of his headlamps. Snowflakes clung to her dark hair and dusted her suit and she was shivering violently. 'I just want to go to the cottage.'

Oliver was about to shout at her for taking such a risk but then he took another look at her and realised that she seemed to be in shock.

And he was rapidly freezing to death.

'You can't walk there,' he said gently, glancing down at her strappy high-heeled shoes with a mixture of disbelief and fascination. If it hadn't been on her foot he wouldn't have known it was a shoe. How did women ever walk anywhere in that sort of foot gear? 'Have you any idea how far it is from here?'

Her teeth were chattering. 'I thought I'd be able to get a taxi from the end of the road.'

Oliver sighed and jerked open the passenger door, guiding her firmly across the slippery drive. 'This is the Lake District, sweetheart, not London. Taxis don't go past the end of the road unless you call them, and even then you usually have to wait for hours while they dig themselves out of a snowdrift.'

She shivered but resisted when he tried to bundle her into the car. 'What are you doing? You can't leave the wedding. You're the best man.'

'And my part is over. Bryony and Jack are leaving to catch their flight soon and the rest of the guests are enjoying themselves.' He gave her a gentle push. 'Get in. I'm taking you home.'

She collapsed into the passenger seat and he closed the door firmly, shaking his head as he saw the marks that her slender heels had made in the snow. It was a wonder she hadn't broken her ankle.

Then he opened the boot and grabbed two thick down jackets from the back seat, vowing that the next time he went to a wedding in early January he was going to wear appropriate dress.

'You might need to rethink your footwear while you're staying here,' he said tactfully as he slid into the car next to her and handed her a jacket. 'Put that on and, please, tell me you have some sensible shoes in your luggage.'

She took the jacket from him, her expression slightly glazed. 'I don't know what's in my luggage. To be honest, I don't know what I stuffed in the case. I dropped it at Bryony's cottage earlier today.'

Oliver eased the car gently down the snowy drive, his teeth gritting as he realised that there was virtually no traction. It was like driving on an ice rink.

'Well, let's hope there's something suitable for tromping around in the snow because we have more than our fair share of it at the moment in this part of the world.'

He pulled onto the main road and cursed slightly as the wheels spun and the car slid away from him. With the ease of experience he turned into the skid, regained control and gently coaxed the car forwards, careful not to touch the brakes.

'Should have brought the four-wheel drive,' he muttered to himself, his large hands strong and steady on the wheel.

'Why didn't you?'

'It's easier to pull when you're driving a flashy car.' He winked at her. 'I thought I might get lucky if I brought the sex machine.'

Helen gave him a wan smile. 'And instead you got stuck with me.'

Her voice faltered slightly and Oliver resisted the temptation to pull over and do something radical to bolster her confidence. The snow was falling thickly and he was afraid that if he stopped the car he might not get it started again.

Assuring himself that he'd be able to concentrate on Helen once he had them both safely home, he flicked on the windscreen wipers, squinting to see through the steady fall of flakes that threatened to obscure his vision.

'If you reach into the back, there's a blanket.' He suddenly realised that, despite his spare coat, she was still shivering. 'Wrap yourself up before you freeze.'

Helen twisted in her seat but before she could do as he'd instructed Oliver caught a flash of red out of the corner of his eye.

Muttering under his breath, he gently brought the car to a halt.

Carefully he reversed a little way back down the road and pulled into a farm gateway. 'Did you see something?'

'No.' Her teeth were chattering now. 'Nothing.'

Convinced that he wasn't imagining things, Oliver flicked on the hazard warning lights and reached into the glove compartment for a torch. 'I'm just going to check. Stay there. I'll keep the engine running and the heater on full.'

He zipped his jacket up and then walked down the road, his footsteps muffled by the fresh snow.

And then he saw it.

A little red car, lying nose first in the ditch.

'Damn.' He sprinted forward and flashed the torch, trying to make out if there were any passengers.

'Is there anyone in the car?'

He turned in surprise to see Helen standing there, swamped in his bulky jacket, a mobile phone in her hand.

'Get back in the car,' he ordered, glancing at her feet and wondering once again how any woman could walk in such high heels. But he was touched that she cared enough not to even think about herself.

'Don't be ridiculous.' She slithered into the ditch beside him. 'You may be Super-Doc but surely even you can't do this on your own. I'm a nurse. I can help. I've turned your engine off, by the way.' She reached out and grabbed the torch from him, directing the beam into the car. 'Oh, no! Oliver, there's a baby!'

She suddenly seemed galvanised out of her almost catatonic state and Oliver blinked in amazement at the change in her. With some difficulty he transferred his attention back to the car.

'And there's a woman in the driver's seat,' he added grimly. 'Call the rescue services and then get back in my car before you freeze or we'll be rescuing you, too.'

He told her which road they were on and then proceeded to yank the driver's door open. At first it refused to budge, buckled by the force of the accident, but Oliver braced his shoulders and yanked again and this time the door groaned and opened with a hideous cracking sound.

'They're on their way,' Helen muttered, and he realised that she was right beside him again.

'You need to get back in the warm.'

'Don't be ridiculous,' Helen said calmly, ignoring him and reaching into the car to remove the keys. Then she made her way to the boot and opened it.

'What are you doing?' Oliver watched in amazement as she hitched up the skirt of her suit and climbed into the back seat, via the boot, displaying an amazing amount of slender leg in the process.

'I'm checking the baby,' she called back to him, 'while you deal with the driver. And there didn't seem to be any other way in without climbing over your patient.'

Stunned by the change in her and temporarily hypnotised by her fabulous legs, Oliver opened his mouth and then shut it again as he heard the injured woman groan.

In a flash he was beside her, his mind back on the job in hand. 'Hi, there.' His voice was firm and reassuring and then suddenly he recognised the driver. 'Michelle? Oh, you poor thing—what have you been doing? Sweetheart, it's Dr Hunter. You're going to be fine. Can you tell me where you hurt?'

The woman gave a moan and gasped for air. 'Oh, Dr Hunter—thank goodness. What about Lauren? Tell me she's OK.'

'If Lauren is this gorgeous baby, she seems to be fine,' Helen said immediately from her position in the back seat. 'She's still strapped in and doesn't appear to be hurt, but I'm not moving her until the paramedics arrive, just to be on the safe side.'

Michelle gave another gasp. 'The car skidded.'

'The roads are terrible,' Oliver agreed, frowning slightly as he heard her laboured breathing. He flashed his torch to see if he could see visible evidence of injury. 'I need to take a look at you, Michelle, before we get you out of this car. Where are you hurting?'

'Chest…' The woman gave a gulp. 'I can't really breathe properly.' She gave a panicky gasp and Oliver flashed the torch again, this time conducting a swift examination. He shone the light on her trachea and noticed that it wasn't quite central.

Damn.

He heard Helen talking quietly to the baby and then heard the shriek of an ambulance siren and saw the vehicle pull up by the edge of the ditch.

'Michelle, I think you've broken a couple of ribs,' he said gently, 'and one of them has punctured your lung. You've got air where it shouldn't be and at the moment it can't escape. That's why you're having trouble breathing.' And her breathing was becoming more and more laboured by the moment. Grimly aware that he was facing a serious medical emergency, Oliver started to undo the buttons of her coat. 'I'm going to release that air and then you'll be able to breathe again.'

And for that he needed access to her chest.

His gaze flickered to Helen and she gave a brief nod of understanding and wriggled her way out of the boot again, this time minus his coat which was now resting carefully over the little baby.

'Needle thoracotomy. I'll get you a large-bore cannula and some oxygen,' she said quietly, and Oliver watched as she scrambled up the snowy bank, wondering what sort of nurse she was. Obviously a very efficient one. He shook his head as he contemplated how cold she must be in her thin suit.

He turned his attention back to Michelle who was gasping for breath. 'I'm just going to move your coat and your jumper, sweetheart, so that I can get to your lungs. Then I'm going to put a little tube in to drain your lungs and that will make it easier for you to breathe on your way to hospital. You're going to be just fine, angel. Trust me.'

'Here. One 16G IV cannula and oxygen.' Helen handed him the equipment he needed and proceeded to quickly adjust Michelle's clothing so that he had access to the side of her chest. 'We can't undress her in this weather so I'll just hold her clothes while you do it.'

Oliver glanced at her. 'The paramedics lent you a jacket.'

'That's right. Just a shame they don't have the same size feet as me,' she said ruefully, and Oliver laughed.

'Michelle, I wish you could see this woman's shoes.' As he spoke he was swabbing the skin and getting ready to insert the cannula. 'You've never seen anything more ridiculous in your life. Just a few pieces of ribbon and a heel that looks like a lethal weapon.'

Michelle gave a weak smile as she breathed through the oxygen mask. 'I love shoes, Dr Hunter,' she rasped, and Oliver rolled his eyes.

'Women! You're incomprehensible.' He used his fingers to find the right position and then gave Helen a quick nod to warn her that he was about to perform the thoracotomy. 'All right, Michelle. This might be a bit uncomfortable for a second but it's really going to help you breathe, sweetheart. Hold Helen's hand for a minute. It will help warm her up. Heaven knows, she needs all the help she can get.'

Somehow Helen managed to hold the patient's clothes out of the way, angle the torch so that he could see what he was doing and provide the necessary comfort and re-assurance.

'How are you doing, Oliver?' One of the paramedics stuck his head through the other side of the car and Oliver gave him a nod.

'Steve, can you get Lauren out and into the warm while I finish up here?' he requested, his expression grim. 'And then we'll need a backboard to be on the safe side. I know about the ribs and the lung but I haven't had a chance to assess the rest of her.'

Because she was going to die if he didn't act soon.

As he spoke, Oliver unsheathed the cannula and used his other hand to feel for the second intercostal space. He would have preferred anaesthetic and sterile conditions but unfortunately neither was available. 'This will hurt a bit, Michelle,' he warned, but she barely flinched as he pushed the needle in. Instantly there was a hiss of gas and Helen released a breath herself.

'Bingo.'

'Give me some light on her face.'

Helen flashed the torch again and Oliver was relieved to see that Michelle's colour had improved immediately and that her breathing was already easier.

'That's quite a party trick,' Helen muttered. 'I thought you were a GP.'

'And that makes me brain-dead?' Oliver glanced at her quizzically. 'Am I supposed to be offended?'

'No.' She laughed and looked a little embarrassed. 'But none of the GPs who I worked for in London would have been able to do what you just did, I'll tell you that now. Have you done A and E?'

'In my youth,' Oliver said, carefully checking Michelle's breathing. 'But I deal with emergencies all the time in the mountain rescue team.'

Despite the steadily falling snow, she was still right beside him, this time holding a roll of tape in her hand. 'Better secure that cannula,' she advised, tearing off some tape and handing it to him. 'Don't want to undo that good work. Inserting chest drains in freezing weather in the dark isn't to be repeated, however impressive it seemed the first time.'

He hid his surprise. Less than an hour ago the woman had been in a sodden heap of misery at his sister's wedding. Now she was brisk and professional, standing right beside him as they dealt with the accident, seemingly oblivious to her high heels and the fact that the weather was bitingly cold.

It was distraction therapy at its most bizarre.

'Do you want to put a tube in here?'

Oliver adjusted the oxygen mask over Michelle's mouth and nose, his hands steady and reassuring.

'No. It's too cold. I want to ship her and the baby out as fast as possible, Steve—' He glanced over his shoulder at the paramedic, who was hovering. 'You can be in the hospital in ten minutes if you don't skid off the road.'

Steve grinned. 'I'll let that one pass because I know you're baiting me.'

'Would I?' Oliver adjusted his position. 'I'm just going to check her over and then we'll get her out.'

Ten minutes later Michelle was safely in the ambulance. Steve looked at Oliver. 'Are you coming?'

Oliver hesitated. He really had no choice. Michelle's condition could deteriorate again on the journey. On the other hand, it would mean taking Helen too because there was no way he was leaving her by the side of the road.

Before he could answer they saw headlights approaching and a car slowed down as it approached them.

'What's going on?' Ben MacAllister, one of the A and E consultants who had been at the wedding, wound down his window. 'I'm on my way to work because they just rang me in desperation. Just dropped off Ellie and the baby. Looks like they're getting another customer. Do you need help?'

Oliver nodded and quickly told him what had happened. 'You could go in the ambulance just in case she needs attention. I should get Helen home. She's not exactly dressed for the hills and I don't want to have to treat her for hypothermia.'

Ben parked his car next to Oliver's and climbed into the ambulance without discussion.

Satisfied that his part in the drama had ended, Oliver grabbed Helen by the wrist and guided her across the slippery road and back to the car.

CHAPTER FOURTEEN

THE cottage was down a narrow country lane but Helen was shivering so violently that she barely noticed where they were going. Now that the emergency was over, she suddenly realised that she was desperately cold.

Oliver pulled up outside the cottage and bundled her inside, flicking on lights as he went and kicking the front door shut behind him.

'Upstairs, straight away.' His expression grim, he hurried her up the staircase into a warm, cosy bathroom. 'Strip.'

Helen stared at him, her teeth chattering. 'Pardon?'

He sighed and raked a hand through his soaked hair. 'Sorry—that didn't come out quite the way I intended it to. You're soaking wet, sweetheart, and we need to get you warmed up. Get in the shower.'

Helen was shivering so violently she couldn't make her fingers move. 'You go downstairs first.'

'No way. This is no time for modesty.' Oliver took a step towards her, strong hands reaching forward and stripping off the jacket that the paramedic had lent her. 'I'm not leaving you until I'm sure you're OK.'

'I'm OK,' Helen protested weakly, wondering if she'd ever feel warm again.

'You will be once you're in that shower and I've made you a hot drink.' He dropped the jacket on the bathroom floor and frowned. 'You're totally soaked through.'

He removed her suit jacket and then started to unbutton her blouse but she covered his hands with hers.

'Stop it! I can't undress with you here.'

Oliver muttered something under his breath. 'I'm a doctor, for goodness' sake.'

He might be a doctor but he was also a man. Six feet two of broad-shouldered, attractive man. There was no way she could undress in front of him.

'I'll be fine,' she muttered, but he ignored her and unzipped her skirt and removed her blouse in a deft movement.

Left standing only in her underwear, she gave a gasp of embarrassment and protest.

'Close your eyes!'

'Oh, for goodness' sake.' He glanced at her impatiently. 'How many naked women do you think I've seen in my time?'

'Millions probably.' She shivered. 'But you've never seen me.'

Muttering under his breath, he tugged the clip out of her damp hair and pushed her towards the shower. 'Move.' His tone was wry. 'I never seduce frozen women. Believe it or not, I prefer them thawed.'

Left with little choice, she stepped into the shower and

closed her eyes with a gasp as the hot water sluiced over her frozen skin, the warmth delicious after the bitter cold of the snow and ice.

'Oh, that's bliss.' She kept her eyes closed as the feeling gradually returned to her toes and her legs and her numb hands.

When she finally opened her eyes and scraped her soaked hair away from her face, the first thing she saw was Oliver standing there, holding a huge fluffy towel.

'Dry yourself off and then get dressed. I've put some clothes on the radiator to warm.'

She switched off the shower and grabbed the towel. 'What about you? You're wet, too.'

He gave a wry smile. 'My jacket was waterproof and I wasn't virtually barefoot. Let's sort you out first.'

She wrapped the towel around herself and stepped out of the shower cubicle but the shivering immediately started again.

'Damn.' Oliver cursed softly and dragged her against him, rubbing her skin with the towel until she gasped.

Then he reached and grabbed some clothes from the towel rail, thrusting them into her arms. 'Here we are. Take off your wet underwear and get dressed in these. They're Bryony's so they should fit. Wear them until you have a chance to sort your own stuff out. There's a hair-dryer on the landing. I'll go and make a hot drink.'

Oliver boiled some milk and reviewed his options.

He'd been expecting to go home after the reception, but he didn't want to leave Helen in this isolated cottage on her own.

The adrenaline rush of dealing with the emergency may have driven her out of her depressed state, but he had little doubt that the recovery was only temporary and there was no way he was leaving her to fester.

He grabbed two mugs from Bryony's cupboard and located the hot chocolate.

Tomorrow was Sunday and technically he wasn't working, although he did plan to make a few impromptu visits on patients who were worrying him.

Like Hilda.

'Hi, there.' Helen stepped up behind him, her cheeks flushed from the warmth of the shower, her dark hair falling soft and loose around her shoulders.

Oliver felt his gut clench as he looked at her.

Without the ridiculous heels she barely reached his shoulder, and now that she was wearing a pair of his sister's thermal pyjamas and a fluffy dressing-gown she looked younger and more vulnerable than ever. Seeing her in proper light for the first time, he detected dark smudges under her blue eyes and lines of tiredness that suggested that she hadn't slept properly for weeks.

He gritted his teeth and resisted the temptation to pull her into his arms.

'Here…' Instead, he handed her a hot-water bottle and pulled out one of the kitchen chairs. 'Sit there and warm up while I finish making us both a drink.'

She sat without argument and Oliver spooned chocolate powder into the mugs and added the milk.

'So you knew that woman in the car? Michelle?' She cuddled the bottle close and hooked her feet around the legs of the chair. 'Is she one of your patients?'

Oliver settled himself opposite her and handed her a mug of chocolate. 'Yes. I look after the whole family. Her baby, her brother and both her parents. Tom delivered Lauren.'

Helen slipped her hands around the mug. 'Bryony has told me about Tom. He's a consultant obstetrician, isn't he?' She took a tentative sip and smiled at him gratefully. 'This is delicious.'

'Didn't you meet Tom at the wedding?'

Helen stared into her mug, her smile fading. 'I didn't meet anyone at the wedding. I spent most of the time avoiding people,' she confessed and then nibbled her lip. 'I was probably horribly rude.'

Oliver cursed himself for bringing up the subject of the wedding. 'You weren't rude, Helen,' he said gruffly, 'you were upset.'

She was silent for a moment and then she put her mug down on the table and looked at him. 'You must be wondering what I'm making all this fuss about.' Her blue eyes were huge in her pale face. 'Bryony didn't tell you, did she?'

'Bryony is a very loyal friend,' Oliver said immediately, 'and you don't have to tell me anything you don't want to. Only if you think it might help.'

'Nothing is going to help.' She gave a wan smile. 'Except maybe extreme violence.'

He laughed, remembering how gentle she'd been with the baby. How she'd ignored the freezing temperatures in order to keep the little scrap warm.

'You don't strike me as a violent person.'

She looked at him, her expression serious. 'Actually, I felt violent,' she confessed, a slight shake in her voice.

'For the first time in my life I really felt like being violent. Isn't that awful?'

'No.' Oliver frowned slightly. 'I expect you had provocation.'

'I think so.' She took a deep breath. 'My fiancé called me from the airport to say that he was on his way to Singapore and that he wouldn't be able to make our wedding after all.' Her tone was light but she was gripping the mug so tightly that her knuckles were white. 'We were due to go to Singapore together after the wedding, you see, first as our honeymoon and then as part of his new promotion. I gave up my job and he rented out his house where I just happened to be living, too.'

Oliver saw the pain and panic in her eyes and suddenly felt pretty violent himself. 'Well, he's obviously a bloody idiot,' he said calmly, pushing her mug towards her. 'Finish it. It will warm you up.'

'That's not all.' She took the mug but she didn't lift it to her lips. 'He took a girl with him. Some young hotshot lawyer he'd been working with. He said that he'd suddenly realised that things weren't going to work out between us. And then he hung up.' She shook her head as if she was still trying to make sense of it. 'That was it. I didn't even get the chance to see him in person.' She looked at him blankly. 'There was so much I wanted to ask him. I wanted to know how long he'd felt like that. It couldn't have been a sudden thing and yet he chose to wait until the day before our wedding.' She lifted a hand and rubbed her forehead. 'I should have spotted something.'

'Stop blaming yourself for his deficiencies.' Oliver

lounged back in his chair and let out a long breath. 'No wonder you found Bry's wedding difficult.'

She gave a wan smile. 'Technically I shouldn't even have been there. I should have been on my own honeymoon.'

Oliver winced slightly, hardly able to imagine how difficult it must have been for her. 'So that's why Bry lent you the cottage.'

'I didn't have anywhere else to go,' she said simply, finally finishing her chocolate and toying with the mug. 'I no longer have a home or a job. When I called Bryony she immediately said that I should come up here, and I have to confess that I jumped at the chance, even though it's the coward's way out. I couldn't bear the thought of seeing all my colleagues in London or facing my relatives.'

Oliver saw the traces of colour leave her pretty face as she contemplated her situation.

'Well, this is a pretty good place to recover,' he said softly, reaching across the table and removing the mug from her fingers. She was gripping it so hard he was afraid she might shatter the china. 'It will work out, Helen. Trust me.'

She gave him a brave, lopsided smile. 'Is that your professional judgement, Dr Hunter?'

'Absolutely.' His eyes gleamed. 'And first thing tomorrow I'm going to sort out your recovery programme. But for now you need sleep.'

'I'm not that great at sleep.'

'You will be tonight,' he assured her. 'Mountain air does it for everyone. Go on up, you look shattered. You're in the bedroom at the front.'

She frowned at him, clearly puzzled. 'What do you mean, I'm in the bedroom at the front?'

'I'll take the spare room,' Oliver said calmly, coming to an instant decision. There was no way he was leaving her. He decided that she needed distraction. 'Or I can sleep with you in yours if you prefer.'

Just as he'd planned, the colour flooded back into her cheeks and she gave a shocked gasp. 'Is that another professional suggestion?'

'Absolutely not.' Oliver gave her a sexy wink. 'It was an extremely *unprofessional* suggestion.'

She gave a hesitant laugh, but her blue eyes were suddenly wary. 'You're staying here? Seriously?'

'Didn't Bry tell you?' Oliver's expression was innocent and he reassured himself that the slight deception was more than justified by the circumstances. 'I'm having some work done on my house and I needed somewhere to live.'

'Oh...' She looked startled. 'What work?'

'I...er...roof,' Oliver said, and then kicked himself. Only an idiot would have their roof done in the middle of a freezing January. He tensed, waiting for her to see through his feeble excuse, but Helen didn't seem at all suspicious and he reminded himself that she was used to London. When did they last see real snow in London? She probably couldn't begin to imagine what a Lake District winter could be like. He exhaled slowly. 'So, actually, I'll probably be here for most of January, too.'

'What—living here?' She frowned slightly and he rose to his feet and scooped up both mugs.

'Sure.' He turned his back on her and kept his tone ca-

sual. 'What's wrong with that? I won't get in your way.'
Well, not much. 'And I don't suppose you'll get in mine.'

He stacked the mugs in the dishwasher, pressed the rinse button and turned to face her, his expression neutral.

'Right.' Her smile faltered slightly, as if she wasn't quite sure how she should be reacting. 'I'm not sure which bedroom is Bryony's…'

'I'll show you.'

He took her upstairs and pushed open a door. 'This is it. You should be comfy in here. You know where the bathroom is. My room is across the landing and this…' he flung open another door '…is Lizzie's room. On second thoughts, maybe I'll sleep in here.' He studied the room thoughtfully and Helen burst into laughter.

'You wouldn't fit in the bed and somehow I can't see you sleeping surrounded by pink.'

'Pink has always been my favourite colour,' Oliver said solemnly, and she leaned against the wall, still laughing.

'Don't tell me—you can't get to sleep without a bedroom full of stuffed toys.'

Oliver decided that he'd endure any amount of pink and stuffed toys if it meant that he could see Helen laugh. For a brief moment her eyes sparkled, a sweet dimple appeared in her cheek and she looked so adorable that he caught his breath, pierced by a sudden need to kiss that soft mouth.

Desire shot through him and he struggled to keep it under control, reminding himself that this woman was seriously on the rebound.

Not a good prospect whichever way you looked at it.

'Oliver?' Her smile faltered. 'You're looking at me oddly.'

'Sorry.' He made a monumental effort to pull himself together. 'Well, I hope you sleep well. Goodnight.'

'Goodnight.' Her reply was soft. 'And thank you for everything tonight.'

He frowned slightly. 'I didn't do anything.'

'You got me through the second most difficult day of my life,' she said simply, and then stepped forward and kissed him on the cheek. 'And I'm very grateful.'

And with that she melted away into Bryony's bedroom, leaving Oliver suffering from a severe attack of lust.

Helen was woken by the delicious smell of fresh coffee and the sound of male voices in the kitchen.

Struggling to shake off the remains of a deep sleep, she glanced at the clock by the bed and realised to her surprise that it was already nine o'clock.

How could she possibly have slept so late?

For the last two weeks she hadn't been able to sleep at all. So why, last night, had she managed to sleep right the way through? Maybe Oliver was right about Lake District air.

She lay there for a moment, warm and snug under the soft duvet, a shaft of light peeping through the curtains as she hovered between sleep and wakefulness.

Male laughter intruded on her doze and she woke fully and sat up.

Since David had called her from the airport, getting out of bed had proved to be the biggest challenge of every day, but today, for some reason that she couldn't identify, it didn't seem so bad.

She dressed quickly and wandered downstairs, curious

as to who Oliver was talking to. Pushing open the kitchen door, she saw him sitting with his feet on the table, chatting to his brother, Tom.

'Good morning…' Feeling suddenly shy and wondering if she was interrupting something, Helen started to back away but Oliver was on his feet in an instant, treating her to that easy, sexy smile that seemed to be his specialty.

'Sit down and I'll pour you some coffee. This is Tom.'

'Hi, there.' Tom gave her a friendly nod and Helen slid into a chair, feeling very self-conscious. Fortunately both brothers dived straight back into their conversation about a rescue that had obviously taken place the week before and, realising that neither of them was taking much notice of her, Helen relaxed and just listened.

Although Tom was a similar build to Oliver and had the same dark hair and blue eyes, he seemed to have a completely different personality. While Oliver was relaxed and friendly, Tom seemed reserved and cool, his handsome face giving away little as he talked.

'We're a dog team down until Ellie's willing to leave the baby,' he was saying, and Oliver nodded, his gaze flickering to Helen.

'In bad weather a dog can search much more effectively than a human,' he explained, leaning over and handing her a steaming mug of coffee. 'Ellie, one of our staff nurses, is a member of SARDA—that's the Search and Rescue Dog Association, but she had a baby a few weeks ago so she's out of action for the time being.'

Helen listened as they chatted about other members of SARDA they'd worked with.

Finally Tom yawned and glanced at his watch. 'I'd better make a move. I'm popping into the hospital. I've got a couple of ladies ready to pod that I'm not entirely sure about.' He glanced at his brother. 'Are you going to be at home later?'

'I might call in,' Oliver said casually, his eyes fixed intently on his brother's face, as if he was trying to communicate something, 'but of course I'm staying here for most of this month because of the work I'm having done on my, er, roof.'

There was a long silence while Tom looked at his brother and then he stirred. 'Your roof.'

'That's right. My roof.' Oliver smiled. 'I'm just lucky Bry's away so that I can stay here while it's happening.'

Tom picked up his coat. 'Amazing planning on your part.' He smiled at Helen. 'See you around. Walk me to the car, Oliver, I need to give you that ice axe.'

'All right, what the hell is going on?' Tom folded his arms across his chest and glanced back at the house. 'You've moved in here?'

'Keep your voice down.' Oliver frowned at him and Tom gave a suggestive smile.

'Well, that's fast, bro, even for you. But, then, she is extremely pretty.'

The fact that his brother found Helen pretty bothered Oliver more than he could possibly have imagined, and he gritted his teeth and consoled himself with the fact that he and Tom never fell for the same type of woman.

'You saw her at the wedding. She was a mess. I didn't want to leave her on her own.'

'Right. So this is, of course, a completely altruistic gesture on your part.' Tom's voice was loaded with irony. 'And what's all this rubbish about your roof?'

Oliver raked long fingers through his cropped hair. 'I needed an excuse to not live in my house. I told her I was having my roof done.'

Tom threw his head back and laughed aloud. 'In the middle of January while it's snowing? And she believed you?'

'She's a southerner. They don't have proper winters in the south,' Oliver said, glancing towards the house to make sure that Helen wasn't listening. 'I was caught on the hop—I didn't know what else to say. I just knew that I couldn't leave her on her own and don't think she has much experience of fixing roofs.'

'For your sake, I hope you're right,' Tom said, waggling his finger at his brother, 'or you are in big trouble. So exactly what form did this comfort take last night? Horizontal?'

Oliver glared. 'Don't be disgusting.'

'Ah…' Tom's eyes glittered with speculation. 'My little brother has come over all protective. So I take it you didn't sleep with her?'

Oliver gritted his teeth. 'I did not. She's been through a bad time.'

'So what she needs is another man to take her mind off the rat who broke her heart,' Tom drawled, unlocking his car and throwing his jacket inside. 'Simple. If you don't think that's you, let me know. I'm sure I could cheer her up.'

Oliver's hands curled into fists. 'Lay one finger on Helen and I'll knock you out cold,' he said icily, and Tom straightened up, the smile fading from his handsome face.

'Whoa.' His voice was soft, all the mockery gone as he put a hand on his brother's shoulder. 'Are you serious about her?'

Oliver sucked in a breath and suddenly realised that he was. 'Crazy isn't it? I've only known her for five minutes.'

Tom's grip tightened momentarily. 'Well, that's all it takes for some people.' He frowned and let his hand drop. 'Be careful, Oliver. If she's been that badly hurt she could be bad news for you.'

'I'll take my chances. To be honest, the biggest problem at the moment is getting her through the next few days. The only time she seemed to function properly was at the accident last night.'

'Accident?'

Oliver related what had happened and Tom shrugged. 'Well, she had something to take her mind off her problems. Sleep with her and it will have the same effect.'

Oliver looked at his brother in naked exasperation, conveniently forgetting the direction his thoughts had taken the night before. 'Do you ever think about anything but sex?'

'Not really.' Tom yawned. 'I'm an obstetrician. I'm confronted by the by-product of sex on a daily basis.'

But Oliver wasn't listening. 'What I need is to find her a job,' he muttered, an idea forming in his mind. 'She's a practice nurse.'

'You've already got a perfectly good practice nurse. You don't have enough work for another one.'

'That's true.' Oliver's expression was thoughtful and Tom gave a sigh.

'What's on your mind?'

'I've got a plan.'

Tom rolled his eyes. 'I thought you might have. And no doubt it involves giving the lovely Helen a job. What are you going to do? Fire Maggie?'

Oliver shook his head. 'No need. I've thought of a much better solution.'

'I daren't even ask,' Tom said wearily, and Oliver looked at him.

'What about you?' He forced himself to ask the question. 'Are you interested in her—seriously?' He held his breath, waiting for his brother to answer, but Tom gave a slow shake of his head.

'No. She's very pretty, but...' He shrugged dismissively and it was Oliver's turn to frown.

'You do realise that you haven't been serious about a woman since Sally, don't you?'

'You sound like one of those daytime chat show hosts.' Tom's eyes were suddenly shuttered, his face blank of expression. 'I'm serious about my career. That's enough.'

Oliver suddenly realised that although they were as close as brothers could be, Tom never, ever talked about Sally. He talked about women and dating and sex, but never about Sally Jenner, despite the fact he'd never been seriously involved with a woman since. Surely after seven years he should be able to talk about her? Unless she still meant something to him. Unless he was regretting the split...

Knowing that he was on dangerous ground, Oliver sucked in a breath. 'Tom...'

'This is a pretty serious conversation to be having outside Bry's cottage on a snowy Sunday morning, don't you think?' Tom drawled lazily, turning back to the car and sliding into the driver's seat. 'If you're still feeling like analysing the meaning of life this evening, you can meet me at the Drunken Fox and we'll get seriously hammered. In the meantime, I've got lives to save.'

He slammed the door, hit the accelerator and roared off at a speed that made Oliver wince.

Making a mental note to force a proper conversation about Sally at some point, Oliver reached into his pocket and grabbed his mobile phone.

His call to Maggie, his practice nurse, yielded the result he was hoping for and he strode back inside the cottage feeling thoroughly satisfied with the way his morning was going.

Pushing open the kitchen door, he was hit by the delicious smell of sizzling bacon. While he'd been outside with Tom, Helen had cooked bacon, made fresh coffee and cut some slices of bread from a loaf.

'I thought you might like breakfast,' she said, and he stared at the plate on the table.

'There's only one plate.'

She flushed. 'I'm not hungry.'

Oliver smiled placidly and settled himself at the table. 'I'll only eat if you eat, too, sweetheart.'

She chewed her lip and lifted the bacon from the pan onto the plate. 'I don't—'

'Helen.' His tone was patient. 'You didn't eat a thing yesterday and you need some energy for what's happening today.'

Her eyes flew to his. 'What's happening today?'

'I need to make some calls and I need you to come with me.'

'Me?' She looked surprised, as well she might. 'Why me?'

Because he had things to do and he had no intention of leaving her sitting brooding in the cottage.

'You were very good at that accident last night,' he said casually, cutting two more slices of bread and putting them on her plate. 'You're obviously a fabulous nurse and once you've eaten something I have a proposition to make.'

She sank into a chair opposite him. 'A proposition?'

'Yes.' Oliver forked bacon onto the bread and pushed the plate towards her. 'Eat.'

'But…'

He smiled placidly and took a huge bite out of his own sandwich. 'Eat.'

She did as she was told, although her bite was more of a nibble. 'What's your proposition?'

'I need a practice nurse.'

She put the sandwich down on her plate. 'I'm not looking for a job, Oliver, I don't think I can.'

'Let me finish.' He smiled at her, wishing that he could do something to bring colour to her cheeks. Even after a decent night's sleep, she still looked pale and tired. 'It would just be temporary. Our practice nurse has gone to Australia for a month to see her new granddaughter. We're pretty desperate.'

Helen frowned. 'But surely if you knew she was going…'

'It was a sudden decision on her part,' Oliver said glibly, consoling himself with the fact that it *had* been a sudden decision, so he wasn't exactly lying. 'It would be impossible to find someone just for a month.'

'You want me to work in your practice for a month?'

'It would be great if you could,' Oliver said fervently,

realising that if she said no he was in serious trouble. He'd just given his delighted practice nurse a month's leave and there was no way he could withdraw the offer. If Helen refused to step in, his partners would lynch him.

'I—I don't know,' she stammered, lifting her coffee mug and then putting it down again without taking a sip. 'I hadn't even thought about work, to be honest.'

'Well, what are you going to do all day if you don't work?'

'I don't know.' She stared at her hands as if she hadn't actually given the subject any thought until that moment. 'I thought I might read a few books, go for walks...'

Oliver remembered her footwear and resolved to check the way she was dressed before she went for a walk. The mountain rescue team spent an inordinate amount of time rescuing people who'd ventured into the hills in unsuitable foot gear.

'I'll take you for walks,' he promised. 'I'll show you the area. When we're not working.'

She coloured slightly. 'But—'

'I'll do you a deal.' His gaze was steady on hers. 'You help me out of my crisis and work in my practice and I'll show you the Lake District. I guarantee that by the time I finish you won't want to set foot in grimy, traffic-clogged London again.'

She smiled and he could tell she was wavering. 'I don't know anything about working in a rural practice.'

Oliver shrugged. 'It's exactly the same as working in any other practice. People still get sick with the same things and have the same problems as they do in London. Our practice nurse runs an asthma clinic once a week and does the immunisations with the health visitors. All the usual sorts of things. And if you have any worries you can always come to me.'

'What about your partners?' She bit her lip. 'Wouldn't they want to interview me or something?'

Oliver shook his head. 'I have two partners—Ally Nicholson, she's the wife of Sean, one of the A and E consultants. They were both at the wedding. And then there's Hugh Bannister. He's great, too. Once I tell them how brilliant you are, Ally and Hugh would just be grateful to you for helping out.'

She sat silent for a moment and he could see that she was weighing up the pros and cons.

'I haven't brought a uniform with me.'

'I'll call Ellie,' Oliver said immediately. 'You two must be about the same size and she won't be using hers for a few months. It will be fine.'

Helen looked at him, clearly unsure what to say now that final excuse had been dealt with.

'All right,' she said finally, 'if you're sure you want me.'

Oh, he definitely wanted her. In his practice and in his bed, preferably every day for the rest of his life.

Reminding himself that he had to take it one step at a time, Oliver pushed her sandwich towards her.

'Great. When you've finished breakfast, get some warm clothes on. There are some patients I want to see.'

CHAPTER FIFTEEN

SHE still couldn't quite believe that she'd agreed to this.

She'd fled to the Lake District expecting to spend a month licking her wounds alone in Bryony's little cottage.

But so far, apart from her long sleep, she hadn't had five minutes alone.

And now she was going to be working in a full-time job and Oliver was living in the cottage with her so there was absolutely no way she was going to be able to find the privacy to brood.

Oh, well, maybe that was a good thing, Helen thought as she climbed into the four-wheel drive next to Oliver. After all, brooding wasn't going to change anything. Brooding wasn't going to bring David back.

She glanced across at Oliver, suddenly very conscious of his hard, powerful brand of masculinity. If she had to find one word to describe him, it would be 'strong.' Everything about Oliver was strong. He was the sort of man who could handle anything. The sort of man that everyone would turn to in a crisis.

Including her.

And if he'd been eye-catching in the formality of a dinner jacket, he was even more handsome in casual clothes.

A pair of ancient jeans clung to the solid muscle of his
thighs and a thick jacket emphasised the breadth of his
shoulders.

Suddenly wondering why she was noticing the way
Oliver looked, Helen fumbled with her seat-belt. It was
just because he was such a dependable person, she told
herself. And she was feeling vulnerable.

'Are you OK?' He smiled at her. 'Boots OK?"

Helen glanced down at her feet, now encased in a pair
of sturdy boots. 'They're great. Surprisingly stylish.'

Oliver grinned. 'Believe it or not, even Bryony refuses to
totally sacrifice style for practicality. Those are her everyday boots. When I take you walking you'll need something
more sturdy. And you'll need to borrow some extra layers.'

'I'm already wearing hundreds of layers.' Helen fingered
the waterproof jacket, still feeling vaguely uncomfortable
at having borrowed her friend's clothes.

'I hope Bryony doesn't mind about this.'

'Well, she's not wearing them,' Oliver said logically,
glancing over his shoulder as he turned the vehicle in the
drive, 'and you're about the same size, fortunately.'

'I could have managed with my own clothes.'

'Helen—' his tone was patient '—your case was full
of London clothes. Great for parties and lunches but we
don't do a lot of that up here. Here you're more likely to be
rescuing a stray sheep from the side of the road and that's
easier if you're not in stilettos.'

She couldn't resist teasing him. 'And you've tried it in stilettos, of course.'

His glance was solemn. 'I ruined my favourite pair doing just that.'

She laughed, amazed by how comfortable she felt with him considering she'd known him for less than twenty-four hours.

He pulled out onto the road and switched on some music, his hands firm and confident on the wheel. 'So did you do a lot of that in London? Parties and lunches?'

'My fiancé—ex-fiancé,' she corrected herself swiftly, 'is a lawyer and he expected me to do lots of entertaining.'

He glanced at her curiously before returning his attention to the road. 'I can't imagine you enjoying all that. Did you?'

Suddenly realising that she'd never even asked herself that question before, Helen was silent for a moment. 'No,' she said finally, 'I don't think I did particularly. It was a lot of pressure and they were nearly always strangers and I was expected to behave in a certain way…' She glanced down at herself again and gave a small smile. 'If David could see me now, he'd throw a fit.'

Oliver winked at her. 'Then maybe we should send him a photo,' he drawled, and she laughed.

'He'd hate me dressed like this, that's for sure. His idea of casual dress is something tartan with a label.'

'Oh, trust me, you're wearing serious labels.' Oliver smiled. 'But they're mountain labels. That gear will gain you instant credibility up here. Everyone will immediately assume that you know how to fasten your crampons.'

Helen looked at him in alarm. 'Then perhaps you'd better tell me what they are.'

Oliver laughed. 'Metal teeth that you fasten to the bottom of your boots when you want to walk on snow or ice.'

Helen looked at him doubtfully. 'Why would I want to walk on snow or ice? It sounds dangerous.'

'It's fun.' Oliver flicked the indicator and turned down a side road, pulling up outside a row of cottages. Then he turned to face her, something glittering in his blue eyes as he looked at her. 'If David would hate you dressed like that then the man is obviously a fool.'

Taken aback by the compliment and the look in his eyes, Helen caught her breath. 'I know you're just trying to make me feel better,' she muttered, 'but thank you anyway.'

'I'm not trying to make you feel better,' Oliver said calmly, undoing his seat-belt and reaching into the back for his coat. 'I think you're the most beautiful woman I've ever seen, apart from the black circles under your eyes-but we'll get rid of those soon.'

The most beautiful woman he'd ever seen?

Helen glanced at him, startled, and then looked away quickly, thoroughly flustered by the warm appraisal in those wicked blue eyes.

'So who are we seeing here?'

'My Hilda,' he said evenly. 'I don't know what to do with her. I'm waiting for inspiration so any suggestions will be gratefully received.'

'What's her problem?'

'She lost her husband last summer and "lost" is the operative word.' He reached into the back of the vehicle for his bag. 'She no longer has a reason to live.'

'That's awful.' Helen felt her heart twist with sympathy. 'It makes me feel very selfish and self-indulgent, stewing in my own worries.'

Oliver turned to her with a frown and his hand covered hers. 'No, don't think that. You're entitled to feel sad and cheated. But you'll recover because David obviously wasn't the right man for you, and once you realise that you'll be fine.' He let go of her hand and jumped out of the car. 'Unfortunately, that isn't the case for Hilda. Barry was wonderful and she adored him. Can you imagine that? Being with the same person for fifty-five years?'

He shook his head and started to walk up the path towards the cottage. Helen followed him, still thinking about what he'd said.

David wasn't the right man for you.

Of course David was the right man. Helen frowned, suddenly feeling confused. She'd loved him. Really loved him. She'd agreed to marry him, for goodness' sake.

But she didn't have time to dwell on Oliver's words because the door to one of the cottages opened suddenly and a woman stood there, her silver-grey hair and her slightly bent posture betraying her age.

'Dr Hunter.' She gave a tired smile and shook her head. 'Don't you have anything better to do than bother me on a Sunday?'

'I'm afraid not.' Oliver spread his hands apologetically. 'There's no food in my house, I'm starving hungry and I thought you might have made one of your amazing chocolate cakes.'

Hilda gave a sigh and looked at Helen. 'He pretends that

I'm doing him a favour when, in fact, we both know that he's just checking up on me.'

'This is Helen. She's my new practice nurse,' Oliver said, gently nudging Hilda back inside the house and gesturing to Helen to follow her inside. 'She's helping me out until Maggie gets back from Australia.'

Hilda looked startled. 'But I saw Maggie yesterday and she didn't say—'

'She managed to get a flight last night,' Oliver interrupted smoothly, 'so finally she's going to see that new granddaughter of hers. It was all very much a last-minute thing.'

'Goodness, it must have been.' Hilda looked startled and then smiled and took them into the small living room. 'Well, that's excellent news,' she said wistfully, and then turned to Helen. 'My family are all down south and it's too far for them to come, although they're very good about phoning. I lost my Barry last year, you see.'

'Dr Hunter told me,' Helen said gently. 'I'm so very sorry.'

'Well, we knew it was coming.' Hilda gave a wan smile. 'He was very ill but thanks to Dr Hunter he didn't suffer. He's an amazing doctor and I owe him so much.' She glanced at Oliver who was looking decidedly uncomfortable. 'I suppose you're too busy for a cup of tea.'

'I'm never too busy for a cup of tea,' Oliver said immediately, and Helen hid her surprise.

In the London practice where she'd worked, she'd never known the doctors accept a cup of tea. In fact, it was pretty rare that they did their own house calls, she reflected. They nearly always handed them over to a deputising service.

But not only was Oliver saying yes to tea, he'd actually wandered through to the kitchen to put the kettle on himself.

'The cake is in the tin, Dr Hunter. You know which shelf,' Hilda called after him, turning back to Helen with a sad smile. 'Poor Oliver.' Her voice was soft. 'He so badly needs to fix everything for everyone. He was the same as a child. Always wanting to put things right. But not everything in this life can be fixed.'

'He's worried about you.'

'I know. He's a dear boy.' Hilda sighed and flexed her fingers, looking down at her wedding ring. 'And he shouldn't keep coming here. There are plenty of sick people out there who need him and there's nothing wrong with me. I'm just lonely.'

'Do you go out at all, Hilda?'

'Well, the bus service isn't that great from here,' the older woman confessed, 'and most of the time I just don't have the energy. And now there's snow on the ground I'm afraid of slipping and breaking something.'

Helen nodded, glancing up as Oliver strolled in carrying a tray loaded with tea and an enormous chocolate cake.

Hilda looked at the cake. 'Did you bring a knife to cut that, dear?'

'No need for a knife,' Oliver said smugly. 'I can eat it as it is.'

Hilda laughed. 'You're just like my Barry. He never could resist my chocolate cake either. What about you, Helen, will you have a slice?'

She'd barely eaten for a fortnight and suddenly, in the space of a few hours, she'd been confronted with a bacon

sandwich and now chocolate cake. Helen opened her mouth
to refuse politely and then caught Oliver's eye.

'I'd love some,' she heard herself saying weakly. 'It's
my favourite and it does look really delicious.'

It *was* delicious, and for someone who didn't think she
had an appetite, Helen devoured her slice with remark-
able ease.

They spent another hour with Hilda, and Oliver talked
openly about things that were happening in the surround-
ing villages, things that he thought might interest Hilda.

Her face lit up as she joined in the conversation, talking about people she'd known since she was a girl. But
when they finally rose to leave there was no missing the
desolation in her eyes and Helen found it hard to tear herself away.

'I don't like leaving her there on her own,' she confessed,
and Oliver sighed wearily.

'I know. It really gets to you, doesn't it?'

'Would she move house? She seemed quite animated
when you talked about things that were happening. This
is a pretty lonely spot. Perhaps if she was in the centre of
town she wouldn't feel so isolated.' Helen frowned, remembering what Hilda had said about being afraid to go
on the bus in the winter.

'She and Barry lived in that house for the whole of their
marriage.'

'But she doesn't have Barry anymore,' Helen said softly.
'She needs company. She needs to get involved in the community.'

Oliver gave her a thoughtful look. 'To be honest, it never
even occurred to me to suggest that she think about mov-

ing. She's lived in that cottage since she married Barry so I assumed that she wouldn't want to leave it.'

'But her life has changed.' Helen brushed a strand of dark hair behind her ear. And perhaps she can't build a new life if she's still surrounded by the old one.'

She frowned, realising that she could be easily talking about herself, and Oliver's blue eyes gleamed with understanding.

'So you think my Hilda should throw out her stiletto heels?'

Helen smiled. 'Something like that.'

'Well, it's certainly a thought.'

'At least you know about her and you're keeping an eye on her.' Helen gave a wry smile. 'I have to confess that in London, I don't think anyone would have checked on her unless she'd called the surgery.'

'Hilda has never called the surgery,' Oliver said dryly, unlocking his car and dumping his bag inside. 'Hilda would rather die quietly than bother anyone. She'd just become steadily more and more depressed.'

But that wasn't going to happen while Oliver was around.

As Oliver fastened his seat-belt his hand brushed hers and Helen looked at him, suddenly noticing the thickness of his dark lashes and the creases around his eyes.

He was gorgeous.

Confused by her own thoughts, she looked away quickly, her heart thudding steadily in her chest.

Two weeks ago she'd assumed that she was going to be spending the rest of her life with David. How could she so quickly find another man attractive?

She'd never been the sort of girl to flit from one romance to another.

David had been her first proper boyfriend.

Quickly she turned her attention back to Hilda. 'I suppose it's important to just keep watching her.'

'Oh, I'm watching her,' Oliver said calmly. 'It's very easy to dismiss depression in the elderly. You say to yourself, "Well, she's old and lonely, what do you expect?" whereas, in fact, a proportion of elderly patients will have a clinical depression that can be helped by medication.'

'But you haven't prescribed anything for her yet?'

Oliver shook his head. 'And I don't want to unless I'm sure she needs it. But I will if I have to.'

Helen nodded. 'If you like, I could do some digging around to see if there are any suitable properties.'

Oliver shot her a curious look. 'You don't know the area.'

'If I'm seriously going to be working here then I'd better hire myself a car,' Helen said practically, 'in which case I'll have the means to get out and explore.'

Oliver was silent for a moment. 'No need to hire a car,' he said finally, starting the engine and releasing the handbrake. 'You can drive this one. I'll drive my sex machine.'

Helen laughed. 'But how will you get any work done with all those women throwing themselves at you?'

'It's a killer,' he admitted ruefully, 'but I'll work it out somehow. I'm sure if I concentrate I can fit them into my busy schedule.'

Helen shook her head, still laughing. She loved his sense of humour. 'It's kind of you, but you've already done too much. I can't steal your car as well.'

He shrugged. 'Macho though I am, even I can't drive two cars at the same time.'

'But, Oliver—'

'Just say yes.'

'But—'

'Do all townies argue as much as you?' he growled, checking in his rearview mirror before pulling out. 'Just say yes.'

She smiled. 'Yes. Are all country guys as much of a bully as you are?'

'We know how to treat our women.' He grinned wickedly and it occurred to her that this man most certainly didn't need a flashy car to pull women. He just had to smile.

'So where are we going next?'

'Into town. I want to check on a baby.' He pulled onto the main road and drove towards town. 'She had a febrile convulsion on Thursday. The mother was pretty shocked by it all.'

'I'm not surprised. Did you admit the child?'

He nodded. 'First febrile convulsion, so yes. We always admit any child under two who has a febrile fit, those with serious infections and those where we can't find a cause for the fever. Otherwise, after the first one, we teach the parents to give rectal diazepam so that they can manage it themselves if the child has further febrile fits.'

He parked in the street and switched off the engine.

'It says "No parking."' Helen peered up at the sign doubtfully, but Oliver just smiled as he pulled his bag from the back seat.

'That's for tourists, sweetheart.'

As if to prove his point, at that moment a female traffic warden wandered down the street and gave them a cheerful nod.

'Good morning, Dr Hunter.'

'Morning, Tracey,' Oliver returned, locking his car. 'How's that ankle doing?'

'Much better since I did those exercises.' She looked at his car. 'I'll keep my eye on that for you, Dr Hunter. We've had some problems along this road in the last few months. Just kids, I suppose, but, still, you can't be too careful.'

'Thanks, Tracey. We're just popping in to see little Pippa Dawson.'

The traffic warden tutted sympathetically. 'I heard that the poor mite was in hospital. Give them my love.'

She gave them a cheery wave and walked on down the street, leaving Helen staring after her open-mouthed.

'She's a *traffic warden?*' She shook her head in disbelief. 'In London they have horns and tails. Scary.'

'Oh, Tracey can be scary.' Oliver laughed as they crossed the road and walked along the snowy pavement. 'You should see her in the summer. The cars are festooned with tickets.'

'So why do you deserve special treatment, Dr Hunter?'

He winked at her. 'That would be telling.' He paused outside a small terraced house and rang the bell. 'This shouldn't take long.'

But Helen noticed that he didn't seem at all resentful to be seeing patients at a weekend. The GPs she'd worked with in London had all grumbled on the rare occasions they'd been on call on a Sunday, but Oliver seemed to be thoroughly enjoying himself.

'Hello there, Lauren.' He greeted the young mother with his usual smile. 'Just popped in to see how little Pippa is.'

'Oh, Dr Hunter, I wasn't expecting you to call.' Visibly flustered, Lauren tried to smooth her hair. 'The house isn't very tidy.'

'I haven't come to make an offer on your house, Lauren,' Oliver said gently, 'and if you think your house is in a mess, you should come and look at mine. And I don't have a sick baby to use as an excuse.'

Lauren relaxed and gave him a wide smile. 'Well, it would be great if you could look at her. We were up all night with her again. She's a lot better, of course, but she's still not right.'

'You poor thing—you must be totally knackered. This is Helen, by the way.' Oliver waved a hand to indicate Helen as they walked into the house. 'She's acting as my practice nurse while Maggie has a well-earned break.'

'Oh, have you finally persuaded her that you can survive without her for five minutes?' Lauren led them into a tiny sitting room. 'Pippa's in here. I put her in her bouncy chair for a change of scene. She was crying so much I didn't know what to do with her.'

'Did the hospital give you a letter for me?'

Lauren nodded and lifted a brown envelope from the top of the television. 'They did all sorts of tests but in the end they just said it must be a virus.'

Oliver smiled sympathetically. 'Irritating isn't it? We train for all these years just to say it's a virus that we can't identify. But those tests will have excluded some worrying infections, Lauren, so in a way that's good news.' He put his bag down and strolled over to the baby who was kicking her legs in her chair.

'I left her in just a vest and nappy because of her temperature,' Lauren said anxiously. 'I'm so terrified she might have another one of those fits. It was awful. I keep worrying about it in case it means she's an epileptic.'

'It doesn't mean that, Lauren,' Oliver said firmly. 'Very young children can't control their temperatures the way you and I can, and that's why they fit. Only a minute percentage go on to develop epilepsy in later life, and although there are no guarantees I'm sure Pippa isn't going to be one of those.'

Lauren bit her lip and shifted a pile of laundry from the sofa. 'But she might be.'

'Well, let's put it like this.' Oliver tilted his head to one side, his expression thoughtful. 'If you buy a lottery ticket tomorrow and I tell you that you have a one in a hundred chance of winning, are you going to go out on a mad spending spree before you hear the numbers?'

Lauren laughed. 'No, of course not. If the odds were one in a hundred then I know for sure that it wouldn't be me.'

'Well, those are the odds,' Oliver said firmly, 'so let's treat it like the lottery, shall we? It's so unlikely to happen that there is no point in planning for it. Now, can I take a look at her?'

Considerably reassured, Lauren bent down and undid the straps that held the baby in the seat while Oliver scanned the letter from the hospital.

'It looks as though they were pretty thorough. Now, then.' He tucked the letter into the pocket of his jeans and dropped to his haunches in front of the baby. 'Hello, sweetheart, you're looking a lot better than you did when Uncle Oliver last saw you.'

Smiling and pulling faces at the baby, he slid large hands around her tiny body and gently lifted her up.

Helen watched, transfixed, intrigued by how comfortable Oliver was with the baby.

'She's so gorgeous, Lauren,' he murmured, holding the baby against his shoulder, running a hand over the downy head, feeling her fontanelle. 'She doesn't feel so hot now. When did she last have Calpol?'

'Not since last night,' Lauren said. 'Her temperature seems to go up in the evenings.'

Oliver nodded. 'That often happens. I'm just going to lay her on the sofa so that I can examine her.'

Helen watched while he worked, noticing how skilled and gentle he was with the baby.

'Stop smiling at me, madam,' he murmured as he undid her nappy. 'It's no good. You are so gorgeous I'm going to have to take you home with me.'

'Well, you're welcome to her at night,' Lauren said dryly. 'I'd give anything for an undisturbed night.'

'What about your mum?' Oliver finished his examination and redid the nappy deftly. 'Can't she have her for a night? I know you're still breast-feeding but you could always express. Do you good to have a night off.'

'I just can't get her to take a bottle.' Lauren gave a helpless shrug. 'I know she's using me as a comforter but it's easier to let her do that than have a screaming battle.'

Oliver pulled a face. 'It's a tough one. Who's your health visitor?'

'Jenny Stevens.'

'Give her a ring,' Oliver suggested, lifting Pippa confidently and giving the little girl a last cuddle. 'Jenny has all sorts of tricks up her sleeve. She might be able to suggest something.'

'I don't want to be a bother.'

Oliver handed the baby back to her. 'You're not a bother, Lauren. You're a tired mum. I think Pippa's on the mend but if you're at all worried you can take her straight back to the hospital. Or you can call me. You've got my mobile number.'

'Stuck by my phone,' Lauren confessed ruefully. 'Thanks, Dr Hunter.'

They walked back to the car and Helen looked at him in amazement. 'You gave her your mobile phone number?'

'That's right.' Oliver slung his bag in the car. 'It saves her having to call several numbers before getting through to me. It's scary seeing your own baby fit. I didn't want her to feel she was alone.'

'None of the doctors I worked for would have given out their phone number,' Helen muttered, and he lifted an eyebrow, clearly puzzled.

'Why not?'

'They would have been too afraid that someone might use it,' Helen said dryly, and he laughed.

'I would have thought that was the general idea, but I'm willing to believe that it's different in London. I suppose, to be honest, I wouldn't give it to any patient I wasn't sure of, but they're pretty good around here and I've known most of them for years.'

She looked at him curiously. 'Did you always want to be a GP?'

'Always. And so did Bryony. We used to play doctors' surgeries when we were little.'

'Not doctors and nurses?'

'Doctor and doctor.' Oliver glanced sideways and gave her a sexy wink. 'But any time you want to play doctors and nurses, let me know. I'm a quick learner and it definitely sounds like my sort of game.'

Helen laughed. He was so open it was impossible to be offended. 'You're going to get yourself in trouble one day, Dr Hunter.'

'Oh, I do seriously hope so.' He chuckled and she rolled her eyes and changed the subject hurriedly.

The more she saw of Oliver Hunter, the more she liked him.

And she was starting to like him a lot.

'Where now?'

'Back home for some lunch and then to the mountain rescue base to check on some new equipment that was due to arrive yesterday.' He drove steadily, his eyes fixed on the road ahead. 'Then we'll create something amazing in the kitchen for our dinner.'

'But you're on call.'

'No I'm not. Time off for good behaviour.' He flashed her a smile. 'Ally is on call this weekend.'

Helen stared at him. 'But you've been seeing patients.'

'Not really. I just saw Hilda because I was worried about her, and I wanted to check up on Pippa because I knew Lauren would be worrying herself sick about her. They weren't emergencies and I certainly wouldn't expect either of my partners to make those calls. Now I'm going back to the Sunday papers.'

He cared enough to check on patients on his day off.

And now he felt he had to entertain her.

'You could just drop me back at the cottage,' she suggested, 'and then you could do whatever it is you usually do on a Sunday.'

'I'm doing what I usually do on a Sunday,' he said easily, 'only this time I have company.'

'I can't imagine you're short of company,' she said, with a wry smile in his direction. Women probably flattened each other in the race to get to him. Why he was wasting time with her was beyond her comprehension. Or maybe it wasn't.

Oliver Hunter obviously had a thing about anything injured or hurting, and at the moment she came under that heading.

She didn't kid herself that he was being anything other than kind.

She was just someone that he had to heal, like his patients.

They were just pulling up outside the cottage when his mobile phone rang. He switched off the engine and answered it.

Even with her limited experience, it was obvious to Helen that someone was in trouble on the mountains.

'I'll be there in ten minutes,' Oliver said tersely, and snapped the phone shut, starting the engine again immediately. He turned to Helen with a frown. 'I'm really sorry, I'm going to have to leave you—someone has been reported overdue. They should have returned from their walk by now but there's no sign of them and the mountain rescue team has been called out.'

'Don't worry about me.' Helen jumped down from the vehicle, conscious that she was slowing him down.

But he didn't immediately drive away. His hard jaw was tense and his eyes searched hers.

'I don't like leaving you.'

She was unbelievably touched. 'Oliver, I'll be fine. I don't need watching. I'll have a quiet afternoon.'

His mouth tightened. 'I don't want you to have a quiet afternoon. You'll brood.'

'I won't brood.' She gave a lopsided smile. 'I'm not that pathetic. I'll make something for our dinner.'

Oliver sighed, visibly torn, and then he muttered something under his breath and raked long fingers through his cropped hair. 'All right, although I've no idea what time I'll be home. Don't wait up for me. Call me if you need to. My mobile number is stuck on Bry's notice-board in the kitchen.'

Oliver didn't arrive home until nine o'clock and by then Helen was chewing her nails and staring out of the window, looking for his headlights.

When he finally walked through the door she flew to meet him. 'I was so worried about you…'

Oliver unzipped his jacket and gave her a curious look. 'That's nice.' His voice was soft. 'No one usually worries about me, apart from my mother.' His eyes settled on hers for a long moment and she flushed, wondering what the matter was with her. She'd known him for less than twenty-four hours and here she was, acting like a clingy wife.

But she'd been scared that something had happened to him—

'Sorry, I—I just thought you'd be back hours ago,' she muttered, suddenly embarrassed, and he stepped towards her and took her face in his hands.

'Don't apologise,' he said gruffly, his thumbs stroking her cheeks. 'It's nice that someone missed me.'

His gaze was warm and assessing and suddenly Helen felt seriously flustered. He dominated the narrow hallway of Bryony's cottage, his shoulders almost filling the space. His jaw was dark with stubble, his cropped hair was damp from the snow and there was no escaping the fact that he was incredibly good-looking.

For a moment he stared down at her and she had a breathless feeling that he was going to kiss her.

'Your hands are freezing.'

He gave a rueful smile and his hands dropped. 'Sorry. It's pretty cold out there.'

'I made you some soup,' Helen said quickly, dragging her gaze away from his and hurrying through to the kitchen. Of course he wouldn't have kissed her. She was imagining things. Why on earth would he kiss her? 'You might not be hungry, but—'

'I'm starving,' he said dryly, hanging up his jacket and following her. 'Believe me, tramping around the fells for nine hours works up an appetite.'

She heated the soup slowly and Oliver sprawled in one of the kitchen chairs and closed his eyes with a groan.

'I'm knackered.'

She shot him a sympathetic look. 'Did you find them?'

His eyes opened and he yawned. 'Eventually. But they weren't where they said they were so that caused some problems.'

'Why were they walking in this weather? There's snow on the ground.' Helen stirred the soup slowly and Oliver laughed.

'Because the snow makes the landscape beautiful, my little city girl. Plenty of people 'round here like to walk and enjoy the hills at this time of year.'

Helen smiled ruefully and poured the soup into a large earthenware bowl. 'I'm sorry. I must seem like an alien to you. I was born in London, I went to university in London and I've worked there ever since.'

Oliver gave a dramatic shudder. 'It's a wonder you're even remotely sane,' he teased, sniffing appreciatively as she placed the bowl on the scrubbed pine table in front of him. 'At least they taught you to cook in London. Smells delicious.'

Helen cut two large slices of bread and Oliver looked at her in surprise. 'That looks home-made.'

'It is.' Helen gave a shrug. 'Not much else to do here in the country when it's snowing outside. I had to find a way of amusing myself and Bryony's cupboards are very well stocked.'

Oliver gave a slow, sensual smile that made her insides tumble. 'We country folk have all sorts of exciting ways of passing the time when the weather is bad.' He picked up the spoon, his eyes twinkling wickedly. 'If you're good, I'll teach you a few.'

Her tummy did a somersault.

He was flirting with her again and she didn't know how to handle it.

Unsettled by her reaction to his good-natured teasing

and feeling totally flustered, Helen flicked on the kettle and generally busied herself around the kitchen.

'So do lots of people go walking in the fells in the middle of January?' She couldn't imagine the appeal and she found it hard to understand that some people would choose to be out in that weather.

'Plenty.' Oliver tore the bread with his fingers. 'And if they're well equipped, that's no problem. Unfortunately the group today didn't have what they needed to survive in this weather. Snow changes things. You can't see the paths. Landmarks look different. It's easy to get lost.'

'But you didn't get lost.' She couldn't imagine Oliver Hunter lost in any situation. He was the sort who others would depend on. Someone who would always lead.

'We have satellite navigation equipment, which helps us pinpoint our exact position.' He looked at her hopefully. 'Is there any more soup?'

Pleased that he was enjoying it so much, she poured the remainder into his bowl. 'But presumably you didn't always have that technology.'

'Before satellite navigation we used compasses and good old-fashioned local knowledge.' Oliver helped himself to more bread. 'And, believe me, you can't beat old-fashioned knowledge. Most of us were brought up in these hills. When Tom and I were kids we used to play a game. We'd identify a fixed point, usually miles away, and then we'd walk to it, memorising landmarks on the way. Then we'd return by the same route, using the landmarks to stop ourselves getting lost.'

Helen looked at him blankly. 'What sort of landmarks?'

Oliver shrugged. 'A rocky outcrop in a funny shape. A

huge boulder with a stream running nearby. Sometimes it was just a patch of sheep dung.'

'And did you ever get it wrong?'

Oliver grinned. 'Never. We had far too much pride to get lost. And by the time we were teenagers we knew the local area so well that we could have walked it with our eyes shut. It was good training for mountain rescue. I'm intimate with an enormous number of boulders between here and Keswick.'

Helen shook her head. 'It's so different from my child-hood.'

'Tell me about your childhood.'

Helen settled herself in the chair opposite him. 'It will sound very boring to you, I'm sure.' She frowned slightly. 'My dad was a lawyer in a London firm. I went to a girls' day school. Mum stayed at home and managed Dad's life.'

'No brothers or sisters?'

'No.' Helen gave a lopsided smile. 'I would have loved a sister, actually.'

Oliver nodded. 'I always imagine that it must be pretty hard to be an only child. All that weight of parental ex-pectation on your head.'

Helen nodded, thinking of her parents' ambitions for her. 'And the trouble is when you disappoint them there's no one else to take the attention away from you.'

'I can't imagine you ever being a disappointment.'

Helen sighed. 'My parents really wanted me to marry David,' she said simply. 'They were totally crushed when it all fell through. Embarrassed, humiliated, angry.' She rubbed her forehead with shaking fingers, suddenly real-ising that the sanctuary she'd found was only temporary.

At some point she was going to have to face people again. 'Their reaction was one of the reasons I escaped up here. I could have stayed at home, but they were both so distraught by what had happened that it made the whole situation even more stressful.'

Oliver looked at her keenly. 'You're talking as if the whole thing was your fault.'

And that was part of the problem, of course. She'd gone over it a million times in her head.

'Well, I must have had something to do with it.'

'For crying out loud, he was the one who rang you from the airport!' Oliver's tone was incredulous. 'He was a total coward. The only good thing about the way he behaved was that it surely showed you that you had a narrow escape.'

'Escape?' Helen looked at him. Up until now she'd just been trying to cope with the shock. Trying to adjust to the fact that her future was no longer the way she'd planned it.

Oliver sighed. 'Would you really want to marry a man who would treat you like that?'

Helen bit her lip. 'I don't suppose it's his fault if he had second thoughts.'

'It's his fault that he didn't stand his ground and face you. He was totally cowardly and he didn't think about your feelings at all. Just himself.'

It was true, of course. David had only been thinking about himself.

'What would you have done?'

'If I'd changed my mind about getting married?' Oliver let out a long breath. 'Well, that's hard to say because I wouldn't make a mistake like that, but if I did then I would definitely have told you face to face.'

Of course he would.

Only a coward would do it the way David had and Oliver Hunter was certainly no coward.

This man wouldn't run from anything.

'My mother thought he was the perfect man.'

Oliver's mouth tightened. 'So why didn't she marry him instead of you?'

Helen smiled. Sometimes she had been a little exasperated, seeing her mother fawn over David.

'She had my best interests at heart. I suppose she worried about me. Her idea of a perfect life was to find a rich man and marry him. She gave up work as soon as she met my dad. She basically ran Dad's life. She wanted the same for me.'

'What about her own life?'

Helen frowned. 'Well, Dad was her life.'

'And that's what you wanted for yourself?' It was Oliver's turn to frown. 'Would you have given up work?'

Helen was silent for a moment. 'David wanted me to, but I loved my job. To be honest, we'd reached the point where we couldn't discuss it. It made him angry. My mother was hoping that once the fuss of the wedding was over, I'd come to my senses and resign.'

'You're a brilliant nurse, Helen. Why would you want to give it up?'

'Sitting here with you, I don't want to give it up,' she confessed, 'but back in London, surrounded by people giving me advice, it isn't quite so easy.'

'Then we need to make sure you don't go back to London.'

She laughed. 'What, you mean hide here with you for-ever?'

'Now, there's a thought.'

Her smile faded. For some ridiculous reason that she couldn't begin to understand, the prospect of hiding here with Oliver filled her with excitement and warmth.

Telling herself that it was just because he was provid-ing a convenient bolthole, she turned the subject back to him. 'Didn't your parents worry about you? Didn't they have expectations?'

'My dad was a climber,' Oliver told her. 'He trained as a doctor, but all he ever wanted to do was climb. He was always disappearing for weeks at a time to try out a new route on some rock or other. He said that climbing was the most fun that anyone could have, and he encouraged the three of us to climb the moment we could walk.'

'And your mum didn't mind?' Helen looked at him cu-riously. It was so different from her own background that she found it hard to even imagine what it must have been like to be a child in the Hunter household.

'Mum loved Dad for who he was, and climbing was part of who he was,' Oliver said simply. 'Of the three of us, Tom was probably most like Dad. Bryony and I were happy to mess around on the fells here. Tom wanted the big stuff. He and Dad climbed together in the Alps and the Himalayas.'

'Didn't your mum worry?'

'I'm sure she worried herself sick.' Oliver gave a wry smile. 'But she would never have stopped any of us doing what we wanted to do. It was always our decision. She probably worried more about Tom than me. I think she had a few pangs when he went to the Himalayas.'

Helen winced. 'I'm sure she did.'

'Mum was very good at letting us follow our own paths,' Oliver said thoughtfully. 'I think she realised that if she tried to stop Tom, he'd do it anyway and then there'd be a rift between them. So she just made sure that he had the very best equipment and that he climbed with people he could trust. At one point we all thought Tom would spend his life climbing. Then suddenly he announced he wanted to be a doctor and that was that. He put the same energy into that as he had into his climbing.'

'He seems young to be a consultant,' Helen observed, and Oliver grinned.

'Don't tell him that. He's arrogant enough as it is. Much as it pains me to admit it, my brother is a bit of a hotshot.'

His pride in his brother was obvious and Helen thought again what a thoroughly nice man he was.

'So, Miss Helen Forrester.' Oliver stood up and lifted his plate and bowl from the table. 'That's my life history.'

'Sit down. I'll clear up.' Helen tried to take the dirty plates from him but he hung onto them firmly.

'You cooked it,' he reminded her, and Helen bit her lip.

'But you've been out all day, and—'

'So?' Oliver's tone was questioning. 'Why does that mean you should be the one to clear up?'

She flushed slightly. 'You've had a hard day, and—'

A muscle flickered in his hard jaw. 'Is that what he used to say to justify sitting on his backside while you ran 'round after him?'

The directness of his question caught her by surprise. 'Yes. No. I mean, his job was much busier than mine and—'

'Helen.' Oliver interrupted her and this time there was no trace of amusement in his voice. 'Don't make excuses for him. And for your information, I don't expect you to clear up after me. While we're living together we share the load.'

Gently but firmly he removed the plates from her fingers and put them in the dishwasher. Then he turned and pushed her towards a chair.

'Your turn to sit down while I make us both a coffee.'

She did as she was told. 'Bryony always used to talk about the mountains,' she said, suddenly eager to change the subject. She didn't want to dwell on David. 'She really missed them when she was in London.'

Oliver nodded. 'Most people who are born here end up coming back. The mountains are in the blood.'

Helen took the coffee he handed her with a smile of thanks. 'I certainly don't feel as though London is in my blood,' she confessed ruefully. 'It's been my home all my life, but I'm not missing it at all.'

But perhaps that was because of everything that had happened.

Oliver sat down opposite her and shot her a curious look. 'Are you not? Well, perhaps we'll convert you to our rural, heathen ways after all. And tomorrow you'll find out what it's like to work in a small GP practice. I hope you like it.'

Helen felt a frisson of anxiety. She was sure she'd like it. But what if she didn't have the necessary skills? Oliver teased her about being a city girl, but what if she just didn't fit into his practice?

She gave herself a sharp talking-to.

He'd been so kind to her and he needed help, she reminded herself firmly. And she'd help him or die in the attempt.

CHAPTER SIXTEEN

THE practice was light and airy, set in a modern building with a huge glass atrium that allowed spectacular views of the mountains.

Helen stared in awe out of the window of the consulting room that she'd been allocated. 'It's so beautiful. How am I ever expected to get any work done?'

'You keep your back to the window,' Oliver advised, flinging open some cupboards to show her where everything was kept. 'We've got everything you're likely to need. If you can't find something, press two on your telephone and that puts you straight through to Pam on Reception. Hit this button on your computer...' he tapped with a long finger '...and you can access your list for the day and the patient records.'

Helen was surprised. 'It's all very high tech.'

'We may be rural but we're not backward.' Oliver's gaze slid down over her figure and a faint frown touched his dark brows. 'That uniform is loose on you,' he said softly, his eyes lifting to hers. 'Ellie is pretty small so I think that means you've lost weight.'

Helen straightened the uniform self-consciously, knowing that he was right. The uniform *was* loose.

'Maybe I could advertise it as a new diet,' she joked feebly. 'The Break-Up Diet. Lose half a stone in two weeks.'

He didn't laugh. 'I'm going to tell Pam to make sure you eat lunch. I'd force-feed you myself but I have a meeting that I can't get out of. But I'll see you tonight at dinner. And I'm cooking.'

With that he left the room, returning moments later with his two partners who both greeted her warmly and thanked her for helping out.

'Maggie does an asthma clinic on a Monday morning,' Ally Nicholson told her. 'Are you OK with that?'

'Definitely.' Helen nodded immediately. 'Asthma was a real problem in the inner-city practice where I worked. I've done the training course and I'm used to running clinics. If I have any worries, I'll call one of you.'

Obviously satisfied that she was going to be able to cope, the other two GPs hurried off to start their morning surgeries and Oliver gave a satisfied nod.

'You're going to be fine,' he said softly. 'Just don't forget to eat.'

Halfway through her asthma clinic Oliver stuck his head around her door. 'I've got a patient I need some help with. I need a different perspective.'

'Go on.'

Having established that she didn't have anyone with her, he walked into the room and closed the door behind him.

'She's another one of my big worries.'

'Oliver, you worry about all your patients,' Helen pointed out calmly, and he grinned.

'I know. But I really worry about this one. She's seventeen and she has asthma but refuses to acknowledge it. The registrar at the hospital just called me. Apparently she was admitted on Friday after a nasty attack but even that wasn't enough to motivate her to do something about her disease. They sounded pretty infuriated with her.'

'That's not very helpful.' Helen looked at him thoughtfully. 'Teenagers have very special needs. Does she have a management plan?'

'In theory. I suspect in practice her management plan involves ignoring her asthma until it's time to call the ambulance.'

Helen sighed. 'I'll talk to her. Is she outside now?'

Oliver nodded. 'With her mother, who is wringing her hands and clearly hasn't slept for two days.'

'Oh, dear.' Helen looked at the list on her computer. 'Well, my next patient hasn't arrived so I could see her now. But can we leave the mother in the waiting room? If we're having a proper conversation about things that matter to teenagers, I suspect it won't be helpful to have her mother in the room.'

'I'll deal with it. Thanks.'

Oliver vanished and then reappeared moments later. Behind him loitered a slim girl with an extremely sulky expression on her pretty face.

'Anna, this is Helen.' Oliver nudged the girl gently into the consulting room. 'She's from London.'

'London?' The girl looked at Helen with an envious expression on her face. 'You lucky thing. I'd do anything to go and live in London. Actually, I'd do anything to live anywhere but here.'

Oliver looked at Helen helplessly and she smiled. 'I expect you have patients to see, Dr Hunter.'

'I do.' He gave her a grateful smile and left the room.

'That man is seriously cool. He could give me the kiss of life any day.' Anna stared after Oliver with a wistful expression on her face and then turned back to Helen. 'I suppose you're going to lecture me, so you might as well make a start.'

'Is that what you think people do?'

'All the time.' Anna slouched in her chair, her expression defiant. 'It's always, "Anna have you done your peak flow?" or, "Anna have you got your inhaler?" just before I go clubbing. And it's always while my friends are standing there.'

'And how does that make you feel?' Helen asked casually.

'Embarrassed. Different. Like some sort of freak.'

'Why don't you tell me what happened on Friday?'

Anna shrugged and picked some imaginary fluff off her sleeve. 'It was hockey. I'm good at hockey. We were winning and then suddenly I couldn't breathe.' She broke off and her eyes filled with tears. 'And the next thing I knew they'd driven an ambulance onto the school field. It was the most humiliating experience of my life.'

'Do you like hockey?'

'Yes, and now I suppose you're going to tell me I can't do it because of my asthma.'

'Not at all.' Helen opened her door and reached for a pad

and pen. 'In fact, you shouldn't have to limit your physical activity at all providing your asthma is controlled—but yours obviously isn't. I like your shoes, by the way.'

Anna glanced down at her feet, obviously taken aback. 'You do?'

'They're great. Everyone is wearing them in London.'

Anna looked at her suspiciously. 'You're different from the usual nurse. She was at school with my mother. You don't look much older than me.'

'I'm twenty-five,' Helen told her, 'so it isn't that long since I was a teenager.'

Anna stared at her for a long moment. 'It isn't just the exercise that gets me.'

'What else?'

'There's this boy.' She bit her lip, her cheeks suddenly flushed. 'He's asked me out a few times but I keep saying no. He's so cool,' Anna breathed, 'but how can I go out with him? He doesn't know I have asthma. Where do I put an inhaler on a date?'

'Well, it depends on the date,' Helen said practically. 'Let's take it one step at a time. Why don't you want him to know you have asthma?'

'He'll think I'm pathetic.'

'Then he's probably not that cool,' Helen said gently. 'And as for where you put the inhaler on a date, what's wrong with your handbag?'

'I don't want anyone to see.'

'The better controlled your asthma, the less likely you are to have an attack like the one last Friday.'

Anna breathed out heavily. 'All right, then. What does it take?'

'We can look at a few things together. We need to monitor your asthma. Do you think you could keep a diary for a couple of weeks? Monitor your peak flow and your symptoms?'

Helen used the pad and paper to illustrate what she was suggesting and talked to Anna about her peak-flow technique.

'And you reckon if I do all that, I can play hockey without dying on the field.'

Helen smiled. 'I would certainly hope so. Why don't we give it a go? Come back and see me again next week. In the meantime, make a note of everything that's worrying you and we'll chat about it.'

Anna stood up. 'And you think I should say yes to that date?'

'If he's that cool, definitely,' Helen said firmly, and Anna grinned.

'I'll keep you posted.'

'You do that.'

Helen waited until Anna had left the room and then went to find Oliver.

'She basically doesn't seem to use her inhalers at all,' she told him, 'because she's so busy hiding them.'

'So how do we get around that?'

Helen smiled. 'We show her she's going to have a much better life if she isn't breathless.'

Oliver's eyes narrowed. 'You think that will work?'

'It's worth a try. Oh, and, Dr Hunter—' Helen turned with her hand on his door, her eyes twinkling '—you probably ought to know that Anna thinks you're seriously cool.'

Oliver grinned and folded his arms across his chest.

'I *am* seriously cool, Nurse Forrester. Have you only just discovered that?'

Helen laughed and went back to her own consulting room, suddenly glad that she'd agreed to take the job.

She hadn't had time to think about David all morning.

By the end of the week Helen had decided that it was more a question of finding time to eat than remembering.

She was extremely busy, and with such a range of problems that she was constantly challenged.

But, as good as his word, Oliver had given her the four-wheel drive, together with a quick driving lesson, and in her lunch breaks she explored the local area, by car and on foot.

And by the end of the week she'd found a wonderful block of flats which she thought might appeal to Hilda.

'There's a warden,' she told Oliver that night over dinner, 'but she'd be as independent as she wanted to be. And although the view over the lake is amazing, she's still only two minutes' walk from town.'

'I'm not sure if she'd want to live in a flat,' Oliver mused. 'She lives in a house at the moment.'

'And she's really struggling with the stairs,' Helen told him, recalling the conversation she'd had with Hilda earlier that week when she'd come in to have her peak flow and blood pressure checked. 'The house has been her home all her married life and it would be easy to assume that she doesn't want to leave it, but I think she does want to leave it.'

Oliver put down his fork and looked at her. 'Go on.'

'Well, she misses Barry dreadfully.' Helen shrugged

helplessly. 'And everything about that house reminds her of him. Obviously, for some people that's a good thing, but for Hilda I don't think that's the case. She doesn't want the constant reminders. She wants to move on.'

'You sound as though you've had quite a chat with her.'

Helen flushed. 'She came in to have her blood pressure checked earlier in the week. She was the last appointment before lunch so I gave her a lift home instead of calling a taxi. She gave me lunch.'

Oliver smiled. 'I'm glad someone is feeding you.' He stifled a yawn. 'I wanted to feed you myself, but it's been a bit of a hairy week. Michelle has been discharged, by the way, and she's doing fine. I popped in to see her at home today. She said to say thank you and she'd love to see your strappy shoes sometime.'

Helen laughed. 'I'll remember to keep them in my boot so that I can show her the next time I'm passing. And, Oliver...' Her smile faded. 'You don't have to feed me. I'm fine.'

He leaned back in his chair, his blue eyes narrowed as they searched her face. 'You're still looking tired and peaky. What you need is fresh air. This weekend I'm taking you into the mountains.'

Helen looked at him with no small degree of consternation. 'Oliver, I'm a town person, remember?'

'But you'll be walking with your own personal guide,' he reminded her, a smug expression on his handsome face. 'I will be responsible for every step you take.'

She bit her lip, wondering if she should admit the truth to him. 'Oliver...'

'What?'

'I'm afraid of heights. I mean, seriously afraid of heights.' She broke off and braced herself for his laughter, but instead he reached across the table and slid his hand over hers. It felt warm, strong and very comforting.

'Will you trust me to take you somewhere you won't feel scared?' His gaze warmed her. 'I promise not to leave you stranded on a ledge or make you walk over anything remotely scary.'

Feeling thoroughly embarrassed by her own inadequacy, Helen looked at him uncertainly. 'I don't know why you would want to take me for a walk. There must be lots of people who would keep you company who aren't afraid of heights.'

'The trouble is,' he said slowly, his expression enigmatic, 'I don't want lots of people. I want you.'

His last sentence was ambiguous and her eyes locked on his. 'Oliver…' Her voice was a croak and he gave a lopsided smile and locked fingers with her.

'Stop worrying, little town mouse. You're going to have a good time.'

And suddenly she found that she wasn't thinking about her fear of heights. She was thinking about spending the weekend with Oliver.

They set out early, but only after Oliver had checked every single item of her clothing.

'If you use a layering system when you dress, it will keep you warmer,' he told her, zipping her into his sister's fleece jacket and then handing her an outer shell. 'This is the waterproof, windproof bit. How are those boots?'

Helen wiggled her toes and stamped on the spot. 'They feel fine.'

'We're lucky that they fit you. If they start to rub let me know but Bryony has them pretty well worn in.'

'I feel like Michelin Man.'

'You look great.' He handed her a hat. 'Put this on.'

She pulled a face. 'I don't look that great in hats.'

'Helen.' His tone was patient. 'You are not going shopping in the King's Road. You are about to brave the elements. Wear the hat.'

She took it from him with a sigh and pulled it onto her head.

He looked at her, his gaze assessing. 'Actually, I disagree. I think you do look great in hats.' He lowered his head and kissed her gently and then turned and picked up a rucksack that looked ridiculously heavy.

Helen stared after him, frozen into stillness by that kiss.

Her whole body tingled even though the contact had been relatively brief.

What had he meant by it?

Why had he kissed her?

And why did she feel so bitterly disappointed that he'd stopped?

Stunned by the thoughts she was having, Helen shook herself. It was natural that she should enjoy the company of an attractive man when her confidence in herself had been so badly rocked. It didn't mean anything. She would have felt the same about anyone who paid her attention.

Why the hell had he kissed her?

Oliver was suffering from a severe case of frustration.

Maybe if he stripped off and rolled in the snow he might be able to cool his aching body, he mused, trying hard to occupy his mind with something—*anything*—that would distract him from the beautiful woman walking behind him.

He'd positioned her behind him because he knew that if she led the way he'd lose all concentration.

She was so sweet and honest.

And the kiss had been a serious mistake.

An impulse which he was now regretting more than he could possibly have imagined because he'd discovered that one relatively chaste kiss was never going to be enough.

He wanted more.

He wanted everything that this woman had to offer.

Which meant that he was in serious trouble because up until two weeks ago she'd been engaged to another man. Three weeks ago, he corrected himself quickly. A whole week had passed and during that time he'd become more and more convinced that David was totally the wrong guy for her.

Somehow he needed her to see that for herself.

He felt her hand tap him on the back and he stopped, turning immediately. 'Are you all right?'

She was out of breath, her cheeks pink with exertion, and he thought he'd never seen a more gorgeous woman in his life. Her eyes sparkled and her soft lips were parted as she gasped for breath.

'Next time I'm going walking with someone with shorter legs.' She took a deep breath and grinned at him. 'You are very fit.'

Oliver had a sudden urge to power her back against the nearest rock and show her just how fit he was.

Instead, he took a step backwards, just in case the temptation to touch her became too great. 'Sorry. My mind was elsewhere.'

'What were you thinking about?'

He shrugged. 'Stuff…' *Her mostly.* 'I'll slow down.' He waved a hand at the scenery. 'So, what do you think of our playground?'

She exhaled slowly, her eyes drifting over the hard lines of the mountains. 'It's really beautiful,' she said quietly, and he felt a rush of relief.

He didn't care that she was a townie. He didn't care that she wasn't fit enough to keep up with him.

But if she'd hated his mountains he would have cared.

'So, do you want to play that game I told you about?'

She laughed and stamped her feet to keep warm. 'What? Spot the boulder?'

He nodded and grasped her shoulders, turning her slightly. 'We're going to walk over there.'

'Towards that ravine?' She looked at him doubtfully and he smiled.

'In the Lake District we call it a ghyll and, yes, we're going to walk over there. But we'll turn back before the path climbs upwards.'

'Path?' Helen squinted down at her feet. 'What path?'

'The one that's under your feet. Come on.' He turned and started to trudge up the mountain that was as familiar to him as his own kitchen. 'Tell me what you see on the way. Landmarks.'

'Lots of snow.' She giggled and he turned and grabbed

her hand, totally unable to resist at least a small degree of physical contact.

'Noticing lots of snow is not going to help you find your way home if you get lost, city girl.' He waited for her to remove her hand and when she didn't, a warm feeling settled inside him. 'How about this rock?'

She was still laughing. 'OK, I've seen it. Hello, rock.'

Oliver was laughing, too, and his grip on her hand tightened. 'Something makes me think you're not taking this entirely seriously.'

'I'm not going to get lost,' she said simply. 'I'm with you.'

Oliver caught his breath and wondered why it was that fate had chosen to present him with the right woman at the wrong time.

Not that it was the wrong time for him, of course. He was more than ready to settle down but Helen was so blinded by her recent trauma that there was no way she would be ready to consider a new relationship so soon.

Consoling himself with the thought that time was on his side, he kept hold of her hand and they walked steadily uphill. The more she told him about David, the more obvious it was to him that she hadn't been in love with the guy. She'd drifted into the engagement because that had been what everyone had expected.

Given time and distance from her family, he was sure that she'd eventually come to realise that for herself.

It had finally stopped snowing and the sun was shining, and they didn't pass another person.

He stopped at a rocky outcrop. 'This is far enough and we can sit here without getting wet. Let's have something to eat.' He swung the pack off his back and delved inside. 'Are you hungry?'

She sank down onto the rock and gave him a wry smile. 'Oliver, we both know that you're going to make me eat whether I'm hungry or not, so it doesn't really matter what I say, does it?'

He smiled placidly and pulled out a flask of hot soup. 'Good point.' He poured the soup into two mugs and handed her one.

She shook her head. 'I'm going to be the size of a block of flats by the time I go back to London.'

The sharp pangs of hunger faded at her words. Suddenly he didn't feel like eating.

Time no longer seemed to be on his side.

'You're going back to London?' He must have looked as horrified as he felt because she gave him a strange look.

'Well, of course I am.' She looked confused. 'Why wouldn't I?'

Because his plan relied on her staying here long enough to realise that she had never been in love with David.

'You've got nothing to go back for.'

She stared across the wild mountain scenery in silence and he saw the pain in her face.

Cursing himself for having been so tactless, he rubbed a hand over the back of his neck. 'I'm sorry,' he groaned, but she shook her head.

'Don't be. It's true.' She took a sip of soup. 'I suppose going back to London isn't something I've even thought about. I gave up my job and the house was David's anyway, so coming up here was an escape.'

'So stay here.'

'I can't hide forever, Oliver, no matter how appealing the thought is.' She gave a sad smile. 'For a start, at some point Bryony is going to want her house back.'

'Not necessarily.' Oliver handed her a sandwich. 'Jack Rothwell owns an enormous pile about three miles from the cottage. I'm sure they'll move in there soon enough. That will leave the cottage empty.'

Helen stared at him and he could tell that the idea hadn't even occurred to her before now.

'Live here…' She stared at the mountains again and let out a long breath. 'That would be like a dream.'

'Then stay.'

'Dreams don't always work in real life,' she said sadly. 'For a start, your practice nurse is only gone for a month,' she reminded him, and he rubbed a hand over his face.

'So we'll find you another job. No problem.'

She smiled. 'Oliver, I don't know anyone here.'

'You know Bryony.' His voice was hoarse. 'And you know me.'

His eyes locked with hers and he could see the question in her eyes.

'Oliver…' Her voice was soft and she looked away, clearly feeling awkward. 'I don't… You can't—'

He sighed. 'Look, I'm going to be honest here so when I've had my say you can black my eye. I like you, Helen. A lot.' Major understatement. 'If you weren't suffering from a very unpleasant break up I would have made a move on you a long time ago.'

Surprise flickered in her blue eyes. 'You've only known me for a week.'

'I've always been decisive. Now it's your turn to be honest. Or are you going to tell me that you haven't felt the chemistry between us?'

She gave a little gasp and the colour seeped into her cheeks. But she didn't deny it. In fact, she didn't speak at all, just turned her head and stared across the valley, leaving him with her profile.

And that didn't tell him anything.

'Helen?' His voice was gentle and he stepped around her so that he could see her face. 'I'm not intending to jump on you, sweetheart. I just wanted to point out that it's there.'

Her eyes locked on his, her expression almost puzzled. 'Two weeks ago I was marrying David.'

'Three weeks,' he corrected her firmly. 'It was three weeks ago, Helen.'

She shook her head and gave a little shrug. 'Three weeks. It still doesn't change the fact that I was marrying another man.'

'But you didn't love him.'

She frowned and shook her head. 'I did. I mean, I do.' She bit her lip, her expression troubled. 'I thought I did—now I don't know any more.'

'All right.' Oliver put both hands on her shoulders and forced her to look at him. 'Let's try something. Tell me what you loved about David.'

'That isn't exactly a fair question.'

'Why not?'

She looked at him helplessly. 'Because right now I'm so angry with him I'm finding it hard to remember.'

Oliver gave a slow smile. 'All right, let's try something different. When did you first realise that you were in love with David?'

'I don't know.' She frowned. 'You make it sound as though it's a light-bulb moment. One minute you're not in love and the next minute you are.'

That's exactly how it had been for him. A light-bulb moment.

The moment he'd seen her in the church he'd known.

Oliver looked at her thoughtfully. 'And it wasn't like that for you?'

'I don't know. I've never really thought about it.' She chewed her lip. 'I started going out with David when I was nineteen—he was my first proper boyfriend, so I suppose I just grew to love him over time.'

Oliver's hands dropped from her shoulders. 'You've been going out with him since you were nineteen?'

She stared at him. 'Why is that so shocking?'

Oliver let out a long breath. 'Because that means you must have been with him for years.'

'Six years.' She nodded. 'What's wrong with that?'

'So when did you decide to marry him?'

'I don't know. It just seemed like the logical next step.'

Oliver looked at her searchingly, wondering if she realised what she was saying.

There didn't seem to have been a single grain of romance in her relationship with David.

'What about you?' She looked at him almost defiantly. 'You're not married so you're obviously not exactly dedicated to commitment.'

'It is precisely my dedication to commitment that has stopped me from marrying the wrong person,' Oliver said calmly. 'I've been waiting for Miss Right.'

Helen smiled. 'But you've never found her?'

'I found her a week ago.'

There was a long silence and a mixture of shock and excitement flickered across her blue eyes. 'Oliver, you don't—'

'If you're about to tell me that I've only known you for a week, then I should probably remind you that I'm a very decisive person. Always have been. I know what I want, and once I know what I want I make a point of making sure that I get it.'

She swallowed hard, her eyes fixed on his. 'And what do you want, Oliver?'

'You,' he said softly, lifting a hand and cupping her face as he looked down into her eyes. 'I want you, Helen. And I'm prepared to wait until you realise that you want me, too.'

'Oliver…' She tried to pull away but he slid his other hand around her waist and anchored her against him.

'Let's just try something, shall we?'

Holding her gently but firmly, he brought his mouth down on hers.

Her lips were soft and sweet and Oliver gave a groan, waiting for her to pull away or slap his face, but instead she gave a little sigh and her mouth opened under his. His last coherent thought was that kissing Helen was going straight to the top of his list of favourite pastimes and then he sank under the surface of an excitement so intense that it couldn't be measured.

His previously clear mind was drugged by sensation and he kissed her fiercely, driven by a ravenous hunger deep inside him.

He felt her arms slide around his neck and Oliver

dragged her closer, frustrated by the thickness of the clothing that separated them, desperate to rip off her layers so that he could feast on her body.

He felt her quiver against him, felt the intensity of her response as she kissed him back, and knew without doubt that this was the woman he was going to spend the rest of his life with.

But he had the sense to know that he couldn't take her there in one enormous leap, and when she suddenly made a little sound and pushed at his chest, he didn't try and stop her.

To be honest, he was too shocked to stop her.

He'd kissed enough women in his life to think that he'd experienced all the different degrees of sexual excitement, but nothing had come close to the way he'd felt kissing Helen. It was as if all the other kisses had been in black and white and this one had been in colour.

And you didn't have to be a genius to know that it had been the same for her.

Her breath was coming in shallow pants and she dropped her eyes, focusing her attention on the middle of his chest. 'I can't believe I just did that.'

'You didn't,' he said calmly. 'I did. I was the one who kissed you.'

'But I kissed you back.'

She sounded so appalled that he smiled.

'Well, just a bit perhaps.'

'Anyone could have seen us.'

'Those sheep over there definitely saw.'

She didn't smile and he gave a sigh and stroked the back of his hand down her cheek in a gesture that was supposed to comfort. 'Is that why you stopped? Because someone might have seen us?'

'Yes. No.' She was deliciously confused and he felt something shift inside him.

'Helen, stop analysing, sweetheart,' he advised softly. 'We kissed and it was—it was…' *What was it?* How on earth did you describe a kiss like that? Explosive? Frightening? 'It was just a kiss.'

She looked at him. 'Two weeks ago I was marrying David.'

'Three weeks ago.' He gritted his teeth. 'It was three weeks ago.'

She gave a lopsided smile. 'You think one more week makes a difference to the fact that I just got carried away with another man?'

'You weren't carried away, Helen,' he said easily. 'You stopped it. If you'd been carried away we'd both now be naked on that rock at severe risk of suffering frostbite.'

She blushed and looked away. 'I can't believe I let you kiss me. That I kissed you back.' Her expression was troubled. 'I've never— I don't know what I was thinking of. Why did I let you?'

'Because I'm irresistible,' he said helpfully, and then sighed when she didn't laugh.

'Relax, sweetheart. It was only a kiss.'

Only for him it hadn't been just a kiss. It had been an affirmation.

'B-but I'm not like that,' she stammered, pushing a strand of dark hair out of her eyes. 'I don't— I mean I've never…'

'You don't go 'round kissing men you find attractive.

Well then perhaps it's time you started,' Oliver said, pulling the edges of her jacket together and zipping it up firmly. 'Come on. Let's go home.'

'I can't have an affair with you, Oliver.'

His hands paused on her jacket. 'Have I asked you to?'

'No. But I'm just making it clear that I can't.'

'Why can't you?'

'For a start, I'm seriously on the rebound.' She gave a wan smile. 'I'm completely confused. To be perfectly honest, I don't know how I feel about David anymore but I do know that I'm not a good bet for any man.'

'Then it's a good job I've always been a risk taker,' Oliver said cheerfully, turning away to stuff the rest of the picnic in the rucksack. 'Don't worry about me.'

'I'll hurt you.'

'In case you haven't noticed, I'm pretty tough.' Oliver heaved the rucksack onto his broad shoulders and paced back to her. 'All right, this is what we're going to do. Call it your rehabilitation programme. You're going to carry on working for me, we're going to carry on living together. You're going to carry on recovering from David and we're going to carry on kissing whenever we feel like it and see where it leads us.'

'It won't lead anywhere. In a few weeks I'll be going back to London.'

'Right.' Oliver gave a bland smile and started down the path, wondering what she'd say if she knew that he had no intention of ever letting her return to London again.

He was going to marry her.

CHAPTER SEVENTEEN

HELEN'S thoughts were so jumbled up for the rest of the weekend that it was a relief to return to work on Monday.

She'd spent most of Sunday trying to avoid Oliver, which was virtually impossible in a cottage the size of Bryony's when the man in question was the size of Oliver.

Every time she'd turned around he'd seemed to be watching her with that lazy, sexy look that made her insides feel funny.

And she couldn't stop thinking about that kiss.

She tried to think of a time when a kiss from David had left her so churned up, and failed. In fact, she couldn't even remember what it felt like to kiss David. Maybe it was just because she'd been kissing David since she was nineteen.

But had his kisses ever felt as though she was on the verge of something deliciously exciting? Had she ever wanted his kisses to carry on and on and never stop?

Because that's how she'd felt with Oliver.

Seriously disturbed, Helen tried to apply some logic to her tumbled feelings.

She was feeling emotionally bruised and battered and Oliver Hunter had been extraordinarily kind to her. It was only natural that she should feel drawn to him. It was nothing more than that.

But it felt like a lot more.

'Are you all right, Helen?' Pam, the receptionist, wandered into her room clutching some notes. 'You look miles away.'

'Just thinking.' Helen forced a smile. 'I'm fine. Are those notes for me?'

Pam nodded. 'I know you've got a full clinic already, but Howard Marks has asked if you'll see him.' She frowned. 'He saw Dr Hunter last week and after he came out of his appointment he was hovering around Reception for ages as if he was trying to pluck up courage to say something. That's why I thought you might agree to see him. I've just got a feeling...'

'Of course I'll see him,' Helen said immediately, taking the set of notes from Pam. 'Perhaps I'll just have a quick word with Dr Hunter first before I call him in. Just so that I have some background.'

'Good idea. He's in between patients at the moment and your next one hasn't turned up so you've been blessed with time to breathe.'

'Thanks, Pam.'

Wondering how it was that she could feel so at home in a practice after only a week, Helen walked across the corridor to Oliver's consulting room and tapped on the door.

She heard his deep voice tell her to enter but her hand paused on the door handle as she braced herself to face him. For the whole weekend all she'd been able to think about had been that kiss.

What if she'd lost the ability to work with him professionally?

Just as she was plucking up the courage to open the door, it was tugged open from the inside and Oliver stood there, his blue eyes questioning as they rested on her face.

'Is something wrong?'

Her eyes dropped to his firm mouth and she forced herself to lift her gaze and look him in the eyes. Something flickered deep in his eyes and then he stood to one side to let her in.

'I wanted to talk about a patient,' she said quickly, just in case he thought she'd knocked on his door with something more personal in mind. 'Someone called Howard Marks has asked to see me. Apparently he saw you last week. I just wondered if you could give me a bit of background.'

Oliver frowned and folded his arms across his chest. 'Howard has asked to see you? I can't imagine what for...' He was silent for a moment and then shook his head. 'No idea. He's a very heavy smoker and he suffers from emphysema. He developed a chest infection over Christmas so I gave him antibiotics. I checked his chest last week and it was free of infection. End of story.'

'That's fine. I just wanted to check that there wasn't anything I should know before I saw him.'

Oliver shook his head. 'Howard is a great guy. He was a friend of my father's—I've known him since I was tiny.'

'Have you?' Helen tilted her head to one side and looked at him thoughtfully. 'I wonder whether that's why he wants to see me.'

'What do you mean?'

'Nothing.' She smiled and walked towards the door. 'Just a thought, and I'm probably wrong anyway so it's stupid to voice it. I'll catch you later, Oliver.'

Suddenly she was breathlessly aware of his broad shoulders and the hard muscle of his thighs outlined by the soft fabric of his trousers. He had a powerful, very masculine physique and without too much effort on her part she could remember just how it had felt to be pressed close to his body.

And she needed to get herself away from his body as fast as possible so that she could somehow regain control of her mind.

Not daring to analyse what was happening to her, she hurried back to the sanctuary of her room and closed the door firmly behind her.

To begin with work had provided a distraction from David. Now it seemed to be providing a distraction from Oliver as well.

She pressed the buzzer to call her next patient and then smiled as a tall, pale-looking man walked into her room.

'Mr Marks? I'm Helen Forrester. Please, have a seat.'

He closed the door carefully and sat down opposite her, his fingers playing nervously in his lap.

'What can I do for you, Mr Marks?'

He shifted awkwardly in his chair and then ran a hand over the back of his neck. 'I have this thing called emphysema…'

Helen nodded. 'Yes. I read your notes. How are you getting on?'

'Well, not great, to be honest.' He pulled a face. 'I have

to breathe in that blessed oxygen sixteen hours a day and then at Christmas I managed to catch something horrible and I was back in bed, coughing my guts up.'

'But the antibiotics that Dr Hunter gave you cleared that up?'

'Oh, ay.' He nodded and glanced at her briefly before looking away again. 'He's a good doctor is young Oliver.'

Helen looked at him thoughtfully. 'And you've known him all your life.'

'Knew his father and mother before they were married.' Howard Marks gave a short laugh. 'Can't believe Oliver is grown up, to be honest.'

'It must be a bit difficult, talking to him about some things,' Helen volunteered, keeping her voice casual, and when he met her eyes she knew that she was right.

'He's a brilliant doctor,' the man said quickly, 'but I remember him as a kid. How can I talk to him about— about—' He broke off and Helen gave a nod.

'About something really personal,' she finished gently, and Howard sighed.

'Stupid, isn't it, really? An old fool like me.'

'If something is worrying you, you should talk about it. Is that why you asked to see me, Mr Marks? Because I'm a stranger?'

He gave her a keen look. 'You're not stupid, are you?'

'I hope not.' Helen smiled. 'And I do understand that it's easier to talk to a stranger about some things.'

'I thought that. That's why I asked to see you.' He broke off and gave a long sigh. 'And now I'm here I don't know how to say it. You'll think I'm completely ridiculous.'

Helen shook her head. 'I won't think that. If the problem is serious enough to bring you here then it's serious enough for me to take it seriously.'

He glanced towards the door as if he was contemplating running through it. 'Your next patient is probably waiting.'

'Then they can wait a bit longer,' Helen said calmly. 'Please, trust me, Mr Marks. Tell me what's worrying you and we'll try and find a solution together.'

'I'm sixty-six,' he wheezed. 'Been married for forty-two years and we've always had a good—well, we've always enjoyed—'

'Sex?' Helen's voice was calm. 'Has it become a problem, Mr Marks?'

He slumped in his chair and ran a hand over his face. 'I can't believe I'm discussing it with you. You're younger than my daughter.'

'But I'm also a professional who cares about your health,' Helen reminded him, 'and sexuality is part of health. If it's any consolation, plenty of patients have discussed exactly the same issue with me. It's very common, particularly in patients who are suffering from respiratory conditions like you.'

He looked at her. 'You've talked to other patients about this?'

'Absolutely. In London there are specialist nurses who deal with this area.'

He gave an embarrassed smile. 'When you get to my age you assume that people think you don't have sex any more.'

'Sex is an important part of a relationship,' Helen said quietly. 'Do you want to tell me exactly what the problem is?'

He rubbed a hand over his face. 'Well, I just run out

of energy. And I suppose I'm frightened because I get breathless.'

'Do you leave your oxygen on when you make love?'

He frowned and shook his head. 'No, of course not.'

'It would probably help if you did. Do you ever go for walks?'

'Sometimes, but I always use my puffer before exercise and that seems to do the trick.'

Helen nodded. 'Treat making love as you would any other exercise,' she advised. 'Have a puff of your bronchodilator before and keep the oxygen on. Have a rest before you make love and it might be wise to avoid alcohol because that can actually inhibit sexual arousal.'

'What about the fact that I get breathless? It scares the wife.'

'Shortness of breath while you're making love is entirely normal,' Helen said simply. 'As long as you are feeling OK you shouldn't worry about it.'

'The wife thinks I'm going to drop dead.'

'Then you can assure her that sudden death during intercourse is extremely uncommon.' Helen reached for her diary and a piece of paper. 'There's a really good leaflet that outlines some sexual positions which help you conserve energy. I used to have a few in the place where I worked last but if you call this number they can send you a copy. In the meantime, this is what I suggest.'

She talked frankly for a few minutes more and then Howard rose to his feet and gave her a grateful smile.

'I can't thank you enough. I feel a lot better.'

'Good.' Helen stood up and walked him to the door. 'Anytime you have any worries just pop back and see me.'

And then she remembered that the chances were she wouldn't be here.

Her life was in London.

She buzzed for her next patient, a frown on her face.

If she was honest with herself she was enjoying this small community where everyone knew about everyone else.

And she was enjoying working with Oliver.

She sucked in a breath and stared out of the window, her eyes on the snow-covered fells that he loved so much.

It was still troubling her that she was becoming so obsessed with Oliver when only a few weeks before she'd been making preparations to spend the rest of her life with David.

It was just self-preservation, she assured herself, pulling herself together as her next patient tapped on her door. David had rejected her so brutally that it was perfectly natural for her to respond when an attractive man flirted with her.

And Oliver wasn't serious. She knew he couldn't be serious.

He'd only known her for just over a week.

That afternoon she finished work on time and went and collected Hilda from her cottage.

'I just want to show you something,' she said, waiting while Hilda picked up her coat and bag. 'And, anyway, it'll be fun to get out and have some fresh air. I've been stuck in a surgery surrounded by germs all morning.'

Hilda smiled. 'I see Dr Hunter has leant you his four-by-four.'

'That's right.' Helen grinned and opened the passenger door for her. 'Although why he trusts us girls with it, I have no idea.'

Hilda laughed and climbed into the vehicle with some discreet help from Helen. 'I suppose this is the point where you tell me you used to be a racing driver.'

'Would you mind if I was?'

'Not at all.' Hilda fastened her seat-belt. 'To be honest, I'm in the market for some excitement.'

'Well, you can relax. I'm not that confident with his car yet,' Helen confessed ruefully, pulling out and setting off towards the town. 'So we'll have to seek our excitement in other directions.'

'So how are you settling down, dear?'

'Very well. Everyone is very kind.'

Hilda glanced across at her. 'And you're living with Dr Hunter…'

Helen blushed. 'We're both staying in his sister's house. I wouldn't exactly say I'm living with him.'

'Sounds as though you're living with him to me,' Hilda said placidly, reaching down and picking up her bag. 'And a good thing, too. We've all waited a long time to see Oliver find the right woman.'

Helen gave a soft gasp. 'Hilda, I'm not the right woman.'

'Judging from the way he was looking at you when he brought you to my house that first weekend, I think he might have a different opinion on that subject.'

Helen shook her head. 'I've known him for less than two weeks.'

'I fell in love with my husband in two minutes,' Hilda said wistfully, pulling a tissue out of her bag and blowing her nose. 'And he was the same. When you know, you know.'

'I probably ought to tell you that until very recently I was engaged to another man.' Helen tightened her fingers on the steering-wheel, wondering why she was disclosing intimate details of her private life to a patient. 'I shouldn't be telling you this...'

'Why not? It does me good to hear about other peoples' lives,' Hilda said calmly. 'Stops me brooding on my own problems. So what happened?'

'He ended it the day before the wedding. He phoned from the airport as he was about to board a plane.' For the first time since it had happened, Helen was able to assess David's behaviour objectively. 'What a rat.'

'A coward of the worse kind,' Hilda agreed fervently, 'but he did you a favour, dear. Whatever pain you might be feeling now, it's nothing compared to waking up every day next to a man you don't love. And there's no way a sweet girl like you could have been in love with a man who could behave like that.'

'I thought I was.'

'Everyone can make a mistake.' Hilda peered curiously out of the window. 'I've never been down this road before. Where are we?'

'If you turn right at the end of the road you end up at the edge of the lake. It's very pretty. And the flat has lovely views of the lake from the sitting room and the main bedroom.'

Hilda looked at her. 'What flat?'

'The flat I'm taking you to see.' Helen bit her lip nervously. 'Please, don't make a judgement until you've seen it. Oliver thinks you won't want to leave the home you lived in with Barry all your life, but I think that home is full of memories for you. Some good, some too painful to live with on a daily basis. I wondered whether you might want to think about a fresh start. Make some new memories somewhere else. And this is a pretty good place to do it. Will you at least look at it?'

There was a long silence while Hilda stared out of the window and then she stirred herself. 'Of course I'll look at it.'

Breathing a huge sigh of relief, Helen switched off the engine.

The warden was waiting for them and Hilda gave a huge smile. 'Well, it's Cathy Janson. How are you, my dear?'

'Brilliant.' Cathy gave the older woman a hug and jangled some keys. 'I didn't realise that it was you who was interested in the flat. It would be fantastic having you living here.'

Helen glanced from one to the other. 'Obviously you know each other.'

'I was the headmistress of the local primary school,' Hilda told her with a wistful smile. 'I taught Cathy. It was a long time ago. She always wore her hair in pigtails then.'

Cathy smiled. 'Come and see the flat.'

She unlocked the door for them and Hilda went first, walking straight to the huge picture window that overlooked the lake. Several boats were moored at a tiny jetty and even though it was bitterly cold, people were strolling along the path that weaved its way along the side of the lake. Behind the lake the mountains rose, filling the background.

'What an amazing view.' Finally Hilda moved, glancing around her with obvious approval. 'And what a lovely warm room. There are times when I think I'm going to freeze to death in my cottage at the moment. The wind seems to howl through every crack. Show me the rest.'

By the time they'd looked around and sat in the living room while Hilda stared at the view, an hour had passed.

Cathy stood up. 'I'm going to have to leave you because I'm picking my Nicky up from school. Just post the keys back through my letter-box when you've finished.' She put a hand on Hilda's shoulder. 'I was so sorry to hear about Barry.'

Hilda let out a breath. 'Life sends us trials and we have to face them. For a while I didn't think I could. But now I think this might be the answer. Change. Something new.'

Cathy and Helen exchanged looks and Cathy made for the door. 'I'll be hearing from you, then.'

The door closed behind her and Hilda stirred. 'Thank you.'

'For what?'

'For daring to suggest what no one else would. The home that I've lived in all my life just doesn't feel like home now that Barry isn't in it with me. If I move here, I can walk the short distance to town, I can chat to Cathy and help pick her daughter up from school. And when it's too cold to go out I can still watch life from this amazing window.'

Helen smiled, a huge feeling of relief washing over her. 'So you want it?'

'Definitely. How hard will it be to arrange everything?'

'Well, you'll need to sell your house.'

'That will be easy enough. The couple next door have been dying to buy it for years. They want to knock the two cottages into one big house. I'll talk to them when I get home. And I'll call Cathy. My son can help me with the details.'

A week later, Hilda had made an offer on the flat and instructed her solicitor to sell her cottage to the couple next door.

On Friday evening Oliver cooked Helen dinner and they cracked open a bottle of wine.

'In three weeks you seem to have sorted out the whole community.' Oliver raised his glass, an odd smile playing around his firm mouth. 'I couldn't believe that Anna actually came back to see you.'

'Twice, actually. In each case complete with diary and peak-flow readings,' Helen said happily, recalling her discussion with the teenager. 'And, more importantly, she's got a date tomorrow.'

'A date?' Oliver blinked. 'How do you know about her love life?'

'Because her love life is actually an important key to her asthma management,' Helen said simply. 'She didn't want the boy to know she was asthmatic. Anyway, she told him yesterday and it turns out that his sister is asthmatic so suddenly everything is rosy. She's going clubbing with him and she even brought her outfit to show me and we found a great place to tuck her inhaler.'

Oliver shook his head. 'You amaze me.' His eyes gleamed wickedly. 'Although I have to confess that someone did warn me that you are the local expert on sexual positions.'

Helen blushed but she held his gaze. 'My conversations with my patients are confidential.'

'They should be,' Oliver agreed dryly, topping up her wine, 'but I have to warn you that it often doesn't stay that way in a small community. According to Howard Marks, you're a cross between Florence Nightingale and—'

'I don't think I want to hear the rest,' Helen interrupted him hastily, her cheeks still pink. 'I just gave him some advice. He didn't want to talk to you because he's known you since you were in nappies. But clearly he didn't mind talking about it afterwards.'

Oliver grinned. 'Man talk. You know how it is.'

Helen rolled her eyes. 'Spare me.'

Oliver's smile faded. 'And thank you for what you've done for Hilda. You wouldn't believe how many sleepless nights I've had over her. I've known her all my life and it just didn't occur to me that she'd want to move. What made you think of it?'

Helen pushed a piece of salmon around her plate. 'The way I feel about moving here, I suppose. When a place is full of memories, it's good to leave it.'

Oliver's blue eyes searched hers. 'So does that mean that you're throwing away your stilettos and staying here?'

In another week Bryony would be back from her honeymoon and Oliver's practice nurse would be back from Australia.

'I don't know.' Helen pulled a face. 'I don't even want to think about it, to be honest. I love it here so much.' She poked her salmon with her fork. 'This is starting to feel like home. I like the people. I like the way their priorities are different.'

'So stay.'

She sighed. 'It isn't that simple, is it?'

'Why not?'

She poked her salmon again. 'Because it feels like running away.' She pulled a face. 'I mean, I know that's exactly what I've done, but sooner or later I have to go home and face the music.'

'Why? Life can be enough of an endurance test without making it worse.' Oliver frowned. 'And what has that salmon ever done to you? You've chopped it into pieces.'

Helen put down her fork and stared at the food on her plate. 'I'm not that hungry.' She looked at him. 'It's funny really. I always had a very clear vision of the way my life would be...'

'And how was that?' Oliver lounged back in his chair and she gave a slight shrug.

'Big house, lots of entertaining, children...'

Oliver gave a twisted smile. 'The corporate wife.'

'I suppose so.'

'And was that your vision or your parents'?'

Helen looked at him, startled. It was a question she'd never asked herself before. 'I suppose I was brought up to think that my life would be like my mother's.'

'So who made the decision to marry David?' Oliver asked evenly. 'You or your parents?'

Helen frowned. 'Me, of course.'

Oliver's expression didn't flicker. 'How did you meet him?'

'He worked for my dad.'

Oliver gave a wry smile. 'And he was deemed a suitable partner for the boss's daughter?'

Helen flushed. 'Something like that. But I liked David.'

'But you don't marry someone because you like them,' Oliver said softly, leaning forward and trapping her eyes with his. 'You marry them because you love them. Did you love him, Helen?'

There was a long silence and she was suddenly aware of the steady beat of her heart and the heat in his eyes.

'I don't know.' She swallowed hard. 'A week ago I would have answered definitely yes, of course I would. If I hadn't loved him, I wouldn't have agreed to marry him.'

'Wouldn't you?' Oliver's gaze was steady on hers. 'You're a sweet girl, Helen. It strikes me that you spend a lot of time doing things for other people. Who were you marrying David for? You or your parents?'

She shook her head. Suddenly the only things she could think about were his unbelievably thick, dark lashes and the lazy, sexy look in his eyes.

'I don't know.' Her voice was barely a whisper and he gave a soft curse and pushed his chair away from the table.

'Oliver?'

He strode around to her side and dragged her to her feet, his mouth descending on hers with a fierce passion that took her by surprise.

She melted instantly, loving the feel of his hard body against hers, this time without the frustrating barrier of outdoor clothing.

As kisses went, this one was crazy, a desperate, driven explosion of sexual chemistry that was stronger than both of them.

'You're driving me nuts,' Oliver groaned against her mouth, one strong hand sliding into the softness of her hair, anchoring her head for his kiss. The other arm dragged her closer still, trapping her against the hardness of his arousal. 'Living and working with you is driving me nuts.'

She gasped and pressed closer still and he slid her uniform up her thighs and lifted her in an easy movement, his mouth still on hers as he sat her on the table. Then he slid both hands over her bottom and tugged her close so that her legs were wrapped around him.

He gave a moan of pure masculine appreciation and reluctantly dragged his mouth away from hers, but only so that he could kiss his way down her neck.

'Have I ever told you that you have fabulous legs?' His voice was husky with passion and his strong hands slid purposefully up her thighs, caressing the smooth skin with deliberate strokes, 'because you have totally, amazing legs—I love your legs.'

'Oliver...'

His mouth smothered her broken plea for satisfaction and she felt the burning heat of his body against hers, felt the warm seduction of his lips and tongue, the skilled touch of his hands. With a moan of frustration she tugged his shirt out of his trousers and her hands slid underneath, exploring warm, male flesh and hard muscle. He had an incredible physique. Suddenly she wanted to feel all of him and she didn't resist when she felt his fingers impatiently freeing the buttons on her dress.

When his fingers slid beneath her flimsy bra and claimed a nipple she gave a tortured gasp and arched against him, feeling the insistent throb of his arousal pressed hard against her, and when he bent his head and replaced his fingers with his mouth she sobbed with a mixture of pleasure and arousal.

Bells rang in her head, loud and insistent, and it was only when Oliver lifted his head with a reluctant groan that she realised that it was the phone.

His breath fractured and his eyes slightly dazed, Oliver slowly released her. 'I've got to answer that,' he said hoarsely, pulling the edges of her dress together with visible reluctance. 'I'm on call.'

Unable to move or think clearly, Helen waited until he'd eased away from her and then tugged her uniform down her thighs, her face scarlet as she reviewed her own behaviour.

What had she been thinking of?

She'd been all set to marry David and yet here she was, only a month later, virtually making love with a man on his kitchen table. And the power of her own response to Oliver shocked her. Never before had she experienced one tenth of the urgency, the need, the *desperation* that she'd experienced with Oliver.

If the phone hadn't rung...

Utterly shocked and confused, Helen fastened her buttons quickly, wondering what had happened to her.

Until tonight she'd never thought of herself as a particularly sexual person. In all her years with David, she'd never felt an overwhelming need for sex. They'd kissed, of course, and made love, but it had always been a very dignified experience, whereas she and Oliver...

They'd virtually ripped each other's clothes off.

Oliver was talking on the phone, asking pointed questions and scribbling a few notes on a pad. When he finally replaced the phone he seemed to have recovered some of his composure. But he kept his eyes on the notepad.

'That was one of my pregnant mums. Lily Henderson.' His voice still sounded gruff and he cleared his throat and ran a hand over the back of his neck as he studied his notes.

Perhaps he wasn't so composed after all.

'She's having severe pains but she doesn't think she's in labour.'

Helen made a valiant attempt at normal conversation. 'Shouldn't she go straight to hospital?'

'Yes, but she had a hideous time with her first one— born down south somewhere—and she's determined to have this one at home.'

'Oh, dear.'

'She only moved to the area a month ago and I haven't managed to persuade her to meet Tom, which was what I had in mind.' Oliver drew in a breath, cursed softly and finally looked at her, his gaze acknowledging what had happened between them. 'I've never had trouble concentrating on my job before.'

Her own breathing was suddenly shallow as she connected with those intense blue eyes. 'So are you going to do a visit?'

Her voice sounded disconnected from the rest of her body. As if somehow it were trying to distance itself from the confusing spiral of emotions that were inside her.

'Yes. I'll take a look at her and try and persuade her to go in. But I was talking about us.' His eyes held hers. 'Or are you going to pretend that that kiss didn't happen?'

She swallowed hard. If only it were that easy.

'Oliver—'

'Because it's probably only fair to warn you that I'm not going to let you.' His voice was soft but grimly determined. He ripped the piece of paper from the pad and tucked it into his pocket. 'I know you think that you're on the rebound but I'm not going to let you dismiss this thing between us just because we've only known each other for two weeks. What we have is too special. When we get back from seeing Lily, we're going to talk about this.'

Her stomach lurched and she looked at him helplessly. 'There's no point. I wouldn't know what to say. All I know is that I've never behaved like that with anyone before. You must think I'm...' She covered her face with her hands, just mortified, and felt him gently tug her hands away.

'You really want to know what I think of you?' His eyes darkened and his gaze dropped to her mouth for a lingering moment. 'On second thoughts, this is not the time to have that conversation. Pretty soon I'm going to tell you what I think of you, Helen,' he promised hoarsely, 'but not two minutes before we go to see a patient.'

He was standing so close to her that she could feel the warmth and strength of his body, see the rough stubble on his hard jaw.

'You want me to come with you?'

He gave her that boyish smile that never failed to charm her. 'I could do with some moral support.'

It was late, she was tired but suddenly all she wanted was to be with Oliver. 'All right.'

Some of the tension seemed to leave him. 'Good. Let's go. She lives in a village on the other side of town.' He grabbed his coat and bag and then turned to look at her, a strange gleam in his blue eyes. 'And, Helen—' his voice was soft '—when we come back, we're having that conversation.'

She stared at him, too confused by her own response to answer him.

She'd thought that the only man in the world for her was David, but suddenly the only man on her mind was Oliver.

CHAPTER EIGHTEEN

LILY HENDERSON opened the door to them but it was obvious that she was in severe pain.

'You should be lying down,' Oliver scolded, and she
gave him a weary smile.

'How? I've just put the other one to bed and Nick isn't
home yet. I've rung him. He's on his way. Come into the
sitting room.'

She flopped down on the sofa and took a deep breath.
'Something's not right, Dr Hunter I can feel it. This pain
isn't right.'

'You've been in labour before, Lily,' Oliver said calmly.
'Does the pain feel like labour pain?'

She shook her head and pulled a face, rubbing a hand
over her swollen abdomen to ease the discomfort. 'No. It
doesn't feel like labour pain. It feels like something else.
But it isn't good. I'm not going into hospital, Dr Hunter.
I'm not going.'

'Let's not worry about that at the moment.' Oliver

grabbed the sonicaid. 'I just want to listen to the baby's heart, and then we'll talk about our options.'

Seconds later the steady, rhythmic pounding of the baby's heart echoed through the room and Lily gave a soft sigh.

'Oh, I'm so glad to hear that.'

Oliver nodded and switched off the machine. 'Your baby's fine at the moment, Lily, but any pain that bothers you that much should be investigated and I can't do that properly at home. You should be scanned and examined.'

Lily shook her head. 'No.'

'We have a brilliant maternity unit here,' Oliver said softly, 'and it has one of the lowest rates of intervention in the country.'

Lily looked at him, her eyes suddenly frightened. 'You know I don't want to go in. I want to have this baby at home.'

Oliver sighed and ran long fingers through his hair. 'I know you had a bad experience with your last delivery, Lily, but you were just unlucky. You never were anybody's idea of a good candidate for home birth, you know that. And you're even less so now.'

Lily's mouth tightened and Helen saw the sparkle of tears in her eyes. 'The doctors didn't know what they were doing,' she muttered. 'You said you'd deliver me at home if you had to. You and the midwife.'

'And if I have to, I will, but how much of a risk are you willing to take with this baby, Lily?' Oliver's voice was soft. 'I can promise that whatever happened to you last time won't happen this time. I'm going to call my brother.

He's the consultant there—remember, I've told you about him? I've told him about you, too.'

'But I don't know him.'

'Fortunately, I've known him for thirty-four years,' Oliver said easily, rising to his feet in a fluid movement and reaching for his phone. 'And he is going to take the very best care of you and this baby.'

Lily started to cry and Oliver gave a soft curse.

'Make your phone call,' Helen said quickly, sliding her arms around Lily and giving her a hug. 'Lily, why don't you tell me what happened last time?'

'He didn't even talk to me,' Lily sobbed, her hand covering her mouth. 'That doctor just strode into the room, yanked the baby out with forceps and left again without saying a single word. He was horrible! And I was in agony for months and months. I couldn't sit for six weeks I was so bruised, and I had to have ultrasound and everything— I just couldn't enjoy the baby.'

Helen winced and hugged her tighter. 'You poor, poor thing,' she said gently. 'But you were just really unlucky, Lily. There is no way Tom Hunter would let that happen.' She didn't even know Tom, but if he was even half as good a doctor as his brother he would be a brilliant obstetrician. 'Trust Dr Hunter, Lily. And think of the baby.'

At that moment the front door flew open and Lily's husband flew in, breathless and visibly stressed.

'Are you all right, pet?' He scooted across the room to his wife and looked at Helen with anxious eyes. 'What's happening?'

'I'm trying to persuade her to go to hospital,' Oliver said, flipping his phone shut and walking over to them.

'I've talked to Tom and he's going to meet us at the hospital. We're going there now.'

'I can't leave Bruce.'

'I've called your mum,' Nick said quickly. 'She's on her way over.'

Lily bit her lip and looked at Oliver. 'Do you promise it won't go wrong?'

Oliver sighed and dropped to his haunches beside her, his handsome face serious. 'What I can promise is that there is no better person than Tom to deliver a baby.'

'But if you were married, would you let him deliver your wife's baby?'

Oliver smiled. 'Oh, yes.'

Helen had a sudden painful vision of Oliver with a pregnant wife and felt a sudden stab of pain in her chest.

He would make a wonderful husband and an even more wonderful father.

Thoroughly unsettled by her own thoughts, Helen forced herself to concentrate on the situation.

Lily looked at him for a long moment and then gave a sniff. 'All right...'

'Good girl.' Oliver straightened in a smooth movement and looked at her husband. 'Has she got a bag packed?'

Lily shook her head. 'No. I didn't bother because I was so determined not to go in.'

Nick slid an arm around her shoulders. 'It'll be all right, babe,' he said firmly, giving Oliver a nod. 'If Dr Hunter trusts his brother, so should we. I'll pack you a bag and I'll follow you to the hospital as soon as your mother arrives.'

Tom Hunter met them in the labour ward. Dressed in

green theatre scrubs, he looked broad-shouldered and handsome, a more serious version of his brother.

'Hello, Lily.' He smiled at his patient, his voice surprisingly gentle. 'I gather you had a rotten time of it when you had your last child. Let's try and do better, shall we?' He lifted his eyebrow towards his brother. 'Need my help, do you Oliver?'

'Someone's got to keep your ego intact,' Oliver replied smoothly, winking at Lily. 'You'd better look after my patient or you'll have me to deal with.'

'Very professional, I'm sure.' Tom jerked his head towards a midwife who was hovering. 'Emma, can you settle Lily in, please? I'll be there in five minutes.'

Oliver turned to Lily and gave her a smile. 'You're going to be fine,' he said firmly. 'I'll see you soon.'

Emma took them down the corridor and Tom looked at Oliver. 'That woman should never have been promised a home delivery.'

Oliver met his gaze full on. 'She's seriously terrified, Tom. It was the only reason I was given access to her house. She's only been in the area for a month. I've promised her that you're the best and nothing will go wrong.'

'No pressure, then,' Tom drawled, taking a chart from a hovering midwife. 'Obstetrics is nothing if not unpredictable, as you well know. Promising a fairy-tale birth might not have been the best approach.'

'You would have rather she bolted the door from the inside and did it by herself?' Oliver's tone was hard. 'Because that's what she would have done, Tom. And she doesn't need a fairy-tale. She just needs to feel that there's someone she can trust. The last guy didn't even speak to her.'

Tom winced. 'Weird, these southerners.' He checked the chart and handed it back to the midwife with a nod. 'That's fine. Call Rob and ask him to come up here, will you? I'm going to be tied up with Lily.'

Oliver let out a sigh of relief. 'You're going to deliver her yourself? Do you promise?'

'I'm not a midwife,' Tom said mildly. 'I'm the guy who steps in when things go wrong. You'd be better with a midwife.'

Oliver shook his head. 'You've got the best instincts of any doctor I've met. If you keep an eye on her all the way through, nothing is going to go wrong.'

Something flickered in Tom's eyes as he looked at his brother. 'Your faith in me is touching.'

'You're the best.' Oliver gave a lopsided smile. 'Arrogant, smug, stubborn and totally self-absorbed, but still the best when it comes to delivering babies.'

Tom laughed. 'I can live with that.' His gaze flickered to Helen and his eyes gleamed wickedly. 'How's your roof coming along, Oliver?'

'Slowly.'

'Of course it is.' For some reason that Helen couldn't fathom, Tom's smile widened and he clapped his brother on the shoulder again. 'All right, I'm off to give your Lily the dream delivery. You owe me a pint. I'll meet you in the pub tomorrow night.'

'Done.'

They left the hospital and drove back to the cottage. Oliver was strangely silent and Helen wondered if he was worrying about Lily.

Or was he thinking about that kiss?

Remembering his promise that they were going to talk about it, Helen was suddenly anxious to delay their arrival home.

She didn't want to have the conversation. She didn't know what she was going to say.

'So your brother doesn't approve of home deliveries?' Perhaps if she kept to work, they could both forget about that kiss.

'Of course not.' Oliver's smile was wry. 'He's an obstetrician. He thinks every birth should take place in a hospital no matter what.'

'And you don't agree?'

He gave a shrug. 'I think a proportion of women are perfectly safe delivering at home providing they understand that in certain circumstances they might need a rapid transfer to hospital. In fact, for some women I think it is definitely the preferred option.'

'Like Lily.'

He pulled a face, his expression troubled. 'Not like Lily, actually. Tom's right. She was always a terrible candidate for home birth, but hers is a classic example of the theory not working in practice. On paper she should definitely have been booked for a hospital delivery, but nowhere on paper does it say how severely traumatised the girl was by her first delivery.'

'Why did she have such a bad experience? Were they negligent?'

'Evidently she had a locum doctor who couldn't be bothered or else wasn't sufficiently experienced. Either way he was very heavy-handed with the forceps and made a terrible mess of her insides. When they first moved here they were refusing any medical help at all.'

'Do you think she'll be OK?'

'Providing Tom doesn't get called away to deal with anything urgent, yes.' Oliver smiled. 'My brother is an amazing obstetrician. He's Mr Super-Cool. You should see him in a crisis. He delivered Ellie, the staff nurse who leant you the uniform—Ben's wife. She had a car accident just before Christmas when she was eight months pregnant. Jack and Tom were both amazing. And Tom's always the same. I think he thrives on crisis. While everyone around him is panicking he barely flickers an eyelid. I'll give him a call later and see how Lily is getting on.'

He pulled up outside the cottage and switched off the engine. For a moment he sat still, staring into the darkness, and then he turned to look at her and tension throbbed between them.

'Helen, we need to talk about what's happening between us.'

Her heart stumbled in her chest. 'Nothing's happening, Oliver. It can't be.'

'Why not?'

'Because five weeks ago I was marrying another man.' But she had to admit that she was thinking less and less of David. Everything had started to blur in her mind. 'It's too soon—we don't even know each other.'

'Yes, we do,' he said softly, sliding a hand behind her head and gently turning her face to his. 'We do know each other, Helen.'

She closed her eyes briefly and shook her head. 'You've been so kind to me. Without you I would have fallen apart.'

Oliver lifted an eyebrow. 'You're suggesting that that episode on the kitchen table was gratitude?'

His voice was husky and masculine and she felt a shiver of excitement pass through her body.

What did this man do to her?

She flushed. 'I can't believe I behaved like that.'

'Well, you did,' Oliver said softly, 'and since it's obvious that you're not in the habit of indulging in rampant sex on the kitchen table I think that should tell you something about the strength of the attraction between us, don't you?'

She stared at him helplessly. 'I don't know what I'm feeling.' She bit her lip. It would have been so tempting to just fall into his arms and take their relationship to its natural conclusion. But she couldn't do that. Not when everything seemed so muddled. 'I can't promise you anything, Oliver. I'm afraid I'll hurt you.'

'That's my problem.'

'No, it isn't. I would never want to hurt you.' She flushed. 'This just isn't the way things happen. I can't be about to marry one man and then—'

'And then fall for another?' Oliver's voice was soft as he finished her sentence. 'Why not?'

'Well, for a start because we haven't met during normal circumstances. We haven't had a normal relationship.'

There was a hint of amusement in his eyes. 'What's a normal relationship?'

She shrugged helplessly. 'Well, dating, I suppose. Getting to know each other. I went out with David for six years.'

The amusement faded. 'I don't need six years to know

that you're the woman for me, Helen. I knew within six seconds.'

His words made her gasp and her heart almost stopped beating. 'Oliver...'

He couldn't possibly mean that.

'Look...' He gave a sigh and slid his fingers through her hair. 'I know that you still haven't sorted out how you feel about David. But sooner or later you're going to realise that he did you a favour. Not the way he did it—that was cruel and cowardly—but what he did. And I happen to think that what you feel for me is real. But I'll hang around while you find that out for yourself and if dating is important to you, then we'll date.'

She was breathlessly aware of every powerful inch of him. 'You said that living and working with me was driving you nuts.'

'And I can think of a very good way of relieving that frustration.' He flashed her a wicked smile. 'But I'm just a simple mountain man. If dating is what it takes then dating is what we'll do. Tomorrow night is quiz night at the Drunken Fox. The pinnacle of our monthly social calendar up here in the wilds. Most of the mountain rescue team should be there. It will rival anything you have in London, city girl.'

At the moment nothing was further from her mind than London.

All she could think about was Oliver. The lazy, sexy look he was giving her from underneath thick, dark lashes, the way a tiny dimple appeared in the corner of his mouth when he smiled.

The way his mouth hovered tantalisingly close to hers.

Her breathing was shallow. He was so close that the temptation just to lift her mouth to his and finish what they'd started was enormous.

'I don't feel like a city girl any more.'

He gave a slow smile that was so unbelievably sexy that she felt her tummy tumble. 'Oh, dear,' he said softly, touching her cheek with his finger. 'In that case, it wouldn't be safe to let you go back to London. The big city is no place for a girl from the country.'

Helen chuckled but there was no escaping the fact that soon she would have to make a decision. She'd been given a month to drift. A month in which Bryony had given her a home and Oliver had given her a job. But that month was up in another week.

And she needed to make a decision about what she was going to do with her life.

Tom dropped by the following morning while they were having breakfast to tell them that Lily had given birth to a little girl in the early hours of the morning.

'Tell me she was OK.' Oliver's expression was strained and Tom gave a long sigh.

'She was fine.' He yawned. 'I was there, wasn't I?'

'You didn't need to section her?'

Tom frowned. 'Why is everyone so obsessed with Caesarian sections these days? Believe it or not, women actually are designed to give birth, you know.' He helped himself to a mug from the cupboard and poured himself a coffee.

'So what happened?'

'You want a report on each contraction?'

Oliver rubbed a hand over the back of his neck and gave a wry smile. 'Am I that bad?'

'Yes.' Tom pulled out a chair and straddled it. 'But I forgive you because it's true that Lily was in a bad state, emotionally at least. She actually did have some damage from the previous delivery and it did cross my mind that I might have to section her, but she was so traumatised by the fact she felt so out of control last time that I decided to take a risk.'

'Her scar could have opened up.'

'In which case I would have repaired it,' Tom said calmly. 'As it is, Emma and I put her in the birthing pool, played her some music, kept her calm and she did it all by herself. Very relaxed. The sort of birth they have in the movies. You would have approved.'

Oliver looked at his brother. 'You stayed with her the whole time.'

'That was your request, I believe,' Tom drawled, leaning forward and helping himself to a piece of toast. 'I'll send you my bill.'

'How did you manage to not get called away? You always get called to handle the difficult stuff. Or wasn't there any difficult stuff?'

'There's always difficult stuff in obstetrics,' Tom said dryly. 'Babies insist on doing the unexpected instead of coming down the right route facing the right way. Last night I delegated. I happened to agree with you that Lily was important. And, actually, my registrar is showing a great deal of promise, which helps.'

'Well, thanks.' Oliver gave his brother a nod, his blue eyes warm. 'I'll buy you a drink tonight.'

'You will indeed.' Tom rose to his feet and reached for his jacket. 'I'm off. I just popped in to tell you about Lily.'

'What are you doing today?'

'Climbing. Ben and I are going together. Ellie has given him time off for good behaviour.'

Oliver grinned. 'Don't fall. I don't want to have to come out and rescue you.'

'Don't push your luck, bro.' Tom nodded to Helen in a friendly way and walked towards the door. 'By the way...' He turned back to Oliver, his eyes gleaming slightly. 'Isn't that roof of yours finished by now?'

Oliver smiled. 'It's coming along well,' he said softly. 'Very well indeed.'

'Glad to hear it because I'm sure I don't need to remind you that Bryony and Jack are back next Saturday.' His eyes flicked to Helen and she smiled.

'I know. It's decision-making time. Find somewhere to live or go back to London.'

Tom looked at her for a long moment. 'I'm sure you wouldn't have any trouble finding somewhere to live if you decide to stay.' He transferred his gaze to his brother. 'I'll see you tonight.'

He walked out and Oliver looked at Helen. 'The sun is shining, the sky is blue and there's snow on the ground. Fancy a walk?'

She nodded. 'It's been a busy week. I was hoping you'd suggest it.'

'Let's get going, then.'

They walked in companionable silence, their footsteps muffled by the snow, the air still and calm.

When they finally stopped for a rest, their breath clouded the freezing air.

Oliver stared up at the sky with a frown. 'The weather is closing in. We should probably turn back soon.' He pulled a flask out of the rucksack and poured them both a drink. He handed a cup to Helen and then muttered under his breath as his mobile phone went off. 'Here…' He handed her his mug, too. 'Hold this for a sec, will you, please?'

While he answered the phone, Helen glanced up at the sky, too. When they'd started out they'd been able to see the tops of all the peaks. Now they were shrouded in mist.

Suddenly she gave a little shiver, relieved that she was with Oliver. It was frightening how quickly the weather could change in the mountains.

Oliver was talking on the phone, screwing up his face slightly as he tried to decipher the crackle. 'You're not very clear.' He listened again and then nodded. 'That's better. OK, where is he?' There was another silence and then Oliver turned and glanced up the path. 'We're about half an hour from there.'

Helen felt herself tense. It was obviously a call from the mountain rescue centre. Was someone in trouble?

Oliver was still listening. 'We can be there faster than that. OK, send them, and I'll give you a call when we find him.'

He snapped the phone shut and retrieved his drink from Helen's fingers. Then he poured it carefully back into the flask, untouched.

'We might be needing this,' he muttered. 'A guy used his mobile phone to call the team. He was slurring his words and not making much sense. He wasn't that coherent and he couldn't be precise about his position, but Angie, who runs the bed and breakfast at the bottom of the valley, says he was seen heading up here first thing this morning. Apparently he's been staying with her for a few days on his own. He's in his fifties and overweight.'

'I hope he hasn't had a heart attack up here. He won't stand a chance, surely?' Helen quickly handed him her drink as well. 'I gather you want to try and find him yourself?'

Oliver let out a long breath. 'Well, they're sending the team out of course, but we're already halfway up his last known route so it seems sensible that we're the advance party. Do you mind? If he is where they think he should be then we can get to him quickly. In this weather time can make the difference between life and death. And I wouldn't do it if I thought there was any risk to you.'

He stroked a hand gently over her cheek and Helen felt her heart turn over.

She couldn't remember anyone ever making her feel so cared for.

She smiled. 'Of course we must go.' Even as she said the words, nerves fluttered in her stomach. She just hoped she didn't let him down.

She watched as he repacked his rucksack and lifted it onto his broad shoulders, trying not to think about the fact that the weather was closing in and fingers of cold were reaching inside her weatherproof jacket.

'That's my girl.' Oliver grinned and his eyes were warm with approval. 'Time to prove yourself, townie. We've been walking for the best part of three hours. It'll take a while for the rest of the team to assemble at base and then get themselves up here. So we're the advance party.'

Helen glanced at him. 'Just remember that I don't know anything about mountain rescue.'

'I'm the mountain rescue bit,' Oliver assured her firmly. 'You're my first-aid partner and general helper. If that man is having a heart attack in the mountains, I'm going to need your help.'

Helen peered doubtfully through the mist, wondering how steep the path became, and as if reading her mind Oliver reached into the rucksack and pulled out some gear.

'There is a bit of a drop up here,' he said honestly, 'but you won't be able to see it because of the mist. Just to make you feel safe, I'm going to clip a rope to you and attach it to myself. OK?'

More than OK.

Helen felt his strong hands fiddle with something at her waist and he jerked straps and adjusted buckles until he finally gave a grunt of satisfaction and clipped a rope to her.

This time Oliver walked with a sense of purpose, his pace steady as they climbed through the mist. Every now and then he stopped and checked their position and Helen stood still, not wanting to distract him and trying not to look over the edge. Because by now there was definitely an edge and she didn't want think about the drop.

'Footprints.' Oliver squatted down for a moment and then straightened. 'Could be his. On the other hand, it hasn't snowed for a couple of days so they could belong to someone else.'

His words were swallowed up by the roar of the waterfall that crashed down next to them and Helen winced as she felt the freezing spray on her face.

'It's really hard to make yourself heard here because of the noise of the waterfall,' Oliver shouted. 'It's virtually non-existent in summer but in the winter it powers down the mountain like a damn with a leak.' He broke off and his jaw tightened. 'Apparently, when he called, they could hear the falls in the background so he must be up this path somewhere if he took a direct route from the bed and breakfast.'

Helen squinted into the mist. 'Could he be the other side of the ghyll?'

Oliver shook his head. 'That's definitely not a tourist route. We'll carry on up here. My guess is we'll find him on this path. I reckon those are probably his footprints.'

But there was no sign of anyone and Oliver's loud calls were virtually drowned by the sound of torrents of water thundering against the rocks.

His expression was grim and he glanced up the path. 'Come on, let's get going. We need to be a bit higher up.'

Higher up?

Helen took a deep breath and told herself that it wasn't possible to be afraid of heights if the mist was concealing the drop. That would be too stupid for words. She just needed to look at Oliver instead of the edge.

So she fixed her eyes on his broad shoulders and made a point of stepping where he stepped.

And then Oliver stopped dead, his gaze fixed on the snowy path.

Helen followed his line of vision. 'What's the matter?'

'Well, the footprints end here—the snow looks crushed.

As if someone fell.' He bent down and touched it with his glove, a frown on his handsome face. 'And some of the snow has been knocked off the edge…'

Realising what he was suggesting, Helen stared at him in horror. 'You think he fell?'

'He was certainly alive when he made the call.' Oliver straightened up, pulled her back away from the edge and unclipped her rope.

'Stand there and don't move,' he said firmly. 'You'll be fine. I just want to see if I can spot him. He may not be there at all, of course, but I have this feeling—'

He removed his rucksack and Helen watched while he pulled out a rope and various other bits and pieces that she couldn't identify.

Then he walked towards the edge and shouted something.

Helen strained her ears to see if she could hear a reply but the roar of the water was almost deafening.

Oliver suddenly vanished from sight and Helen felt her heart lurch. Without his reassuring presence the mountains suddenly seemed less welcoming. She glanced around her but the mist created an unnerving stillness that made her shiver.

She looked hopefully towards the edge again but there was no sign of Oliver.

There was no point in shouting because she knew he couldn't hear her so she stayed where she was for a few more minutes and then gingerly inched towards the edge.

Telling herself that he might need her help, Helen forced herself forwards until she could peer into the ghyll. The mist prevented her from seeing very far and the roar of the water was almost deafening. Huge rocks loomed into her vision, shiny from the spray of water and interspersed with patches of frozen snow. And finally she saw Oliver below her, balanced on a rock, holding onto the body of a man.

At first Helen thought the man must be unconscious but then she saw him move and felt a flood of relief.

At least they weren't dealing with a body.

She watched in horror as Oliver dragged the slumped figure as far away from the edge as possible, his face damp from the spray of the water.

She closed her eyes briefly, forcing herself to face the inevitable. It was perfectly obvious that he needed help and the only help available was her. Which meant going down the rock to him.

Could she do that?

She stared down at the glistening surface and decided that there seemed to be quite a few handholds.

Without allowing time for her fright to grow any further, she took a deep breath and turned around, lowering herself gingerly over the rock. At least it was misty so she couldn't see the extent of the drop.

Trying to ignore the biting cold, she moved slowly, lowering herself carefully, only moving a hand when she was sure that both feet were firmly placed on something solid. Once she slipped and her insides dropped with fear until she felt her feet once more rest safely on the rock.

Her heart still pounding ridiculously fast, she risked a hesitant glance downwards and for a brief moment the mist cleared, showing her the steep, vertiginous drop to the bottom.

Oh, dear God...

Her vision blurred and she closed her eyes immediately, clinging to the rock as panic swamped her usually rational brain.

'It's all right, angel, I've got you.' Oliver's voice, firm and masculine, came from right underneath her. The next moment he was next to her, one strong arm fastened firmly around her waist, securing her to the rock. 'I've got you, sweetheart. You're not going to fall. Take a few deep breaths and don't look down.'

He felt solid and safe and Helen felt herself relax slightly.

Then she remembered what was below her.

'I know I'm being pathetic, but I don't think I can move, Oliver,' she said shakily, hating herself for being so useless but horribly aware of the vicious drop that lay below them.

'I don't want you to move until I tell you to.'

She felt his hand at her waist. Felt him clip a rope onto her harness. But mostly she felt him, warm and amazingly reassuring right behind her. He was like a safety blanket between her and terror.

'Good girl. You've been very brave,' he murmured in her ear. 'And I'm glad you did it because I need your help. This man needs your help. You're almost down, Helen. Just a few more steps and you're there.'

Her eyes were still tightly shut. 'I can't do it—I'm going to fall.'

'You're not going to fall. You're attached to me and I have no intention of going anywhere.' He gave her shoulder a final squeeze and then moved his arm. 'I'm going to go first, and then I'm going to tell you where to put your hands and feet. Just do exactly what I say.'

He did just that and she climbed down the rest of the

way like a robot, following his instructions, taking his hand whenever he offered it.

And finally she was safe.

If standing on an exposed rock, facing a furious waterfall could be described as safe.

Trying not to think about it, Helen gradually released her grip on Oliver's hand.

'OK—brilliant. Now, don't go near the edge because it's slippery.'

Helen managed a smile. 'Oliver, you don't need to tell me not to go near the edge,' she said and he grinned in return.

'Maybe I don't. In that case, let's see what we can do to help this chap. I've told the team where we are. Some of them should be here pretty shortly. He's conscious but only just. I haven't had a chance to have a proper look at him yet.'

The man was slumped against the rock, his eyes glazed. He tried to say something but his words slurred together. He gave a groan and his eyes drifted shut.

'Apparently his name is Brian Andrews. Can you hear me, Mr Andrews?' Oliver tried to rouse the man who opened his eyes with what seemed to be a supreme effort. 'Brian? I'm a doctor. Can you talk to me? Are you in pain?'

The man mumbled something incomprehensible and knocked Oliver's hand away when he tried to take his pulse.

'Whoa. Calm down—we're here to help you.' Oliver backed off slightly and Helen dropped to her knees beside him, anxious to help.

'Do you have any pain, Mr Andrews?' Her voice was

soft and gentle and the man turned his head towards her, his eyes glazed as he tried to focus.

'Need to go home.' He swung his arms wildly and tried to get up, but Oliver restrained him.

'You need to keep as still ask you can for a moment,' he advised. 'There's a steep drop down there.'

The man swung his arms again and Helen looked at Oliver in confusion.

'Why is he behaving like this when we're trying to help him?' she asked, her eyes swivelling back to the man. 'He's very pale and sweaty.'

'Yeah. I need to examine him.'

But it didn't look as though that was going to be a possibility. The man snarled at them aggressively and suddenly he reminded Helen of a patient she'd once treated.

She gave a soft gasp. 'Oliver, do we have any hot chocolate left in that flask?'

'Yes.' His eyes lifted to hers as he interpreted the reason for her question. 'You think he's diabetic?'

'I don't know. But his symptoms remind me of a patient I nursed once. Everyone thought he was drunk but he was hypoglycaemic. He was slurring his words like this and he was sweaty and pale. And I seem to remember that he was also pretty irritable.'

Oliver took another look at the man and gave a short laugh. 'Well, it's certainly worth a try.' Rocking back on his heels, he delved into the rucksack and pulled out the flask. 'I hope you're right. See if you can find some sort of SOS bracelet or any medication on him.'

Helen leaned forward, her voice gentle. 'Are you a diabetic, Mr Andrews?' She spoke soothingly to the man, her fingers rolling back the sleeves of his jacket as she searched for clues. This time the man lay unresisting. 'No bracelet, no chain, nothing. But his pulse is very fast. I'm sure he's a diabetic, Oliver.'

Oliver nodded. 'I'm beginning to agree with you and we're definitely going to give it a try. There's not much else we can do until the team arrives anyway. We can't get him off this rock by ourselves. All right, give me a hand to hold him while I get him to drink this. We're lucky. Any longer and he wouldn't have been in a state to eat anything, and I'm not in the habit of carrying injectable glucose when I go for a walk.'

They propped the man in a sitting position and then Oliver poured a small amount of their hot chocolate into a plastic mug.

'Make sure it isn't too hot,' Helen warned anxiously, and Oliver tested the liquid quickly.

'It's fine. It's not going to burn anyone. Just very sweet, which is exactly what he needs if his problem is what you think it is. He needs fast-acting oral carbohydrate.'

Helen bit her lip, her heart thudding hard against her chest. She hoped desperately that she was right.

But surely, if he was a diabetic, the man would have been wearing a bracelet?

'Can you drink this for me?' Oliver murmured, pressing the cup to the man's lips and encouraging him to take sips. 'That's great. And more if you can. That's it. I think this is going to help.'

Oliver persisted until the mug was empty and then turned to Helen. 'There's some chocolate in the front pocket of my rucksack. Let's give him that, too.'

It was a slow process but gradually the man cooperated and ate the chocolate and his condition started to improve markedly.

Fifteen minutes after they'd given him the hot chocolate he was able to talk clearly. 'Thanks.' He wiped a shaking hand across his mouth. 'I seem to have got myself in a spot of trouble...'

Helen shot Oliver an incredulous glance. As understatements went, it was impressive. The man had been incredibly lucky. Had they not been in the area he might have died before help had arrived.

'You're a diabetic,' Helen said gently, 'but I couldn't find a bracelet or anything to tell us that.'

The man's eyes drifted shut and he let out a long breath. 'Don't want to be labelled,' he muttered, shaking his head slightly. 'Don't want it to interfere with my life. Just want to get on and do the things I've always done.'

'Right.' Oliver ran a hand over the back of his neck. 'Well, you can do most of the things you've always done, providing you control your blood sugar properly. You've just done a fairly strenuous walk. Did you bring food with you?'

The man shook his head. 'Didn't plan to be out that long.'

'You were suffering from something called hypoglycaemia,' Oliver explained, 'which basically means that your blood sugar was dangerously low. It usually happens when you take more exercise than you were planning or when you delay a meal. Or sometimes if you give yourself too much insulin. Presumably you attend a diabetic clinic?'

The man gave a grunt. 'Load of bloody busybodies—always telling you what to do and checking up on you.'

'They're trying to help you control your diabetes,' Helen said gently, giving his hand a squeeze, but he brushed her hand away.

'I can control it by myself.'

Helen opened her mouth to speak but Oliver caught her eye and gave a discreet shake of his head.

'All right.' His voice was calm and even. 'Well, you're clearly feeling better in yourself but you had quite a fall. You obviously lost your balance on the path and managed to tumble down here. It's amazing that you didn't fall all the way to the bottom. Are you hurting anywhere?'

The man struggled to his feet, brushing away all offers of help. 'No. I'm fine. I just went for a stroll and I started to feel dizzy.'

At that moment there was a shout from above and Sean Nicholson, the A and E consultant, abseiled quickly down a rope, landing neatly next to them.

Helen stared at him in awe, remembering how long it had taken her to climb down that same route.

'I've never seen anyone do that before.' She smiled at him in admiration. 'I must say it looked a great deal more entertaining than clinging to slippery rocks with finger-nails, which was my experience.'

Oliver winked and took some equipment from Sean. 'Hell on the nail varnish, don't you find, Sean?'

'Nightmare. That's why I chose the easy route. Good afternoon, Mr Andrews.' Sean gave the patient a friendly nod, listening while Oliver related what had happened.

'If you're going to nag me, then please don't bother,' the man said grumpily and Sean frowned slightly.

'My job is just to get you down safely from this mountain,' he said smoothly. 'And to recommend that you get yourself checked out at the hospital before you carry on with your holiday.' He glanced at Helen and then looked at Oliver. 'You two should probably make a move. Helen's looking cold. We can manage here easily enough now. You've done the hard bit.'

And Helen realised that she was actually freezing.

Sitting still on that rock, the chill had suddenly penetrated her bones and she started to shiver.

'Oliver…' A disturbing thought had struck her and she glanced upwards, a horrified expression on her face. 'Am I going to have to climb back up the way I came down?'

'No. From this point it's quicker to carry on to the bottom,' Sean said immediately. 'You turn right and meet up with the path. Oliver knows the way.'

'Down?'

Remembering the drop, she glanced at them in horror.

'Sean's right,' Oliver said quickly, fastening his rucksack and swinging it onto his back. 'It isn't far from here. You've done the worst bit.'

Without giving her time to brood, he clipped a rope to her waist, gave her harness a tug and guided her towards the edge of the rocks.

The sound of the waterfall was so loud they could hardly make themselves heard and Oliver glanced back at Sean who was coordinating with the rest of the team.

'Drunken Fox, tonight?'

Sean grinned. 'You're buying.'

Oliver went first and then guided Helen down until finally they reached the bottom and picked up the path.

'How long will it take them to get him off the mountain?' Helen asked, tugging her hood up to protect her head from the steadily falling snow. 'Will they be all right?'

Oliver glanced at her in amusement. 'They'll be fine. And it shouldn't take them long. Couple of hours?'

'And then what?' Helen frowned as she huddled deeper inside her coat. 'He's obviously determined to ignore his disease. Will they try and persuade him to take it more seriously?'

'Helen, we're the mountain rescue team,' Oliver reminded her gently. 'We rescue people from mountains. It's not our job to sort out the rest of their lives, however much we might like to. Sean will try and persuade him to go to hospital to be checked and he'll certainly tell him that he needs to see his GP, but after that it's out of our hands.'

'Well, it was a very exciting walk. And I must admit I was shocked by how quickly the mist came down,' Helen said with a shudder. 'One minute we had virtually blue skies, the next we could barely see. But that might have been a good thing, I suppose. If I'd been able to see all the way to the bottom of that ghyll I never would have plucked up the courage to climb over those rocks.'

They reached the car and Oliver shrugged the rucksack off his back.

'You were great. I would never have known you were born and bred in the city.'

Helen stood still, her eyes on the mountains that she was steadily growing to love. 'It's going to be really hard to leave.'

Oliver heaved his rucksack into the boot, slammed it shut and turned to face her. 'Then don't.' His voice was hoarse. 'Don't leave, Helen. Stay.'

He cupped her face in his hands and lowered his mouth to hers, his kiss so hot and urgent that she felt flames reach up from deep within and devour her self-control.

She felt the erotic lick of his tongue, felt his strong hands drawing her against him, felt the flash of energy and passion that exploded between them.

With the temperature dropping rapidly, she should have felt cold, but all she felt was warmth.

When he finally eased away from her, she felt bereft and looked at him in disbelief and confusion.

How could he bring an end to something so perfect?

'It will be dark soon. We need to get home.'

Helen hid her disappointment, uncomfortably aware that she wouldn't have been able to end that kiss even if an avalanche had engulfed them both.

'Right...' She tried to look suitably indifferent. As if kisses like that came and went all the time.

He gave a humourless laugh and ran a hand over the back of her neck. 'If you're for one moment thinking that I found it easy to stop that kiss, there's something I ought to tell you.' He curved a hand under her chin and forced her to look at him. 'Next time I kiss you, townie, I'm not stopping.'

CHAPTER NINETEEN

THE Drunken Fox was crowded with people that evening, but for Helen there was only Oliver.

She couldn't remember ever being so aware of a man.

They'd finished their walk in virtual silence and when they'd arrived back at the cottage, Oliver had pushed her gently towards the stairs.

'You have the first shower,' he'd said gruffly. 'We're going out in less than an hour.'

And now they were both in the pub and all Helen could think about was going home again.

Realising that in just a few hours they would be alone in the cottage together with no threat of interruptions, Helen felt her tummy tumble with a mixture of nerves and anticipation.

Oliver had made it perfectly clear that he wanted their relationship to go all the way.

Did she?

From the moment they'd entered the pub, Oliver hadn't strayed from her side, and even now she could feel the brush of his muscular shoulder against hers as he lounged casually against the bar, chatting to Tom.

It came as no surprise that he seemed to know everyone in the pub, and after three weeks in the Lake District Helen was starting to get used to the fact that everyone seemed to know everyone else's business. And she liked it. Liked the fact that people cared about each other.

She glanced around the cosy pub, loving the warm, intimate atmosphere created by a flickering log fire and a bunch of people who clearly knew each other extremely well. It smelt of wood smoke and welcome, a place to relax after a hard day.

She felt Oliver's arm slide around her waist, trapping her against him as he stood chatting to his brother at the bar.

He was wearing a pair of worn jeans that moulded themselves perfectly to the hard muscle of his thighs and a soft wool jumper that emphasised the breadth and power of his shoulders.

He looked so sexy and male that she was finding it hard to breathe.

And he seemed so relaxed it was hard to believe that he was the same man who'd kissed her breathless earlier.

Perhaps he'd changed his mind about the way he felt.

And then he turned to say something to her and something in his gaze made her realise that he wasn't relaxed at all. And he certainly hadn't changed his mind.

He was biding his time.

So it came as no surprise when he finally looked at his watch and reached for his jacket.

'Time to go home,' he said easily, taking her hand and nodding to his brother. 'See you tomorrow.'

Still holding her hand tightly, he led her out of the pub and they walked to his car.

They drove home in silence and by the time he finally pulled up outside Bryony's cottage, the tension between them had reached an almost intolerable level.

Oliver switched off the engine and stared into the darkness for a moment.

Then he turned and his eyes burned into hers. 'Helen, we both know what's going to happen once we walk inside that door so if this isn't what you want...'

Delicious, forbidden excitement squirmed low in her stomach and suddenly she found the answer she'd been searching for. 'It's what I want.'

She didn't understand why, but Helen had moved beyond trying to understand what it was that she felt for Oliver.

'Then let's go inside.'

He unlocked the door of the cottage but instead of putting on the lights he walked straight through to the cosy living room.

'Oliver?' She followed him through, stopping in the doorway as she realised that the room was full of candles. And Oliver already had half of them alight.

He must have set them up before they left for the evening and she hadn't even noticed.

The flickering light gave a seductive, mysterious glow and Helen watched as he lit the log fire.

She was still wearing her coat and he crossed the room towards her and slid it from her shoulders, his eyes holding hers.

'I happen to love this room, but if you're cold then we can go upstairs...'

'I'm not cold.'

'You're shivering.'

'That's not because I'm cold.' She closed her eyes, aware that his clever fingers were making short work of the tiny buttons on her cardigan.

'So why are you shivering?' His voice was low and husky and she felt the seductive brush of his fingers against her flesh and suddenly she was standing there in only her lacy bra and her jeans. 'Why, Helen?'

She swallowed, her heart pounding as she stared up at him. 'Because I want you. But I'm scared, Oliver.'

His hands stilled. 'Scared?'

'Scared of hurting you.' Her voice was a whisper. 'I don't know what I want. I don't—'

'Shh…' He covered her lips with a gentle finger. 'No more talking.'

And just to make doubly sure that she couldn't talk, he lowered his mouth to hers.

And his kiss snapped the last of her feeble resistance.

Stifled by sexual anticipation, her heart thudding out of control, Helen lifted her hands to his jumper and instantly he took over, dragging his mouth away from hers and stripping himself naked to the waist.

Her pulse rocketed and her breathing stopped. For the past few weeks she seemed to have become more and more aware of Oliver's body but even those increasingly frequent glances hadn't prepared her for the reality. And she hadn't known it was possible to want a man with such fierce desperation.

Her eyes slid down his muscular chest, following the line of curling dark hairs that trailed downwards and vanished under the waistband of his jeans. And then her gaze slid lower still to the very visible evidence of his erection straining against the unforgiving fabric.

'See what you do to me?' He slid a strong hand behind her head, sliding his fingers into the softness of her hair and holding her firmly. 'You've been doing that to me since the first moment I saw you.'

Without giving her a chance to reply, he guided her head towards him and met her halfway, his mouth descending on hers with hot, restless purpose.

Wild, intoxicating excitement exploded inside her and she kissed him back, exchanging bite for bite and lick for lick. He tortured with his mouth and teased with his hands until she realised that somehow they were both naked.

Without stopping to wonder how he'd accomplished that without her noticing, Helen pressed closer to him, shivering at the first touch of his flesh against hers.

She felt warmth and heat and pounding excitement and then he scooped her off her feet and carried her to the rug in front of the fire.

He lowered her gently and then came down on top of her and she sobbed with pleasure as she felt the solid weight of his body on hers, felt his skilled, clever fingers seeking the burning heat of her femininity.

He muttered something into her hair and then slid down her quivering, writhing body and fastened his mouth on her breast. The skilled flick of his tongue over her already hardened nipple made her gasp and arch against him and she dug her nails into the hard muscle of his shoulders, tortured by sensation.

His fingers explored her intimately but it wasn't enough and she sobbed his name in a plea for more.

He lifted his head, his gaze burning into hers. 'What?'

'Please, Oliver...' Her voice sounded broken and she slid one hand down his body and closed her slender fingers over his pulsing arousal. 'Please, now...'

His gaze darkened and his breathing became harsh and rapid as he slid an arm under hips. 'Look at me Helen, I want you to look at me.'

Didn't he know that she wasn't capable of anything else? At that precise moment she wanted to spend the rest of her life drowning in Oliver's blue gaze, feeling the heat of his body on hers.

With a flicker of delicious anticipation she felt the hard throb of his erection touching her intimately and then he entered her with a powerful thrust, driven by the almost intolerable need that consumed both of them.

Her vision blurred and she shuddered as she felt him thrust again, felt his strength and power deep within her. Her muscles tensed and then rippled, drawing him in.

'Don't move,' he pleaded hoarsely, his breathing fractured as he struggled for control. 'Just stay still for a minute.'

But she couldn't stay still. She shifted under him, rotating her hips, and he groaned and thrust deep in response to her provocative movements, losing the battle he'd been fighting for control.

And still their gazes held. Held as they moved together, held as their flesh grew slick and damp and held as he drove them both to a climax so intense and all-consuming that Helen forgot about everything except Oliver.

For a single, breathless moment in time she belonged to him.

She was part of him.

And finally he closed his eyes and buried his face in her hair.

'I love you, Helen.'

His soft words brought a gasp to her throat and tears to her eyes. She opened her mouth to say the words back to him but no sound emerged.

It had felt so special but she couldn't work out why.

What was the magic ingredient? Why had it felt so different?

'Oliver...'

He lifted his head and kissed her gently, a wry smile of understanding in his blue eyes. 'It's all right—I know it's all too soon for you.'

So why was she lying underneath him feeling as though she never, ever wanted to move?

Helen nursed a cup of coffee and stared out of the kitchen window towards the mountains, wondering how everything in her life could have changed so much in just three weeks.

Her aching body was a delicious reminder of the night before and she ran a hand from her waist to her hips, as if aware of herself for the first time.

I love you.

She closed her eyes briefly, reliving the moment when he'd said those words with a thrill of excitement.

And then she remembered David.

David had said those words, too. Just before he'd caught a plane to Singapore with another woman.

Words were, after all, just words. Anyone could say them. Especially when sharing the intimacies that she and Oliver had the night before.

If David hadn't meant those words after six years, how could she expect Oliver to after only three weeks? No one fell in love in three weeks. It wasn't possible. Love needed time to grow.

She was still brooding when there was a loud knock on the door.

Assuming it would be Tom, Helen put down her coffee and walked quickly to the door, opening it with a smile on her face.

David stood there.

Helen's smile faded and emotion rushed through her with the force of a tornado.

Something must have shown on her face because he gave a slight grimace and ran a hand through his hair. 'If you're going to hit me, perhaps you'd better do it now and get it over with. But at least let me talk. I've been driving all night.'

Noticing that he was wearing a thin suit and footwear totally unsuitable for the weather, Helen stood to one side.

It didn't occur to her that three weeks previously she wouldn't have noticed such a thing.

'You'd better come in before you freeze.' Her voice was strangely flat. Five weeks ago all she'd wanted had been the opportunity to talk to David. To find out why he'd done what he had. Now she couldn't remember what it was she'd wanted to say to him.

He walked past her into the cottage and paused in the hallway. 'Helen...'

'Let's go into the kitchen,' she said quickly, glancing anxiously towards the stairs. For some reason it seemed extremely important that Oliver didn't come downstairs yet. At some point during the night the fire had gone out and they'd moved to the bedroom.

And Oliver was still asleep...

David frowned slightly but shrugged and followed her through to the kitchen, his expression wary as she turned to face him.

'I'm going to come straight to the point.' He gave her that lopsided smile that she'd once found so attractive. 'I made a mistake, Helen. A huge mistake. And I admit it. We never should have split up.'

Helen stirred. '*We* didn't split up,' she said politely. 'You left me at the altar.'

Bright spots of colour appeared on his cheekbones and he shifted his weight uncomfortably. 'Well, not exactly. I—'

'I hadn't actually arrived at the church,' Helen agreed helpfully, 'but it was a close thing.'

David gave a sigh and ran a hand over his face. 'Look— you have every right to be angry. But we were together for six years. Is that really something that you can throw away lightly?'

'You did,' Helen pointed out calmly, and David frowned.

'What's wrong with you? You've changed,' he said quietly. 'You never used to answer back or be confrontational.'

'Well, maybe you just didn't know me, David.'

'Listen, sweetie.' He spread his hands in a gesture of

apology. 'Everyone makes a mistake at some point in their lives. Well, this was mine. And now I'm going to put it right. I want you back.'

He wanted her back?

Helen stared at him, waiting to feel a rush of relief and pleasure. Waiting for the impulse to throw her arms around him.

Nothing happened.

Her eyes slid over him, noting his perfectly groomed appearance. Despite the fact he claimed to have driven all night, there was no trace of stubble on his freshly shaved jaw. He looked as though he'd just stepped out of the court-room—his tie neatly adjusted, the flash designer watch gleaming on his wrist.

He looked rich, sophisticated and self-confident. Most women's idea of a perfect partner. And he wanted her back.

It seemed that shattered dreams could be glued together again after all.

She looked at him, searching her brain and her heart for the answer.

However much he'd hurt her, they had been together for six years.

She'd been expecting to exchange vows with this man.

She could still have the life she'd mapped out for herself.

Oliver woke to find the other half of the bed empty.

He rolled over, his body reacting instantly to the subtle scent of Helen's perfume still clinging to her pillow.

Where was she?

They'd made love all night, so ravenous for each other that they hadn't broken contact until the light had started to intrude through the curtains. They'd savoured and lingered and feasted on each other until, clinging together in blissful, satiated exhaustion, they'd finally fallen asleep.

And for the first time in his life he'd laid himself bare emotionally. Stripped himself naked in every sense, willing to trust this precious woman with his heart.

For the first time in his life, he'd said *I love you*.

He covered his eyes with his forearm and cursed softly, grimly aware that despite the unbelievable physical intimacies they'd shared, Helen hadn't once said those words back to him.

But, then, Helen didn't think that love could happen so quickly.

Or did she still think that she was in love with David?

Deciding that he'd given her enough space, Oliver pulled on jeans and a jumper and padded downstairs, pausing on the bottom step as he heard Helen's voice coming from the kitchen.

He frowned.

He hadn't heard the door.

'I'm really glad you came, David,' she was saying and Oliver froze.

David? *She was talking to David?*

And she was glad he'd come?

Unprepared for the pain that seared his chest, Oliver pushed open the door of his sister's kitchen and saw Helen wrapped in a man's arms.

David's arms.

'Excuse me.' If he'd had his way he wouldn't even have announced himself, but to make his escape he needed his jacket and his car keys and both were in the kitchen.

He cast one long look over the man who had once been Helen's fiancé and who was obviously destined to hold that position again. If he hadn't heard those words himself—*I'm really glad you came, David*—he would have flattened the guy for the way he'd treated Helen.

But clearly such heroics were uncalled for.

So instead he walked calmly into the kitchen, trying not to notice that Helen was still in her dressing-gown. The thought that she was still naked under there filled him with almost unbearable tension.

Last night she'd been his.

Every warm, feminine inch of her.

'Oliver...' Helen pulled away from David and turned towards him, clearly embarrassed and Oliver managed a smile. In fact, he was fairly proud of the smile. Considering the way he was feeling, it was a hell of a convincing smile.

But he didn't want Helen feeling guilty.

He knew better than anyone how confused she'd felt over David and if she wanted him back in her life he certainly wasn't going to stand in her way.

'I need to go to the surgery.'

'But you're not working.'

He gave a shrug and reached for his keys and his coat. 'You know me by now, Helen. I'm always working.'

And he no longer had a reason to stay.

Helen stared after Oliver and suddenly everything was clear.

Like the mist lifting from the mountains, she suddenly saw what she wanted her future to be with perfect clarity.

But was it too late?

Was Oliver just going to walk away from what they'd shared the night before?

She stood frozen to the spot and then the heavy slam of the front door galvanised her into action and she sprinted after him, desperate to talk to him, totally oblivious of the fact that David was still standing in the kitchen.

She tugged open the front door, frantic to get to Oliver, but Oliver put his foot down, scattering shingle and snow as he drove away at speed.

'No!' Feeling utterly desolate, Helen's slim shoulders slumped and she stared after him helplessly. Then she noticed the four-wheel drive.

He'd taken the sex machine. Which meant she could go after him.

Lost in thought, she gave a start as she felt a hand on her shoulder.

She'd totally forgotten about David.

He stared after Oliver's car with disapproval. 'Who was that? He was driving far too fast for the road conditions.'

'That,' she said quietly, 'is the man I love. And he's used to the road conditions. He's lived here all his life.'

She turned, noticing how ridiculous David looked in his expensive suit. She'd always thought he was good-looking but suddenly she found herself noticing that his shoulders weren't as broad as Oliver's and he didn't smile with his eyes. In fact, no matter which way you looked at it, he just wasn't Oliver.

She tried to imagine David climbing into a ditch to save a woman's life or making a call on a Sunday unless he was being paid an exorbitant hourly rate.

She tried to imagine David making love to her the way Oliver had the night before.

Her face heated at the memory and she gave a soft smile.

Love.

That was the secret ingredient.

That was the reason it had felt different.

'Are you seriously suggesting that you love that man? You can't possibly love him.' David looked at her in bemusement. 'You can't have known the guy for more than a few weeks.'

'But time doesn't have anything to do with it, does it David?' she said quietly, suddenly desperate to go after Oliver and talk to him. 'You and I were together for six years, but I don't think you ever knew the real me. And I don't think I knew you either.'

David looked thoroughly out of his depth. 'Shall we continue this conversation indoors?' he suggested, glancing up at the sky with a frown. 'It's freezing out here.'

Helen shook her head. 'Actually, I like it out here. The air is really clean and there isn't anything more to be said. I'm really glad you came, David, because it helped me realise that we are not a good match.'

'That's ridiculous.' David looked at her. 'You would have made a perfect lawyer's wife.'

'No.' Helen lifted her chin. 'I'm me, David. I'm not here to make your life easier. If that's what you want, find yourself a secretary. And now I need to get dressed.'

And with that she hurried back into the cottage and up the stairs.

She needed to see Oliver.

* * *

She found him in the surgery, absorbed by something on the computer.

'Oliver?'

He lifted his head, his expression distant. 'Hi, there.'

She remembered just how close they'd been the night before, how he'd held her and made love to her, and wondered how he could be so reserved.

Her heart plummeted.

That cool reserve hurt her more than she could possibly have imagined.

Had she misread the situation?

'Listen, about David—'

'It doesn't matter, Helen.' His tone was steady and he turned his attention back to the computer. 'You must be thrilled that he came back.'

She looked for signs of jealousy. Anything that suggested that he minded, but there was nothing.

Misery spread through her.

If he didn't mind that David had come back, that could only mean one thing.

'Oliver—'

'Our relationship probably helped you put your feelings for him in perspective. It was just a bit of fun. I hope you're not feeling guilty about it.'

Helen stared at him, really shocked by his almost indifferent response.

Last night he'd kissed every inch of her quivering body.

Last night they'd whispered intimacies and shared secrets.

Last night he'd told her that he loved her.

And now he was talking to her as though she were a patient.

'Tell me honestly…' Her voice was croaky and suddenly she found that her hands were shaking. 'Do you regret last night?'

There was a long silence and when he finally turned to face her she noticed the lines of tiredness around his kind blue eyes. 'Yes,' he said quietly, 'I suppose I do.'

Pain stifled her breathing and she backed away from him. She'd heard all she needed to hear.

'I'm sorry.' Her voice was barely audible and she grabbed the door handle for support. 'If it's any consolation it won't matter because I've decided to go back to London. I'm catching the train tonight. You won't have to see me again.'

He gave a brief nod, not in the slightest surprised, and Helen was astonished by the depth of her own disappointment.

What had she expected?

That he'd try and stop her? That he'd beg her to stay?

He'd already told her that he regretted their relationship.

There was nothing left to say except goodbye.

But the words stuck in her throat and Oliver seemed more interested in his computer than her.

So Helen quietly put his car keys on his desk, slid out of the room and walked out of the surgery with tears in her eyes.

She'd get a taxi back to the cottage, pick up her bags and go to the station before Bryony and Jack arrived home. That way she wouldn't be a wet blanket.

She stood for a moment in the car park, staring at the

mountains, thinking that in a month she'd recovered from David.

All she had to do now was recover from Oliver.

But she knew that what she felt for Oliver would be with her forever.

CHAPTER TWENTY

OLIVER stared blindly at the monitor, fighting the temptation to put his fist through it.

It had taken every ounce of will-power on his part not to crash his way through his desk and grab Helen.

But the image of her in David's arms had stayed with him.

He tried to console himself with the fact that four weeks ago his life had been happy.

Four weeks ago his life had been fine.

But that had been before he'd met Helen.

The door to his consulting room flew open and he glanced up eagerly, his broad shoulders sagging slightly when he saw his brother standing there.

'What's wrong?'

Tom strolled into the room, pushing the door shut behind him. 'Bryony just rang from the airport. She's on her way back. I came to warn you so that you can rethink accommodation for you and Helen.'

'Thanks, but it's all sorted. I'm going home after I've finished here.'

'Home to your home?' Tom lifted an eyebrow mockingly. 'And what about your roof?'

Oliver didn't smile. 'My roof is finished.'

Tom looked at him searchingly. 'And Helen?'

There was a long silence and when Oliver finally spoke his voice sounded rusty. 'David has turned up.'

'David? The guy who left her?'

'The same.'

'And she slapped his face, yes?'

'Not when I was there,' Oliver said evenly. 'In fact, they were looking pretty cosy. She came here to say goodbye. She's on her way back to London, presumably to begin the life she had planned before he ditched her at the altar. He's about to make her a very happy woman.'

'Are you sure about that?' Tom frowned. 'I just saw her climbing into a taxi, looking as though her best friend had died. She certainly didn't look like a woman who'd rediscovered the love of her life.'

Oliver gave a twisted smile. 'Helen's a sweet girl. I expect she was worrying that she'd hurt me. I tried to pretend that it was all just a bit of fun and that none of it mattered, but I don't think I was very convincing.'

Tom looked at him, his eyes searching. 'And you're sure you didn't misunderstand?'

'I heard her say that she was glad to see him,' Oliver muttered, running a hand over his face and slumping in his chair. 'Damn, Tom. I never thought it would hurt this much.'

'Love?' Tom gave a harsh laugh. 'Love is the worst pain known to man.'

Momentarily distracted, Oliver looked at his brother, realising that the statement had deeper implications. 'I assume you're talking about Sally. I've always wanted to know why you ended it.'

'Because I thought she was too young to make that sort of commitment...' Tom paused for a moment and his firm mouth curved into a smile of self-mockery. 'And I was stupid,' he finished softly. 'Incredibly stupid.'

Knowing that Tom never talked about Sally, Oliver held his breath. 'And if you could put the clock back?'

'It's too late for that,' Tom said harshly, glancing quickly at his watch, 'but it isn't too late for you. I suggest you go back to the cottage and knock him down. Then drag the maiden back to your lair and have your wicked way with her.'

He'd done that the night before.

It didn't seem to have made even the slightest difference to her final decision.

Oliver gave a weary smile. 'Helen's made her choice.'

Tom frowned. 'That doesn't sound like you. If you love her, fight for her! You've always fought for everything you believed in. Literally, when you were younger. You had permanent black eyes at one point.'

Oliver shook his head. 'The one thing I can't fight is her love for another man, Tom. It has to be her decision. And she's made it.'

* * *

Helen stood on the freezing platform, wishing the train would arrive.

Once she was safely on her way, maybe she'd lose the desperate urge to run back to Oliver.

She glanced around her, realising that she was the only person waiting for the train.

Five more minutes. Five more minutes and then the Lake District would be part of her past.

And so would Oliver.

From the tiny station car park she heard the slam of a car door, a masculine shout and then footsteps. Her heart lifted, only to plummet again as she saw Tom striding towards her.

'Is something wrong?' She looked around her but the platform was still empty, which meant that she could be the only reason for the visit.

'Plenty.' Tom raked long fingers through his dark hair. 'Look, I'm probably going to say the wrong thing here—heaven knows, I've made a complete mess of my own love life so I'm certainly not qualified to tamper with anyone else's—' He broke off and took a deep breath. 'Do you love Oliver?'

Helen looked at him, startled. 'Sorry?'

Tom gritted his teeth impatiently. 'Do you love my brother?'

'Well, I—'

'It's a simple question, Helen. Yes or no?'

'Yes,' she croaked, rubbing the toe of her boot on the frosty surface of the platform. 'Yes, I do. But it was just a bit of fun for him.'

Tom gave a disbelieving laugh. 'You may love him, but

you don't know him very well, do you? He thinks you're reunited with David. He doesn't want you to feel guilty about going back to him. He's making things easy for you. It's pure Oliver.'

'Easy?' Helen stared at him and swallowed hard. 'Seeing Oliver so cool this morning was the hardest thing I've ever had to bear, particularly after last night—' She broke off and blushed, realising what she'd just said, but Tom gripped her shoulders, forcing her to look at him.

'So you're not going back to David?'

She shook her head. 'No. I couldn't. I love Oliver.'

'Then why are you going back to London?'

Helen glanced down the track and saw the train approaching. 'Because I can't live here and see Oliver every day. It would hurt too much, knowing that he doesn't love me.'

'He does love you.' Tom swore under his breath and stared at the approaching train with something close to desperation. 'No wonder the path of true love never runs smoothly,' he muttered. 'People don't tell each other the truth.'

'Oliver has only known me for three weeks.'

'Oliver loved you from the first moment he saw you,' Tom said. 'He moved into Bryony's cottage, for goodness' sake, just so that he could be with you because he couldn't bring himself to leave you on your own.'

Helen frowned, suddenly confused. 'He was having his roof done.'

Tom sighed. 'Helen, Oliver's roof is fine. Rock solid. Not a leak in sight.'

Helen stared at him. 'But—'

'He was determined to watch over you. Pure Oliver again.'

Helen's mind was racing. Oliver had stayed in the cottage just so that he could be with her? 'That doesn't mean he loves me. That just means he's kind. As you say, "Pure Oliver." He would have done the same thing for anyone.'

'You need more evidence?' Tom thrust his hands in his pocket. 'In order to create a job for you, he bought his practice nurse a flight to Australia so that she could afford to visit her daughter.'

Helen shook her head. 'But she'd wanted to go for ages.'

'But she couldn't afford it,' Tom said gently. 'Oliver paid for the ticket and gave you the job because he decided that you needed the distraction of working to get you out of bed in the morning. He was afraid that if he left you on your own all day, you'd brood.'

Suddenly Helen remembered Hilda's surprise at hearing that Maggie had decided to go to Australia at such short notice.

'He didn't need a practice nurse?'

'Maggie is a perfectly good practice nurse.'

Helen swallowed in disbelief as she assimilated the enormity of the gesture. 'He did that for me?'

Tom nodded. 'He loves you, Helen. Enough to let you go because he thinks you love David.'

Helen stared at the train as it slowed and then turned her eyes back to Tom. 'He loves me?'

'And you love him.' Tom picked up her bags. 'So I suggest you cash in that ticket you bought and let me drop you back in the village. Last time I saw him he was dragging on his walking gear. It's what he always does when something stresses him. He takes to the hills.'

Helen was digesting everything that he'd said.

Had Oliver really thought she was going back to David?

Had he thought that he was making the decision easier for her?

She stood for a minute and then gave Tom a smile. 'Do you know where he's gone?'

'I've got a good idea.'

Helen breathed a sigh of relief. 'In that case, do you think you can drop me at the cottage so that I can borrow Bryony's walking clothes one more time? And then I need you to point me in the right direction.'

She found Oliver by the lake, at a place they'd walked to together several times over the past month.

He was sitting on a rock, throwing stones into the water. He stood up as she approached, his expression neutral.

'You shouldn't walk in the mountains by yourself—you might get lost.'

Helen shrugged. 'I was careful. You see, I have this friend who taught me a game.'

The wind played with his dark hair. 'And what game is that?'

'You memorise different landmarks on the way.' Helen turned to look back down the path she'd taken. 'I passed a boulder shaped like a sheep, a patch of ice shaped like Africa. If I had to find my way back without getting lost, I could.'

He was silent for a moment, a muscle working in his lean

jaw. When he finally spoke his voice was slightly hoarse. 'What are you doing here, Helen?'

'Looking for you.' She closed her eyes and breathed in the air. 'It's lovely here.'

'Helen…'

He looked so remote, so unlike Oliver, that for a moment her courage faltered. And then she remembered everything that Tom had told her and that gave her the strength she needed.

'Actually, I'm here because I need to ask you a question. If I ask you a question, will you give me an honest answer, Oliver?'

His expression was wary. 'That depends on the question.'

As a response it was less than encouraging, but she ploughed on anyway. This time she wasn't going to give up until she'd told him how she felt.

'Do you love me, Oliver?'

He flinched as though she'd struck him and dragged his eyes away from hers, staring out across the mountains. 'What sort of a question is that?'

'An important one.' Suddenly her hands were shaking and she had butterflies in her stomach, but still she carried on, trying not to be put off by the fact that his hands were thrust firmly in his pockets. 'Last night you told me you loved me. I want to know if you meant it, or if it was something you say to every woman you make love to.'

He didn't move and he didn't look at her. 'I don't say it to every woman.'

'So, is that a yes?'

His hard jaw tensed and for a moment she thought he wasn't going to answer.

Then he stirred. 'Yes. I love you. Now what?'

Her heart lifted but he still didn't turn to face her so she walked around until she was in front of him.

'Now you can ask me a question.'

Finally his eyes met hers. 'Helen, I—'

'I expect you want to ask me about David,' she said quietly, 'so I'll just tell you anyway. I don't love David, Oliver. I'm not going with David. In fact, I should probably tell you that I intend to settle down in the Lake District with my family.'

Oliver was silent for a long moment, his blue eyes fixed on hers, his expression unreadable. Then he cleared his throat. 'Your family?'

'That's right.' She was taking a huge risk but she'd decided that it was worth it. 'For a while there's just going to be me and the man I love, but pretty soon I'm sure we'll have babies because I'm dying to be a mother and he's going to be a great dad. And if we're going to have lots of children we need to make a start.'

There was a long, pulsing silence and Oliver finally stirred. 'This man you love…'

'Yes?'

'He doesn't live in London?'

She gave a smile. 'He'd hate living in London. The man I love was born to live in the mountains. They're part of who he is.'

'Sounds a pretty weird choice of partner to me.' Oliver's voice was hoarse and he still hadn't touched her. 'Why would a London girl like you love a man like that?'

'You want to know what I love about him?' Helen's voice was soft. 'I love the fact that he cares so much about everyone. I love the fact he cares enough to see patients on his day off and pretend his roof needs fixing just so that he can keep an eye on a friend of his sister's that he doesn't even know.'

Oliver sucked in a breath. 'Helen—'

'I love the way he laughs all the time and I love the way he kisses.' Helen paused, digging her nails into her palms. 'And I love the way he pretends that he doesn't love me so that I can leave without feeling guilty.'

Oliver's eyes locked on hers. 'But you don't want to leave?'

She shook her head. 'Never again.' She huddled deeper inside her coat and stamped her feet to keep warm. *Surely he'd touch her soon?* 'My home is here. With you. If you want me, that is.'

And finally the tension seemed to drain out of him.

He gave a groan and dragged her into his arms, his voice muffled as he buried his face in her neck. 'Oh, God, Helen, I thought I'd lost you. When I saw you with David I thought I'd lost you.' He squeezed her tightly and then pushed her away slightly so that he could look at her. 'Once I heard you say you were glad he'd come, I thought that was it.'

'When you walked out, I almost died.' Helen put her arms around his neck, sliding her fingers into his hair, loving the way it felt. 'I couldn't get rid of David fast enough. But then I came to the surgery and you were so cold...'

'It was the only way I could stop myself from breaking down and begging you to stay,' he confessed in a raw tone, 'and I didn't want to do that to you. I wanted you to make the decision yourself, without pressure from me. I thought you'd already made that decision.'

'I'd already sent David away when I found you at the practice. I came to tell you that I loved you,' Helen told him, oblivious to the biting wind which buffeted both of them. 'But after you told me that last night was a mistake, there didn't seem much point.'

Oliver groaned and cupped her face in his hands. 'Last night wasn't a mistake, angel.' He lowered his mouth to hers, his kiss so hot and full of promise that she felt her body shiver. Only when both of them were struggling for breath did he lift his head. 'Last night was the single most perfect thing that has ever happened to me. When I woke up this morning and you were already downstairs, I assumed I'd frightened you away by telling you that I loved you.'

'I think I frightened myself,' Helen admitted, colour rising in her cheeks. 'It was so... I mean, I never—'

'Neither did I.' Oliver kissed her again. 'And when I saw you with David...'

'I told him that I was glad he'd come, because I thought there were things I wanted to know,' Helen said quietly. 'I wanted to know how he could have ended our relationship the way he did, without seeing me face to face. Then I saw him and realised that actually I didn't even care anymore. I didn't care why he did it that way. All I cared about was you.'

'You were in his arms.'

'He pulled me there. I left them very quickly,' Helen said and Oliver let out a long breath.

'He's rich, Helen.'

She glanced around her, breathing in the air and sighing with pleasure as she looked at the mountains. 'What's rich?' She turned back to him. 'Rich is being with the person you love.'

He cupped her face in his hands. 'I thought you didn't believe that love could happen quickly.'

'I've learned a lot of things in the past few weeks,' she said softly. 'Like the fact that I love mountains. And that I don't want to go back to London. And that love can happen in a breath and when you're least expecting it. I arrived here broken-hearted but you made me see that what I felt for David wasn't love. Love is what I feel for you.'

'And is it enough?' His voice was hoarse and he stroked a hand around her face and tilted her chin. 'Is it enough to make you leave behind the stilettos and the suits? Your big city life? Is it asking too much of you to make you live here?'

She smiled. 'I want to live here. I want to be here when Hilda moves into her new flat. I want to know how things go with Anna and her new boyfriend and—' her eyes twinkled '—I even want to know about Howard Marks's sex life.'

Oliver grinned. 'I can assure you, you don't!'

Helen laughed. 'Well, what I mean is, I want to be part of this great community. I know I can't carry on being your practice nurse, but I still want to be part of everything.'

'Ah.' Something flickered in Oliver's eyes. 'About the practice nurse job…'

Helen's gaze softened. 'I can't believe you paid for Maggie to visit her daughter just to create a job for me.'

Oliver rubbed a hand across the back of his neck. 'It seems my generous gesture has rather backfired.'

'How?'

Oliver gave a wry smile. 'Maggie called this morning to say that she's enjoying herself so much she'd like extended leave of absence. I need a new practice nurse.'

Helen's mouth fell open. 'Oh!'

'Yes—"oh."' He shook his head. 'I must admit I didn't have the best morning. First I saw you with David and then my practice nurse decides not to come back.'

Helen kissed him. 'But the day is improving,' she said softly, 'because I happen to know someone who would make a great practice nurse. If only in the short term.'

Oliver dragged his mouth away from hers reluctantly. 'Short term?' His voice was husky and his eyes were still on her lips. 'Why short term?'

She blushed slightly. 'Because we were both a little carried away last night, that family of ours may be arriving sooner rather than later.'

Oliver stared at her and then a huge smile spread across his face. 'I might have made you pregnant—'

'Stop sounding so smug. If you have, you'll soon be interviewing a new practice nurse.'

'I don't care.' Oliver gave a groan and kissed her gently. 'I hope I did make you pregnant. I want to have lots of babies. I probably should have told you that before.'

Her insides melted. 'If you're the father, I want lots of babies, too. I love you.'

'And I love you, too.' He glanced back along the path she'd taken. 'Can you remember the way home?'

'Of course. Boulder shaped like a sheep and ice like Africa. 'Why?'

His blue eyes gleamed wickedly. 'Because I don't think we should leave this baby thing to chance. We should go home and try again.'

She lifted her mouth to his. 'That, Dr Hunter, sounds like a very good idea.'

* * * * *

Sad the story's over?

Don't worry, there's still heaps more heart-warming, sparkling Sarah Morgan Christmas magic to be read!

Did you fall in love with Tom? Wonder what the secrets were between him and Sally? Then don't miss their story in the exclusive ebook

SNOWKISSED!

Remember that summer when everything changed?

Katy: Days away from marrying a man she doesn't love, Katy's shocked when fate throws her in the path of Jago Rodriguez—he may have left her years before, but now he's back...

Libby: Spirited, impulsive and independent, Libby has no interest in relationships, until she comes face to face with a man who won't give up and a date she can't turn down!

Alex: Wanted by every woman he's ever met, Alex is totally unprepared when a stranger appears on his doorstep with a baby in her arms.

www.millsandboon.co.uk

713/MB425

Come home to the magic of Nora Roberts

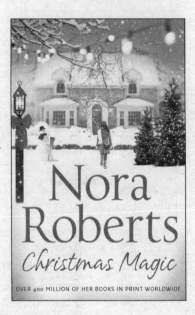

Identical twin boys Zeke and Zach wished for only one gift from Santa this year: a new mum! But convincing their love-wary dad that their music teacher, Miss Davis, is his destiny and part of Santa's plan isn't as easy as they'd hoped…

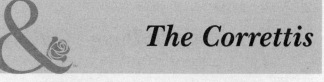

The Correttis

Introducing the Correttis, Sicily's most scandalous family!

On sale 3rd May

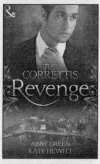

On sale 7th June

On sale 5th July

On sale 2nd August

Mills & Boon® Modern™ invites you to step over the threshold
and enter the Correttis' dark and dazzling world...

Find the collection at
www.millsandboon.co.uk/specialreleases

*Visit us
Online*

0513/MB415

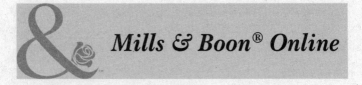

Mills & Boon® Online

Discover more romance at
www.millsandboon.co.uk

- **FREE** online reads
- **Books** up to one month before shops
- **Browse our books** before you buy

...and much more!

For exclusive competitions and instant updates:

 Like us on **facebook.com/millsandboon**

 Follow us on **twitter.com/millsandboon**

 Join us on **community.millsandboon.co.uk**

Visit us Online Sign up for our FREE eNewsletter at **www.millsandboon.co.uk**

WEB/M&B/RTL5